Acclaim for V

"... a fun read for both mystery a...

—R... ...EW

FOR *MURDER TIGHTLY KNIT*

"[Chapman] adeptly fleshes out her characters and weaves in facts about the Amish faith without overwhelming the narrative. Readers of inspirational fiction and fans of Beverly Lewis will delight in this gentle mystery."

—*LIBRARY JOURNAL*, FOR *MURDER TIGHTLY KNIT*

"Readers will enjoy figuring out the murder mystery while also growing close to the characters as they fall in love, learn more about one another, and grow deeper in their faith."

—*BOOKLIST*, FOR *MURDER TIGHTLY KNIT*

"Vannetta Chapman keeps the action suspenseful, and the who-done-it mostly unpredictable as her Amish and English characters work together to solve the mystery. Out of even such dreadful circumstances come moments of grace: between Amber and her Amish employee Hannah and between Amber and Tate, who had each given up on love."

—*BOOKPAGE.COM*, FOR *MURDER SIMPLY BREWED*

"Vannetta Chapman has crafted a tightly woven tale in the best tradition of the cozy mystery ... Chapman's light touch and thoughtful representation of the Amish culture make *Murder Simply Brewed* a delightful read for an evening by a warm fire, a cup of tea in hand."

—KELLY IRVIN, AUTHOR OF *THE BEEKEEPER'S SON* AND THE BLISS CREEK AMISH SERIES

"*Murder Simply Brewed* combines all the coziness of an Amish home with the twists and turns of a great suspense. With a little romance thrown it, you can't go wrong! Vannetta Chapman has crafted a charming story that shows things aren't always as they first appear."

—BETH SHRIVER, BESTSELLING AUTHOR OF THE TOUCH OF GRACE TRILOGY

Other Books by Vannetta Chapman

THE AMISH VILLAGE MYSTERY SERIES

Murder Simply Brewed
Murder Tightly Knit
Murder Freshly Baked

THE SHIPSHEWANA AMISH MYSTERY SERIES

Falling to Pieces
A Perfect Square
Material Witness

STORIES

Where Healing Blooms included in *An Amish Garden*
An Unexpected Blessing included in *An Amish Cradle*
Mischief in the Autumn Air included in *An Amish Harvest*
Love in Store included in *An Amish Market*

Material Witness

A Shipshewana Amish Mystery

VANNETTA CHAPMAN

ZONDERVAN

Material Witness
Copyright © 2012 by Vannetta Chapman

This title is also available as a Zondervan ebook.
Visit www.zondervan.com/ebooks.

This title is also available in a Zondervan audio edition.
Visit www.zondervan.fm.

Requests for information should be addressed to:
Zondervan, *Grand Rapids, Michigan 49530*

ISBN 978-0-7852-1715-2 (repack)

Library of Congress Cataloging-in-Publication Data

Chapman, Vannetta.
    Material witness / Vannetta Chapman.
        p. cm.—(A Shipshewana Amish mystery ; bk. 3)
     ISBN 978-0-310-33045-5
      1. Amish—Fiction. 2. Shipshewana (Ind.)—Fiction. I. Title.
  PS3603.H3744M38 2012
  813'.6—dc23   2012003447

All Scripture quotations, unless otherwise indicated, are taken from the King James
Version of the Bible.

Any Internet addresses (websites, blogs, etc.) and telephone numbers in this book
are offered as a resource. They are not intended in any way to be or imply an
endorsement by Zondervan, nor does Zondervan vouch for the content of these
sites and numbers for the life of this book.

Cover design: Anderson Design Group

Printed in the United States of America

---

18 19 20 21 22 23 24 /LSC/ 20 19 18 17 16 15 14 13 12 11 10 9 8 7 6 5 4 3 2 1

In memory of my grandparents:
John and Rose Allen

WHILE THIS NOVEL is set against the real backdrop of Shipshewana, Indiana, the characters are fictional. There is no intended resemblance between the characters in this book and any real members of the Amish and Mennonite communities. As with any work of fiction, I've taken license in some areas of research as a means of creating the necessary circumstances for my characters. My research was thorough; however, it would be impossible to be completely accurate in details and descriptions, since each and every community differs. Therefore, any inaccuracies in the Amish and Mennonite lifestyles portrayed in this book are completely due to fictional license.

Glossary

ack—oh

aenti—aunt

bedauerlich—sad

boppli—baby

bopplin—babies

bruder—brother

daadi—grandfather, informal

daed—father

danki—thank you

dat—dad

Dietsch—Pennsylvania Dutch

dochder—daughter

dochdern—daughters

eck—corner

Englischer—non-Amish person

fraa—wife

freind—friend

freinden—friends

gelassenheit—calmness, composure, placidity

gern gschehne—you're welcome

Gotte's wille—God's will

grandkinner—grandchildren

grossdaddi—grandfather

grossdochdern—granddaughters

grossmammi—grandmother

gudemariye—good morning

gut—good

in lieb—in love

kaffi—coffee

kapp—prayer covering

kind—child

kinner—children

mamm—mom

mammi—grandmother, informal

naerfich—nervous

narrisch—crazy

nein—no

onkel—uncle

Ordnung—set of rules for Amish living

rumspringa—running around; time before an Amish young person has officially joined the church, provides a bridge between childhood and adulthood

schweschder—sister

was iss letz—what is wrong

wunderbaar—wonderful

ya—yes

Families in Material Witness

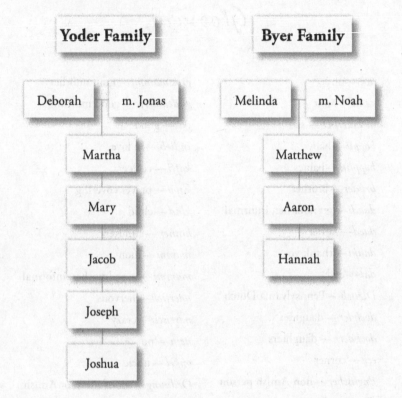

Yoder Family

Deborah — m. Jonas

Martha

Mary

Jacob

Joseph

Joshua

Byer Family

Melinda — m. Noah

Matthew

Aaron

Hannah

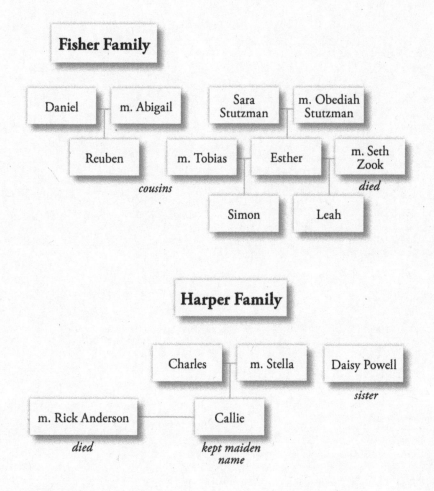

Fisher Family

Daniel — m. Abigail

Sara Stutzman — m. Obediah Stutzman

Reuben — m. Tobias — Esther — m. Seth Zook

cousins

died

Simon — Leah

Harper Family

Charles — m. Stella

Daisy Powell

sister

m. Rick Anderson — Callie

died

kept maiden name

Prologue

SHIPSHEWANA, INDIANA

MID-SEPTEMBER

"AM I LATE?" Callie pushed the door closed against the September wind, grateful to see her three best friends waiting for her.

Deborah, Melinda, and Esther surrounded her like the fall flowers in her garden circled the pavestone walk.

"Bishop Elam wouldn't have started without you," Deborah said. Thirty-three years old, three inches taller than Callie's five foot, three inches, and weighing somewhere around 140 pounds, Deborah was healthy and beautiful. Her blondish-brown hair was neatly tucked into her prayer *kapp*, and her amber eyes nearly always expressed her calm, pleasant character.

Callie had begun to think of Deborah as her sister, but she understood they looked like complete opposites. Callie tried to gain weight but couldn't, had dark hair that refused to behave—especially now that she was growing it past her collar—and large eyes such a deep brown someone had once told her they looked black. No amount of makeup could minimize Callie's eyes—she'd tried. They still dominated her face.

She often found herself glancing at Deborah, wishing she could be like her. She'd confessed that once, and Deborah had reminded her God had a reason for making each person exactly as they were. Perhaps one day he'd let her in on the secret.

1

"Did you have trouble finding the place?" Melinda reached forward and patted down Callie's hair, which Callie imagined now resembled something out of a punk-rock video. Melinda was small and precious like a bird—a bird who wore glasses that always managed to slip down her nose.

"No. No problem. Your directions were good. Max treed a squirrel and refused to come inside. I finally left him in the side yard barking as if he hadn't a brain cell in his head."

Esther cradled her infant in her arms. Tall, dark blonde, with beautiful blue eyes, she looked happier than Callie had ever seen her.

"May I?" Callie reached for baby Simon before Esther had time to answer. Six weeks old, he smelled of powder and warm blankets and love. She wanted to find a chair and stare at the miracle of his little face.

"We should move to the kitchen." Esther nudged her toward the dining room table.

"*Ya*, Bishop Elam is gathering everyone," Deborah agreed.

Callie barely heard, she was so focused on the infant. Truthfully she didn't know why she'd even been included in the reading of Mrs. Hochstetler's will.

Melinda was closest to the elderly woman. Glancing over at her friend, Callie noticed that her eyes seemed misty behind her glasses. She didn't know the entire story behind Melinda and Mrs. Hochstetler's friendship; when she'd asked, Melinda had only said, "She was special—very special to me."

Callie had known Mrs. Hochstetler, though not well. The elderly Amish woman was nearly ninety, but she'd still stopped by the shop regularly, purchasing fabric and thread—never kits. She claimed that the day she needed a kit to piece together a quilt, she'd stop sewing.

Personally Callie liked the quilting kits. She was now working on her second quilt, and she'd chosen one of the new baby quilt kits that had appliqués of farm animals. It was to be a present for Simon. With a little luck she'd finish it before he got too old.

Somehow everyone fit around the table—all seven of Mrs. Hochstetler's grown children; Deborah, Esther, Melinda, and Callie; the banker, Mrs. Barnwell; and the bishop. To Callie, it seemed they made an odd group. The bishop was saying a few words about Mrs. Hochstetler, so Callie used the time to glance around the house.

Like most Amish homes it was clean and unadorned—the countertops free of clutter. No curtains hung on the windows, but there were shades that could be pulled down against the night. A big cast-iron stove sat between the sitting room and the kitchen, no doubt used for heating the rooms. A newer gas-powered stove sat against the east wall of the kitchen, opposite the gas-powered refrigerator.

Callie was so busy admiring the rooms, thinking of how little she knew about her customers, she didn't realize Bishop Elam had begun reading the final will and testament. But she did notice everyone around her sit up straighter.

The bishop read from a single sheet of paper.

Mrs. Hochstetler had left simple and direct instructions—the house to one son, the animals to another, some money to a third. No one was left out. As the bishop continued in his soft German accent, Callie found herself focusing again on the infant in her arms. She forgot about dying and wills and stopped wondering why she was there. She focused on the miracle of life in her arms. For a moment.

Until she was suddenly jarred from the tranquil place she had slipped into by the sound of her name.

"Daisy Powell's niece, Miss Callie Harper, is to receive the three quilts in the chest next to my bed. Once restored, they may be sold at Callie's discretion. Money from the sale of the quilts will be split five ways—one portion each to Esther Fisher, Deborah

Yoder, and Melinda Byer, who will each help with the restoration, and one part to Callie, who will oversee the sales. The final portion of money will be deposited in the previously established account at First Bank Shipshewana to be used as arranged with my banker, Mrs. Barnwell."

Bishop Elam removed his reading glasses and set them on top of the single sheet of paper on the table. "If there are no questions, I suggest we all share a cup of tea."

Chairs were scooted away from the table, and conversations slowly started back up again.

Callie glanced from Deborah to Esther to Melinda. "Quilt restorations?"

"It's hard work," Esther admitted.

Deborah reached for the baby. "And not always worth the time."

"She never mentioned old quilts to me." Melinda pushed up her glasses. "I've been to see her many times, but I never—"

"What type of quilt could possibly require its own bank account for a mere twenty percent?" Callie gazed around at her friends, wondering for the first time if perhaps Mrs. Hochstetler had suffered from a touch of dementia. Before she could think of a way to tactfully raise the question, Sadie Hochstetler, the wife of Levi Hochstetler, walked over to their group.

"I'll take you to see the quilts if you'd like." Sadie was in her early fifties, a little on the heavy side, quiet and shy. Though she regularly came into the shop, she rarely said more than good morning and thank you.

Restoring quilts? Splitting the profits five ways? Would there even be profits? And as to those specific instructions, why a separate bank account? What made these quilts special? So many questions swirled in Callie's mind, colliding together, that they stirred up quite a cloud of confusion.

Callie, Esther, Melinda, and Deborah followed Sadie to the

bedroom and gathered around the cedar chest at the foot of the
old bed. Silently they waited as she raised the lid on the chest ...
and tenderly pulled out one family heirloom after another.

By the time she reached the third quilt, Callie still had plenty
of questions, but as to why the quilts were special — that she definitely understood.

Chapter 1

DEBORAH UNROLLED THE BOLT OF FABRIC: a fall calico print of small pumpkins intermingled with leaves and cornstalks. It wasn't something she would purchase. Amish only quilted with solid colors, but she could certainly see why it was a hot seller tonight.

"Four yards?" she asked.

The woman from Chicago tapped her manicured nail against her lips, both painted a dark rose. "I'm not sure. Nancy, what do you think? Three or four yards?"

Nancy Jarrell wound her way through the crowd gathered in Callie's shop. Though Nancy was also from Chicago and definitely clung to her big-city ways, Deborah felt closer to her since she and Callie had visited the museum last month. God indeed worked in surprising ways. She never would have imagined that quilts sewn by herself, Melinda, and Esther would be exhibited in the textile rooms of the Chicago Museum of Arts.

At first, the bishop had decided it would be prideful to do so. Upon hearing that, Callie had asked to meet with him personally and argued that considering the women's work too good for others to see was more akin to pride. The humble thing to do would be to allow Nancy Jarrell to show the quilts. It was a backwards sort of logic, but it worked. As a result, the quilts had sold at a high price—money that helped Deborah and her *freinden*. And Deborah had grown closer to the woman standing in front of her. She wouldn't call it friendship exactly—it wasn't that strong—but definitely closer than mere acquaintances.

Nancy smiled and nodded toward Deborah. "Tell her what you're making. She'll know how much you need. Deborah's the one who sewed the quilt you purchased. She and her friends."

The woman's eyes widened and her hand flew to her neck, fingers resting on the diamond necklace around her throat. "You're the one who stitched the diamond-patterned masterpiece that Nancy showcased a month ago? Oh my. I was hoping I would have the chance to meet you, but I had no idea you'd be working in a shop. Your quilt was exquisite. I had a special frame made and hung it on the wall in my family room."

Deborah smiled politely, though the thought of her quilt—their quilt—hanging on a wall made her a tad uncomfortable. Quilts were for warmth. They belonged on beds to give comfort, not on walls to be gawked at. She thanked the woman and turned the conversation back to her purchase, even as her eyes caught sight of Melinda and her oldest boy helping Lydia out at the register. Matt had turned eleven this year, the same age as Deborah's oldest child, Martha.

The Fall Crafters' Fair—or Fall Festival as old-timers called it—had begun a few hours earlier. It was Shipshewana's largest festival of the year. Tonight was a warm-up of sorts and the reason Callie had extended her hours. Normally stores in Shipshe closed their doors and tucked in the welcome mat at six p.m. sharp, but for festivals, hours were extended. If the number of people in the shop was any indication of the crowds they would encounter, they were in for a record-setting weekend.

Who would have thought quilting could be such a profitable business? Yet it had become one for her and her friends. God had answered their prayers and had provided for their needs. He'd brought Callie, with her energy and inventive methods for attracting customers, and he'd blessed Deborah, Melinda, and Esther with the gift of piecing quilts in unique ways.

It brought them money they all needed. Deborah's gaze fell on Aaron, Melinda's middle child, who was waiting near the door in his wheelchair, and she breathed a quick prayer of gratitude. The money earned from the quilts they'd sold in Chicago had helped pay for testing Doctor Bernie insisted Aaron needed.

Aaron had been diagnosed with chicken breast disease when he was very young. It was a muscular disorder among the Amish. Children with chicken breast disease lacked a structural protein, and most eventually became too weak to breathe. The great majority didn't live past the age of two. Doc Bernie called Aaron a miracle child.

The woman Deborah was helping thanked her for the fabric and murmured again about how much she loved the diamond-patterned quilt she'd purchased.

Who was Deborah to criticize how the quilts were used? So what if this woman enjoyed displaying them on a wall rather than huddling under them on a cold winter night? It wasn't for her to judge.

Martha rushed to her side, cheeks pink and slightly breathless. "*Mamm*? Aaron and Matthew are going to watch the chain-saw carvers who are giving an early demonstration in the central tent. May I go with them?"

Deborah placed the bolt of cloth on the pile of items waiting to be reshelved and turned to help the next customer. "Your *dat* doesn't need you?"

"No. He took the boys home."

"Why would he take them home before we were ready to leave?"

"They fell in the mud. All three of them. Mary's clean, but she wanted to go with them. She was tired."

Deborah closed her eyes. She tried not to picture what happened all too often, but in a flash an image of her seven-year-old twins and two-and-a-half-year-old son covered in mud came to mind.

"They were watching the musicians practice for tomorrow, and the boys—"

"Don't tell me anymore." Deborah held up a hand. "I'd rather not know the details. He took the large buggy?"

"*Ya*. I asked to stay and help with Max. Miss Callie said he needs a walk. We thought we'd take him along with us if you agreed we could go to where the booths are."

Deborah glanced toward Callie, who was winding her way through the crowd in the shop, weaving her way toward Deborah. She was wearing the new dress they'd sewn together. Made of harvest-green fabric, a very popular color this season, it accented her dark hair and light complexion. Callie looked beautiful and more than a little harried.

Had the shop ever been this full of people before?

Market days were always busy, and the Labor Day sale had been very successful, but this was *over the top*, as her friend liked to say.

Losing three children, a wheelchair, and one rather large dog would probably help.

"All right, but be back before dark."

"Yes!" Martha bounced away, but Deborah snagged her arm before she was out of reach. Leaning down, she whispered in her ear, "Take special care with Aaron."

"'Course we will." Martha's brown eyes turned solemn for a moment.

Deborah almost regretted robbing her daughter of that moment of sheer childhood delight. Then she glanced over at Aaron, realizing again how fragile the seven-year-old was. Nearly eight. He was nearly eight, and they would be celebrating that birthday with prayers of thanksgiving. She released Martha, knowing she'd done the right thing.

"Where are they headed?" Callie asked as she began sorting the bolts of fabric Deborah was finished with.

"Out to see the preparations for the festival. It'll be *gut* for them to play a while and give us more room."

"This crowd is amazing, isn't it?" Callie's eyes sparkled. "Wanna bet old lady Knepp doesn't have nearly this many customers?"

"Callie—"

"I strolled by Quilts and Needles this morning. Her display wasn't as cute as the one Lydia fixed up for us."

"Mrs. Knepp sticks with the old ways."

"The old ways must include rudeness. She returned the fall flowers I sent over." Callie had gathered six bolts of fabric into her arms by now, and she seemed as if she were about to tumble backward.

"Is she still angry that Max tore up her flower bed?"

"It's my fault I suppose. I was talking to Trent and let the leash slip out of my hands. Even so, I don't understand why the woman hates me as much as she does. I thought the Amish were all about forgiveness."

"We each forgive in our own way."

"Humph. Admit it. She wishes I'd never moved here from Texas, never taken over my Aunt Daisy's shop." Callie did an about-face, nearly knocking over a display of magazines, then trotted down the aisle to return the cloth to its proper section.

Lydia would have done it, but Deborah knew Callie liked to be out working the floor. She enjoyed being out among the customers, which was why Lydia was on the register. It was one more way she was different from Mrs. Knepp and one more reason her shop did well.

Deborah began helping the next customer, who wanted three yards of a striped print. Sliding her scissors through the fabric, she glanced up and out the front plateglass window and saw the children were just then passing under the store's raspberry-colored canopy, which covered the front walk. Already a throng of people filled the sidewalk, though the fair had begun only a few hours before.

The weather was beautiful—cool but not cold. People were happy to congregate together in their little town of six hundred. This weekend, their population would swell to well over thirty thousand. The local police would have their hands full directing traffic.

Deborah watched the children thread their way through the crowd. Martha guided the wheelchair, leaning down to say something to Aaron, who laughed, then tugged on his jacket. Matthew walked close beside them, holding onto Max's leash. The yellow Labrador trotted beside them, his head held high, nose pushed into the air sniffing the festival smells.

A warning alarm sounded in Deborah's mind, but she pushed it away. In no time at all, the children would be back safe and sound.

Nearly an hour later, as Martha guided his chair, Aaron stared up at the twinkling lights in the trees that lined the sidewalks of Shipshewana's shopping district. The artificial lights reminded him of the stars, and he wondered why the *Englischers* had bothered to wrap them around the tree branches.

Perhaps because they lived in town, where *Gotte*'s lights weren't as easy to see.

That's what his *daadi* would say anyway.

Today had been very nearly perfect.

He'd received an *A* on his spelling test in school and a *B* on his math quiz. Maybe he could have earned an *A*, but Jacob and Joseph had been popping peas at the girls in the next row, and

Aaron had started laughing, which led to wheezing. By the time he got his breathing under control, time was up, and he hadn't been able to finish the last two questions.

It had been worth it to see Annie King squirm back and forth, trying to pull the peas out from between her dress and her apron. Aaron liked Annie all right, but she could be a little annoying at times. He'd told his *mamm* that once, and she'd explained he would like girls more when he was older.

That was hard to imagine.

Except for Martha. She was nice, but then again, she was different. More like his *mamm*.

"Drat." His *bruder* stopped suddenly in the middle of the sidewalk, causing Martha to nearly trip and pull back on his wheelchair. It felt like the time he'd ridden his *dat*'s horse, in the saddle, and the horse had suddenly reversed. Aaron had fallen, but his *dat* had caught him before he'd hit the ground—something they still hadn't told his *mamm*.

"Forget something?" Martha asked.

"*Ya*. I think I left my wallet at one of the last places we stopped."

"When we bought the candy apples?" Martha peered around at Aaron's half-eaten apple.

"Maybe. I took it out and set it on the counter of the booth."

"Wasn't your cousin Mary Ellen working there?"

"*Ya*. I'm sure she would have set it aside for me if I did leave it after I paid."

Martha pointed to the sack in his right hand. "After that we bought your new slingshot."

"True, but I think I paid for that with money out of my pocket, from the change Mary Ellen gave me. Now I can't remember." Matthew took off his wool cap and rubbed his hand over his head, front to back, then back to front—something Aaron knew he did when he was *naerfich*.

13

"Matt, you go and see Mary Ellen." Aaron pulled in a deep breath, then continued. "Martha, you go and check the slingshot booth. I'll wait here with Max."

"Are you sure?" Matthew glanced from Martha to Aaron and back again.

"I'm not . . . ," another deep breath, "going back to the quilting shop without you." He reached for Max and gave the dog a reassuring pat. "*Mamm* would have both our hides."

"All right. She told us to be back by dark, and there's still a little light left. If we hurry — "

"We can be there and back in ten minutes." Martha moved to the front of his chair, squatted down so she was eye to eye with him. "Sure you'll be fine?"

"*Ya*. Move me to the side." He glanced over to where a bench had been placed next to a large shrub. "There."

"Okay. We'll be back before you even know we're gone."

"Stop worrying." Aaron looped Max's leash around his wrist. "I'm not a . . ."

Matt glanced back over his shoulder, then at Aaron, a smile trying to win over the worry.

". . . little kid," Aaron finished.

"'Course you're not," Martha whispered.

He saw the look that passed between Martha and his *bruder*, but decided he'd rather ignore it than deal with their concern. Today had been very nearly perfect.

"He's *gut*," Matthew said. "Let's hurry."

They took off through the crowd, which was already beginning to thin. In fact, this end of the street was much less busy than the rest, probably because Daisy's Quilt Shop wasn't at the center of town.

Aaron was always calling it Callie's Quilt Shop in his head. He remembered Daisy, the lady who'd been Callie's *aenti*. She'd always kept little pieces of candy behind the counter for them. Callie didn't

14

know about the candy, but it didn't matter. He liked her as much as Daisy. She had a funny accent, like something he'd heard in a Western movie he'd watched at his neighbor's house once.

Justin, the boy who lived at the farmhouse next door, was a year older than Aaron. He went to the *Englisch* school and loved old Westerns. Justin was from New Mexico, and he said John Wayne was the best cowboy who had ever ridden a horse. Sometimes Aaron's *mamm* paid Justin's *mamm* to drive Aaron to the hospital or Doc Bernie's office. Justin's *mamm* didn't want to take the money—he'd heard them discuss it time and again—so sometimes Aaron's *mamm* paid in fresh vegetables from their garden. Once she'd tried to give them a quilt, but Justin's *mamm* had insisted on paying for that.

Aaron didn't understand grown-up girls any more than he understood the ones in his classroom. He also didn't understand why sometimes Doc Bernie came to their house, but other times they had to go to the big city, to Doc's office in Fort Wayne. Actually he didn't mind the city. It was interesting.

So Aaron and Justin hung out together on doctor days, what with all that riding back and forth in the family van—which wasn't as cool as a buggy, but had its advantages on the large, crowded *Englisch* roads. The drives were long and when they returned back to Justin's house, his *mamm* and Justin's *mamm* would sit in the kitchen and drink tea and talk. Occasionally Aaron was allowed to go into Justin's room to play. Not always, but sometimes.

A few times they'd managed to sneak into the back bedroom and boot up Justin's laptop computer. Aaron's *mamm* didn't know he'd watched the old black-and-white movies, and he wasn't going to be the one to tell her. She tended to fuss about those sorts of things, like she fussed when he had trouble pulling in a deep breath.

Doc Bernie said that was normal behavior for *mamms*.

She definitely didn't know about the Western movies, but it

wasn't like they played video games or watched television. Justin's *mamm* was pretty strict for an *Englischer*. Justin's Internet didn't work unless he plugged it into the wall in the living room, and he didn't have a television in his room like he said some kids did.

But the old Western movies were something his *onkel* had given him. They'd merely had to slip them into the computer to watch them when they were bored, when Aaron's *mamm* had left him there and Justin's *mamm* had gone off to run errands.

And Aaron never mentioned it to his *mamm*. There were a lot of things his *mamm* didn't know.

The crowd on the sidewalk dwindled to nothing as the minutes ticked by, and Aaron finished the candy apple while he watched the front of Daisy's Quilt Shop.

Too bad he didn't have a watch.

Max lay down next to his chair, his head on his paws, his ears relaxed and touching the ground. When Aaron thought about the future, he thought about working with animals like Max. Animals seemed more comfortable around him than people did.

Why was that?

The sun had set, though it still wasn't full dark.

He could make out the front of the shop and the garden on the far side of it. The street lamps came on, casting a funny glow. Staring down the sidewalk, down toward the garden where Max liked to play, something shiny caught the light so it winked back at him.

The bushes bordering the garden on the far side of the parking lot moved slightly.

Holding out his hand, Aaron tested the air.

No breeze.

None.

The bushes moved again.

Aaron leaned over in his chair to see better.

There was someone standing in the bushes. All he could see was the bottom half of the person—the top half was hidden by the shrubs. Had to be a lady. Aaron could see the color of her dress. He didn't know any man who would wear a pair of pants that color of green.

Why was some lady hiding in Miss Callie's bushes?

She was staring in the direction of the shop, kind of angled toward Aaron, but more toward the windows of the shop.

Probably she couldn't see Aaron from where she was.

He rolled his chair forward one, then two rounds of the wheels. Max moved forward with him, then resettled next to his wheel. Aaron scooted to the front of his chair, careful not to tip it over.

Max raised his head and looked at him quizzically.

Aaron put one finger to his lips, then stared back toward the woman in the bushes. At first he thought she was gone, but then he spotted her dark green dress again. She'd be hard to see, except every few seconds she shuffled her feet, and he could make out her black shoes.

Aaron was so focused on watching her feet and not losing sight of her he didn't see the man walk up behind her.

Everything that happened next, happened very quickly.

The woman pitched forward, out of the bushes and onto the pavement, landing facedown with her arms beside her as if she'd meant to give someone a hug before falling. Her body seemed to twitch once, then again, then her arms and her body lay perfectly still, like one of his sister's dolls thrown in the dirt. No blood spread out around her, but somehow Aaron knew she was dead.

He knew, because he'd seen that in the Western too.

The man stepped forward. With one hand he stuck something into his back pocket. Then he lunged over the woman, grabbed her purse, and reached forward to pick up an item off the ground. Then his head jerked up and he was staring straight at Aaron and Max, who had begun barking madly.

Finally, he turned and he fled into the darkening night.

Chapter 2

CALLIE HAD LEFT FOR A QUICK ERRAND. They had used up all of the cash-register tape—a silly thing to run out of on the biggest weekend sale of the year. She'd dashed out to buy some from the General Store, needing to feel the coolness of the fall evening on her face. Though the shop had been crowded when she left, Melinda, Deborah, and Lydia were there to help with customers. Callie had been gone fifteen minutes tops and was less than a block away when she heard Max barking. Clutching her small shopping bag and purse, she began sprinting toward her shop.

Why was Max barking as if someone's life depended on it?

Her garden came into sight, followed by the lights of her shop. She slowed and breathed a sigh of relief.

No fire. No police lights. Perhaps Max had merely treed a squirrel again.

Then she realized his barking wasn't coming from the yard. He was past the yard, near the bench on the far side of the shop, near Aaron, who had rolled out to the middle of the sidewalk and was sitting there alone, gesturing to the dog.

Max was running back and forth, first toward her, then back to Aaron, barking the whole time as if he were sounding an alarm.

She started to run again—toward Aaron this time. Perhaps

he was having trouble breathing. It was hard to tell in the fading light. But then she was close enough to see that he was waving her back, waving her in the direction of her garden.

So she spun around, slowing down to search for what she'd missed during her sprint toward the shop.

A cry caught in her throat when she saw the woman lying half in, half out of her shrubs, lying with her arms spread out as if she'd literally taken a flying leap onto the pavement, lying perfectly still and facedown.

Callie glanced around, hoping to see someone who might be close at hand to help, but the crowds had moved toward the center of town. No one else seemed to have noticed the tragedy occurring at the corner of her shop's parking lot.

She crept closer, peering at the woman.

Callie knew that face. She'd scrutinized it often enough through the front windows of Quilts and Needles. How was this possible? She was staring at the lifeless form of her nemesis, her archrival, the person she'd spent the past year trying to win over to her side. As a final act of retribution, Mrs. Knepp had died in her parking lot.

Callie knelt down and put her fingers gently on Mrs. Knepp's neck to feel for a pulse. The woman's skin was fragile and thin beneath Callie's fingers. It reminded her of the archived papers she sometimes stopped by to read at the Shipshewana Visitor's Center. For over a year now, she'd sparred with this woman, but she'd never actually touched her—the realization hit Callie like a blow.

Mrs. Knepp was still warm to the touch. She couldn't have been dead long, and Callie couldn't feel a pulse.

Had she been standing near the shrubs and stopped breathing—perhaps choked on something or suffered a heart attack? But her hands weren't clutching her neck or her heart. They were flung out to her side.

Mrs. Knepp had never struck Callie as particularly fragile. The old lady was tough as a drill sergeant. Why would she drop dead on such a pleasant September night?

Or had she?

Perhaps something more sinister had happened?

If so, Callie knew from past experience she needed to be careful not to mess up Shane's crime scene.

With the first tendrils of fear sneaking down her spine, she backed away slowly. With Max's barks still ringing loud and insistent in her ears, she turned and ran toward Aaron. As she darted past the front window of her shop, she glanced in and was amazed to see customers still milling around, folks still talking and laughing.

Didn't they know?

Hadn't they heard Max's cries for help?

Couldn't they tell that death, possibly murder, had once more invaded the town limits of Shipshewana?

She reached Aaron at the same time Matthew and Martha did.

"What's wrong? Why's Max barking?" Matt squatted down on the right-hand side of his brother, his face red from having run and the questions coming in a rush as he tried to catch his breath.

Martha tugged on the strings of her prayer *kapp*. "Are you all right, Miss Callie? You're shaking and—"

"Listen to me, Martha. I want you to go inside. Don't go anywhere but inside. Keep your eyes on the store as you walk in. Do you understand me?"

"*Ya*."

"Once inside, I want you to have your *mamm* call 9-1-1. She needs to tell the dispatcher to send help quickly. She needs to notify them someone's died."

Martha's eyes widened, but she didn't ask any further questions, only turned and hurried into the shop.

Max had stopped barking when Callie arrived. Now he sat

between her and Aaron, the hair on the back of his neck raised and a low growl emanating from his throat.

Aaron reached forward and touched between his ears. "It's okay, boy. You did *gut*."

Max turned and licked Aaron's hand once, then refocused on the scene in front of him—eyes and ears still on alert.

"We weren't even gone for ten minutes. Are you sure you're okay?" Matt removed his wool cap and rubbed his hand over his hair. "What happened, Aaron?"

"I'm not ..." Aaron pulled in a deep breath, and Callie wondered how much the shock of Mrs. Knepp's death had affected him. "I'm not sure."

Melinda tumbled out of the shop, her shoes slapping against the pavement as she ran to her son's side. "What is it? Aaron, are you okay?"

She'd always been so calm, so completely composed about Aaron and his condition. The stark fear in her eyes was something Callie had to glance away from. Instead she focused on Max and on calming him down. He continued to whine deep in his throat, his gaze focused on the lifeless form at the far end of the parking lot.

"I can't breathe—"

"Are you having an attack? Do we need to call the doctor?"

"No. It's that you're clutching me so ..." Aaron pulled back, his face flushed. "Tight!"

Melinda stood and straightened her apron over her dress, but she didn't step away from her son's chair. She did peer up at Callie. "You wanted Deborah to call the police? She said there's been a death. Are you sure?"

"I hope she didn't alert the customers." Callie tucked her hair behind her ears.

"No. Deborah took the cordless phone into the supply room and used it there. The customers are staring out the window because I ran. I was afraid for Aaron. Afraid that—"

21

"I'm fine," Aaron insisted.

"Who died?" Matt stood and tried to see around his mother. "I don't understand how this could have happened. We left him no more than ten minutes ago."

"You left your *bruder*? Here? Alone?" The questions came like hail falling on a roof, causing Matt to flinch and stare down at his shoes.

While he explained to his mother where they'd gone, Callie wrapped Max's leash around her wrist, then walked to the door of her shop and whispered to Deborah about what she'd found. Fortunately it was full dark now, and the customers couldn't see the lifeless form that awaited Shipshewana's finest.

A cruiser pulled up, red lights blazing and siren blaring.

Callie winced.

There would be no keeping Mrs. Knepp's death a secret now. Her mind ran back over the same questions like a tongue seeking out a sore tooth. Mrs. Knepp was old. Could she have died of natural causes? Or did someone harm her?

There was something else bothering Callie about what she'd seen, something her mind kept reaching for, but like a fading dream she couldn't quite remember what it was.

What had she seen?

Matt continued to squirm under his mother's gaze, scuffing his right shoe against the sidewalk, leaving streaks of mud.

That was it. Suddenly what she'd seen came back with crystal clarity, but instead of feeling relief, a shiver crept down her spine, causing her to draw her sweater tighter around her shoulders.

A light storm had passed through the evening before. She recalled waking in the middle of the night to the sound of rain dripping on her roof. As she rolled over, reached out, and stroked Max, she'd breathed a prayer of gratefulness she wouldn't need to water her garden before work.

Rain.

And gardens.

And mud.

Minutes earlier, when she'd first arrived and seen Mrs. Knepp, when she'd first run toward her, the initial thing she'd seen, even before it had registered that the woman was dead, were large muddy footprints, one on each side of the body.

Almost as if someone had stood directly over her lifeless form. Which left Callie with two questions.

What was Mrs. Knepp doing in the bushes of Callie's shop?

And who had stood over the old lady as she died?

Callie watched Andrew Gavin step out of the cruiser. A second police vehicle arrived, which held Captain Taylor. She knew both men quite well, given her history with the police department since her arrival in Shipshewana fifteen months ago.

Gavin was a teddy bear at heart, though physically he looked to Callie like he'd been discharged from the Marines just last week. Thirty-one years old with blue eyes that could turn to ice if you were threatening the citizens of Shipshe, all six feet of Andrew Gavin was muscular in a military way. It was something he hadn't lost from the four years he'd spent serving overseas for Uncle Sam. His brown hair was still cut regulation length, and his brows framed eyes filled with concern as he hurried in her direction.

Captain Stan Taylor followed a few steps behind.

Callie barely remembered her grandfather, but she imagined he might have looked a lot like Officer Taylor. Warm brown eyes, bushy white brows, and a protruding stomach gave him a grandfatherly look. Taylor's wife constantly implemented new plans to reduce his waistline, but none had been successful to date. More importantly, he'd been kind to Callie when she'd first been under suspicion of murder her first summer in Shipshe.

Taylor took the lead. "Did we receive that call correctly, Callie? Has there been a death?"

She'd remained fairly calm since hearing Max's furious barking, but now that Gavin and Taylor were here, her sense of detachment fled.

She raised her hand to point toward the body at the far side of her parking area and—now that she knew her friends were safe, that her worst fears were allayed—her entire arm began to shake uncontrollably.

"Over there, facedown on the pavement." Callie began walking with them to the body. "She might have ... she might have fallen over."

"She didn't fall," Aaron said. "A man pushed her."

Everyone turned to stare at the small boy in the wheelchair. He didn't blink and didn't look away. He waited—eyes wide, wool cap pulled down over his ears, right hand resting on the wheel of his chair.

The shaking spread to Callie's legs, and she had to sit down in the middle of the sidewalk.

Did Aaron just say someone had pushed Mrs. Knepp?

But pushing someone onto the concrete wouldn't kill them. Would it? How could it?

Yet she was dead.

Mrs. Knepp was dead.

Whoever had pushed her had left her body less than fifty feet from the front door of Callie's shop.

And whoever had done it was still running around loose.

Chapter 3

DEBORAH WAS CONTENT staying inside the door of the quilt shop, even after Callie had whispered that she'd found a body on the corner of the lot.

When Martha had first come in, she'd sent her oldest directly to the fabric table to help with orders, then hurried to the back to make the emergency phone call.

All the while her mind had insisted there must be some mistake. This couldn't be happening again.

Then Melinda had fled out the door to check on her boys, Callie had come to talk to her ever so briefly, and the officers had arrived in their police cruiser and walked over to Callie.

Deborah was a practical woman. She understood death was part of life. She'd personally sat beside death's door several times in her thirty-three years. But it had been less than twelve months ago that she and Esther had stopped by Reuben's pond and found an Amish girl floating facedown in it. Five months before that, Callie had been suspected of killing the town's newspaper editor. Surely there was a limit to the amount of violence in the world. It didn't make sense that they would find themselves in the middle of a death once again—and so soon.

Something about the way Captain Taylor rested his hand on the

25

butt of his weapon while he was talking to Aaron, Melinda, and Callie gave Deborah the feeling this was indeed what was happening. Gavin was scanning the area too. *Almost as if the two officers thought ... as if they expected to find a dangerous person lurking about.*

Deborah had not actually accepted that there was a dead person outside the shop. She'd hoped perhaps it was a mistake.

Perhaps children were playing a prank or someone had taken ill and merely looked dead.

Watching the officers, the thought crossed her mind that maybe it was more than a death. Maybe it was another murder.

Nein.

She couldn't accept that it had happened again — in their town, near their children, and in the midst of their lives.

She refused to believe it.

Until she saw Callie walk away from Melinda and Aaron and point toward parking area of the shop, after which she crumpled onto the front sidewalk. Until she saw Max try to nuzzle Callie's face. Then Deborah knew that death had once more found its way into their protected circle.

She dropped the bolt of fabric she'd been holding, pushed through the crowd in the store, and ran outside to kneel beside Callie.

"Was iss letz?"

"I've lived here almost a year and a half, and sometimes I still can't understand a word you say." Callie's voice was muffled, since her head remained between her knees. Her knees were propped up, making a tent of the new dark green dress they'd sewn together.

"She'll be all right, Deborah. It's only the shock." Gavin touched their shoulders as he walked by, then turned toward the crowd of people who were spilling out of the shop.

"I'm going to need everyone to remain calm and go back inside."

"What's happened?" one of the customers called out.

"Why do we have to go back inside?" another asked. "I'm done shopping."

"I need to go home to my family." Deborah thought that sounded like Mrs. Drisban, one of their regular customers.

"I understand, but we're going to have to ask you a few questions first." Gavin turned to catch instructions from Taylor, then relayed them to the small crowd gathering at the door of the shop. "The Captain has asked everyone not to leave until we can have you fill out some forms."

"Forms? Why do we have to fill out forms?"

"Because it's a requirement in these situations. Now please move back into the building." Gavin crossed his arms and took up a military stance outside the door.

Deborah had seen a few soldiers in uniform when she and Callie had gone to the museum in Chicago. The soldiers had stopped at a diner where they were eating lunch. Callie had explained to her then that Gavin still acted exactly like them. They'd had a laugh over it, because they'd both been able to picture him in the middle of the group of men, in uniform. He wouldn't even have needed a new haircut.

But looking at him now, watching him take up that protective stance outside Callie's door, she realized that what he hadn't lost when he'd left the military was more than physical bearing or hairstyle. What he hadn't lost was the inclination to watch over those in his care.

But who was he protecting now?

One thing was certain. No one would leave unless they thought they could go through Andrew Gavin, which they couldn't. The grumbling continued at the entrance of the shop, but there wasn't a single person who attempted to move to the parking area.

"We'll pass out the forms once you're back inside," Captain Taylor explained, pocketing his cell phone and walking in front of Gavin. "They ask you to provide your contact information and answer a few simple questions. Officer Gavin will remain here to ensure no one leaves. I have another officer posted at the back door. This is going to take us an hour or more, so I suggest you all move away from the door and settle down. The more cooperative you are, the faster we can proceed."

"Proceed with what?"

"Has there been a burglary?"

The questions flew at him rapidly.

"My daughter texted me that you've found a dead body."

Deborah and Callie both glanced up at the same time. The first officers to arrive had quickly cordoned off the sidewalk and parking lot adjacent to the shop. Yellow crime-scene tape now stretched from where Melinda and her boys waited to the end of Callie's garden area. They'd marked off her entire section of the block. But that didn't stop a growing crowd of onlookers from gathering outside the crime-scene tape. Quite a few of them had cell phones out. Some were texting, others were talking, and several were taking pictures.

The shoppers reluctantly went back inside as a county vehicle arrived. Two crime-scene techs spoke quickly with Captain Taylor and then began setting up mobile lights.

When they switched them on, Deborah saw the body, the black shoes, dark stockings, apron hem, and plain dress.

Her stomach clenched as if she were seized with a heavy labor pain. "Who is that, Callie?"

"It's Mrs. Knepp."

"You're sure?"

"Yes, I'm sure." Callie placed her head back between her knees as Trent McCallister pulled his truck to the curb, then ducked under the crime-scene tape.

He made his way straight to them. Tall, with light-colored hair that reached past his collar, he always reminded Deborah of a teenage boy. It was more than the carefree smile and the clothes that looked as if he'd stolen them off one of the skateboarders down at the park—tonight ragged blue jeans and a "GET FIT"

T-shirt. It was that his hazel eyes seemed to refuse to grow up in spite of the things he photographed as editor, writer, and photographer of the town paper. Or maybe—the thought startled Deborah as she knelt beside Callie—maybe because of them.

"You two all right?" Trent asked.

"We're fine, but she's not doing so well." Deborah nodded toward Mrs. Knepp.

"Almost looks as if she tried to fly from the top of the tree and met a hard landing." Trent raised his new Nikon digital camera, one with a lens big enough to capture more detail than Deborah cared to see. He clicked off three pictures, then turned back to them. "Were you here when it happened, Callie?"

She shook her head no, but didn't raise her eyes to meet his.

"What's wrong with her?"

"Gavin says she's in shock."

"Huh. You'd think she'd be used to this by now." Trent snapped two more pictures and turned back toward Melinda and the boys. "Why are they waiting outside?"

"Oh, my gosh." Callie's head popped up. "I forgot about them." She jumped to her feet, nearly tripping herself on the hem of her fashionable dress. "I wonder why they're still waiting by the bench."

"Callie, I need you to stay over here." Taylor stepped between her and Melinda. "I know you want to go to her, but she's fine. They're all fine. Can you wait here until we take your statement?"

Callie nodded but turned to Deborah as soon as Taylor walked back over to his men. "Why can't we go to her? What harm would it do?"

"He probably wants to make sure you don't color each other's statements. If you talk to each other, you'll begin to echo what the other says." Deborah glanced over at Melinda, who now sat on the bench next to Aaron. Matthew sat beside her, staring at the growing collection of officers.

"Melinda didn't see it," Callie reminded her. "Aaron did. Aaron was here before I was."

"Then Aaron is their primary witness." Trent reached in his pocket and pulled out a treat for Max. "What?" he asked, in response to Deborah's stare. "I'm a reporter. It makes sense for me to carry dog treats. You never know when I'm going to cross a hostile canine."

Whistling softly, he walked away.

"He only does that for Max, doesn't he?" Deborah reached forward, scratching Max between the ears.

"Yes. I think my dog is gaining weight."

"Are you okay now? Your color's coming back, but I was worried there for a minute."

Callie reached down and placed both arms around Max, giving him a giant hug. Then she stood and looked Deborah straight in the eyes. When she did, Deborah realized why Callie had been sitting with her head between her knees.

It wasn't merely the shock of what she'd seen.

It was the realization of what was to come.

"Deborah, I'd thought maybe Mrs. Knepp had just collapsed—died of a sudden aneurysm or heart problem."

"Except you don't collapse with both your arms out."

"True. It's an odd position. There's more though." Callie told Deborah about the shoe prints on each side of the body and about Aaron seeing a man push the old lady.

"Who would push her?"

"I don't know."

"Well, a shove—even onto concrete—can't kill someone."

"Deborah, it's so creepy—someone who I've been in a feud with dying. I always thought I'd have time to win her over, but now..."

"It's not your fault, and you did attempt to gain her friendship. More than once. You know this."

"Maybe I should have tried harder." Callie glanced over at Mrs. Knepp's body, and Deborah noticed the color draining from her face again.

"None of us are able to choose our day, Callie. Don't look at her that way. Don't look at her as if it's your fault."

"It's more than her being dead and on the corner of my lot. Whoever Aaron saw push her is still out there. They probably ran away because of Max's barking." Callie reached for Deborah's hands. "And think of this—they were bold enough to harm her so close to my shop, on one of the busiest nights of the year. What kind of person does that? And why?"

Deborah didn't know how to answer that question, didn't know where to begin. Before she could think of what to say though, another car pulled up on the street—a car teenage boys refer to as a hot rod. Yellow with a black stripe over the hood, it blocked in several other vehicles, and Deborah could just make out Shane Black sitting behind the wheel.

She'd heard Callie's questions, but she had no answers for her. She also heard Callie's sharp intake of breath at the sound of Shane's car, and she had no answer for that either. Something had been going on between those two for some time. Something neither one was willing to admit.

Thoughts of home flitted through her mind, but Deborah pushed them away. She realized Martha would need to catch a ride to their farm with her *aenti* who had a booth tonight in the downtown area. She couldn't possibly leave Callie and Melinda until they were cleared to go home as well. And Callie might need a place to sleep for the evening if she didn't want to remain here.

Though Deborah had risen early to prepare for what was supposed to be one of the biggest festivals of the year, the day had taken an unexpected turn. With a sinking feeling, Deborah realized her own bed was a place she wouldn't see for many hours.

Chapter 4

SHANE FORCED HIMSELF to remain in his car and survey the scene. It wasn't what he wanted to do. He wanted to push through the growing crowd until he reached Callie's side, and then pull her into his arms and assure himself she wasn't hurt.

But plainly she was not hurt.

He could see that from where he sat. Plus dispatch had reported one deceased and that would be the lady facedown in the parking lot with her arms splayed out to her sides. The woman appeared to be Amish, but Shane knew from his years as a county detective that clothing didn't prove a thing.

Floodlights had already been set up by the crime-tech team. They revealed large muddy footsteps tracking away from the body and down the sidewalk to the south. Apparently this wasn't the work of a professional. Either that or this guy wanted to be followed. By the size of those footprints, Shane concluded the perp was a he. But, given it was an old lady who had been attacked and Shane didn't see her handbag lying around, he would have bet his 1971 Buick GSX the perp was a he without even examining the footprints.

And Shane didn't anticipate parting with his classic Buick.

Possibly this hadn't been a crime. Shane pulled his Chicago

Cubs ball cap down farther on his head and considered the possibility.

Could be that someone found her dead and ran, but that was unlikely. Most folks in this town stuck around, called for help, and answered the officers' questions. Even the Amish — who didn't care to have their pictures snapped by a reporter from the *Gazette* — would answer questions. They might not answer with the detail Shane wanted, but still, they wouldn't have left a body there for someone else to stumble over.

No. If the person who had been on the scene first had run, he was hiding something.

Shane surveyed the rest of the area surrounding the shop. These few minutes in his car would be the only quiet he'd have in the next twenty-four hours, and sometimes — for him — first impressions formed the cornerstone of the investigation.

Deborah stood beside Callie and the dog. He wished Callie Harper would allow him to get as close to her as she let the Labrador. The thought rudely intruded into his analysis of the scene, and Shane pushed it away as the beginnings of a headache drummed at his temples.

Andrew Gavin and Stan Taylor stood near the front of the shop, shooing witnesses back inside. It was doubtful anyone in the shop would have seen much of anything useful given the angle of the windows, which fronted out to the street — to the west. The placement of the body was to the south. Anyone inside the shop likely wouldn't have noticed a thing unless they were hanging out the door, but he'd pursue any possible lead. Cases had turned on less.

He returned his attention to Callie and Deborah and noticed they were staring north — almost as if they wanted to move that direction but weren't sure if Gavin and Taylor would allow it.

He followed their gaze and spotted what they were looking at, or rather whom — Melinda Byer and her two sons, Matthew and Aaron. All three huddled on a bench, though of course Aaron was in his wheelchair beside it. Matthew stared at his shoes, misery etched on his young face. Melinda kept one hand firmly on Aaron's chair, the other on Matthew, like she needed to protect the two boys. She looked worried. Matthew looked guilty.

But Aaron—Aaron looked completely lost. His face was devoid of color and his eyes continually darted from the officers to the body at the far end of the lot. He chewed on the thumbnail of his left hand and his right knee jiggled nervously on the footrest of the wheelchair.

Aaron was the person Shane needed to talk to.

Aaron was his witness.

First things first though.

He slammed the Buick's door loudly enough to draw some attention.

"Keep McCallister away from the deceased," he growled, walking over for a quick assessment of the body. He hoped he never became accustomed to seeing the violence one person could do to another. This one seemed pretty senseless. Closer inspection seemed to confirm she was in fact a little, old Amish woman, struck down on a cool September night.

"I have feelings, Black. When have I ever compromised one of your crime scenes?" Trent stuck his hand out and Shane shook it.

Hard as it was to admit such a thing, Shane liked the editor of the *Gazette*. Normally he stayed clear of the press, but Trent was different. He'd kept the girls safe on more than one occasion, though he'd managed to pull a few good headlines out of it in the process.

"There's always a first time," Shane mumbled. "How do you manage to beat me to every crime scene?"

"Maybe because I live in Shipshe."

"Yeah. Your lack of travel time is giving you a leg up."

Trent nodded toward the corpse. "Seems lately, we're having more than our fair share of murders."

"We don't know it's a murder," Shane muttered, though Trent had no doubt reached the same conclusion he had. "If it is, I wouldn't call three cases in fifteen months a crime wave."

He scowled as Trent began scribbling in his book. As far as quotes went though, that was a relatively harmless one. He started to walk away, then turned around and pointed a finger at Trent.

"No pictures of the deceased."

"No identifying pictures. I know the rules."

"Be sure you follow them." Shane turned and approached a crime-scene tech.

"Cause of death?"

"Good evening to you too, Shane." Leroy Jackson's white teeth practically glowed when he smiled—his dark-skinned face melting into the night. Short, thin, and balding, he was the best crime tech Shane had ever known—and he'd known more than a few.

"Suppose it could be worse. Could have several senior citizens falling out of the bushes."

"Wouldn't say she fell, given the angle of her body." Leroy was taking measurements and writing them down in his book. Most techs used recorders now, but Leroy used a book, like the old-timers. Shane had asked him why once, and Leroy admitted knowing a guy who had a recorder break on him. The killer had gone free because forensics couldn't stand up to the defense during the trial.

"So she was pushed?"

"Not exactly."

"I don't understand."

"Neither do I. It's more like she jumped or something jolted her."

"Taser?"

"That's what I was thinking, but there are no obvious signs

of it—would have to be one of the newer, wireless models. An autopsy should be able to tell us."

Shane stared down at the scene, sighed, and ran his hand over the back of his neck. Like he'd figured . . . it was going to be a long night. "Send pics of those shoeprints to my email along with anything else you find."

"You got it."

Shane finally strode to Callie.

When she turned her face up toward his, it was all he could do not to reach forward and wipe the fear off her face, smooth the worry lines away, kiss her as softly as he had outside the Lapps' barn back in Goshen. Had that been last winter? He'd been trying to take their relationship to the next level for months, but she'd been avoiding his calls. To be honest, they didn't have a relationship— you couldn't call meeting over criminal investigations dates.

So Shane didn't kiss her or touch her face. He settled for catching her hand in his.

"You okay?"

"Everyone keeps asking me that." She stared at the ground as she spoke. "At least I think that's what Deborah asked me."

"Is that a yes or no?" He ran his thumb up and down the inside of her palm.

When she still didn't glance up, Deborah answered for her. "She's better than she was five minutes ago. At least she's standing now."

"True?" Shane asked.

"True." Callie's voice was soft, with a slight tremor.

"Did you find the body?"

"Yes." She glanced at him then, her brown eyes brimming with tears, but she blinked them back. She looked away, staring out at the crowd gathering across the street.

He put his hand under her chin, waited until her dark eyes met his. "Don't worry. We'll catch him."

"Him?"

"Not likely that a woman would bump off an old lady in public. Women tend to be sneakier—use poison or the dinnerware. Plus there's the size of the shoeprints tracking away from the body. You'd have to be talking about a warrior woman, someone from the Amazon, and she would be fairly easy to spot. My bet is our perp's a male."

"So you do think it was murder? Not an . . . an accident?" Callie's eyes filled with a wild terror he'd seen before, seen too often in victims of crime, and it tore at his heart to see it in her.

She'd been through a lot since coming to Shipshe, and she'd always been strong. His mind flashed back to the first time he'd arrested her, and he nearly smiled. Callie Harper was one tough woman. She had experience around dead bodies. But he'd never seen her quite so rattled before.

Why the meltdown now?

Why was this murder affecting her so deeply?

"I suppose she could have picked your parking lot to have a heart attack, but other evidence—" He stopped himself, knowing he shouldn't share the details with her and Deborah. They weren't on the police department staff and weren't part of the team, even if they did find a way of showing up during every murder investigation. "My guess is foul play. We'll know in the next few hours. And if it is murder, I'm betting the perp was a he—"

"He's still out there, Shane. Whoever did this." Callie started to say more, then pressed her fingers to her lips.

Shane glanced at Aaron, and then back at her, wondering where he should start.

"Go to Aaron," she whispered. "I think he might have seen what happened. I just heard . . . I just heard Max barking as I was coming back from an errand." She held up a bag from the General Store. "I started running as soon as I heard him barking. I knew something was wrong."

"So you came from ..."

"The south." Callie turned and pointed. "I'd been to purchase register tape. Max was with Aaron. When I heard him barking, I ran and I ... I didn't see her at first ... then Aaron waved me back, and that's when I noticed her."

"Exactly as she is now?"

"Yes. I checked for a pulse, but there was none. Mrs. Knepp was already dead."

Deborah sighed. "I wonder if her daughter has heard."

"You're sure the deceased is Mrs. Knepp?" Shane asked, as every muscle in his back grew more rigid.

"Yeah. I'm sure."

"How do you know her?" Shane frowned, pulled down his ball cap. He didn't like that Callie knew the deceased. Didn't like that her involvement in the murder was already growing more complicated.

"She's the owner of Quilts and Needles," Callie explained. "It's the other quilt shop in town." She stopped, gazed around as if the killer might jump out of the bushes. "Max and Aaron were already here when it happened—I guess. That must be why Max was b-b-barking."

The final words were hard to make out, her teeth were chattering so badly.

"Deborah, take her over to the ambulance."

"I'm f-f-fine."

"You're in shock, Callie." The words came out sharper than he intended. He pulled in a deep breath and forced his aggravation down. It wasn't her fault it happened here. And it wasn't her fault she knew the victim. "Go with Deborah and let the paramedics check you over."

When she continued to shake her head, the last of Shane's patience snapped. "Go now or I'll carry you there myself."

Callie's eyes flashed with a small spark of the anger he was used to, and the worry gnawing at the base of his neck backed off a tad.

"She can walk," Deborah murmured.

Callie tried to yank her hand out of his grasp, but he pulled her back to him. "They'll give you a blanket and some water. Sit down in their rig for a few minutes and let your adrenaline return to normal. I'll check on Aaron."

Shane had been trying to get close to Callie Harper since the morning they'd spent at the top of Timothy Lapp's silo — the morning he'd been terrified a nineteen-year-old boy would pull a trigger and end her life. He'd been patient because he cared for her and he didn't believe in rushing things, but seeing her standing there beneath the streetlights with another dead body only a hundred feet away, he couldn't help himself.

Before he could question whether it was the right thing to do, he turned her face toward his and kissed her softly on the lips. Then, without another word, he walked away.

As Aaron watched the entire scene unfold, his emotions hopped all over the place, like the grease that popped in the iron pan when his *mamm* fried chicken. Right now what he was feeling most was surprise, but sometimes fear crept in, and then suddenly he'd find himself curious about what was happening. Grease popping in the pan — that's what he was.

This was nothing like that Western movie starring John Wayne.

In *The Cowboys*, John Wayne was okay, even after the cattle rustlers showed up and shot him in the back. He hadn't looked okay to Aaron — not with blood coming out of his elbow and his shoulder and his stomach. Aaron had been upset the first time he'd watched the movie, and it had taken all of his concentration not to cry when the boys and Mr. Nightlinger had buried John

Wayne on the hillside. Then Justin had shown him how they could hit the replay button and see that the old cowboy was fine. The movie would start over and things on the screen were like before. The killing in John Wayne movies was all pretend.

Tonight was different.

Everything—from the body on the pavement to the crime-scene tape to the *Englischer* walking toward him—everything told him this was real.

"Melinda." The *Englischer* stopped in front of them, waited for his *mamm* to say something.

"Detective Black."

"Are the boys all right?"

"They seem to be. We waited here because Officer Taylor asked us to. This is where Aaron was when ..." His mother clutched his chair more tightly, so tight he could feel it shake a bit under the pressure. "When it happened, I think. I ran out to check on him after Martha came in the shop to ask Deborah to call 9-1-1. Matt was out here with him. Then we all waited here."

Detective Black turned and studied the scene once more, then focused on Aaron's *mamm* again. "That's good. That was the right thing to do."

He stuck his hands in his back pockets and sighed heavily, like he had to give bad news. Aaron's teacher sighed that way sometimes, and good things never followed. "Callie says the deceased is Mrs. Knepp. Did you know her?"

Aaron couldn't see his *mamm*, but he heard her pull in her breath sharp-like. "*Ya*. 'Course I do. When Callie's shop was closed, we all had to go there for our quilting needs."

"Do you know anyone who would want to harm her?"

"No. Mrs. Knepp, she's lived in Shipshe for as long as I can remember. She was cranky, but no one took offense to it. That was simply her way."

"All right. I'm going to need to ask the boys a few questions now."

His *mamm* loosened her grip on the chair a bit, leaned forward, and gave them both her serious look. "Boys, this is Detective Black. Answer his questions directly. Don't add to your answers at all to make your stories better. He needs to know exactly what you saw so he can do his job."

Aaron nodded that he understood and noticed Matt did the same.

"*Ya*, Detective Black." Matt stood up tall.

"All right, Detective Black." Aaron tried to sit straighter in his chair.

"You can both call me Shane, since we're working together on this." The officer squatted down in front of Aaron's chair. 'Course Aaron had seen him around town before, but he'd never seen him this close. He didn't wear a uniform like the other officers. He was wearing a baseball cap, which seemed funny. But it was obvious — even to Aaron, and he was only seven, nearly eight — that Shane was The Law. He was tall and thin, but you could tell he was strong too.

Strong like Aaron's *dat* was strong.

Most *Englischers* he knew weren't near as strong as his *dat*. His *mamm* said that was because his *dat* worked in the field all day. Detective Black didn't work in the field, but it was still plain as could be — he was tough enough to do anything that needed doing. Probably he could build the barns and move the animals, same as Aaron's *daed* did.

Aaron stared down at his legs, at how useless they were, and the old feelings of shame and regret bubbled up from somewhere near his stomach.

Then Detective Black — or rather Shane — started talking to Aaron's *bruder*, and Aaron forgot about feeling bad. It was like watching the movie again, and he wanted to know what was going to happen next. He had questions too.

This officer was different from the others. He did things Aaron didn't understand. Aaron had watched him walk over to Mrs. Knepp, but he only paused for an awfully short time, which seemed odd. Didn't he need to study her body closer?

Then he'd talked with Miss Callie and Martha's *mamm* longer. Why was that?

Questions swirled through Aaron's mind as he looked into the man's pitch-black eyes. The questions nearly made him dizzy, like when he watched his kite tossing back and forth on a windy day—'course he could only hold the spool of string while his *bruder* ran with the kite, but he still liked to stare up into the sky and watch it take flight.

And honestly Aaron didn't mind studying Detective Black now, if it weren't for the dead woman at the other side of the parking lot. He should feel bad though. He'd just seen someone hurt someone else. Violence was wrong. How could he be interested in what was happening with Detective Black like Matt was interested in reading the sports page of the local paper? This wasn't something he should be thinking about right now.

He wondered if that made him a very bad person.

He wondered if he should talk to his *mamm* and *dat* about that—maybe later when they were home and he was ready to say his evening prayers.

"Matthew, did you see what happened?"

"*Nein.* I . . . I had left. I shouldn't have. I lost my wallet, and I went back to find it." Matt stared at a spot on the ground, and Aaron knew he was wondering if he could have stopped the bad man if he'd been here.

But he couldn't have.

Aaron had seen the hatred on the man's face. Remembering it made the candy apple he'd eaten earlier turn sour in his stomach, made him think he might need to throw up in the bushes, but he didn't want to puke in front of everyone. His *mamm* would fuss for sure and insist he go straight to bed. He swallowed and pushed the sour apple back down.

Matt couldn't have stopped the man. Probably no one could have, except maybe John Wayne.

Maybe Shane.

"All right. So you wheeled Aaron here first. The two of you were here alone and—"

"No. Martha was with us. I realized I'd left my wallet somewhere, but wasn't sure where. So we decided to go back and find it."

"That was my idea," Aaron piped in. "Remember? I suggested that Martha go to where you bought the slingshot and you go to where you bought the candy apple. It was my idea that you leave."

Matt licked his lips. "I'm the oldest. I should have known better than to leave you alone."

"I wasn't alone. You left me with Max."

Matt didn't answer that. Instead he went back to staring at the spot on the ground.

"What time do you think that was?"

"Wasn't dark yet." Matt looked up and out across the crowd that had gathered down the street. "But the lights in the trees had already come on, so it was tending toward dark."

"All right, we can check the timer on those."

"I've got it!" Matt sat up straighter and smacked has right fist into his left palm, exactly like when he was warming up to catch a baseball. Aaron loved that sound. "It was seven o'clock exactly when we left him. I know because I heard the clock tower—the one down by the train station—strike seven times. I thought, *If I run, I can be to that booth before the seventh strike.*"

Shane waited for Aaron's *mamm* to confirm the time.

She nodded once. "Sounds about right. It was growing dark when I first heard Max bark. I thought he'd seen a squirrel or a bird. After that, Martha came running inside telling us to call for help."

"We were gone ten, maybe fifteen, minutes. No more than that. I heard Max barking too, and I started running back." Matt turned and pointed to the north. "You can hear Max from a long way when he's *bedauerlich* or *naerfich*."

Shane glanced toward Melinda.

She mouthed the words *sad* and *nervous* to him.

"Good. Those are good details. Now this is very important." Shane looked each person in the eye, making sure he had their attention, then he focused on Aaron. "You were waiting here alone with Max—say, from seven to seven-fifteen. Tell me what you saw first."

Aaron felt everyone's attention on him. He tried not to squirm in his seat. "I was staring straight ahead, and I saw someone's shoes, then dark green cloth. I thought, *That can't be a man, because no man would have pants that color.*"

Shane stood and backed up so he was looking toward the body from Aaron's vantage point. "You could only see the woman's shoes?"

"And the bottom of her dress."

"Why was that?"

"Because she was hiding in the bushes."

Shane stood there for a minute, staring at the same thing Aaron was staring at—which at the moment was a lot of crime techs crowded around a dead body. Then he walked in front of him again, a frown pulling down the corners of his mouth. "Are you sure about that?"

"*Ya.* I thought it was strange, and Max and I, we leaned out to see better. She kept disappearing, because of the light and because her dress was sort of the same color as the leaves of the bush."

"Huh."

Aaron realized that was the first thing any of them had said that had surprised the officer. He hadn't expected that. And come to think of it, why *had* Mrs. Knepp been hiding?

As if he were echoing his thoughts, Shane asked, "Any idea what she was doing there, hiding in the bushes?"

Aaron began to chew on his thumbnail, though there wasn't much of it left.

"Aaron?"

"I wouldn't want to speak badly of anyone. And she's dead, right? It's not pretend, like ... like in the movies?"

Beside him, he felt his *mamm* stiffen.

"No. It's not pretend." Shane didn't seem surprised at all that Aaron had asked the question. "Whatever you tell me, it stays between us, Aaron. But maybe—" Shane glanced up and over to where Mrs. Knepp lay. "Maybe it will help me catch whoever did this to her. So probably she wouldn't mind."

"Well ..." Aaron ran his hand over the top rim of one of his wheels, another thing he did sometimes to calm himself. "It looked to me like she was spying on Miss Callie's shop. She was holding something up to her eyes, you know?"

Then he mimicked making two circles with his hands and holding them in front of his eyes.

"I know it was almost dark, but did you see any reflection coming from her direction?"

Aaron glanced at his *mamm*, unsure what Shane was asking.

"Reflection," his *mamm* repeated. He noticed her eyes were shiny behind her glasses, and he wondered if what he had done was going to make her cry. "Reflections are like the sun shining off water."

"Oh, *ya*. When she'd put her hands up, there would be a shiny sparkle for a minute. I suppose that's what made me notice her to begin with. It was sort of like a game spotting her hiding there, but then ... but then the big *Englisch* man came. He came up behind her and maybe pushed her. I'm not sure about that part."

"Go on," Shane said softly.

"Well, she sort of jumped, sort of fell then. Like when we catch a fish and *Dat* cleans it. 'Cept once I was helping and didn't hold the fish tight enough. *Dat* put his knife in, and the fish jumped." Aaron stole a peek at his *bruder*, but Matt only shrugged. "Like that, I guess. She jumped sort of, then lay there, like the fish lies there after *Dat* finishes gutting it."

Aaron felt coldness spread inside him then, and he didn't know what it meant. All he knew was that he wanted to go home.

Maybe he shouldn't be here.

Maybe he shouldn't have seen all he had seen.

Maybe it was because he'd watched the movies with Justin and now he was paying for that sin.

"She never did move again. The man didn't even seem surprised." When no one said anything, Aaron pushed on. "*Dat*, he's kind with the fish, the ones we throw back and the ones we keep. He says *gut* things to them and talks of how we need to eat and how *Gotte* provides for us. The *Englisch* man, well, he didn't seem kind at all, and he didn't say anything. He stood over her, then reached forward and grabbed her bag and maybe ..." Pulling in a big breath that rattled against his ribs and squeezed his heart, Aaron forced himself to finish his sentence. "Maybe he did pick up something else too. It was getting toward dark then, and I couldn't see so well. Then he walked away. Like she meant less than a fish. Like she meant nothing."

Aaron didn't realize he was crying until Shane patted his knee, stood up, and told him he'd done well, that he and Matt had both done well. There was a big roaring in Aaron's ears, and then his mother was standing behind his chair, both of her hands on his shoulders.

Chapter 5

MELINDA WATCHED HER SON answer Shane Black's questions, and the pain was nearly more than what she'd experienced birthing her boys. Hannah had been easy, barely any labor at all, but both her boys were delivered after hours of long, excruciating agony. Rebecca, the district's midwife, had assured her the babies weren't in danger, but she'd seen the worried looks exchanged between Rebecca and her own mother.

Nothing about those first two births had been normal.

The pain of watching Aaron's telling was as real and as hurtful as what she'd experienced when the boys were born.

Why couldn't she protect them?

Why couldn't she stand between them and the world a little longer?

As a teenager her parents had sheltered her. She'd never strained against it as some of her friends had. Part of being Amish was being separate. She accepted that easier than some, she supposed.

As a parent, she'd done her best to keep her children within the safe haven of the Amish community. She protected Matt. He was her first, and it was a natural thing to do. But when Aaron was born . . .

A lump rose in her throat, and she fought against the fears hammering in her chest—fears that were always a mere heartbeat away.

To think her son had witnessed the death of someone, possibly a murder.

To think he was a few feet away when such a terrible thing had happened.

She wanted to grab him in her arms and run, run back to their farm. She wanted Noah by her side, and she wanted him here now.

Aaron drew in a deep breath. She thought she could hear his lungs rattling. What if the shock was too much? What if it caused him to regress?

She gripped the back of his chair more firmly with both of her hands and refused to shy away from Shane Black's intense gaze. Forcing all the strength she could muster into her voice, she declared, "We have to go home now."

Shane nodded as if he understood. "You and Matthew can go, but I need Aaron to stay a little longer."

"I'm not leaving him here." She pushed up on her glasses.

"I need to take Callie's statement, maybe Deborah's." Shane studied the crime scene as he rubbed the muscles along the back of his neck. "I also need to see what the crime techs have for me. Then I need to look through the reports from people in the shop. Shouldn't take more than an hour, maybe two."

"We're going home."

"Sure. When we're finished."

"We're going home now."

"He's my primary witness, Melinda. He's my material witness."

"He's a child."

"What he saw will affect the outcome of this case."

Melinda didn't see Noah walk up, but she sensed it the moment he was there. She knew it by the scent of the soap he washed with, by the soft touch of his hand at her back, and most importantly, by the way her fear settled like a colt suddenly calmed.

"Problem with the boys?" he asked, handing her Hannah. Their youngest was nearly two now and not really a baby any-more, but Melinda still thought of her that way. Her daughter reached for Melinda's *kapp*, then snuggled into her neck.

Melinda closed her eyes and pulled in deep, cleansing breaths as the panic finally settled for the first time since hearing Martha tell Deborah to call 9-1-1.

"*Dat!*" Matthew jumped up, grabbed his father's hand.

Aaron squirmed around in his chair, offered his father a genu-ine smile as he reached for his baby sister's foot.

"Evening, Noah."

"Shane."

"There's no problem with the boys," Melinda said, answering Noah's original question. "I was explaining to Shane that it's get-ting late, and it's time to take the boys home."

"Can't do it." Shane held up his hand to ward off her argu-ments. "I understand. I do. But your son's the single witness who saw the perpetrator, and the guy's still out there. We need to bring our sketch artist over here and have her work with Aaron while his memory is fresh."

"*Ya*, I heard about the death. So it's true, son? You saw what happened?"

Melinda noticed that Aaron nodded but didn't offer to repeat the details to his father.

"Can it be done in the office?" Noah asked. "This cool night air isn't *gut* for his breathing."

Shane nodded. "Sure. Yeah. We can do it at the station. Is that okay with you, Aaron?"

Aaron nodded as he squirmed back around in his seat. "I don't have to go alone, do I?"

"'Course not. One of your parents can come with you."

"I'll go," Melinda assured him, kissing Hannah and handing her back to Noah.

"We'll be home as soon as we can," she whispered. "No one's eaten yet."

"I'll see to Matt and Hannah. Be sure to grab a bite for you and Aaron."

"We keep some snack food at the station." Shane nodded to Melinda and her family, then turned to answer a question from one of the crime techs, who had been waiting patiently behind him for a few minutes.

"I'm sure Shane will do his best to hurry things along here." Noah squeezed Melinda's arm softly, ruffled Aaron's hair, then put his hand to Matt's back and walked him away from the site.

It was a small comfort, but at least Melinda knew two of her children were out of harm's way. Now to finish with what Shane needed and see Aaron safely home. She had no desire to hinder the police investigation, but neither did she want her son to be in the middle of it.

Go to the station, sit with the artist, and then this thing will be over, she thought to herself.

Deborah sat across from Callie in the otherwise empty waiting room of the Shipshewana Police Department. Martha had gone home with her *aenti* an hour ago.

Callie and Deborah had decided to skip dinner, since neither had any appetite. Deborah knitted as Callie stared at the pages of the latest Agatha Christie novel she was reading.

"You haven't turned a page in nearly twenty minutes," Deborah observed.

"Yes, well, you keep pulling out that row of stitches. Maybe I should try knitting and you should try reading this story." Callie slapped the book shut and drummed her fingers against the cover.

"I'm distracted," Deborah admitted. "And you seem *naerfich*. Do you want to talk about it?"

"No."

"At least Esther wasn't at the store tonight. I wouldn't have wanted her waiting inside with all the grumbling customers while they filled out Gavin's forms."

Callie smiled, but it was a sad thing. "Tobias would have come up and pulled baby Simon out through a back window."

"*Ya*, I believe you're right. He's considerably protective of that *boppli*."

"Who can blame him after all they've been through?"

Deborah's mind drifted back over the last murder investigation, back to the young girl she and Esther had found in Reuben and Tobias' pond, and back to Samuel Eby—the boy who was now working building cabinets in the RV factory twenty miles to the northwest.

" 'For as the heavens are higher than the earth, so are my ways higher than your ways, and my thoughts than your thoughts.' " She didn't realize she'd spoken aloud until Callie bumped her with her foot.

"Amish proverb?"

"Nope. Scripture."

"I don't remember that one."

Callie reached down and ran her fingers through Max's coat. The Labrador rolled over on his side and groaned in his sleep. Deborah wondered if the Shipshe police allowed everyone to bring their canines into the station or if they made an exception for Callie. She was certainly becoming a frequent visitor—they both were.

"I should have let it go," Callie whispered, still staring at Max. "You told me to drop it. Lydia told me to. Even Esther told me to. All I could think of was making my shop better than hers. All I could think of was competing, and now she's dead."

Deborah stood, holding her knitting by her side, and moved to the seat beside Callie. Max opened one eye and gazed at her, but didn't bother changing positions.

"You did try in the beginning, remember? You went and visited Mrs. Knepp. You even sent cookies to her shop once. Wasn't that last Christmas?"

"Yes." Callie pulled in a shaky breath, then wiped her nose on the sleeve of her dress.

"That's new, and you're soiling it. Use this." Deborah handed her a handkerchief, which made Callie's tears fall faster. "Tell me the real reason you're *bedauerlich*."

"She was a cranky old woman, and no matter how hard I tried, I couldn't win her over. So it became a game of sorts. You know? Like in high school when you couldn't get in with a group, so you decided it wouldn't matter—except it did matter. You only had to pretend that it didn't."

Deborah nodded, though in truth she wasn't sure exactly what Callie was talking about.

"If she wouldn't like me, I decided I would make a sport of it. So I walked by and scoped out her displays, and a few times a week, I'd catch her walking by to check out mine. She was always crabby. I never saw her smile, and not once did she say a kind word to me."

"You're saying you'll miss her?"

"I will miss her." Callie blew her nose in the handkerchief. "In my mind there was always going to be a day—sometime in the future—when we would call a truce. Then we'd find a way to work together, to make Shipshewana the quilt capital of Indiana. Now she's dead, and she died in my parking lot. Someone did something to her—"

"We don't know that."

"You think she died naturally as she was hiding in my bushes?"

"Probably not."

"Do you think the person who pushed her was playing around and then ran off?"

"No. I don't think that at all."

"Do you think Shane would bother with a sketch artist unless he was convinced this person was dangerous?"

"All right," Deborah acknowledged, though the admission sent a weariness through every part of her body and soul.

"Someone killed her."

"*Ya*. I suppose you're right."

"Someone killed her, and they didn't even wait until it was dark. Who does that? He walked up behind her and somehow struck her down so that she fell in the middle of the pavement without any dignity at all. No one deserves to die that way, least of all a little old lady whose biggest crime was ..."

Callie's tears came again in earnest. Max rolled over on his stomach, laid his head on his paws, and stared at her with what Deborah thought seemed like great sorrow in his eyes. "Her biggest crime was being old and cranky. Maybe she was ... lonely. Maybe I should have taken her a casserole!"

Deborah put her arm around Callie and rubbed her shoulder. "I believe you're tired. You've worked hard preparing for this weekend."

"That's some of it, yes."

"And perhaps you're experiencing regret. My *mamm* always said, 'To forgive heals the wound; to forget heals the scar.' "

Callie frowned, rubbed at her forehead with the fingertips of both hands. "Is that one of your Amish proverbs?"

"I suppose *Englischers* might call it that. It's one of those things my *mamm* said when I worried a thing too long."

"But what does it even mean?"

"Rather depended on the situation."

"But you think it applies here?"

Deborah smiled, patted her on the back a final time. "*Ya*. Perhaps."

"I rarely understand the things Amish folk say." Callie blew her nose, but she did sit up straighter.

"She used to say this in German, so you wouldn't have understood her at all." Deborah reached for her knitting and began again. "I think what she meant, though, is that if you forgive the harm someone has done to you, then a wound will stop aching and heal, but the scar will remain."

"I know I'm supposed to forgive. Everyone is taught that it's the right thing to do ..." Callie hung her head, appearing as lost as a calf without a momma, but at least she'd stopped crying.

"*Ya*, forgiveness is *gut*, but the second part of the saying is just as important. If you forget the harm, then not only will the ache be gone, but the scar will disappear as well. You'll have no recollection of the injury to tarnish your memory of the person."

Callie frowned, reminding Deborah so much of her twin boys that she almost laughed out loud. "Mrs. Knepp's dead body has barely been scooped up off my pavement, and you're telling me I should—"

But before she had a chance to finish the thought, the door to the back room opened, and Melinda walked out, pushing Aaron's wheelchair. The boy was fast asleep.

They were followed by Shane. He needed a shave and his shirt was rumpled, but he seemed pleased with what they'd accomplished.

And though Deborah thought Melinda looked exhausted, there was also an expression of satisfaction on her face.

"How long has he been out?" Callie asked, as Max nudged the wheelchair, checking on Aaron.

"Nearly thirty minutes." Melinda leaned forward, moving Aaron's cap off of his eyes. "We were waiting until the artist finished."

"He did well, Melinda. Tell him this will help a lot." Shane held up a letter-sized sheet of paper as he spoke. "I've already instructed officers to post copies around town, and Gavin has sent it out on the wire as well."

"May I?" Deborah reached for the sketch at the same time Callie did.

They both stared down at a white male with thick brows, long-ish hair, and a prominent nose. A scowl covered his face. He had no facial hair, though he did have long sideburns. Something in the jawline or maybe the set of the eyes reminded Deborah of . . .

Who did they remind her of?

A friend?

An acquaintance?

Someone she'd passed on the street?

"So he's an *Englischer*?" Callie asked.

"Because he has no hat or beard?" Shane shook his head. "Can't jump to that conclusion."

Deborah continued to stare at the drawing.

"Recognize him?" Shane asked.

"No," they said simultaneously.

"But there might be something familiar about him." Deborah held the drawing out at arm's length, as if distance could jog her memory.

"Do you think perhaps you've seen him before?"

"No, that's not it. I can't quite put my finger on it. The feeling reminds me of when I study one quilt pattern that is similar to another."

"Maybe he's related to someone you know."

Callie crossed her arms, hugging them to herself. "The sheet says he was dressed in blue jeans and a flannel shirt. Sounds like an *Englischer*."

"He may have wanted to appear that way, but we can't know for certain." Shane put his hand on Callie's back as he walked them toward the front door. "Thanks for waiting so long. I know Melinda appreciates it."

"*Ya*, I do, but it wasn't necessary."

"Do you want me to send an officer to escort you ladies home?"

Deborah pulled her sewing bag over her shoulder as she shook her head. "*Nein*. I'll follow Melinda to her lane, then it's not much farther to my place. I'm sure we'll be fine."

"And I'm less than a mile away." Callie started to walk out with them, but Shane pulled her back.

"I'd like to talk to you. It won't take long."

"Can it wait until tomorrow?"

"No. Give me five minutes."

"All right, but I wanted to help with Aaron."

"We have this, Callie. You stay here with Shane if he needs you." Deborah pulled Callie into a hug, reached down, and gave Max a pat good-bye. "I'll be there to help early in the morning. It's a school holiday for the children, so as soon as the chores are tended to I can be at the shop."

"Maybe you should call her first," Shane suggested.

Deborah stopped so abruptly Melinda bumped into her.

"To be sure the shop is ready to open," Shane said.

"Surely the crime team will be done by morning—" Callie's voice rose a full octave and Aaron began to stir in his chair.

"That's one of the things I wanted to talk to you about," Shane explained. "Deborah, can you call her before you come in?"

"Sure. I can call from the phone shack at the end of the road." Callie scowled but nodded in agreement.

Melinda gave everyone a small wave and pushed the wheelchair through the door. Deborah glanced over her shoulder as she followed Melinda and Aaron out into the night. The last glimpse she had of Callie was Shane leading her back to the chairs they had just been sitting in.

Everything about the man, from the tightness around his shoulders to the scowl on his face, said the news he was about to deliver was going to make her friend very unhappy.

Chapter 6

SHANE SAT CLOSE ENOUGH that his arm brushed against Callie's, close enough he could feel the weariness rolling off her in waves.

If there was one thing Shane Black wasn't, it was a hypocrite. He knew he wasn't a spiritual example to anyone. He and God had been at a standstill for years. So far, God hadn't blinked.

Shane was good with that.

So why did Callie Harper make him want to drop his head into his hands and ask God, "Why? Why is the one woman I care about in harm's way again?" And in the same breath he wanted to breathe a prayer of thanksgiving that she had walked away unscathed.

This from a man who only darkened a church's door when he was visiting his parents during the holidays.

"I wanted to be sure you're okay."

"Of course I am."

He pulled her hands into his, wondering how best to proceed. Callie wasn't known for being reasonable, especially when she was tired. Right now her eyes told him she'd passed exhaustion at least an hour ago. Her hands were freezing, and he rubbed them with his thumbs, trying to restore her circulation. "The paramedics checked your vitals?"

"Yes."

"Tell me what's going on, Callie."

"Tell me why you think my shop won't be open tomorrow."

Instead of answering, he asked again. "Are you sure you're all right?"

"I wasn't even the one hurt. Why all the questions?" She wouldn't hold his gaze for long, and when she did, she kept blinking rapidly.

Exhausted? Or still frightened?

"This is our third homicide together, and I've never seen you react this way."

Max watched their conversation silently, his head moving back and forth as if he were viewing a game of volleyball. Too many times when Shane was with Callie, it seemed they were engaged in a verbal match of some sort.

Why did he have trouble showing her he cared?

Why couldn't he come out and say it?

Callie's eyes brimmed with tears, and she stared at a stain on the chair across from her.

"Callie?"

"This one feels more personal, that's all!" The words burst from her like a confession.

"Why does it feel personal?"

"Mrs. Knepp was my adversary. We were competitors. This jerk ..." She pointed at the poster he'd placed on a nearby table. "He took her out. Why would he do that, Shane? What did a little old lady ever do to him?"

"We're checking into that. Seems to be a burglary."

"Who kills someone on a public sidewalk for a purse? Why not grab it from her and be gone?"

"Happens all the time—"

"In New York, maybe, or Houston. When was the last time it happened in Shipshe?"

"I have the same questions that you do." He waited three beats, then pushed forward. "You don't know of any other enemies she had? Other than you?"

Callie's eyes narrowed. "Don't tell me I'm a suspect."

"Nope. I already checked out your alibi. It held." He refused to let go of her hands when she tried to pull them away. "I'm serious. You may have known her better than anyone else—other than her family who aren't giving me much. They're Amish though, and right now they're in shock and don't trust me. What did you know about Mrs. Knepp?"

"She was cranky and rude and didn't play well."

He waited for more.

"Which is still no reason to kill her in the middle of town."

"There aren't that many reasons for murder, period. When it comes down to it, when it comes to a violent murder like this one—"

"Why are you saying violent? I didn't see any blood . . ."

"You know I can't share details of the investigation with you." Shane let go of her hands. "And I'm asking *you* the questions, remember?"

"You're asking me for a motive, and I can't think of one."

"Well the usual ones are relatively few." Shane relaxed back into his seat, his arms across the back of their chairs, and studied her. How could she still look beautiful after two-and-a-half hours inside a police station and considering all she'd been through?

Callie held up her fingers and began ticking them off. "Money, passion, revenge—"

"Still reading Agatha Christie?" he asked.

"Shows, huh?"

"*Murder on the Orient Express* is sticking out of your bag."

She rolled her eyes, pushed the book farther down in her purse, and stood to go.

Max jumped up too, eager to finally be on the move.

"It's too bad a homicide is going to cause you to miss this year's Fall Festival," he said, walking her to the door.

"What are you talking about?" She turned on him like a storm.

"What do you mean what am I talking about?"

"Why would I miss the festival?"

"Because there was a murder on your property." Shane reached for a strand of her hair, pushed it out of her eyes. "I know tonight you think you want to open tomorrow. But in the morning, you'll realize how tired you are. Tonight you're in shock. Tomorrow—"

"You can't be thinking of closing me down. In fact, you have no grounds to close me down. Adalyn Landt stopped by earlier to tell me she was headed out of town for the weekend, but she said for me to call her if I need her. She said she'd turn around and come back." She began pawing through her bag for her phone.

"Hold on, sweetheart. No need to call your lawyer." Shane closed his eyes and pulled in a long breath. Would this night never ease up? "I was only saying that you must be tired, and that perhaps it would feel odd to conduct business mere hours after someone was slain on your doorstep."

"Which technically wasn't my fault." Now Callie's old fire was back in spades. While Shane wanted to be irritated with her, it comforted him to see her spark return. He should have known if there was one thing that could erase the fear and exhaustion in her eyes, any mention of her shop would do it.

He moved closer, until there wasn't even a whisper of space between them, until he was close enough to feel her next breath, close enough to calm the fear that had nearly consumed him since the call first came in.

Max nosed his way between them, but didn't growl any warning. If Shane was going to date Callie Harper, and some part of him seemed intent on doing just that, he and the dog were going to have to come to an understanding.

"It wasn't my fault," she whispered again.

"I never said it was your fault. Would you settle down and let me worry about you occasionally?" He traced her cheekbone, let his fingers work their way through her hair. She stood for it all of five seconds before pulling away.

"We'll be open tomorrow. Be sure your men are out of my way."

"They're already gone. Left less than an hour ago. We did have to leave crime tape around the exact location of the deceased."

"I don't sell much merchandise from the garden." Callie sailed through the door, without glancing back. Shane wanted to laugh, but there was something about this case that wasn't funny at all.

It wasn't just the murder—he'd seen his share of those. But Callie had been right about one thing: murder in Shipshewana was rare. Murder for a purse that had already been found discarded a mere four blocks away from the murder scene just didn't add up.

The fact that there were no fingerprints on the purse didn't sit well with him either. This wasn't going to be an easy case, but then again, what case ever had been?

What exactly was this perp up to?

Shane had a stack of witness sheets to wade through, so he made his way to the coffeepot. Maybe someone had seen something he hadn't noticed when he'd glanced through them the first time.

He would read while the crime techs analyzed their data and Callie slept.

And he'd pray that tomorrow would be a better day.

Callie noticed Max was acting strangely as soon as she pulled up to the darkened parking area outside her shop, but she thought it was because of the strange scents left from all the police, crime-scene techs, and the so-recent death. She took him into the garden—careful to walk a wide circle around the corner with the yellow tape—and waited for him to take care of his business.

Instead of padding around, Max slunk near the far side of the yard with his nose to the ground, growling occasionally and pausing once to raise his nose at the nearly pitch-black sky to howl.

"It's all right, boy. They're gone now. There's no one here but the two of us." When he returned to her and she clipped his leash onto his collar, he strained at it as if a rabbit were darting across the parking lot. Callie briefly wondered if she'd be able to lead him to the back door. Max had bulked up since she'd inherited him, and his early morning runs with Gavin had added muscle where before there'd been fatty weight.

"Maybe I should consider joining you two for a jog," she muttered, opening the garden gate. The words had no sooner left her lips than Max jerked the leash out of her hand, a snarl tearing from his throat. Every hair on her neck bristled in alarm, but Max had already disappeared into the night—the one indication of where he'd gone being the sound of his leash dragging against the pavement.

Callie took off in pursuit. Though one part of her mind screamed a warning, it was a warning she ignored. She couldn't help it. Her legs flew, running after Max.

He burst across the parking area, past the front of the store, and around the corner of the building, streaking by the trellis and rose bushes that still held a few white fall blooms. He would have made it to the back alley, but he pulled up short at the property line, his bark angry and rabid.

Callie came in sight of him and stopped when she saw what he was barking at—two figures both clad in black. They stood in the dim light cast by the lone bulb dangling above the dumpster near the back lot of Pots and Pans. She opened her mouth to scream for Max to back away, but by then the first figure had already raised his weapon and found his mark.

Max made one final leap, then crumpled to the ground, his cry dying midbark.

Not again. This can't be happening again.

Images of Trent McCallister kneeling over Max, his shirt soaked with blood, flashed across Callie's memory. Before she could holler, before she could even stop to think about whether she ought to save her dog or run for help, the figure turned to point his weapon at her.

Unable to move, Callie stared back, frozen.

She stared and time stopped.

But instead of feeling the sting of a bullet, the man lowered his weapon, grinned, pointed a finger at her, then turned and walked off into the night, his boots echoing down the alley. His partner followed close behind.

Callie's pulse thundered in her ears.

What had happened?

Who were those people?

Why hadn't they shot her?

Why *had* they shot her dog?

They'd shot her dog. The thought startled Callie into motion, and she ran to Max, kneeling beside him on the pavement. Her hands went to work, searching to find the bloody hole, searching in the dim alley light to see if he was still alive.

Instead, her fingers bumped into a dart sticking out of Max's side. She grasped it and pulled, careful not to stick herself with the tip of the syringe. Placing her ear to Max's chest she counted his respirations.

What was normal breathing for a sixty-five–pound Lab? His breathing seemed fast, and he wasn't moving. But Callie wasn't sure if the rapid breathing was an issue or if it just meant he was asleep.

She'd dropped her purse somewhere as she ran, but now she needed to go back and find it. She needed to call for help.

"Don't you die on me, Maxie. I need you." She kissed him once, stood, and ran into the darkness.

Were they waiting for her there? The brief thought darted through Callie's mind, but it was followed by another question: *Why would they be?*

They'd passed up a perfect chance to shoot her at the same time they'd shot Max. With a tranq dart? That's what she was holding, right?

She slowed as she turned the corner around the front of her building. The street was now silent — no cars, no people, no one to hear or help her. Sweat poured from her as she crept down the front walk until she could make out her bag, contents spilled under a streetlight.

Her cell phone was there.

She could call Shane.

Call for help.

But she'd have to stand under the glaring light, and she'd once again be a perfect target.

The image of Max lying near the alley, an unknown drug running through his veins, spurred her forward.

She reached her bag, snatched it off the sidewalk, scooped up her things, and had turned to sprint back to Max when she looked toward the front door of her shop.

What if someone else was in there? What if while she was kneeling by Max they attacked again?

Clutching her bag so she could clobber an intruder with it, she stepped slowly toward the front of the shop.

The door had been pushed open at least four inches — maybe not noticeable to someone driving by, but if you were standing on the sidewalk, you couldn't miss it.

Drawn toward that door, knowing she should walk away, should walk back to Max to call Shane, she instead pushed the door wide open. The first thing she did was reach for the switch and flood her shop with light. A plain white envelope lay on the floor in front of her. Nothing was written on the outside. With shaking hands, Callie picked it up and tore it open.

The words were typed on a single sheet of white paper.

As she slid to the floor, she felt herself tumbling down a dark hole.

Don't call anyone about Max or you could be next.
You'll receive further instructions within the hour.

She hesitated for less than a moment, and then placed the note on the counter next to the register, not bothering to see if anyone was there. Something told her they weren't.

They were cowards.

Only cowards shot a dog with a tranq gun then fled.

Only cowards preyed on old women in parking lots.

And Callie thought surely this was the same person. Hadn't the man standing under the light been approximately the same height and weight as the man Aaron had described?

Her anger built and her terror subsided as she snatched her keys from her purse and made her way through the darkness outside, picking her way carefully along the brick path to the garden shed. She fumbled with the lock and opened the door, which creaked as it always did. Why hadn't she oiled it? Pulling out the tarp she used for moving dirt and rocks around the backyard, she walked quickly back around the building, pausing only once to glance down the road. But the lights revealed nothing except a car passing at the end of the street.

Callie hurried on to the alley.

Max hadn't moved at all, but she hadn't expected him to. It had been two years since she'd been a pharmaceutical rep, but she still received the trade magazines. They made for good late-night reading when she couldn't sleep. Her mind cycled through the

most common drugs used in tranq darts: Domosedan and ...
what was the other? Something that started with an *F*. There
was a third as well, but now her mind had gone blank. These
people did not strike her as professionals. They could have used
the wrong drug and the wrong dosage. As she pulled Max onto
the tarp, then dragged the tarp to the back door of the shop, she
kept her tears at bay. He wasn't dead. If they'd used the wrong
dosage or the wrong drug, he'd already be dead.

Unlocking the back door to her shop, she pulled him up the
small loading ramp the deliverymen used before closing and lock-
ing the door behind her. Hurrying through the shop, which was
silent except for the sounds coming from the low hum of her
appliances, she closed and locked the front door as well.

Then she stood completely still and listened.

It didn't sound as if anyone were inside with her.

It didn't *feel* as if anyone were inside with her.

She picked up an umbrella by the front door — it was the old-
fashioned kind, left here from when Aunt Daisy was still alive.
She hadn't had the heart to throw it away. Weighing over a pound
and nearly thirty inches long, the end was metal and so sharp Callie once considered using it to spear trash as she walked around
the yard.

Tonight she might need it for something else.

Chapter 7

First Callie checked on Max, who still lay in the hall by the back door. No more than fifteen minutes had passed since he'd been hit with the tranquilizer dart. His breathing had evened out, but he continued to sleep soundly—unnaturally. She had no idea if he'd be out for twenty minutes or for twelve hours. She didn't know enough about these types of drugs and how they worked on dogs.

What she needed to do was boot up her laptop.

What she needed to do was call her vet.

Or Shane.

Instead, she covered Max with the lap blanket from one of the chairs in the sitting area, picked up her monster umbrella, slung it over her shoulder like a bat, and began walking through the shop, from aisle to aisle, checking for intruders.

No one was there, but the register drawer was open, its contents spilled on the floor.

A peek in her office revealed the computer was on. The screen saver cycled back and forth from a photo of the girls' quilts on display at the Chicago Museum of Arts to one of her and Max sitting in the garden. She'd taken that one with the self-portrait feature of her new camera and had uploaded it to the computer less than a week ago. Was it the last photo she'd have of her and Max?

Pushing the thought away, she reached forward and moved the mouse. The monitor displayed all of her folders, files, and accounts. Who had been on her computer? Who knew the password to log on? She had the computer set to *sleep* after thirty minutes of inactivity, so had someone been in her office and on her computer less than thirty minutes ago?

Tightening her grip on the umbrella, Callie stepped out of the office and into the hall. She tried the door to her apartment, found it unlocked, and started cautiously up the stairs.

The eighth stair creaked when she stepped on it, and she froze, holding her breath while she listened for any movement. It was hard to hear anything above her pulse thundering in her ears.

After waiting two minutes, she wiped her hands on her dress—they were so slick with sweat, she was sure she would drop the umbrella—before continuing her climb to the top of the steps. When she rounded the corner and took the first look at her apartment, her legs nearly failed her.

She clapped her hand over her mouth, but there was no preventing the cry that escaped her lips.

Every drawer was open, every object within them spilled out onto the floor. Cushions had been pulled from the couch, and her bedding had been ripped off the mattress, which itself had been tipped off the bed frame.

Callie slumped back against the doorjamb and stared at the mess in front of her.

Who had done this?

The man in the alley?

When? Wouldn't it have taken a while to cause this much chaos? Shane had said the crime team finished up less than an hour ago. Whoever did this had been watching and waiting and had moved very quickly or . . .

Callie suddenly knew she was going to be sick.

She stood, stumbled through the disorder that had been her

home and made it to the kitchen sink. She leaned over it for one minute, then two, but nothing came up. She hadn't eaten. There was nothing in her stomach.

Running the cold tap, she splashed water on her face, then on her neck.

Was it even possible?

Could they have been up here in her apartment while she was downstairs helping customers? How? She hadn't recognized the person in Shane's sketch, so it couldn't have been a customer in her store. But what if they'd sneaked in and made their way upstairs while she was busy with someone else? She might not have heard them over the noise of the crowd.

She kept the door to her apartment locked when the shop was open, but obviously her perp knew how to pick a lock.

Though Max would have heard them — heard them and alerted Callie.

Which meant they had to have come between the time the children left for their walk downtown and the time the police had arrived. They could have slipped in when she was out for register tape, sneaked by Deborah and Lydia. So who killed Mrs. Knepp?

Callie grabbed a rag, wet it with cold water, and pressed it to her forehead.

She needed to talk to someone, and she needed to see to Max.

But what about the note?

The thought had no sooner crossed her mind, than the phone in the shop began to ring. She ran down the stairs to answer it.

The display on the caller ID lit up, but the word scrolling across read *Unknown*.

She picked up the receiver, but didn't say anything.

"It'll take a while for the sedatives to clear his system. But you'd know that, having sold drugs and all." The voice was male and middle-aged. It was the voice of a creeper.

69

Callie would have liked to kick his teeth in.

"Why did you do this to him?"

"Chill, Harper." The man's voice lost some of its amusement. "Max is fine—this time. Dogs bother me though, so don't expect me to be kind twice. He'll be awake in an hour, if you tell us what we want to know. Now turn the lights off, so we can talk."

He was watching her?

From where?

She walked to the main light switch and flipped the downstairs lights off. Shafts of light from the street lamps shone through the front windows. Would Gavin or Shane notice that her shop was in darkness? She tried to resist, but she stepped away from the counter, so she could see the street better, see if help was coming.

"The good officer, Gavin, passed by right before I shot your dog, so you can stop gazing out the window."

Callie ducked back behind the counter. Had he seen her? How was that possible? Infrared glasses? No way this creep was that well equipped.

"Everything appeared to be locked up nice and tight from the street. I made sure he couldn't see the door was open as he drove by. You had to be standing on the sidewalk to see that—trick of light. I'm good with tricks. I wanted you to find my note, not Officer Gavin. I wouldn't expect help from that direction. He only checks once every ninety minutes, and by then, you better pray I have the information I want."

A deep fright filled Callie's belly, like ice water swallowed on an empty stomach. But at the same time her anger began to boil. The temper her mother had often warned her about threatened to erupt. This person had no right to violate her private space, shoot her dog, and then think he could hold her ransom.

For information? What information? What could she possibly know that he would want so badly?

Then another thought leapt in front of the others. The same

thought she'd had earlier, but this time it came back stronger, more certain.

"You killed Mrs. Knepp." She practically spat the words.

Instead of denying it, the man on the other end of the phone laughed. She heard the strike of a match, a deep inhalation, and then the scrape of a chair against concrete.

"Yeah, I did, and I won't stop there. So listen real close. You can save yourself and the mutt too. Tell me where the money is."

"The money—"

"We know it's not in your register, your safe, or your apartment."

They'd been searching for money?

She didn't have any. The shop was making a profit, but barely.

"We even know it's not in your bank account." He took another drag from his cigarette. She could practically smell the smoke. "Found your little notebook with all your passwords. Might want to keep that somewhere else in the future. Next to your keyboard isn't the smartest place—you know, in case you're burglarized."

A woman giggled in the background. That sound was so out of place, clashed so completely with all that had happened in the last six hours, that Callie nearly fell apart then and there. Surely this was all a terrible nightmare.

She would wake and find Max lying beside her, conscious and safe.

She would wake and find her life put back together.

"Why ..." Her voice cracked on the word. She swallowed and tried again. "Why did you kill her?"

Creeper blew out one last long, exasperated breath. It was followed by the sound of his boot grinding against the ground, probably crushing out his cigarette. Then the sound of a chair scraping across floor, as though he had stood up. "One hour—have the money in the alley or when we come back Max dies."

"But—"

"If you try to contact anyone, you will both die."

Panic surged through her veins. She imagined him about to disconnect the line. Knew she had to find some way to keep him talking. "I . . . I hid it."

He grunted. "Hid it," he repeated.

Callie squeezed her eyes shut, tried to think of the biggest lie that would buy her the most time. "I didn't want to report it to the IRS. So I hid it instead."

"All right. Tell us where, and we'll retrieve it and be out of your way."

"It's not here. Do you think I'd keep that much money close by?"

Creeper's voice faded as he spoke to someone else, no doubt the giggling woman he'd chosen for an accomplice. "I told you she was smart. Didn't I tell you she was smart?"

Pressing her forehead against the wall, Callie tried to think up more details to this preposterous scenario before he could ask her questions.

"Give me directions, and we'll go and get it."

"Can't." Callie thrashed around in her mind for an excuse. "Even I couldn't find it in the dark. And every cop in the county is hunting for you."

The woman in the background began arguing. Now Callie could make out her words. She definitely had a Chicago accent. "I told you not to use the Taser. You shouldn't have killed—"

Creeper screamed an obscenity and the woman shut up. Silence filled both rooms, and Callie suddenly became aware of her computer humming, the clock over the register ticking, and her own pulse thumping.

"Are you playing with us?"

"Do you think I'm stupid?"

Mrs. Knepp's murderer was quiet for five, then ten seconds. "Nah. You're not stupid."

He struck another match, and she wondered why he didn't use a lighter. Would the police be able to track the smell of nicotine, discarded matches, and a room with a concrete floor?

"How long do you need?"

"I'm not sure." Callie felt sweat trickle down her back. What should she say? She needed to get him off the phone and find a way to contact Shane. How much time would it take to search for money she didn't even have?

Creeper lowered his voice to a whisper. "I like feisty, but not too feisty."

"You want me to do this without attracting police attention?" Callie fought through the fear, forced herself to make up a believable scenario. "I'll have to keep the shop open, or they'll know something's wrong. Which means I can't go out until after I close the shop, and then it will take time to dig it up."

"We'll help you."

"No."

"You're not in a position to give orders, remember?" Again the deep inhalation as he sucked up nicotine.

"I remember, and I'll get you your money. But I ..." She allowed some of the tears she'd been holding back to escape, allowed her voice to tremble with the fear threatening to consume her. But she held the rage and anger that were building in check, forced herself to keep it inside a little longer. "I want my dog to be okay, and I want my house back to normal. I don't want to ever hear from you again."

He laughed softly. "We can arrange that. Long as you turn over the money. By the time the cops catch on to us ... we'll be gone, like smoke."

The woman cackled with him, the sound echoing in the night.

"Don't take too long, Harper. I'll be watching you." His boots clomped against the concrete. She thought he'd disconnected, thought it was finally over, when he whispered his parting shot into the phone.

"We can see more than you think—I can see you hiding behind the counter right now—and we can hear more too." He paused and sighed in what seemed to Callie like frustration. "You find the money. Find what's mine. In the meantime, we'll check with a few other people who might have a portion of what needs to be returned, what I mean to have back."

Then the line went dead.

Callie hit the End button on her cordless receiver and had just pulled in her first full breath when the phone began ringing again. She stared at the phone in her hand and finally pushed the Talk button on the sixth ring—though she didn't say a word.

"One last thought, Harper. That little kid in the wheelchair might be able to identify me, which is a worry. You want to have that money to me quick-like so it won't be a problem. And as far as your boyfriend, the invest-tee-gator? Tell him something—anything—to keep him off my back."

Then Creeper hung up again, and this time he didn't ring back.

She listened closely, straining to hear the sound of a car door or even the tinkle of the bell over the door of her shop. But there was nothing.

Eventually she became aware, once more, of the hum of the computer. She reached under the counter, behind the curtain that covered her supplies, and checked for the black box, the surveillance system her aunt had purchased several years ago. It was gone. She'd known it would be, but still another part of her heart cracked.

She stood, her legs numb from kneeling on the floor, and moved to where she'd left Max. He still lay in the same position.

Watching her dog, she noted the slight rise and fall of his chest. Sobs began building in her throat, wanting to escape, but she refused to give in to them.

A dozen questions and answers collided in her mind as she watched Max.

Why did he shoot her dog if they'd already been through her place? *Because he wanted to show her he could.*

Why didn't he kill her like he'd killed Mrs. Knepp? *Because he wanted his money.*

What would he do to Aaron if she didn't deliver it? *He'd kill him.*

She knew the answers, knew them every time her mind conjured up the sketch Shane had shown her, every time she remembered the sound of his voice in her ear.

But the one question she couldn't find an answer to, the one question that spun round and round as Max finally began to stir, was the question she knew she'd have to answer and answer soon.

What money was he talking about?

Shane stared down at the text message once more before exiting his vehicle. The message was odd enough on its own, but the fact Callie had sent it at two a.m. was completely unexplainable.

Can't sleep. Might b late 4 r bfast date. 6:30 instead? Am sure Margie will hold our tbl. Gnight.

He'd wanted to call immediately to talk to her, but he'd resisted because of that last word—it sat there, like a nail in a firmly sealed coffin. Everything about her message sent warning bells screaming through his head and heart, but that last word plainly indicated he was not supposed to call her.

Gavin had reported that all of Callie's lights were off when she had gotten home and every ninety minutes after that as well. So the part about not sleeping made no sense.

And Shane and Callie had never made plans to meet for breakfast. Why was she pretending they had? Why was she pretending she needed to move the time to six thirty? It was as if she were speaking in code, as if she expected her message to be intercepted—which was ridiculous—and needed him to read between the lines.

It was only six fifteen, but he'd decided to go with his instinct and scope out the only place he knew of where someone named Margie might hold a breakfast table for them. He snapped his phone shut and walked toward The Kaffi Shop. Between the murder and the cozy mysteries Callie had been reading, perhaps she'd developed a little paranoia.

Still, Shane scanned the street as he pushed open the door. The odor of fresh coffee—which in no way resembled what he'd been drinking at the police station—and baked breads nearly knocked him back out to the sidewalk. For one second, he forgot why he was there as his stomach responded to his more primal needs.

"Morning, Shane." Margie glanced up in surprise. Bright red hair framed a face spotted with freckles, even though she was in her late-thirties. He'd yet to see her when she wasn't smiling. Margie was one of the most contented persons Shane had ever met—and definitely a morning person.

"Morning, Margie."

"Surprise seeing you here so early."

He ordered a coffee and a cinnamon roll, placed his money on the counter, then leaned in closer and lowered his voice. "Have you seen Callie today?"

Margie shook her head, causing her long, green earrings to bounce and glitter. "Nope. Callie's not much of an early bird. She usually drops by at lunch or in the evenings after she closes her place."

"Got it." He grabbed a copy of the *Gazette*, which had a photo of yesterday's murder splashed across the front, and placed another dollar on the counter. "I'll be at the back if anyone needs me."

Ten minutes later, at exactly six twenty-eight, Callie pulled up across the street. She had Max with her, and Shane knew as soon as they both stepped out of the car that something was wrong.

For one thing, Max usually bounded out of a car. This morning Callie had to reach in, pick him up, and set him down on the ground as if he might break. The dog sniffed around, gazed up at his owner, then began to walk gingerly—but when he took his first step, he wobbled.

What was that about? It looked like her dog was dizzy.

Callie wore a knee-length jean skirt, her Texas boots, and a long-sleeved brown suede top. In other words, she looked like the country girl who was in the process of stealing his heart. As she moved toward the shop, walking stiffly with her head never glancing left or right, her eyes focused completely on him, Shane stood. He began to move in her direction, but she shook her head, or at least he thought she did. The shake was so small, he could have imagined it.

And then she was opening the door.

"Morning, Callie. What can I get you?"

But Callie didn't answer Margie. She just walked toward Shane. And then he noticed her lack of color, the dark smudges under her eyes. His pulse kicked up a notch, and his mind began to shift through all the things that might have happened since he saw her last night.

Before he could choose one though, before he could begin to guess what might be wrong, she walked straight into his arms.

"Callie, what?"

"Hold me," she whispered. The tremor in her voice was nearly his undoing.

His arms closed around her, and he could feel her trembling. He wanted to pull away, wanted to look into her eyes, but something told him she would fall onto Margie's floor if he didn't hold her up.

After a minute, no more, she disentangled herself and walked to the booth where he'd been sitting. She sat on the side he'd occupied only moments before, facing the front of the shop.

Which forced him to take the seat with his back to the windows.

"Nice seeing you so early, Callie. Still want a double shot of espresso in your coffee and whipped cream on top?"

"Yes. Thank you, Margie."

"Sure thing." She studied them curiously. "I think I have some dog treats behind the counter for Max."

"That would be great."

Max lay with his head down on her feet, showing no interest in the people around him. He didn't even bother to sniff Shane or respond to Margie's voice. To Shane he seemed more than unresponsive. It almost seemed like he had been drugged.

"Listen and don't ask too many questions." She licked her lips, tried to speak, but couldn't. Clearing her throat, she started again. "They could be watching from outside, and I don't want them to see your expression. I don't think they could possibly have microphones here. They can't put mics everywhere. How could they? How would they know where we might meet or who Margie is even if they were somehow monitoring my texts?"

Sweat was now pouring down Shane's back. He leaned forward and captured her hands, which were shredding his napkin. "Slow down and breathe."

So she did. And then the horrible story began to spill out. At first he had trouble believing what she was telling him. But it synced too well with what he was seeing—Max's lethargy, her shock, the evidence at the scene. Mrs. Knepp had technically died of a heart attack, but preliminary autopsy reports indicated an electrical shock caused the heart attack. A small mark at the base of her neck, half an inch below her prayer *kapp*, was indicative of a Taser.

There were no dart-like electrodes left in her skin though, only the single mark. The killer had used a Taser, but he'd used a model with drive-stun capability, which was not supposed to incapacitate—unless the person being tased was in her eighties. Shane's preliminary meeting with Knepp's family had revealed that Knepp had an irregular heartbeat and was taking medication for the condition. Apparently the shock of the night before was too much. "What about the security machine in your shop?"

"It's gone. The entire device is missing." She stared at him, fear mixing with dread.

And then there was the thing, that single thing that had been scratching the edge of his consciousness for the past twelve hours, and it finally broke through.

"The dress you had on yesterday—"

"What about it?"

"The material, a dark green, was it something new? Something from your shop?"

"Yes. Deborah helped me with the pattern." Her hands shook as she tried to drink the coffee Margie had brought. "I made it from our new fall fabrics. Shane, I don't think that's important. We need to figure out—"

"You said he admitted killing Mrs. Knepp, and then later in the conversation you heard a woman arguing with him?"

Callie nodded. "Right. Something about a Taser and that he should have used something else. I didn't understand it. I was trying to think of a way out of the conversation, but it almost sounded as if things hadn't gone according to plan. As if he hadn't meant to do that at all."

"I don't think he did." Shane considered holding back what he'd pieced together, but Callie needed to know as much as possible now. She had shown great courage coming to him. He needed to be straight with her, and he needed to find a way to protect her until this psycho was caught. "Callie, I think he meant to attack *you*. If he had used a Taser on you, it would have knocked you out, but it wouldn't have killed you. Mrs. Knepp was old, and her heart couldn't take the stress. Think about it. Both you and Mrs.

Knepp wore a dark green dress. He approached from behind, saw a shoulder or hemline, and thought it was you."

"But she was so old." Her voice rose in indignation. "Are you telling me I look like an old Amish woman? I have much better hair than she does, and my skin ... You can't be serious, Shane."

"You don't resemble each other from the front. He attacked from the back, and there wasn't much light."

"Her *kapp*—"

"He might not have seen it with her hiding in the shrubbery, though I still don't understand why she would have been spying on your shop."

"It was just something we did. There was no real harm in it."

"Until last night ..."

Callie's eyes flooded with fear for a moment, then anger won once again. "We have to stop them."

"We will, but until then I want you to let me send you away. I don't know why he's focusing on you or what this talk of money is, but we can protect you—"

"No."

The stubborn woman Shane knew so well stared at him, and though the fear was still there, lurking below the surface, he knew arguing with her would be useless. "No. I won't do it. I won't run and hide while Aaron is in danger."

"Then we'll hide Aaron too."

"And his entire family? How do we know they won't go after Deborah or Esther or a dozen other families in Shipshe? No. This stops with me. So far he's already accidentally killed an old woman and tranq'd my dog."

"And tossed your apartment."

Callie's eyes nearly closed in anger. "If you catch him, promise me ten minutes alone with this creep."

"*When* we catch him. It might take us a while, but we will catch him." Shane felt a sudden urge to hit something—a punching bag, a wall, this perp's face. "Have you forgotten how many people are in town this weekend? This won't be easy."

"He's not leaving until he gets what he wants, and he wants his money."

Shane sighed, realizing again how much the woman sitting across from him had found her way into his heart. She was stubborn, yes; but she was also smart, even when she was scared. "I'll put up perimeter security."

"That won't work. They'll be watching. He told me he could see everything."

Shane smiled for the first time since receiving her text. "That was probably a bluff."

"But he knew where I was sitting—"

"A good guess. He knew where the phone was located, so of course you'd be nearby."

"But he knew"—her hand came out of her lap, waving, nearly knocking over their coffee mugs—"other things."

"He may have had binoculars or infrareds on the place, but I doubt it. I think we have a Vegas player here. Someone who knows how to bluff and how to bluff well."

"So how do we catch him?"

"Use the festival to our advantage."

"But you said it would be hard to find him with so many people."

"True, but there are good things about it being the busiest weekend of the year. There are people everywhere." Shane tapped a beat on the table. "He can't watch us all, and he's not the only one who can wear a disguise—if what he had on when Aaron saw him was a disguise, and I'm betting it was. You're not going to be out of my sight until your creeper is behind bars. I will catch this guy, and when I do—only God will be able to help him."

Chapter 8

MELINDA SET HANNAH in her high chair and placed two toys on the tray, then turned to the sink full of breakfast dishes. She took her time with the plates and cups, allowing her hands to linger in the warm, sudsy water.

Every day included chores, but holidays like Fall Festival seemed to bring extra work for each member of her family—including both boys.

Matt was in the barn, mucking out stalls.

And Aaron, well ... Noah had a plan to see what Aaron was capable of doing.

The kitchen window looked out over the side yard as well as an area Noah had put together for the chicken pen. He'd even smoothed a path for Aaron's wheelchair.

Though Melinda understood Aaron needed chores like everyone else, it was still difficult for her to watch him struggle to remove the lid from the barrel, scoop out the correct amount of feed into the bucket he had fastened across his lap, then work his thin arms, wheeling the chair down the path.

Noah had also set the pen up with two gates, knowing Aaron wouldn't be fast enough to keep the chickens from escaping if there was only one. The dishwater grew cold as she watched Aaron open the first gate, wheel through and shut it, then open the second. He was instantly surrounded by noisy, hungry chickens. He scattered feed with one hand as he wheeled slowly with the other, attempting to spread the food out for the large group of hens, just as his father had shown him.

"How's he doing?" Noah's soft voice in her ear caused Melinda to jump, sending suds and water flying.

"He's fine." She grabbed the dishtowel and wiped her apron. "But it seems so hard for him. I could have done it myself in half the time, and you know I don't mind."

Noah took the towel from her hands, turned her so she was facing the kitchen rather than the window, and wiped the water off her neck. "*Ya*, you were always *gut* at feeding the chickens."

He smiled and kissed her gently on the lips, which sent a stream of warm feelings down through her stomach all the way to her toes. "It's not you that needs to learn though, and it's not you that needs to grow stronger."

Melinda closed her eyes, forced herself to lay aside her fears for one more day. "I know you're right. Still ... I worry."

"Which is one more thing that makes you a *gut mamm*."

Reaching past her to hang up the dishtowel, he gave her the smile that had the power to settle her world, then walked over to the high chair and picked up Hannah. "Thought I might take this little girl to check the crops with me."

Hannah squealed and reached for her daddy's beard.

"Want to ride with your *dat*? Want to ride behind the big work horse?"

At the word *horse*, Hannah began hollering, "Down. Down, *dat*. Down."

"You've done it now. She means to go and find her shoes."

"A *gut* idea, baby girl."

When Hannah had toddled out of the room as fast as her chubby legs would take her, Melinda confessed to Noah what had been bothering her from the moment her eyes had opened earlier that morning. "After last night, after what Aaron saw, I was wondering if I should allow him to rest today."

"It was a terrible thing for him to witness, for sure. If he has questions or worries, I believe he'll talk to us, Melinda. Besides, do you think he'd be better off inside chasing it round and round in his head?" Noah scooped Hannah up as she came tumbling back into the room carrying her shoes. Before he walked out the door, he stepped closer to Melinda, kissed her once more, and whispered, "Look at your son now, *Mamm*. I think he's going to be fine."

Melinda turned and looked out the window. The picture that met her eyes was a bright fall morning, like so many others in her heart. It caused her breath to catch in her throat and her hand to fly to her lips. There wasn't a day that went by when she didn't thank God for her family—even with all the worries and fears Aaron's special condition brought. Even though she watched Hannah constantly, concerned perhaps she too would have the same disease. Melinda trusted God, trusted his provision and care. When she thought of having another child though, a part of her heart shrank back—afraid.

Could she bear watching another child suffer as Aaron suffered?

Still, when she looked out the window as Noah had told her to, she couldn't help but know Aaron was blessed by God. She couldn't help but be grateful he was a part of her life.

The sun had broken through the clouds that the weather forecast had said would scatter by noon, and her son sat in a patch of sunlight. The hens were all busy with the feed Aaron had managed to scatter, and he had somehow reached down and caught one of the baby chicks. He was holding it carefully in one hand and petting it with the other. Even though she couldn't see it from this distance, she knew that a look of pure wonder covered his face. It was only a chick and the boy who had managed to surprise it away from its mother. Melinda knew Aaron had held plenty of chicks before; she'd handed him one last week. But he'd managed to catch this one himself. It was his secret, and hopefully, even if only in some small way, it would help heal a portion of what had happened to Aaron the night before.

As she watched, he set the chick carefully on the ground, put his skinny hands on the wheels of his chair, and made his way slowly, laboriously, back through the gates and along the path—a look of marked determination on his face.

It was a few minutes before noon when Esther pulled up to Melinda's house. Simon was sound asleep in the wooden carrier Reuben had designed that fit perfectly on the floorboards in the back. Esther hoped she wouldn't wake him carrying him inside, but she needed to talk to Melinda, and she needed to do it before continuing to town. So she picked up her bag of quilting supplies, then reached for her infant son.

She'd barely stepped away from the buggy when Melinda was at her side.

"Let me help you. I'll take him."

"*Danki*. Where are the boys?"

"They finished their chores a little while ago and have gone to fish at the pond behind the barn. Is Leah with your parents?"

"*Ya*."

"I can fix you some lunch if you'd like."

"No. I ate an early lunch with Tobias. Then I dropped Leah off, and Simon fell asleep before we'd even made it to the main road." They walked up the steps of the front porch and into the sitting room.

"Hannah's down for her nap as well. I can't believe how this *boppli* is growing, Esther."

"Tobias says he's longer each week, but I refuse to believe it. I want him to stay exactly this size for a while."

"He's beautiful."

Melinda traced Simon's face with her finger, a wistful look shining in her eyes—a look Esther recognized all too well. Esther had waited a long time to have another child, waited a long time for Tobias to come along. She certainly never thought she'd be happily married again after the death of her first husband, but God had had other plans for her.

"I was on the way into town to stop at the shop to see if Callie could use my help."

"I suppose you heard about yesterday."

"*Ya.* Aaron's okay?"

Melinda sighed and adjusted Simon in the crook of her arms as she sat back on the couch. "Aaron appears to be fine. Don't ask me how. I would probably be having nightmares if I saw a woman killed." She shook her head, causing her *kapp* strings to brush against Simon's baby blanket.

"Last night Aaron was able to relay facts to Shane, and for the most part he didn't become upset—not until the very end. He did seem more tired than usual, falling asleep in his chair before I could put him in the buggy. I can't remember the last time he did that. But otherwise, it's as if he can put the events he witnessed behind him."

Esther barely flinched at the mention of Shane's name—another sign God was still in the business of changing hearts. But then, without Shane, her marriage to Tobias would be an entirely different thing. His cousin Reuben might be serving a life sentence in jail right now. Shane had solved the case of Katie's death. He was the reason her family was whole.

Esther pushed away the memories of last fall's tragedy.

"Tell me what happened. I want to hear it from you. My *mamm* wasn't very clear."

After Melinda had related the night's events, Esther stared at her in disbelief. "How can this be happening to us again?"

"I know. It doesn't seem possible."

"At least none of us are wanted for this murder. I suppose that's a blessing."

"*Ya.*" Simon began to stir and root around, so Melinda handed him back, a grin spreading across her face. "I believe he's looking for you. I'll go and grab us two mugs of tea while you allow him to nurse."

"Tea would be great. Do you have something herbal?"

"*Ya.* Of course."

By the time Melinda returned with the drinks, Esther remembered the other reason she'd stopped by. "I wanted to talk to you about these quilts that we're restoring. The work's more challenging than I expected."

"Yours too? I can see why they're valuable—the stitching is exquisite, but I can't figure out the pattern on the border."

"I agree. That's why I brought mine over. I've never seen a quilt pieced together like this before. I asked my *mamm* about it, and she said it looks like a storybook quilt to her."

Melinda pushed up her glasses and cocked her head at the same time. "Hadn't thought of that. I've never seen an actual storybook quilt, though I have heard of them. Hang on a minute."

When Melinda returned with her quilt, Simon was done nursing. He burped, then smiled at them both.

"That boy is as charming as his father." Esther spread Simon's quilt on the floor and placed him on it, then stacked pillows around him.

"Here's the quilt I'm supposed to restore. I've gotten as far as reinforcing the stitching on the first few panels."

"But the border makes no sense on yours either."

Melinda frowned. "The top and bottom do. I had no problem there."

"Which is odd in and of itself. When was the last time you saw a quilt that had a border change on two sides? I don't even know what I'm sewing on my quilt." Esther bent over the tiny stitches that constituted the side borders. "At first I thought it was a type of pattern work, but it doesn't repeat in any way that makes sense. Look at mine. It's the same."

Esther went to her sewing bag and pulled out the quilt top of the piece she'd agreed to restore. "Now the workmanship is excellent, as you pointed out. I'd say it's better than what even you or I or Deborah are able to do."

"*Ya*, some of the older women had a real gift. My *mamm* said that Mrs. Hochstetler was the finest quilter she had ever known — that she taught many of her generation how to quilt and that plain women from several counties once came to learn stitching from her."

Esther frowned. "Why don't I remember any of this?"

"I believe she stopped quilting before we started. You know I visited with her more than you did because my *mamm*'s *aenti* and Mrs. Hochstetler's *schweschder* were *freinden*. I was never clear on how they knew each other. But she would show up at our family gatherings, and she'd always comment on my quilts or offer to show me how to improve my stitching. She couldn't sew very much herself at that point because of the arthritis in her hands. It was quite crippling."

Melinda's expression grew distant, a look Esther had seen far too often on her friend's face.

"What is it? What did you remember just then?"

Smiling, Melinda stared down at the quilt again. "Mrs. Hochstetler had a special way with Aaron. Where other people would ask about him in general or maybe shy away from the topic, she would want to know specifics — like whether he'd managed to pull himself up yet, or if he could put on his own clothes. She wasn't being nosy either. She took a real interest. She was a sweet lady, and I'm going to miss her."

Esther reached out and patted her friend on the arm, but then she remembered the problem facing them. "I wish she'd thought to tell you more about these quilts before she passed. I have no idea what to do with this border. Honestly, mine is as big a mess as yours, and it's going to have to be redone before we can sell them. Look at this—"

As she was talking, she'd laid her quilt top down beside Melinda's on the floor, laid it down so that they could see how one quilt was in as bad a shape as the other.

Instead, what they saw was that, when laid together, the two quilts looked like two pieces taken from the same puzzle—except they didn't quite fit together.

"It still doesn't make any sense." Esther stood and frowned at the two quilts. "It almost looks like—"

"I'll tell you what it almost looks like." Melinda's voice filled with wonder, sounded exactly like Tobias' when he spoke to his newborn son. Melinda stayed on the floor, kneeling beside the two quilts, but she reached for Esther's quilt and turned it so that the top borders were now side by side and the side borders—the borders that were indecipherable—now touched.

"It almost looks like the borders we couldn't figure out form an old German script." Melinda glanced up, a smile tugging at the corners of her lips.

"Script that is divided between two quilts."

"So you can't read it, unless you put the two quilts side by side." Melinda's smile widened.

They stared at each other in surprise.

"Your quilt has the top half of the words," Esther whispered.

"And your quilt has the bottom."

"Exactly like a puzzle."

Chapter 9

DEBORAH DIRECTED HER BROWN MARE, Cinnamon, into the parking lot of Daisy's Quilt Shop just as the downtown clock was striking noon. As she pulled in, she remembered she was supposed to have called first. Well, obviously the shop was open, so no harm done. She'd hoped to arrive an hour earlier, but Joshua had put her behind schedule. Her two-and-a-half-year-old had decided to pull off his diaper and run around the house naked, which had resulted in not one but two accidents. It was definitely time to potty train her youngest, and she intended to — soon. But festival weekend wasn't the ideal time.

Joshua smiled and put two chubby hands on her face as she lifted him out of the buggy.

"We see Callie?"

"Yes, sweetie. We're going to see Callie."

"We see Max?"

"Yes, we'll see Max, but you be *gut*. Keep your pants on, young man."

Joshua patted her cheeks. "Pants on."

"Exactly." She wondered again if she should have accepted Martha's offer to come along, but Deborah knew her oldest had actually wanted to play with her cousins. The Fall Festival was an exciting weekend in Shipshewana. It didn't seem fair to stick Martha with babysitting instead.

Jonas had assured her he would see that the children finished the day's chores before noon, before Miriam, Deborah's closest sister, arrived to take the children into town. His last words to her before she left had been, "Help your *freinden*, but be careful in the crowds, Deb." A soft touch, and then he was gone to work in the fields. He'd join them in town later that afternoon.

So though she could have used Martha's help, she knew her daughter would have more fun playing and attending the festival with her cousins.

She placed Joshua on the ground, pulled his wool cap down so he wouldn't lose it, then reached for his hand as he toddled toward the front door of Callie's shop. The parking lot was full in spite of last night's excitement. A ribbon of yellow crime-scene tape at the far side of the lot was the single telltale sign of Mrs. Knepp's murder.

Deborah guided Joshua down the crowded sidewalk, under the berry-colored canopy that shaded the windows, and up to the front door of the shop. She had barely reached for the handle of the door when Callie pulled it open, causing the bell to ring merrily.

"You can't come in," she said.

"What?"

"I'm sorry. Read the sign. Things are crazy, and I had to make some new guidelines. You understand."

"Understand—"

"It's on the sign." Callie pointed at a handwritten sheet of paper taped to the front door, as she emphasized the word *sign*, like it held some special meaning. Then she began to push the door shut.

"What ... Wait. What are you doing?"

Joshua reached forward and tugged on Callie's jean skirt. "Max? Joshua see Max."

"I'm sorry, Deb. It's just for this weekend." Something like regret and a steely stubbornness shot through Callie's eyes, then she nudged Joshua out of the way, back into Deborah's dress, before slamming the door shut, rattling the glass.

Deborah was left standing on the stoop, gazing at the sheet of paper that read, "No children under three years of age permitted in store during Fall Crafters' Fair."

She read it again, but the words didn't change.

What in the world?

Why was this sign on Callie's door?

Why had her friend shut the door in her face?

Two *Englisch* women murmured apologies and brushed past Deborah, into Callie's shop.

Deborah wanted to stamp her foot. She wanted to march inside and demand to know what was going on. Instead she reached down, picked up Joshua, and made her way back to her buggy, to Cinnamon, and—she supposed—to home.

Except she didn't want to go home.

The festival was in full swing around her. So she found herself on the sidewalk, in the growing crowd of people, moving toward downtown.

What could have come over Callie?

Deborah had never seen her act rudely before.

Her mind raced back over the previous night. Joshua hadn't even been with her. He'd been home with Jonas and the twins. Martha had been at the shop with Aaron and Matthew. Had that been the problem? Too many children in the store?

But the sign had specifically said "No children under three years of age." And only for this weekend!

Deborah was so deep in thought, so busy trying to puzzle out the abrupt change in Callie's behavior, and at the same time so busy trying to weave her way through the crowd while holding onto Joshua, that she practically ran into a chain-saw carver walking straight toward her.

Wearing an unbuttoned plaid shirt, the T-shirt underneath read "Will carve for food." He was carrying a small chain saw and wore a ball cap that boasted a handsaw and covered badly kept hair that fell to his shoulders. Unshaven stubble added to his already unkempt look and sideburns stretched down to his jawline.

"Excuse me," she murmured, stepping around him.

But instead of allowing her to pass, he reversed direction and fell into step beside her. "Mind if I walk with you?"

The voice was familiar, but it didn't match—

"Don't stare," Shane murmured. "Keep walking until we reach my booth."

"Your booth?" Deborah's voice squeaked, causing a few people to turn and stare.

"I'm a chain-saw carver. Can't you tell?"

"You know how to chainsaw?"

"I live in Indiana. I'm a man. I can chainsaw."

"But why—"

"Just keep walking."

"I think I've fallen down the rabbit hole Martha read about in school." Deborah hugged Joshua to her, stopping in the middle of the sidewalk so the pedestrian traffic streamed around her like water in a river flowed around a large boulder.

"Don't stop, Deborah. We need to act normal. It's just a little farther."

She looked into his eyes then, and when she did, the times they'd depended on each other surged forward in her memory. His disguise fell away, and she was no longer in the midst of a crowd, confused and jostled up against a person she didn't recognize. Instead she was standing next to someone she could trust—she was standing beside her friend.

"*Ya*, okay. I can do that."

Five minutes later they were at his booth. Joshua was seated in the corner, playing with a toy truck someone had carved, and she was listening to Shane explain what had happened to Callie, how they were going to help her, and what they needed to do to catch Mrs. Knepp's killer.

The entire story sounded insane.

"You believe me. Don't you?" Shane's voice was urgent, and his eyes pinned Deborah to the stool she was perched on.

"I suppose. Yes. But Shane, why can't you simply call in more help? Take Callie out of the shop if they're watching her. Take her somewhere she'll be safe. Then catch this terrible person some other way." She ran her hand up and down one of the strings of her prayer *kapp*, knowing she wasn't going to like his answer.

"I almost did." Shane scratched the sideburns that must have been fake but certainly looked real. He hadn't shaved either, that much was evident. It occurred to her that he probably hadn't rested at all since the 9-1-1 call she'd placed the night before. "I almost insisted she close the shop and come into protective custody. She didn't want to, but I could have found a way to force her. And I still would, except for Aaron."

When a couple stopped to watch him carve, he held up his chain saw and smiled at them. "Booth will open in another hour, folks."

They nodded and moved on.

"Whose booth is this?"

"Don't worry about it. I paid him to rent it to me when I need it. He'll show back up when I text him."

Deborah closed her eyes, trying to make Shane's words come together in some pattern, trying to make them make sense. Opening her eyes, she checked once more on Joshua, then scooted her stool closer to Shane, lowering her voice. "What is your worry about Aaron? That he's a witness?"

"Yes. And the person who killed Mrs. Knepp, tranq'd Max, and called Callie last night also directly threatened Aaron. It wouldn't take him fifteen minutes in this town to figure out where Aaron lives."

"You could hide Aaron too, at least until you catch this man ..." Deborah's voice wavered as she realized what she was suggesting.

"Do you think Melinda and Noah would allow that? Would they hide as well? You understand the Amish mind-set better than I do, Deborah, but as much as I've worked with them, I'd guess no. I don't think they would. I believe they'd say—"

"They'd say it's *Gotte's wille*, that they're under *Gotte's* protection." Deborah stared at her son, rolling a wooden truck back and forth. "They'd say that they're safer where they are than trusting *Englischers*."

"So you agree my plan is the best way?"

Deborah studied Shane closely then. His disguise couldn't hide his piercing black eyes, haggard expression, and the intensity that he didn't know he possessed. His plan was rather crazy, but it might work.

Except for one thing.

One thing he didn't realize, but she did. It was as clear as the feeling of excitement going through the crowd that passed his wood-carving booth. Shane Black had fallen in love with Callie Harper.

When had it happened?

Her mind sifted back through the months since Callie had arrived in town, flipped through them like so many pages in a book. She supposed it didn't matter when he had crossed the line from dealing with her as a detective to being her friend to hoping their relationship would grow more intimate. What mattered was that this man cared about one of her best friends. He cared about her deeply.

He'd do his job, and he'd do it professionally.

He'd find a way to protect both Callie and Aaron.

And she had no doubt he'd find a way to bring the man and woman who were responsible for this awful situation to justice.

But would he understand that the weight he was carrying was his love for the woman working in the shop a half-mile down the road?

That was something Deborah wasn't so sure about. As she gathered Joshua and hurried back to Cinnamon, hurried to carry out her portion of Shane's plan, she also realized it was something that would have to wait.

"You want to go, don't you?" Matt's voice didn't leave much room for arguing. It was more a statement than a question.

They were making their way back from the pond. Aaron held the fishing rods out in front of him, as if he were still planning on reeling one in. He studied the rods and took his time answering.

"Well?"

"I'm thinking."

"What's there to think about? It's the biggest day of the year. Chain-saw carvers, musicians, more food booths than last night, cloggers, painters—"

"I remember what's all there."

"Not to mention everyone from school."

"Ya." Truthfully Aaron did want to go. At least he didn't want to stay home, which was the same as wanting to go. Wasn't it?

"So what's the problem?"

Matt stopped wheeling, stopped while they were still out of range of the house. His *mamm* would be gone already, gone to help at the quilt shop more than likely. His *dat* would be working near the barn, watching for them. They needed to wash up and then they could be on their way.

"So what's the problem?" Matt asked again.

"There's not a problem. Not really." Aaron ran his hand over the wheel of his chair. He liked the way it felt. He enjoyed the warmth of it and even the way it picked up dirt from the trail.

Matt began pushing the chair again, pushed it to their spot—a place near the top of the hill. A place where they could see nearly all the homestead but still feel hidden. Once he'd pushed the chair into the shade of the huge old tree, Matt moved around in front of him and sat on a large rock that had been there for as long as Aaron could remember.

"I know you better than anyone, Aaron. Maybe better than you know yourself. So what is it? What haven't you told them yet?"

Aaron thought about keeping it in, but somebody needed to understand the danger he was up against. What if the man came back and killed him and hid his body? No one would find out what had happened.

He should tell someone—someone he could trust.

He should tell his *bruder*.

Plus, Matt always seemed to know what to do.

Taking a deep breath, he pushed the words out. "He saw me."

His *bruder* didn't question him, didn't laugh, didn't even answer right away. Instead he looked out over their family's farm.

Thought on it for a good minute or two.

"I didn't move, didn't make any noise, but Max was with me, and he was pretty upset. I think he smelled death. Do you think that's possible?"

"Sure. Animals have instincts like that."

"He started barking like crazy, went wild like he had to scare the man away from his territory."

"The man looked up?"

"*Ya.*"

"And he looked at you."

Aaron nodded.

"Now think about this, Aaron. Maybe he didn't notice you

were sitting in a wheelchair. Maybe he just saw a kid sitting. You were close to that bench."

Aaron's mind slid back to the night before, to the way he'd wheeled the chair out so that he could see better.

"Probably he did see the chair."

"All right." Matt didn't move, continued to think on it awhile. Finally he asked, "And you didn't tell the officers this?"

"No. *Mamm* was right there the entire time. You know how she is, barely leaving my side, as if I'm going to fall over or something. She'd have croaked of a heart attack if I'd admitted the man looked right at me after he attacked Mrs. Knepp."

Matt nodded. "Probably you're right. It was *gut* thinking to protect our *mamm*. She's got plenty enough to worry on what with all the work she does here and the quilting and *boppli* Hannah."

Some of the tightness melted out of Aaron. He'd wondered if he'd done the right thing. Though he was still plenty scared, it helped to have his *bruder* agree with what he'd done.

Matt stood up and began pushing the chair again.

"That's why I wasn't sure if I should go to the festival or not. Think we should talk to *Dat* about it?"

"Could. If things get any worse we will. Right now, he has his hands awful full with the crops. I'd hate to bother him if we don't have to."

Aaron looked over at the fields as they drew closer to the barn. His *dat* was a hard worker. He wondered what it would be like to be able to drive the horses the way his *dat* did, to be able to work in the fields and carry the bags of feed without it hurting his chest at all. The last thing he wanted to do was add to his *dat*'s troubles. "Maybe I should stay home, pretend I have a stomachache or something. Just until Shane is able to catch him."

"*Nein.* Him seeing you, that's all the more reason for us to go to town, wander around the festival a while." Matt's voice took on a hard sound, like it did whenever one of the kids at school tried to give Aaron a hard time. Didn't happen often anymore, but sometimes, when a new person moved in, Matt sounded that way for a day or so. Then things settled down.

Aaron wondered if this was the same. He wondered if his *bruder* could handle the man who'd been outside Callie's shop.

"We need to go to town," Matt repeated. "That's exactly what we need to do. We need to find out if this guy is still hanging around, and if he is—we need to decide what we're going to do about it."

Chapter 10

CALLIE'S SHOULDERS ACHED, and though the clock said it was only just 12:32 p.m., she was sure it should be past two by now. She'd never had a day pass so slowly.

Each time the bell over the door jingled, she jumped, expecting the horrible man on the phone to burst through, minus his giggling accomplice. For some reason, she knew she wouldn't see the woman. The woman was a prop—like a lamp set on a stage for a play.

The woman wouldn't show up even if the man did.

Customers filled every square foot of the store, but Max lay at her feet, still barely moving. Like her, he kept one eye on the door. She noticed he watched it as if he, too, expected trouble. He didn't bother to greet anyone. Neither people he knew nor any of the strangers.

Whatever they'd drugged her dog with, they'd measured the dosage wrong. He clearly wasn't throwing off the effects as quickly as he should. She'd laid a hand on his side several times to check his breathing, and he seemed all right. The lethargy was not normal though, at least not according to what she'd been able to find on the Internet.

He wouldn't eat, and he showed little interest in his surroundings.

She wanted to call Doc England, her vet, but apparently Creeper was watching her cell phone as well as her business line. How had he found her cell number? From a phone bill in her office? Somehow he'd stolen it. Earlier she had received a text from him—a text that had left her freaked out and paranoid.

Contact no 1. We r watching. Find the $.

What money was she supposed to find?

When would they call again?

How was she going to protect her friends?

And then, always, like a county-fair Ferris wheel, her mind circled back to the first question—what if Max didn't improve?

The one thing outpacing her fear was her anger. If something didn't change soon, she was afraid the anger would burst out of her like rain from a Texas thunderstorm.

She was surprised Shane hadn't been by the store. His last words to her before they'd parted earlier this morning was that he had a plan and for her to trust him. He told her he'd share it with her as soon as he had "things in place." Now what did that mean?

One more question to add to her bag full of questions. Not what she needed. She slammed her order pad on the counter and Lydia jumped.

"Are you okay?" Lydia gently touched her sleeve.

"Yes. No. I'm not sure." She pulled the pad toward her and began doodling in the margins. "Why are all these people milling around? They should either purchase something or leave. They're making me nervous."

Lydia's eyes widened, but she didn't say anything.

"What? You're looking at me like I've grown antennas."

"No. No antennae. It's—"

"Spit it out," Callie growled.

"I've never seen you this way," Lydia admitted. The girl had recently turned eighteen years old, and Callie expected her to announce that she was to be married any day now. The marrying season. It would probably steal away her one good assistant. Callie pushed the worry away.

"I'm sorry. I'm—" she bit back the truth, "—tired is all."

Lydia let out a breath. "*Ya*. Festival does that to shop owners. Maybe next week you can take off a day or two."

"Maybe. We are seriously crowded, and it's not because everyone is here to shop. Look at that old man in the corner. I think he's been here all morning. Go and see if you can help him or shoo him out. We need to make room for customers who want to purchase something."

As Lydia hurried off, Callie turned to ring up a customer who had approached the register, but her thoughts returned to Shane.

Where was he?

It wasn't like he could walk in flashing his badge, but she'd hoped he might find a way to check on her. Of course, he was conducting a murder investigation. Still, she thought she'd seen something in his eyes this morning, something more than concern for one of the citizens under his care.

Or had she just been *hoping* to see that?

Being stuck in this shop with all these people was driving her crazy. Some of them seemed determined to stand around drinking her coffee and tea. Why couldn't they leave? Or, better yet, purchase something?

She watched as Lydia made her way to the old man in the corner. Why was he even here? Old men occasionally purchased things, but if they did, it was usually a quick stop in with a supply list from their wives. This man did not appear to have a list. She tried to mentally pair him up with one of the women present, but someone stepped between them, handing her a bolt of calico and asking for three yards.

Walking to the cutting table, she slammed the bolt of Christmas print down on the counter and jerked her scissors out of her apron pocket. "Three yards?" she practically barked at the out-of-towner standing in front of her.

"Yes, three, please," the woman murmured nervously. "Or two if you don't have three left. Whatever you have is fine."

The woman's eyes darted from the scissors to the material to Callie's face and then back again. What was wrong with this lady? She acted as if *she* feared being attacked.

Glancing down, Callie realized she had her fingers wrapped around the scissors the same way someone might clutch a knife. She set them on the table, wiped her hands on her apron, and smiled at the customer. "Of course you can have three yards."

Picking the scissors back up, Callie forced herself to relax. Just because the culprit might be watching didn't mean she had to scare off every potential customer by acting like a maniac.

Shane was probably right. It was probably a bluff. Who could see over this crowd anyway? And even if they could, it didn't mean they knew what she was thinking, it didn't mean they could hurt her.

The bell over the door rang and she jerked up on the scissors, slicing diagonally across the middle of the fabric. Max whimpered, but he still didn't move.

"Is your dog all right?" the customer asked.

"Yes." Callie glanced down at Max. "But I'm going to have to ask Lydia to help you with this fabric."

After calling Lydia over to the table, Callie hurried to the front counter where Esther's husband, Tobias, waited patiently—a smile on his face, his eyes calm and focused on her as she hurried across the room.

"Tobias. I didn't expect to see you here today."

"*Ya.* Don't usually stop by for fabric and such, but I was in town and Doc England asked me to come and pick up Max."

"Max?"

"He had an opening this afternoon after all. You were wanting to update Max's shots and have that toenail looked at?" Tobias had removed his black hat and now gripped it casually with both of his hands — big hands even for a man who was over six feet tall. He interlaced his fingers around the top of the hat, which he held upside down, almost as if he had his hands wrapped around a cup of coffee.

Callie glanced down and saw Shane's business card taped to the inside of Tobias' hat. Tobias held the hat in such a way that it probably couldn't be seen by anyone or anything else.

Written on the card was a brief note.

"Doc England ..." Callie licked her lips and tried again. "He ... he told me that he couldn't possibly see Max until next week."

"Guess with folks going to the festival and all, he had some cancellations. I ran into him while I was at the feedstore, told him I could come down and pick up Max since you'd probably be too busy."

"Okay. Ummm. Let me go find his leash then." Callie wiped her sweating hands on her skirt, then hurried to her office where she kept Max's things. She resisted the urge to look over her shoulder, though she wanted to badly. She wanted to see if anyone was watching through the windows or maybe scoping her out through the decorative glass of her front door.

She should try to control her paranoia.

He was bluffing. Surely Creeper had been bluffing.

So why was Shane being so careful? And why did he want Max?

When she came back and clipped the leash to Max's collar, he didn't even stand.

"I guess you may need to carry him." Callie felt her throat close around tears she refused to shed. She wanted to be there, wanted to explain to Doc England herself what was wrong with her dog.

Instead she watched Tobias bend down, pick up her sixty-five pound Labrador as if he weighed no more than a bolt of cloth, and carry him out the door. As he walked away, Tobias winked. "Don't worry about him, Callie. Doc England's the best vet in the county."

Then the bell rang again, three more customers walked in, and she was left in the store full of customers, left trying to make some sense of the words on Shane's card.

Give him Max.
Talk to the old man near the window.

Melinda was on her way into town, finally, when she passed Deborah's buggy on the road.

Deborah began waving wildly and pulled over to the side. Come to think of it, why was Deborah headed the wrong direction? She couldn't be leaving town already. It wasn't even two o'clock. Activities were in full swing. Why would she be going home?

Melinda glanced over at the boxes of pies she was to deliver to her sister's booth. They'd made every flavor imaginable, including Dutch apple, chocolate, and of course, shoofly. She needed to hurry before the afternoon rush hit.

Leaning out of the buggy, she watched Deborah.

Her friend had already turned around and started back toward her. The pies would keep for a few minutes. Clucking to Ginger, Melinda directed her own mare off the road. By the time she'd made her way out of the buggy, Deborah had pulled over as well. Usually calm, collected, and composed, Deborah practically tumbled out of the buggy, then pulled her dress up to keep from tripping and ran toward her.

Melinda was so surprised, she stood there staring at her, not moving at all.

"I'm so glad you stopped." Deborah arrived breathless, her hair escaping from her *kapp*. "I tried to call the phone shack, but the neighbor said your buggy had already left your *schweschder*'s."

"What's wrong? You look all—" Melinda's hands fluttered out as she took in Deborah's appearance.

"*Ya*. I know. I'm a sight."

"Is Joshua all right?"

"He's fine. Fell asleep before we were even out of town." Glancing left, then right, as if they might not be alone there on the side of the road, Deborah lowered her voice, then stepped even closer. "It's Callie. She's in trouble. Actually we all are."

"Trouble?"

"The man who killed Mrs. Knepp ..."

"What? Is he back?"

"And Melinda," Deborah reached out and touched her arm, as if she were the one who needed supporting, "he knows about Aaron."

"Aaron? My Aaron?" The fear that always hid in Melinda's heart blossomed, clawed its way up her throat.

"I'm not saying this well. Shane can explain it better. But we need to gather everyone and meet at Reuben's barn tonight. I already sent Esther there."

"You're not making any sense." Melinda tried to calm her heart, which had started beating triple speed at her son's name. "Who knows about Aaron? And what sort of danger is Callie in? Maybe you should come and sit in my buggy."

"*Nein*. There's no ... no time. There are other things ... other things I have to do. Already it's late. The day ... it's slipping away."

Melinda waited until Deborah's words had stumbled to a stop. Taking hold of both Deborah's arms, Melinda spoke slowly. "You didn't answer me. What about Aaron? Tell me who knows about Aaron. Explain what you're talking about."

Deborah nodded, swallowed once, and tucked some hair back

into her prayer *kapp*. "The man who killed Mrs. Knepp, he called Callie last night, after he'd shot Max."

"Shot Max?" Melinda reached for the side of her buggy.

"He's fine. It was a ... what did Shane call it? A tranquilizer. He shot it from a gun, like the men would a bullet from their hunting rifles. If she doesn't give him the money he wants—money she knows nothing about—he'll do something terrible. I don't know what. And he said—" Deborah glanced away, but then looked back at Melinda, her eyes never wavering from her friend's face and her voice resolute. "He said that he knew about the kid in the wheelchair."

Melinda felt the earth shift under her feet.

"You should sit down."

"No. Tell me the rest." She leaned back until her shoulders were pressed against the warmth and solidity of the buggy. "Tell me what you know."

"Shane wanted to put you all into hiding—you and the *kinner*. Callie too." She paused, then rushed on. "But he didn't think you'd go. He'll ask again tonight. You need to talk to Noah."

"Noah!" Melinda's hand clutched her throat. "He's taking the boys to the festival. They might be there already. I had to stop at my *schweschder*'s to pick up the pies. I left Hannah with her, picked up the desserts, and I'm supposed to deliver them to the booth. What am I to do with the pies, Deborah?"

"Give them to me. I think it's better that I go back into town, and you go home to find Noah and the boys."

"But should we take the time to switch them?"

They both peered into her buggy. Boxes of pies covered every surface.

"If Noah passes us on the road, he'll see us pulled over and stop. We haven't really lost any time, and I don't mind taking the pies back in."

"What if he's already in town?"

"If I see him, I'll send him home."

"*Ya*, okay. I suppose that works."

By the time they'd switched the pies to Deborah's buggy, Melinda could feel sweat soaking through her dress. "*Danki.* You're a *gut freind.*"

"*Gern gschehne.* Now you go, but drive carefully. Go home and find your family. Bring them to Reuben's." Deborah reached out and straightened her friend's *kapp*, which had come unpinned in the front. "Shane has a plan, Melinda—a *gut* plan. I think it's our best chance."

Melinda turned Ginger around and headed home, unsure if she'd find her family there or an empty house.

How had this happened?

She'd spent her entire adult life trying to protect her boys. Now it seemed they stood in the midst of harm's way.

Her mind raced ahead to all the things that could go wrong, but Ginger's slow, steady pace gradually calmed her nerves. Surely God had not saved Aaron from the terrible chicken breast disease—how she hated that name—so she could watch him perish at the hands of an evil man.

No. That wasn't possible.

God had plans for Aaron. Plans "*of peace, and not of evil.*" She'd known that from the moment she'd first held him in her arms. God had plans for each of her children. She could trust in the truth of his promises. Even when she pulled into her lane and confirmed her fears—that Noah's buggy was already gone—she didn't immediately turn and rush Ginger back into town.

Instead she pulled the buggy up to the barn, stepped down into the shade, and checked her mare. Ginger was dependable— more like a family pet than a workhorse. A light golden-brown, she wasn't as spry as when they'd first purchased her nine years ago, but Noah said not to worry, that Ginger still had many years of service left. Buggy mares had been known to last seventeen, even up to twenty years. If they were treated well. If they were cared for correctly.

As Ginger nudged Melinda's hand searching for a treat, it was plain from her labored breathing to the way she shuffled her feet that she actually needed some water and a few minutes' rest.

So Melinda unharnessed her from the buggy, pulled her into the coolness of the barn, and dropped a cupful of feed into her bucket. Then she made sure there was plenty of water for her to drink. Going through the motions of the chores calmed Melinda, forced her to think rather than react.

Her instinct was to turn and hurry back to town as quickly as possible, but hurrying wasn't always the wisest course of action. Hurrying could get her family killed.

She needed to stop, let the horse rest, and think.

She needed to focus and determine how best to prepare for the hours and days ahead.

She needed to pray.

Deborah was already on her way into town, on her way to finding Melinda's family and warning Melinda's husband of what needed to be done. They would be here soon. If she stayed put, Ginger would be well rested by the time they needed to leave again.

Melinda walked into the house, retrieved a small pad of paper and a pen from the kitchen drawer, and walked back out to the porch. Sitting on the steps where she had a good view of the lane leading up to the house, she began to make her list.

She listed things they would need at Reuben's this evening. Tapping her pen against the paper, she drew another column. In that column, she listed things they would need for the weekend, in case Noah decided it was wiser they stay that long. She didn't think he'd say that, but it was best to be prepared.

Twenty minutes later, Noah's buggy still hadn't appeared on the lane. Twenty minutes. Probably Deborah was just arriving in town, just tying up Cinnamon and going to look for Noah and the boys. Melinda forced her worries down and turned the page of her small pad.

Her third list was sadly short. No matter how she focused, she couldn't come up with more than three lines to write under the title—so she stood, tucked the pad into her apron pocket, and began collecting the things they'd need to take to Reuben's. But her mind kept running over the last list, determined to lengthen it.

There had to be more possibilities.

She'd pulled out two extra traveling blankets from the closet when a fourth possibility occurred to her. She dropped the blankets on the floor, pulled out the pad, and wrote it down.

Obviously, it wasn't Callie's money. Callie didn't know where or what it was.

But they could help her find it. If it would lure this evil man out of hiding, bring him to a place where Shane could capture him and take him away, then they would find the money.

Find the money, capture the murderer, and their lives could return to normal again.

It was but another puzzle—a mystery of sorts.

And together, their circle of friends had become quite good at solving them, especially when lives were at stake.

Chapter 11

SHANE SLID INTO THE CHAIR across from Stan Taylor in the Shipshewana Police Station. He'd snuck in through the back door, careful to remove his wood-carving disguise before he'd come within a block of the station.

"You look horrible, son." Taylor pushed a bottle of water into his hands, then sat down behind his desk, the chair groaning under his weight—which might not have been a testament to his weight as much as it was to the age of the chair.

"Yeah, it's part of the disguise." Shane stared at the water. "Did we run out of coffee?"

"We did not, but if you keep drinking it, you're going to crash. Drink some water instead. I'm guessing you didn't sleep at all?"

Shane ignored the question, focused instead on opening the bottle and guzzling half of it.

"So catch me up. Your texts make sense less than half the time. Or maybe you've forgotten how to spell."

Shane didn't bother to explain to Taylor that texting consisted of abbreviated spelling. Instead he took another long swig from the water bottle and sank back against the cracked plastic chair.

"I'm meeting with the Byers and Yoders tonight at Reuben's farm."

111

"Think you can get Callie out?"

"Yes. Tobias took the dog to Doc England's an hour ago. We plan to put Perla in Callie's spot as soon as darkness falls."

"How will that fool anyone? Perla doesn't exactly look like Callie."

Shane leaned forward, rubbed at the tension headache developing along the back of his neck. "She's the best we've got. She's good with her firearm, and she's approximately Callie's height."

"I'm guessing Perla weighs five pounds more—"

"Ten."

"And she's Hispanic."

"It'll be dark." Shane finished the bottle and tossed it in the recycle box beside Taylor's desk. "Look. It's not a perfect plan, but I think it will work. They're the same height. If our perp's watching—and I'm not sure he will be—I don't think he'll be able to notice the weight difference or the skin color from a distance in the dark."

"All right. Then what?"

"After the switch, I'll hustle Callie out to Reuben's. Once the group is together, we'll work on figuring out what money he's looking for. If we can, we'll find the money, find the identity of our man."

Taylor sat up straighter. "Great. While you're all at Reuben's, I'll be in town with the extra county personnel." He unrolled a detailed map of Shipshewana on the desk between them. "We'll place people here, here, and here."

Shane shook his head. "I want you to back off that alley."

"Didn't you say that's where she saw him?"

"Exactly. If that's his spot, if that's where he's comfortable, I want to leave it open for him." He grabbed a highlighter from the pencil holder on Taylor's desk. "Pull your people back to here and place extra reinforcement over at the corner."

Taylor studied Shane's marks for a minute, then nodded. "All right, but we have two problems. During the day, these areas are crowded, and we won't be able to see much."

"Agreed, there's no reason to set up before six tonight. The switch will happen closer to nightfall."

"Once it's full dark, our people are going to look conspicuous standing around."

Shane tapped the map with the highlighter. "Put them in landscaping clothes. Keep them in place after dark, like they didn't finish their work. They'll be better able to blend into the shrubbery that way too."

Taylor rubbed at his eyebrows, something Shane knew he did when he was concerned or exhausted, or in this case—both. "Prelim autopsy confirm the stun gun?"

"Not conclusively. But there was a mark on Mrs. Knepp's upper torso consistent to the marks a Taser with drive-stun capability would make. She definitely died of a heart attack, and her lab reports show she received an electrical shock from an unknown source."

"So someone tased her."

"Yeah. I'd say so."

"What does Leroy have so far?"

"No fingerprints. He can tell from the shoe prints that our perpetrator is roughly six feet tall. Shoe size was a ten."

"Everything check with the kid's story?"

"Yeah. Yeah, it does."

Taylor sat forward, placed his hands flat against the desk. "I'm a cop, Shane. I think I'm a good one. You're the guy who chases murderers, and I appreciate the times you've helped us before. Seth Zook ... that was a tough case."

"I'm still not happy about how it wasn't resolved either."

"Then there was Stakehorn's murder."

"Perp's still in jail."

"And finally Katie Lapp."

Shane didn't bother answering.

"I realize you have other work outside of Shipshewana, but you've always done a good job for us, for our citizens, and my point is that I appreciate it. Now do you have any theories as to what we're dealing with this time?"

"You want my hunch? Without the proof?"

"Yeah. I do."

"I think the murder was a mistake all around—mistaken identity, mistaken outcome. He was after Callie. Probably the woman she heard in the background of the phone conversation, the woman she heard laughing, was in the quilt shop shortly before the time of Mrs. Knepp's attack."

Taylor considered that for a minute, then grunted in agreement. "She saw Callie leave and gave our killer a heads up."

"Exactly. He might have followed her, but the street was busy. Somehow he messed up, confused Mrs. Knepp for Callie."

Taylor leaned back, the chair squeaking once again under his weight. "Because of the dresses. Because they were the same color."

"It's the best explanation."

"Didn't he wonder why she was in the bushes, spying on her own shop?"

"People do strange things, Captain. And I don't think our perp's exactly normal. Who knows what was going through his mind. But he sees the dress, sees someone roughly the same height and build, and he makes his move. When he uses the Taser, he doesn't think it will kill her—"

"Because he doesn't realize she's eighty-two years old."

"He grabs the purse."

"Which he thinks has the money."

"Or information leading to the money." Shane thought of this psycho attacking Callie and his anger spiked. This case was quickly becoming personal, and when it was personal, he risked making a mistake, which meant he needed to control his emotions.

"Enough money to kill for?" Taylor's question pulled him back to the conversation.

"That amount varies for different people. And remember he probably didn't realize he was killing someone when he tased Mrs. Knepp. Once someone kills though? Experience has taught me that the second time is easier."

Taylor sighed, stood, and attempted to hitch his pants up over his protruding stomach. A thought flitted through Shane's mind about suggesting Weight Watchers online, but he decided the middle of an investigation might be a bad time to recommend a new dieting plan.

"Why would he think Callie knows where the money is?"

"Maybe because she does. She just doesn't know it yet."

Deborah had no trouble spotting Noah's horse and buggy. He preferred to tie it up on the far end of town, down by the old train station, which was no longer in use. Probably he'd dropped the boys off somewhere closer to town.

The question was where.

How would she ever find them in this crowd?

Joshua was awake now. Awake, hungry for his afternoon snack, and needing to find a bathroom fast or he'd be pulling off those pants and diaper quicker than the twins could find trouble. Why couldn't her son use his diaper for one more week? She wasn't ready to potty train him today, but he was a stubborn one.

"Keep your pants on, son."

"Josh potty."

"We're almost there. Wait one minute, please."

She walked quickly around the corner and saw The Kaffi Shop. Noah wouldn't be there, but it did have a bathroom and carried juice, milk, and pastries. Anything to prevent a meltdown while she looked for Melinda's family.

A copy of the wanted poster Shane and Aaron had created was taped to the window, right beside the open door. Deborah didn't pause to look at it, but she did notice several people standing there, discussing what a pity it was for a sweet old lady to have her life ended in such a senseless way.

They didn't appear overly worried. It didn't seem to have kept anyone home, possibly because extra officers had been brought in from the county office. And it certainly wasn't hurting their appetites. They sipped their coffee and munched on pastries as one claimed she'd heard there had been three bullet holes and the other adamantly insisted it was a knife attack.

Deborah slipped past them, hoping Joshua didn't pick up on any of the things they were describing. She needn't have worried.

He was too busy trying to pull off his pants and diaper.

"Not yet," she whispered.

"Potty. Joshua potty."

Kristen, one of the local high school girls, was working the counter.

The place was crazy crowded, but Kristen waved at Deborah, who pushed her way through the mob of people and hurried back to the bathroom. Once there, Joshua looked up at her as he danced in a circle around her legs.

"Now?"

"Yes, son. Now."

He wiggled out of his pants and pulled the tabs on the diaper, a grin spreading across his face as she helped him onto the toilet.

Unfortunately, his good mood didn't last.

As soon as they left the bathroom and he smelled the chocolate chip cookies, he pushed between the legs of the people in the shop and pressed his face against the glass counter of the display.

"Joshua, come back here." Deborah excused herself, made her

way to the front of the line, and finally caught hold of his hand. With some effort she dragged him away from the display.

"Joshua hungry." He looked at her with eyes as round as the large fresh cookies stacked behind the case. "*Mamm.* Cookies."

"Josh, honey. The line is much too long." Deborah squatted beside her son and attempted to reason with him. When it was obvious he wasn't hearing a word she had to say, she tried to take his hand in hers and head outside once more. Joshua was having none of it. The cookies were plainly inside, and that was where he wanted to be. He sank to the ground as if he had no bones, dragging his feet and pointing toward the counter of baked goods and iced drinks.

"Joshua thirsty. Josh hungry."

A few tourists sent her *the look*—the one that said, "Control your child or take him home."

She wished it were so simple.

By the time she'd dragged him out to the sidewalk he was in full-blown meltdown.

Fortunately there was a vending machine across the street.

"Let's buy you some cold water."

"Cookies. Joshua wants cookies."

Cookies! She'd left the pies in the buggy. What had she been thinking? The murderer, Callie, Melinda's boys ... her mind was so full, she'd completely forgotten the pies.

Feeding a dollar into the slot of the drink machine, she snatched the cold bottle of water from the bin below, and twisted the cap open. Joshua stopped crying as soon as his lips settled around the cold bottle.

"Joshua like water."

"I know you do, sweetie."

He took a big drink, dribbling some on his shirt. "And cookies."

"How about some pie instead?"

Picking him up, she hurried toward her buggy. Was it really mid-afternoon? The day was passing too quickly. She needed for time to slow down.

Joshua clutched the water bottle as they neared the buggy, hurrying. Deborah wondered if the pies were ruined.

She'd finally come within sight of her buggy when an old man stepped out from between two *Englisch* cars. Deborah moved to the left to scoot around him, but he moved in the same direction.

Heart racing, she moved to the right. He was now close enough that she could see his face, the hand that reached out to stop her, the vaguely familiar eyes looking into hers.

"Deborah. It's me—Gavin."

"Oh, my heavens." Deborah stopped and picked Joshua up, needing to feel him against her to slow the beating of her heart. "Andrew? Is that ... you?"

"Good disguise, huh?"

She peered closer. He wore baggy clothes, a wig, and some sort of powder over his skin that made him appear wrinkled—from a distance. Up close, it just made him look dirty.

"*Ya.* I thought you were a person in need of a home."

Gavin smiled slightly at that. She had no idea why.

"I even knew you were dressing as an older man. Shane told me, but I didn't quite envision ... this."

Joshua reached out to pull on the hair that draped around Gavin's face, giggling as he did so.

"Something wrong with your little guy? I thought I heard him crying as you came around the corner."

"He's hungry and probably doesn't feel like walking."

"What are you doing back here? I thought you were headed to our alternate location."

Deborah shook her head as she continued moving toward her buggy. "It's a mess. The entire day has been nothing but one giant catastrophe."

"No one's been hurt, have they?" Andrew reached out and touched her arm. Deborah couldn't help patting him on the hand, even if it did mean she got some of his mysterious powder all over her fingers.

"I think everyone's fine. I caught Esther and Melinda in time. Melinda turned around and headed back home, so I brought her pies in for her and then forgot about them." Opening her buggy door, they both peered inside. "Oh, dear."

"Looks okay to me." Gavin took Joshua as she reached inside and pulled out a meringue pie.

"Meringue isn't supposed to look like a crater. It's supposed to be ... fluffy."

"Where do all these go?"

"Booth twenty-nine, Melinda's sister. I was in such a hurry to look for Aaron, Matt, and Noah that I forgot about delivering the pies."

"The boys are here?" Gavin's voice dropped to a rumble.

"*Ya.* I think so. I spotted Noah's buggy. Noah came separately from Melinda. That's why I turned around and came back. Melinda went on to the house to see if they were still there and wait if necessary, and I came into town to deliver the pies and look for Noah and the boys ..." Her voice drifted off as she closed her eyes. The pies were a mess. What now?

"All right. I'll call it in to the team—that way we'll have everyone looking. You take these pies on to the booth. It'll look more natural to be moving merchandise while you're looking for them, and you'll be able to see better from the buggy anyway." Andrew placed Joshua in the buggy's seat, then touched Deborah on the shoulder, waited for her to turn and look at him. "Try not to worry. We're lucky to have run into each other. This way we can work together."

Deborah started to say that maybe it wasn't luck. Maybe it was *Gotte's wille.* But before she could get the words out, Andrew leapt for the buggy.

He reached Joshua too late.

"Pie. Joshua like pie."

One hand in the shoofly, the other in his mouth, he smiled up at her. Deborah knew she should be angry, but then she remembered he hadn't had much of a lunch and no afternoon snack. She reminded herself that a dangerous man was stalking them, and the priority was to find Melinda's family.

"Yes, Joshua likes pie, sweetie." Turning him around in the front seat so he was sitting and holding the small pie in his lap, she kissed him once on the cheek.

Climbing into the buggy, she waited for Andrew to untie Cinnamon, then made her way back into the crowd, toward booth twenty-nine. While she slowly crept forward, she watched the people for any sign of Aaron, Matt, or Noah. She searched the faces for a glimpse of the person drawn by the police sketch artist.

And she occasionally glanced over at her son, perfectly content with his shoofly pie.

Something about the way he smiled at her convinced her they were going to find a way out of this maze.

Chapter 12

ONCE AARON STARTED ROLLING through the festival crowds, he forgot to be afraid.

For one thing, he and Matt ran into Annie King. She didn't even ask about the murder, though there were posters in every shop window. Instead she started teasing him right off.

"Thought your *mamm* would make you stay home and study your math, Aaron."

"Why would she do that?" He squinted up at her, the sun making it hard to see the expression on her face. Not that he needed to see it. Her tone was enough to know she'd have that smirky smile.

"Why? Because your folks don't abide *B*'s, same as mine don't. 'Course I don't make *B*'s so it's not a problem." She plumped out the apron over her dress, then glanced at Matt, who was talking to a few of the older boys from their school.

"I could tutor you." She ran her fingers down the strings of her prayer *kapp*, then twirled them around. Why did she do that? Were the strings bothering her? "If you want me to. Since you're having problems."

"*Nein.*"

"*Nein*, you don't want me to? Or *nein*, you're not having problems? Which do you mean?"

"I didn't mean neither one."

"You didn't mean *either* one." Her expression suddenly resembled his teacher's. Except on Annie King's face, it made Aaron's head hurt.

Suddenly Aaron wanted to be moving through the crowd again. Even the risk of being caught by a murderer seemed better than Annie's questions.

"I don't know what you're talking about, Annie, but I don't need you coming over to show me numbers." At precisely that moment, Matt and his *freinden* stopped talking and started listening. Suddenly, everyone was completely silent, then everyone laughed—everyone except Annie.

"Fine. Excuse me for offering to help." She flipped the strings of her prayer *kapp* behind her and disappeared into the crowd.

"I will never understand girls," Aaron muttered.

Matt said good-bye to his *freinden* and began pushing Aaron's chair. "It doesn't get any easier that I can see."

"Don't notice *Mamm* and *Dat* going at it."

"True enough, but then maybe they've had time to settle down. Look at how old they are."

Aaron hadn't ever thought about it. Were his parents old? They were just his parents. They were the age they were supposed to be.

Old was Bishop Elam or his *grossdaddi* or the woman who had died outside Miss Callie's shop.

The image came back like a sudden headache brought on by eating ice cream too quickly. The woman looking at the shop, then the *Englischer* sneaking up behind her. The woman leaping forward, leaping to her death. It replayed through his head over and over in an endless loop.

"Are you even listening to me?"

"*Ya*, 'course I am."

"Then tell me which way you'd rather go."

"Doesn't matter." Aaron pushed away the memories of the

night before and tried to focus on what Matt was saying. "*Dat* said we had an hour before we were to meet him. He was taking Hannah to see the clog dancers."

They waited, indecision freezing them in the crowd.

"I wouldn't mind seeing clog dancers," Aaron admitted as they began moving forward again.

"*Ya*, but we're supposed to be walking around, looking for—"

"I remember who we're looking for." Aaron jerked to the left in his chair as a big *Englisch* woman with an even bigger purse nearly whopped him on the side of the head.

The crowds were larger than ever this year. Or maybe he didn't remember last year as well as he thought he did. Would they even be able to spot the man from last night if he were walking down the sidewalk next to them? "I can't see anything from here except elbows. Maybe we should try across the street."

"*Gut* idea. I think the booths are drawing all the crowds over to this side." Matt pulled Aaron's chair to a stop in front of a red light, but as he did, the light changed to green.

They started across the busy street, and that's when Aaron saw it. He saw it at the same moment his *bruder* did, at the same moment Matt drew in a big breath, and yanked back on the handles of the chair, nearly throwing Aaron out of it with the sudden change in direction.

Aaron's eyes were glued on the small blue car barreling toward them and the man and woman seated behind the windshield. Their faces were all wrong, as if they had been covered with paint or mud.

But the eyes—he would know the eyes of the driver anywhere. He'd seen them—a little less than twenty-four hours ago, and then again in his nightmares.

Shane had experienced many such moments before, but few of them had involved children.

Moments when everything happened at once.

Moments when all other things came to a crashing halt.

The moment when he first made contact with the perp.

He was walking with his chain saw, headed toward Callie's shop. It wasn't his designated time to stop by. The shop was currently covered by one of Taylor's men who was supposed to be wandering around the store shopping from his wife's list. Shane had talked to him not five minutes before, and everything was quiet.

So why was he headed over there?

Why was he stepping outside of his own plan to calm the worries racing through his mind?

Because he couldn't resist the need to confirm with his own eyes that she was fine.

So he'd closed the tent flap on the booth he'd appropriated from the local vendor and headed toward the quilt shop.

He noticed the blue Smart Car approaching from the north immediately. The cars were a curiosity—more like a child's toy than an actual vehicle. He'd seen a few in Fort Wayne, but there weren't any registered in Shipshewana that he was aware of.

But he didn't immediately notice the two people in the vehicle were wearing masks. He was too far back.

Sunlight glinted off metal.

He looked to the west, saw Aaron's wheelchair with Matt pushing it on the edge of the walkway. He had time to register that the boys weren't supposed to be here. Deborah ought to have intercepted them outside of town. So he changed course, determined to reach Melinda's boys before they crossed the street. But then the light changed to green and Matt started to push Aaron's wheelchair as traffic traveling north to south stopped.

Except for the blue Smart Car.

It accelerated.

And it was headed straight for the boys.

Matt pulled back on the wheelchair at the exact moment Shane pulled out his Glock, stepped forward, and shouted, "Police! Everybody down!"

The Smart Car swerved in order to hit the boys, but a vendor with a cartful of ice cream either realized what was happening or abandoned his cart out of instinct. He pushed the cart into the street and it careened off the little blue car, sending it in the wrong direction.

Shane raised his gun and aimed at Callie's "Creeper"—he knew without a doubt that this was who he was facing—but he quickly realized he couldn't discharge his weapon in a crowd of people.

The driver of the car hadn't slowed down after being hit by the ice-cream cart. As he barreled forward, Shane could see the man was wearing a skintight mask. For a fraction of a second, Shane had a perfect shot, but if he hit the driver, the car would be completely out of control on a crowded street.

He lowered his weapon.

As they sped past, Shane focused on the ghoulish black mask the driver was wearing—and the single spot of white that came from his smile. The woman in the passenger seat wore something similar, but her mask was a chalky gray. Based on what little Shane could see, she looked flat-out angry. Bright eyes peeked out from eye holes, and nostrils flared.

They were impressions made in a split second, but the overall effect was bizarre.

Shane pulled out his phone. "I want all available vehicles to pursue a blue Smart Car headed south past the square. No license plate visible from the back, but the front bumper is dented on the driver's side."

He listened for less than ten seconds before interrupting Taylor. "Yes, I'm sure it's him. He's arrogant. He's rubbing it in our faces—that's why he chose such a conspicuous car."

This time he had to hold the phone away from his ear. The captain didn't holler for long. "I didn't fire my weapon, but my cover is blown. Now put our units on every route to the toll road and alert the security team at the toll-road authority office to watch the cameras."

Snapping the phone shut, he returned it to his pocket, then checked his Glock and attempted to move the crowd away from the sight. "Everyone's okay, folks. The danger's passed, and you shouldn't be standing in the middle of the street, so go on with your business."

"My ice-cream cart is ruined." An older gentleman with a completely bald head stood looking at his cart, which was now caved-in on the side that said *Fresh Homemade Ice Cream.*

"I need to check on the kids, Fred."

"I need to sell this ice cream before it melts. And when did the police start dressing like chain-saw carvers?"

Shane ignored the question and hurried over to the boys.

"That was him, wasn't it?" Aaron's voice was ragged and his eyes were huge, but he didn't appear to be hurt.

Matt looked angry—not that Shane could blame him. Getting mowed down by a Smart Car in broad daylight would raise most anyone's temper—child or adult.

"Yeah, I think it was. You boys okay?" He didn't see any sign of injury.

"He looked different."

"He was wearing a mask," Shane explained.

"I've never seen a mask like that before." Matt pulled Aaron's chair farther out of the sidewalk traffic. "Lots of *Englisch* kids wear masks around Halloween. Never seen any like that, and I had a pretty close look at those two in the car since they practically ran over us."

"From where I was, seemed like they were wearing the more expensive skintight type. They conform precisely to your features, but still manage to mask your identity. The effect can be fairly disturbing." Shane inspected both boys. "You're sure you're okay?"

Aaron nodded.

Matt frowned even more. "*Ya.* We're getting used to this stuff."

Shane looked out at the crowd, most of which had dispersed. A few folks continued to mill around, talking, some even pointing at Shane and the children. "Deborah was supposed to find you before you made it to town. I didn't want you here today. Where are your parents?"

"*Dat*'s with Hannah over by the dancers." Matt drummed his fingers against the chair. "Our *mamm* was going to arrive a little later. She had to pick up some pies, take them to our *aenti*'s booth."

"All right. I want you to stay with me. We're going together to find your dad, and he's going to get you out of here."

Shane started to lead them away, but Aaron reached up and stopped him. When his hand closed around Shane's arm, something inside of Shane began to melt like a scoop of Fred's ice cream dropped on the pavement on a warm summer day.

He'd done his best to remain detached.

On every case he kept an emotional distance, because he thought it made him more objective, helped him to do a better job.

But when Aaron wrapped his fingers around Shane's arm and looked up into his eyes—looked up with fear but also hope—Shane knew he wouldn't be able to keep all of his barriers in place during this investigation.

"You don't think he'll try to kill us again, do you?"

"Not today."

"That's a relief," Matt muttered. "At least we can grab some food in peace."

Shane recognized the anger and frustration in the boy's voice, but he didn't call him on it. In fact, Matt reminded Shane of himself. He'd been the same age as this boy when he'd been caught up in a similar drama, a drama he'd rather not dwell on.

But Shane understood the need to protect one's family ran deep.

When you couldn't protect your family, when you were too young or too weak, it broke something in you. Something it sometimes took years to heal.

Chapter 13

ESTHER WAS IN THE KITCHEN, scrubbing vegetables in the sink, when she saw the first of the buggies traveling down the lane. By the time they trundled past the pond, the same pond where she'd once stopped to pick flowers and found a young girl's body, she was standing on the front porch, wiping her hands on a dishtowel.

"Simon asleep?" Tobias asked her, loping up onto the porch in three long strides. He stood close, as if he needed to protect her, but they both knew the buggies approaching carried friends.

Friends who needed their help.

"He's awake, but in his crib. I thought it best to leave him there for the moment."

Tobias glanced back through the screen door.

"Don't worry." Esther reached up, touched the beard that had come in so thick during the past year. "We'll hear him through the open window if he cries."

A grin spread across Tobias' face. "*Ya*. His cry is healthy."

"How would you know? You jump up in the middle of the night before his second yelp is out of his mouth." She meant it half as a tease and half as a scold. She feared her husband was spoiling their son, and Esther was not one to indulge a child. But Tobias didn't even bother to deny it. The smile on his face grew, and he even chuckled. He was impossible. He was worse than Leah on Christmas.

"*Mamm*, is everyone coming to dinner?" Leah, Esther's three-year-old daughter from her first marriage, put down the two dolls she'd been playing with on the porch swing and walked over to join them.

"Yes, Leah."

"Like on Sundays?"

"Just like on Sundays," Tobias said.

There were now four buggies in sight, and Esther wouldn't relax until at least one *Englisch* car had been added to the mix. She wanted her friends near her and safe. She wanted this thing to be over.

Melinda pulled up first. All three children were riding with her. Noah had brought the second buggy, and Esther wondered about that. Did it mean he wasn't intending to stay?

Behind them Deborah drove her smaller buggy, and Jonas drove the large buggy filled with all five of their children.

They'd barely come to a stop when Reuben walked out of the barn he insisted on living in despite the fact that there was plenty of room in the house. Over dinner last night she'd once again asked him why he wouldn't move into the extra bedroom, but Reuben had simply scratched his sideburns, winked, and said he expected that room would be full before very long.

Reuben was Tobias' cousin, but the two might as well have been brothers. They'd worked the farm together for years. Perhaps they were close because they'd both waited to marry, which was unusual in their community. Reuben was still single. Sometimes she wondered if he would always be single. There was a story there Esther still hadn't heard—a story Tobias claimed he didn't know. She hoped Reuben would share it with her one day, but she realized it might remain a mystery. He was private about some things.

One thing Esther was sure of: his heart had been broken long ago and he hadn't allowed himself to love again.

But despite how close they were, Reuben and Tobias didn't look alike—both were tall men, but any similarities ended there. Whereas Tobias was thin like a poplar tree, Reuben reminded Esther of the sycamore. He was a big man with the most tender heart she'd ever encountered. That he'd nearly been convicted of a murder he didn't commit and nearly had to spend his entire life in jail still astounded her. That he would be willing to be convicted in order to save a young Amish man from the *Englisch* justice system was something she didn't understand at all. Esther was raised to embrace and practice grace; yet Reuben's actions exceeded anything she'd ever encountered. Even her own dealings with the boys who had accidentally killed her first husband weren't the same. In that accident, those involved had come directly to her almost immediately to confess and ask her forgiveness.

Reuben's situation was entirely different.

Wasn't it?

Before she could worry over the questions any longer, Melinda's and Deborah's children tumbled out of their respective buggies— Aaron helped into his wheelchair by Noah.

The men immediately turned to tending to the mares.

"I should go help with the horses," Tobias murmured. He ran his hand across the back of her neck, and then he was gone.

Even after a year, she wasn't accustomed to his devotion.

Even after a year, she sometimes woke afraid it was all a dream and that she would find herself still alone.

"Has anyone heard from Callie?" Esther asked, meeting them halfway between their buggies and the house.

"Shane told Noah they'd be here in time for dinner," Melinda said.

"We stopped at the phone shack," Deborah added. "There were no messages."

As Esther watched the children, she could almost believe it

was a normal evening. She wanted to believe that, but her heart told her otherwise.

"Yes, you may go and play," Melinda said to Matthew. "But stay close so you'll hear us call."

"Martha, will you take Joshua?" Deborah asked as her youngest ran to his big sister.

"Sure," Martha said.

"*Mamm*, may I pick some of Esther's flowers?" Mary asked, tugging on her mother's hand.

"Not the ones from the garden."

"The wild ones? In the field?"

"As long as you watch for snakes."

"We'll walk with her," Martha assured Deborah.

"We brought a baseball and a bat," Matt interrupted, pointing to a canvas bag in Aaron's lap.

"Baseball or flowers?" Martha asked Mary.

"Can we do both?"

"If we hurry."

"Best place for baseball is behind the barn." Esther nodded toward the east pasture.

"Yes!" Jacob and Joseph, Deborah's six-year-old twins, bounded away.

"Stay clear of any mud," Deborah called out after them.

Esther pressed her fingers to her lips, trying to stop the laugh that wanted out. These were not laughing times, but Deborah's boys... they did have a way of finding trouble.

"Why are you smiling, Esther Fisher?" Deborah climbed the steps and dropped onto the wooden swing.

"I'm not." She did her best to appear serious.

"You might as well confess. We both saw you," Melinda said.

"It's your boys, Deborah."

"They would make any sane person laugh," Deborah agreed.

"Or cry." Melinda set Hannah down on a blanket, dug a picture book from her bag, and handed it to her.

"It's not that they're bad," Deborah said. "It's that they seem to be able to create work, no matter how hard they try not to."

"I was thinking ..." Esther trailed off and shook her head.

"Say it." Deborah set the swing in motion. "After today I could use the distraction."

"I was thinking how much they remind me of Jonas. Do you remember when we were their age? How he would always go out at recess. We'd be playing, and he'd—"

"Disappear." Melinda looked up from her place on the blanket beside Hannah. "I always wondered where he went."

"To the creek? To the water pump? Who knows. I was busy playing with you two, so it never occurred to me to ask him. I didn't know I was going to marry him and bear his children." Deborah laughed.

"He always came back muddy or with a critter or—"

"With something bleeding or broken." Deborah stopped the swing with her foot. "You're right. I should have known. They take after their father."

Somehow the moment of shared memories eased the worries of the day. They smiled, the three of them, and Esther felt the knot of worry that had been building at the base of her neck relax.

"I was washing vegetables. I left them in the sink."

"I'll help," Deborah said.

A piercing cry split the afternoon's peace.

"Bring me that sweet *boppli* before Tobias gets here and steals him away," Melinda said. "I'll be happy to rock him."

"You're lucky to have the chance," Esther said to Melinda.

As they walked inside to pick up Simon and finish the vegetables, she admitted to Deborah, "I told Melinda earlier. Tobias is spoiling this child. I barely have the chance to hold him myself—mostly when Tobias is in the field."

"Remember, it's his first."

"*Ya*. With Leah I did jump as soon as she cried—in the

beginning." Esther gazed down at her son. He was beautiful. "Then *Mamm* told me that I didn't have to hurry so. That it wouldn't hurt her if I walked slowly from the clothesline into the house to answer cries. She wasn't hurt, only calling me, and as long as she knew I would answer, it was all right to go at a measured pace."

Deborah leaned over the crib, reached forward, and caressed the top of Simon's head. "Be glad that Tobias cares for him so much, Esther, and that he's willing to help. Some men aren't."

"You're right. It's only that I don't want a child who's rotten." She laughed. "You've seen them, Deborah, so don't look at me so. We've both seen them—Amish and *Englisch*."

"I have, and I know you won't have one. Look at Leah. You've done a fine job with her."

Esther smiled. She loved her daughter, and she was grateful God had given her this second chance to have a family. Deborah was right—she shouldn't worry so. It seemed with babies there was always something to be anxious about.

As she picked up Simon, carried him to Melinda, and returned to finish preparing dinner, it occurred to her that she'd rather fret over those everyday things.

They helped to take her mind off the thought of a murderer traipsing around Shipshewana searching for Melinda's son.

Callie stared at her cell phone until it said 7:15 p.m., then she walked out the door, pulling it shut behind her and testing the knob to be sure it was locked. Her eyes were on the garden though. Gavin had told her to walk there at 7:15 exactly—not a minute before or after.

He'd also told her to be sure to lock the shop's front door behind her.

She'd wanted to laugh earlier this afternoon when she'd

walked up to the elderly man sitting by the windows—as Shane's note had directed—and asked him if he needed any help. He'd lowered the quilting magazine he was supposedly reading, smiled slightly, and said, "Tea would be nice."

If she hadn't already been standing close enough to see through the old-man clothing and dusty powder that aged his skin, those four words would have given him away. Gavin's voice flowed over her like a welcome fall thunderstorm after a long rainless summer.

They'd hustled over to the small kitchen, where they'd huddled in the corner for five minutes and he'd explained the plan. The disguise he'd worn had been great from a distance, but up close, Callie wanted to take a wet cloth and wipe the powder off his face.

She wanted to remove the hat and replace it with the ball cap he wore when jogging with Max.

She wanted to put her head against his chest and weep.

Instead she squared her shoulders and agreed to a plan she did not understand. She stayed in her shop all day, tending to customers. She stopped worrying Creeper would find a way inside and instead tried picking out who replaced Gavin as her guardian. Gavin had assured her Shane was rotating people into the shop every ninety minutes. It became a game of sorts to figure out which "customer" was really an undercover officer.

Callie knew her customers well and had become adept at recognizing the out-of-town types. Who-doesn't-fit-here wasn't so hard once one knew what to look for. Then there was the fact that since she'd moved to Shipshe, she'd become quite familiar with most of the officers working for the Shipshewana Police Department. A few of her guardians were from neighboring towns, but they all had the same watchful look—no matter how they tried to conceal it. Makeup could hide age. A wig could change hair color and style, but when someone was protecting another person's life, their entire physique took on another bearing. An undercover cop could hide behind a newspaper, slouch against a wall, even sit and text on a cell phone. But their eyes? Their eyes were ever vigilant. Soon Callie found she could pick them out within ten minutes of their entering the shop.

The question was: would Creeper also be able to pick them out of a crowd? Probably not. Certainly not if he was looking through binoculars. At least Callie didn't think so. The fact that someone was in the store with her, aware of her problem, and armed was enough to calm Callie's nerves and allow her to focus on running the shop.

She ate lunch standing at the counter, and she watched over Lydia like a mother hen. It had crossed her mind to tell Lydia to take the day off, but there was no way the girl would have agreed. It did help ease Callie's mind that she'd found a way to bar Deborah and baby Joshua from the store.

She shooed all of her customers out at six p.m. sharp and straightened the shop like she did every night, then she changed into jeans and her baggiest black T-shirt as if she were planning to take a walk around her garden, maybe mourn the fact that Max hadn't returned.

Looking lost without Max was easy enough to fake, since it was true. Doc England had called and said her dog was doing fine, but the toenail removal needed watching overnight to ensure there wasn't any infection. There was no toenail removal, and Callie wanted to know if Max had fully recovered from the tranquilizer's drugs. But she didn't dare ask in case one of the customers in the store was Creeper or his accomplice, though she still didn't expect to see either one. Better be safe and follow Shane's plan, which included silence on the subject of Max. Instead she thanked her vet, assured him she'd check back again the next day, and hung up the phone.

Now she walked across the parking lot toward her garden. She refused to look toward the area still marked off with crime-scene tape. Instead she concentrated on the cool breeze. She hadn't stepped outside all day, had been afraid to leave Lydia alone even for a moment. The breeze spoke of freedom and eased some of the anxiety in her shoulders.

Darkness settled around her.

She forgot to wonder what might happen next.

Then she heard a rustling in the corner of her garden and instinctively grabbed the hoe leaning against her fence.

Perla's voice was soft, musical, and not terribly amused at the moment. "Put it down, Callie. Last thing I need is a hoe upside my head."

When she stepped through the brush, Callie could see that Perla was wearing clothes identical to what Callie was currently wearing—blue jeans and a black T-shirt.

"What are you doing here?"

"Being you. Did you leave the back door unlocked like Gavin said?"

"Yes, and I locked the front. Why do you have to be me?"

"Because you're not staying here tonight." Perla glanced toward the far side of the garden and Callie spotted him.

Shane held back, but enough light remained to see his outline. He'd lost the chain-saw disguise Gavin had told her about and was once again wearing jeans, a T-shirt, and a Cubs ball cap. Callie had the strongest desire to go to him and melt into his arms.

Instead she stayed where she was, clutching the hoe.

"Put the hoe down and get out of here. Won't look right with there being two of us."

"Two of us?"

Shane remained in the shadows, beckoning her without a move, without lifting a muscle.

"Tienes que ir." Perla moved toward the back door of the shop as Callie glanced toward Shane. *"No es necesario entender."*

Callie's Spanish had grown rusty since leaving Texas, but she understood what Perla was saying well enough. There was little about this mess that made sense to her, but she knew to follow Perla's instructions.

She moved toward Shane—slowly first, but then more quickly as she saw the look of concern in his eyes. When she reached him he took her hand in his, wordlessly, and pulled her deeper into the darkness.

They didn't speak until they'd crept three blocks, wound their way down two alleys, and found his car. Once the doors were closed and he'd locked them—manually, the Buick was too old to sport automatic locks—Callie turned toward him in the darkness, trying to decide which question to ask first.

She never had a chance.

He pulled her into his arms, pulled her right across the front leather seat, and pressed his lips to hers. She didn't have time to think about whether it was right or wrong.

All thoughts of the perpetrator fled.

Her mind focused on Shane and the feel of his arms around her.

Shane, running his fingers through her hair.

Shane and the night and the darkness acting like a blanket pulled close, wrapping her in their warmth.

When he finally released her, he still didn't start the car. Instead he sat there, staring out the front window, his arm still wrapped around her shoulder.

"What was that about?" she whispered.

"I have no idea."

"Seriously?"

"Look—" She sensed him shaking his head in the darkness. "—I didn't mean to do that."

"Great."

"Not what I meant." He pulled her even closer, ran a hand up and down her arm, sending shivers all the way to her toes. "I know

now isn't the right time, but I needed ..." He blew out a sigh. "I needed it, all right? I needed to know you were fine."

"That was a health check? Kissing me?" She was pretty sure she should be offended.

He turned toward her, kissed her again, but this time softly, lightly. "Yeah. I guess."

Pulling in a deep breath, she closed her eyes, envisioned a field of Texas wildflowers, then released the breath slowly. It did nothing for the butterflies in her stomach, but it did help clear her mind somewhat. "I'm glad I could ease your worries, Black."

"I wanted to stop by earlier, but then a Smart Car tried to run over Melinda's boys."

"Gavin stopped by after his shift and told me about that. He also assured me everyone was fine."

"They are." He started the car and buckled his seat belt, but when she attempted to move toward the passenger door he stopped her, showed her where the middle seat buckle was.

Once they were both safely fastened—as if that could save them from a criminal bent on murder should he try to smash them with a miniature car—Shane pulled out into the street and turned on his lights.

Callie forced herself to forget the kiss and the emotions tumbling from her head to her heart to her stomach. What mattered right now was the investigation.

"It was Creeper?"

"I'm willing to bet it was the same perp. He was wearing a mask, but who else would it be? Look ... we need to get out to Reuben's."

"Reuben's?"

The part of town they were driving through was closed up for the night. Any pedestrian traffic was farther downtown. He pulled up to a stop sign. Beneath the streetlight Callie could make out Shane's features, the worry in his eyes, and how the last twenty-four hours had taken their toll. He turned to her, framed her face with his hands, and wouldn't look away until she met his eyes.

"Melinda, Deborah, Esther, all the kids—the men too— they're all at Reuben's. Gavin's on shift right now, but he and Taylor will be out later. We're going to figure this out, Callie. You believe me, right?"

She tried not to lose herself in his gaze. She wasn't ready for this relationship. She'd thought maybe she was, after what had happened with Reuben, after the scene outside Timothy and Rachel Lapp's house in Goshen. The first few times he'd called over the last year, they'd talked for hours, but it had frightened her. So the next time he called, she hadn't answered. It had been immature of her, but Callie hadn't known what else to do.

Those talks had made her realize how alone she felt.

They'd made her dare to want more, but wanting more was dangerous.

She'd had more with Rick, and she'd lost everything.

As Shane cupped her face in his hands, she found she couldn't look away. And she didn't want to. As she gazed straight into Shane's dark eyes she lost her footing, felt herself falling, and she didn't care anymore.

There was no middle ground. It was either trust and take the leap, or back up and somehow endure this thing alone.

"Yeah, I trust you." That wasn't what he'd asked her. She realized that, and when he kissed her again, she knew he realized that as well. Believing him was one thing—that was actually easy. Trusting him? For Callie, that was a leap of faith.

Shane turned his attention back to his driving, the sound of the Buick filled the night, and Callie understood this time she had no choice.

She needed him.

Chapter 14

THE WEATHER WAS PLEASANTLY WARM for late September. Warm enough to serve dinner in the barn instead of the house.

The side of the barn Reuben lived in had minimal heat— very minimal. Melinda realized the *Englischers* thought Amish homes were cold without electric or gas heat, but the way their kitchen and sitting areas were laid out actually kept them comfortably warm. This was not the case with Reuben's living arrangement.

When he and Tobias had moved into the old barn, they'd walled off one-third of it. The third they lived in was still cavernous and impossible to adequately heat. They'd laughed and said it was more like the outdoors, where they were comfortable. A cast-iron stove sat in the corner, but Melinda wasn't sure how it kept Reuben from freezing during the coldest months.

For tonight though, it was still comfortable.

She held Esther's baby against her right shoulder and clasped Hannah's fingers with her left hand. Hannah skipped along beside her, as if this were an everyday event, and why should she think any differently? The older children helped Deborah and Esther carry casserole dishes filled with ham, roasted vegetables, and fresh bread from the house.

She'd barely made it to the door of the barn when she heard an automobile making its way down Reuben's lane. Her pulse raced, and she cradled Simon closer, squeezed Hannah's hand, and looked frantically for Aaron.

"He's fine. Inside playing and waiting for dinner."

How was it Noah managed to appear whenever her worries spiked? Had they been married so long he had developed a sixth sense?

"Besides, it's Shane in his old car."

"Is Callie with him?"

"*Ya*. I'm sure she is."

Melinda breathed a sigh of relief. Turning to Noah, she handed him baby Simon. "Stay with your *dat*, Hannah."

Melinda hurried through the darkness toward the car.

Callie hadn't unbuckled yet by the time she reached it, so Melinda waited for her to stand and straighten her baggy clothes before stepping forward and enfolding her in a hug.

"How are you?"

"Fine."

"I wanted to come and see you, but Deborah said we shouldn't."

"No, I didn't want—"

"I heard. No children in the store."

"Yes, well. That was a ruse to—"

"You're always trying to protect us. How are we to help you if you won't let us near?"

Melinda pulled Callie toward the barn and didn't actually take any notice of Shane until he caught up with them, his voice a deep rumbling like thunder on the horizon. "Callie and I decided that it was better that way."

"So you were in on this together."

"You could say that." Callie stopped halfway to the barn, looked back toward the house where the light from two lanterns shone in the main room. "We're not going to Esther's?"

"Not enough room inside the house for everyone. Come on. We were starting dinner."

"Why are we passing the new barn?"

"That's where the horses are. You wouldn't want to eat there."

"So we're eating in the old barn?"

Melinda noticed Callie hesitate as they moved closer to the old structure. "It's still in *gut* shape. It was too small for the farming work, but it was built by their *grossdaddi*. Nearly seventy years old and still standing strong."

When Melinda, Callie, and Shane stepped inside, the various conversations stopped. Everyone turned to look at them.

Melinda could feel it then — all their shared history, their present predicament, and the future they didn't yet understand all coming together in that moment.

This was the place where Shane had arrested Reuben, or rather where Reuben had allowed himself to be taken into custody so Samuel Eby could go free.

These people formed a group as close as the family Melinda had been raised in, a group that loved one another and would look after one another. A group of nineteen people, and yes, the children were included in that number, because somehow the children had been caught up in this too.

A group of plain and *Englisch*.

What was *Gotte's wille*?

How could God possibly be involved in this terrible thing?

But she knew then. She realized as each person turned to look at them. With Callie's hand in hers and Shane standing beside her, she understood God had brought them together and had provided for their needs — with one another.

She looked into her son's eyes; she couldn't protect him from all the harm that might befall him. This was the son she had spent so many nights praying over, so many nights worrying he wouldn't live to see three years of age, then four. Now he was nearing eight. "A miracle," Doc Bernie had said.

"*Gotte's wille.*" That's what Noah said.

That's what her *mamm* reminded her about each time Melinda went to her with an aching heart.

But today a man had tried to kill Aaron — tried to mow him over with a miniature *Englisch* car — and Melinda hadn't been there to protect him.

Shane had done that for her. Shane or God.

Either way, God had provided.

Everyone began speaking and the moment was broken.

Deborah waved Callie over.

Children found places around the table that had been set up in the middle of Reuben's living area. When heads were bowed for prayer, Melinda's heart was so full of fear, of questions, and of thankfulness that once again they were together, that she could only sit with Noah's hand in hers, unable to form a single clear thought.

Deborah insisted on helping with the dishes, though Jonas said the children could do it.

"Not in the house, Jonas. It's too far. Anything could happen."

"Martha can do them here, in Reuben's sink." He tucked some wayward strands of hair into her prayer *kapp*, trailed his hand down her face, her neck, her arm. His fingers on her skin settled her nerves.

She took a deep breath and nodded in agreement. "I'll help them, and then Martha can take the younger *kinner* to the other side of the barn, where we can at least hear them."

"*Ya.* That sounds like a *gut* compromise. What can I do?" Jonas asked.

"Distract Shane so he doesn't make any decisions until I get back to the table."

She began gathering plates as Martha ran the water. When Callie stood to help, Deborah tried to stop her but was quickly persuaded to let her join.

"I need some time with the women," Callie whispered.

Deborah smiled and waved Callie forward.

Once they were in the half of the room that served as a kitchen, which was less than five feet from the table, Callie glanced over her shoulder, then started speaking. "Surely he can't hear me over the clatter of these dishes."

"Who?" Deborah asked.

"Shane! He's sticking to me like glue. You'd think he expects the killer to swoop down from the sky and snap me up from in front of his eyes."

"Is that possible, Callie?" Melinda pushed up on her glasses and reached for a dish towel.

"No. How could he when I'm surrounded by half the Shipshe force at all times? I think what happened with Mrs. Knepp was an accident."

"An accident?" Esther held baby Simon to her shoulder, rubbing his back in tiny circles, trying to coax a burp. "How do you kill someone by accident?"

"For some people, apparently it isn't that hard."

Martha looked up from her washing, her arms elbow-deep in bubbly water. "Jacob and Joseph killed a baby pig by accident. Remember?"

Callie looked at Deborah with one eyebrow raised.

Deborah shrugged as she accepted the dishes Melinda dried and stacked them neatly for carrying back to the house. "The boys built a crate to house the new piglets, but they didn't build it with the slats close enough together. One of the piglets escaped and wandered under the feet of the workhorse."

"That's terrible."

"*Ya*, for the piglet it was awful. Remember, sows have eight to twelve piglets per litter, so the boys are learning fast, and they've been much more careful because of that incident. The remaining piglets were well cared for and there's been another litter since—with no accidents. I'd say any future litters those boys have a hand in raising will be among the best-kept pigs in LaGrange County. But the one—dead for sure. Not even enough left of him for bacon."

"So they killed it by accident," Martha repeated.

"Sounds like a case of negligent homicide." Shane leaned against what passed for a kitchen cabinet in Reuben's eyes.

All four women turned and stared at him. Martha suddenly became very focused on her dishwater.

"I'm kidding." He raised both hands, palms out. "I think we're just about ready to start. Gavin just arrived and Taylor is outside on his cell phone, finishing up a conversation with the men in town."

Deborah stacked the final plate and asked Martha to go with the older children to the other side of the barn.

"I don't get to stay?" Martha squeaked.

"You're old enough to know everything, but I'll tell you later. Right now, I want the younger *kinner* away from the details."

"Makes sense," Martha admitted. "I like plain ways, but there are days I wish we had a nanny."

"There are days I'd agree with you."

Deborah moved to the table and grabbed the seat beside Callie.

Shane had already taken his place on the other side of her. Was the danger so great or was something else working here? Deborah still sensed romance in the air. Maybe. The other possibility was one her mind was shying away from. Their group was in danger because a murderer was on the loose—again.

Andrew Gavin and Stan Taylor stepped through the door,

ushered in by Reuben. They weren't alone though. Gavin held Max's leash in his hand. When Max saw Callie he let out a single bark and bounded toward her, dragging his leash across the floor.

Callie nearly fell out of her chair in her attempt to reach her dog. She buried her face in his fur, wrapped her arms around his neck, and hugged him tightly. It was a wonder the dog stood for it.

Deborah's eyes met Shane's, and she nearly laughed out loud at the naked look of aggravation on his face. He was jealous of a dog? Shane glanced away quickly, but not quickly enough.

Her suspicions confirmed, Deborah wondered if Callie even realized what was going on with the man. Her friend could be clueless regarding men's intentions at times. She hadn't picked up on the fact that both Trent McCallister and Andrew Gavin were interested. When Deborah had pointed it out during their last murder investigation, Callie had quickly changed the subject. But later she'd admitted that though a few dates with Trent had left her laughing, he was more interested in his next news story than a relationship. Gavin was easier for Callie to figure out. More and more she thought of him as a brother.

Callie sat back down, Max now under her chair. "He's much better than before," she whispered to Deborah.

"That's *gut*. Doc England always knows what to do." But before they could discuss Max's recovery further, all eyes turned to the head of the table, where Captain Taylor was standing.

There were no more places to sit. Deborah wondered if they'd have to take this discussion outside or over to the feed barn, but Gavin remained standing, backed up to the wall, though he didn't lean against it. She'd never seen the man actually lean. He stood erect as always, arms crossed.

Reuben moved to the head of the table beside Taylor.

Reuben clapped the man on the back, then began speaking. "Captain Taylor's here to give us an update of what's going on in town. I want to add before we start that you all know you're welcome on our farm for as long as you need to stay. Our way isn't to fight, but that doesn't mean we have to stand in the town square waiting for trouble to find us either. Tobias and I would be glad to have you until this thing is settled."

He sat down and reached for his coffee cup. Deborah couldn't help but notice that it looked like a child's plaything in Reuben's hands. He was such a big man. Did this *Englisch* fellow, this Creeper, as Callie called him, know what he was up against? Would it matter? It was well known that Amish took a vow of nonviolence. Was that why he had moved so boldly among their town's people?

Taylor met each gaze around the table before he began speaking. "We put Perla in Callie's apartment at seven-fifteen this evening. She was the closest officer we had to Callie's size on such short notice. If our suspect is watching from a distance, we believe the decoy will work. If he tries to approach, he won't have a chance to see that he's wrong. Perla's prepared to take him down and is trained in self-defense. We also have additional men around the perimeter of the building."

"Is that what you think will happen? You think he'll go back into Callie's shop?" Deborah reached over and laced Callie's fingers with her own.

"We don't know, but it's a possibility. It's also the reason we didn't want Max there. The dog won't settle with Perla like he does with Callie. His uneasiness could arouse suspicion."

Deborah smiled when Callie squeezed her hand and reached down for Max with her other.

"Have you confirmed if it was the same person who tried to run over Aaron and Matthew?" Melinda leaned forward, her arms crossed and on the table, her hands clutching her elbows.

"As you know, we don't have traffic-light cameras in Shipshe. However, some of the shops do have outside surveillance. We were able to catch a break at two places—the bank's outside cameras and the toll-road entrance. Both caught the Smart Car—had to be the same one, because the front bumper was damaged, and it's the only Smart Car spotted in the region."

"And? Was it him?" Callie pulled her hand out of Deborah's and began to turn her coffee cup around and around.

"Yes. It was. He had a mask on when he went by the bank, but he'd taken it off by the time he made it to the toll road headed west."

"Did he take the toll road all the way to Chicago?" Tobias asked.

"No. We might have caught him if he had, which indicates he knew that. He took it to the next exit, then we lost him."

"Can't be hard to find a car like Aaron and Matthew described." It was the first time Noah had spoken. "I've never seen one around here or in Goshen or Middlebury. I've never seen one at all."

"We found the car." Taylor shook his head as everyone started talking at once, held up his hand. "It had been stolen from a couple over in Middlebury. Our perp left it near the university in South Bend. There was nothing in it, and no prints at all, which means he was wearing gloves. I wouldn't say he's a professional, but there are certain things he understands."

"No DNA evidence?" Reuben glanced up, met Deborah's stare.

She was remembering the courtroom in Fort Wayne, Reuben's trial, and how they'd tried to use his DNA as proof that he'd committed a crime that he hadn't done. Was he thinking of the same thing?

"None that we've found, but as you know, there are more types of DNA than fingerprints. It will take time, but we'll likely come up with something." Shane pushed back his chair and walked to the front of the table, standing beside Taylor.

Deborah was reminded again of the burden these men carried, protecting the entire town of Shipshe.

"We're closer than we were twenty-four hours ago when we first discovered that Mrs. Knepp was murdered," Taylor said. "We have wanted posters up and distributed across the state. We have photo identification now that confirms Aaron's description was good, and we know our perpetrator is determined to stay in the area until he gets what he wants."

Taylor nodded to Shane and moved to stand beside Gavin.

"What he wants is money." Shane frowned, then added, "Apparently a large sum of it."

"He seemed to think I would know where it is, but I don't." Callie looked straight at Deborah first, her gaze traveling around the room to each person, then finally settling on Shane. "I'm barely getting by each month. I still have a little put aside from Aunt Daisy's will, but it's not much. Not enough to murder someone for. I have a feeling he discovered that when he hacked into my computer."

She shook her head, pulled her hands into her lap, but Deborah could see that they were shaking now. "The way he talked, it was a lot of money. I can't imagine why he thinks I have it or why he thinks I would even know where it is."

"Somehow the money is connected to you, Callie," Shane said. "Or he thinks it is. He could be misinformed. Or maybe you do know something, and you don't remember it."

"You would think something like that wouldn't slip my mind."

Shane tapped the table. "Tomorrow is the last day of the festival. I'm assuming you want to keep the shop open?"

"Yes. If I close it, wouldn't that make him suspicious?"

"We could keep Perla in as your double."

Callie started shaking her head and turned to Deborah for support.

"That might work at night when no one is in the store, Shane." Deborah chose her words carefully. "I don't see how it would work during the day when there are customers."

Shane nodded once, but the muscle along his jawline hardened, and Deborah realized this wasn't going to be easy for him. He wouldn't allow himself to rest at all as long as Callie was putting herself in harm's way.

"What you did today worked fine," Melinda offered.

"True, but our perp will become more restless and less reasonable with each hour that passes. Today he was willing to wait because he thought you'd find the money tonight." When no one challenged Shane's dire prediction, he added, "I'd like to take twenty minutes and break up into two groups. Ladies, you know more about what needs to happen at the quilt shop. Make me a list of ideas and what you need to keep it open tomorrow — keep it open safely. While you're at it, try to come up with some ideas of where this money could be."

Deborah, Callie, Esther, and Melinda murmured their agreement.

"In the meantime, I'd like the men to meet with me, Gavin, and Captain Taylor. We'll come up with a plan to keep the children safe through the weekend —"

"Through the weekend? What happens on Monday?" Esther had started to rise from her chair. She was still holding a sleeping Simon.

"This ends before the week starts. I wouldn't be surprised if this ends by Saturday night."

"How can you be so sure, Shane?" Deborah asked it quietly, not as a challenge, but out of curiosity.

"Crowds leave on Saturday. I don't think he's going to want to be caught here in a town of six hundred. It's hard to hide if you're not one of our own."

Chapter 15

AARON PUSHED HIS WHEELCHAIR over to his *bruder* as soon as Matt walked through the door of the barn. He didn't want Martha getting to him first. He actually hoped Martha wouldn't notice them at all. They didn't need a girl's help with this, not that he could see. "What did they say? Could you hear them at all? Because I can't hear a thing from this side of the partition. That wall Reuben built is solid."

"*Ya*, I could hear. I was standing right outside the window."

"So?"

"So they're talking about protecting us, like we're a bunch of piglets that need to stay in a crate."

"We are like a bunch of piglets."

They both jumped at the sound of Martha's voice.

"I thought you were going to the bathroom."

"You're not my *mamm*, Martha Yoder. In fact, we're the same age, so don't be thinking—"

"Save it, Matthew. They'll be here in a minute. Hurry and tell us what you heard."

Aaron twisted around in his chair and stared at her in surprise. "Us?"

"*Ya*, us. We were all three there when this thing started. I

152

figure we're all in this until the end. And keep your voice low so you don't frighten the younger ones." She nodded toward her twin *bruders*, Joshua, Leah, and Hannah—all of whom were playing a game of hopscotch a few feet away.

Matthew tugged off his wool cap, ran his hand over his head—front to back, back to front. "Shane was saying he thinks the man won't stick around past Saturday night or Sunday."

"I guess that makes sense. So if we can keep you two from being run over tomorrow, you should be fine."

Aaron scowled at her. He didn't like remembering the car coming at him. It had been a small car, but he'd still felt like a chicken on a chopping block sitting there in his chair, waiting for it to smash him flat on the pavement.

"They won't let us go into town tomorrow, even if we wanted to. We'll probably be stuck out here babysitting or doing chores." Aaron picked at a seam on his pants leg. For some reason he thought again of the boys in the Western movie. They'd wanted to go on the trail ride, but John Wayne had told them no. They'd had to sneak their way in at first, especially the youngest one. "We're going to miss the busiest day of the festival, and we're going to miss any chance to catch this *Englischer*."

"Don't know how we could catch him anyway," Matthew pointed out. "All we did today was cause a scene and upset Fred. He was still hollering about what happened to his ice-cream cart when *Dat* found us and pulled us away from the intersection."

"Did you see the way Shane stepped out into the open, steadied his pistol, and almost shot that car? I think he would have taken a shot if so many people hadn't been around." Aaron was remembering Shane, but somehow he was picturing John Wayne again. He hadn't realized it until that moment, but the two men had a lot in common—both carried a pistol, were stubborn, and didn't have any *kinner* of their own.

"Think about it." Martha flopped onto a hay bale. "When you two showed up, Creeper showed up."

"Creeper?" Aaron glanced at her. His mind had been on the Western again. He knew it was a movie—not real life. But John Wayne had been a real man, and Aaron was busy wondering: What would the real John Wayne have done if he were in their shoes? How would he have caught the bad guy? He sure wouldn't have hung around the barn taking care of *bopplin* and feeding chickens.

"Yeah, Creeper. That's what I heard Miss Callie calling him when we were washing dishes. It kind of fits, for a name."

"Gives me the creeps every time I think of him," Aaron mumbled in agreement.

"What I was saying was he busted out of hiding when you two came into town."

"Maybe that was a coincidence," Matt said. He'd pulled out his slingshot and was popping it. Aaron noticed he seemed to be practicing with it a lot the last day or so, like he might need it for something.

"Could be. It's not like he could have known where you two would be, unless he'd been following you or looking for you."

"Why would he be looking for us?" Aaron's voice squeaked like a mouse. He cleared his throat and tried again. "What did I ever do to him? I'm a *kind*."

"You're the one who can identify him, remember? Even Miss Callie didn't *see* him. She heard his voice, but you saw him at the scene of the crime. You saw him kill Mrs. Knepp."

"No, I didn't. I only saw him stand behind her. Then she fell over."

Martha and Matthew stared at him.

"Okay, I saw him kill her."

All three grew silent. The echo of a pebble hitting the chalk outline in the corner and the sounds of the younger *kinner* skipping as they continued with their game of hopscotch filled the night.

Finally Martha said what they were each thinking. "The question is, what are we going to do about it?"

"Don't see how we can do anything." Aaron pulled at the seam on his pants leg so hard he tore a small hole in it. "*Mamm*'s going to keep such a close eye on me, I'll be lucky if she doesn't slip a lead rope around my chair."

"Unless..." Matt stopped midsentence, but he began popping his slingshot again.

"Say it. Unless what?"

"He has that look in his eye," Aaron mumbled. "Usually means one of us will be in trouble soon."

"Unless we pulled the swap."

"Oh no." Aaron began rolling his chair back and forth.

"What's the swap?"

"Last time we did that, they caught us, and we both had extra chores for a month."

"But they probably won't catch us this time, because they're focused on other things. Even if they do catch us, well, it won't matter by then." Matthew was grinning now, and Aaron knew it meant his mind was already made up.

"Are you going to tell me what you're talking about?" Martha put her hands on her hips. When she did, she looked older. Maybe they shouldn't tell her, but before he could decide, Matt was explaining.

"The swap is where one of us tells *Mamm* one thing and the other tells *Dat* something else—"

"That's lying." Martha clamped her mouth shut and crossed her arms.

"Not exactly. Not if you do it right."

"He means, not if you don't get caught."

"Tomorrow Aaron tells *Mamm* that we're going to take the cart and pony to *Dat*."

"Wait. You mean you're staying here tonight?"

"I think we all are, even our *daeds*. They're more worried about nighttime for some reason. Harder to see the Creeper creeping." Matt grimaced at his own joke, then continued. "Our *dat* will leave to do chores very early, before it's full light. Once we're done with breakfast, Aaron could ask Esther if we can borrow her cart and pony to go and help *dat*."

"And when you never show?"

"We'll show, but we won't stay long. I'll tell *Dat* that *Mamm* wants us back, because she's worried—which technically will be the truth. Instead, we'll go into town." Matt smiled as if he'd figured out the hardest arithmetic problem their teacher had to offer.

"It's still lying. Why do you call it the swap?"

"Because each of us swap a little part of the story out. It's not lying so much as it is . . . you know, swapping." Aaron stopped rolling his chair. "Why are we going into town?"

"To catch the Creeper. He'll see you in your chair, and he'll come right out."

"This is your *gut* idea?" Martha shook her head, eyes closed.

"Sure. Because I'm going to be waiting for him this time." Matt held up the slingshot, and when he threw his arm around him, Aaron started thinking the plan might work. It did sound like the sort of ambush John Wayne's cook and the boys had set up. He was beginning to wish he'd never seen that movie. There had to be a way to get it out of his head.

"Are you serious?" Martha asked, hands on hips. "Because this sounds *narrisch*."

"I can see why you'd think so," Aaron said. "But you haven't seen how *gut* Matt is with the slingshot. *Mamm* doesn't like him to use it, but I've watched him practice. He can hit a squirrel when I can't even see it. Creeper won't be any problem for him."

"But, we don't believe in violence. Bishop Elam says—"

"I know what the bishop says." Matt's voice took on a hard edge again. "And I know what this man wants to do to my *bruder*.

I'm not going to aim to hurt Creeper—not permanently. But I will stop him until Shane can get there."

Martha sighed heavily, but a mulish look came over her face. "Guess you're going to need me to come along then."

"What? No. We don't need a—" Aaron almost said the word *girl*, but the glare from Martha stopped him.

"Someone has to call Shane when you two set your trap. I happen to know where we can borrow a cell phone."

Which pretty much sealed the deal. Now it was a matter of surviving the night, waiting until daylight, and then implementing the swap.

Aaron could hardly wait.

Shane had no trouble building a consensus among the men.

After thirty minutes, they'd hammered out the details. Now came the difficult part.

"Should we each speak with our families privately?" Noah asked. "Melinda might need some convincing."

"I wish we had time for that, but I expect our assailant to call back at any time—"

"Or show up, if he's managed to follow one of you out here." Reuben's expression was calm, passive almost, but Shane knew he could count on him to help if it came to the safety of the women and children.

"I have two more men at the border of your property by the road," Shane reminded him.

"With us taking shifts outside the house and the barn, the women and *kinner* will be safe," Jonas said.

Jonas had listened well, though he hadn't said much. Shane had been worried he might have his own ideas about how to handle the situation, that he might want to implement a separate plan. "Are you on board with this, Jonas? If you think there's another way ..."

"For tonight, I think what you have outlined is *gut*. My family will need to take it one day at a time. Though we don't know *Gotte's wille* in all things, he will provide direction as we need it."

It was the most Shane had ever heard him say. He wasn't completely happy with the man's level of commitment, but then he had five children and a wife to worry about. Technically he didn't even have to be here since they weren't eyewitnesses to the crime. Melinda was closest to Deborah and Esther. What was the perp's level of commitment? Would he start chasing down every lead? Shane didn't know. But it felt right to keep the three families hidden on Reuben's farm until he caught this guy. Deborah's close ties to Melinda and Callie were what kept them at Reuben's tonight, and Shane respected that. So he nodded to Jonas, thanked him, and led the group back inside to face the women.

The four women were sitting at one end of the table. Deborah and Melinda were poring over a copy of the *Gazette*. Esther was writing on a yellow-lined tablet, and Callie was holding the baby. Her eyes met his, and he remembered the kiss in the car—remembered it and wished suddenly he could take her away from here.

Maybe if he took her away the danger would disappear.

Maybe if he took her away she'd be safe.

Captain Taylor had left to check with the men on patrol. Gavin walked to the end of the table with him. Tobias, Reuben, Jonas, and Noah took places at the opposite end of the table.

"We came up with a security plan for the evening." Shane shared the rotation schedule with them.

"So we all stay here?" Callie asked.

"Women and children in the house. Men here at Reuben's, when they're not working."

"Is that really necessary?" Melinda put down the pen she'd been using to mark items in the paper.

"Probably not for Deborah and her family." Shane nodded toward Jonas.

"There's a possibility we're more trouble than we're worth, with our five *kinner*. But Deborah and I talked about it on the way over. If it's helpful for us to stay, then we'd like to stay. We consider you all to be our family."

A few seconds of silence passed before Esther said, "Always room for seven more. I vote you stay."

Murmurs of agreement sounded around the table.

"What happens tomorrow?" Esther asked.

"Can't neglect the animals at home, so we'll have to be going back at first light," Noah said. "At least the men will."

"I would rather keep the women and children here." Shane knew this would be a sticking point. Amish folk were hard workers. You could settle them down for an evening, but come daylight, they wanted to be back at their business.

"I'm going into town," Callie said. "That's the whole point of this ruse, right? We made a list of ways to keep the shop open and secure like you told us to."

Instead of answering, Shane eyeballed the men for help.

"Could be I'll need the twins to return to the farm with me tomorrow. If everything looks safe," Jonas added. "They have quite a few pigs that need seeing to."

"I can probably do our work alone." Noah ran his hand under his suspenders.

Everyone began talking at once, and Shane could feel himself losing control of the meeting. He held up his hands, palms out, to stop everyone. "We can meet back here an hour before sunrise, decide who should stay and if it's safe for some to leave."

"We can't stay here forever, Shane." Melinda worried the pen she was holding, spinning it in circles.

"I realize that, but I still think our perpetrator will make his move this weekend."

Melinda glanced over at Noah, who nodded once. "All right. We had some ideas that might help in that area. We think the money he was looking for may have been advertised in the *Gazette*."

Shane felt a twitch at the back of his neck. He held very still, because his first reaction was to reject the idea straightaway. "Listen before you reject an idea," his father had always said. Shane had been quick to turn away from something as a boy, and it was an inclination he had to fight against as a detective. "Why would you think that?"

"The first reason is that it's a sizeable amount of money." Callie pulled Simon's baby blanket tighter and snuggled him to her. "I've already admitted that my savings account isn't all that lucrative. Our assailant knows that, because he found my password book."

"How much are we talking about, Callie?" Tobias stroked his beard. "If you don't mind my asking."

"I don't mind at all. You are all risking your lives for me. You have a right to know what this guy is after. I have less than five thousand in savings, and another ten thousand from my Aunt Daisy's probate in a Certificate of Deposit. Since that wasn't enough to make him go away, whatever he's after has to be more than fifteen thousand dollars."

"So how does the *Gazette* figure in?" Shane once again pushed his impatience down. Obviously the girls were excited about this, and they had helped to catch two murderers on his watch—albeit one by accident.

"Remember when we asked Trent to plant the story so that Stakehorn would think Callie had a lot of money in her safe?" Deborah smiled as if those were the good old days.

"I remember. I didn't approve then, and please don't tell me you're thinking about doing it again."

"No." Melinda shook her head, causing the strings of her prayer *kapp* to brush against the pages of the paper. "But what if Creeper saw something in the paper, something that made him think Callie had a large sum of money."

"Money that in his mind rightfully belonged to him." Esther crossed her arms and frowned.

"Since he picked Callie, we're thinking it must have something to do with either her personally or her quilt shop." Deborah leaned forward and tapped her finger against the paper. "We looked through the old copies we found on Reuben's shelf, and we marked anything that could even possibly be misconstrued. It's what you might call ... a long shot, but better perhaps than nothing."

Shane wanted to resist their logic, but the women had set the hook in his mouth as skillfully as he could land a five-pound bass with the right lure.

It *was* a long shot, but nothing else was working. They had no fingerprints to work with, and so far no DNA had shown up from the crime scene or the Smart Car. He knew the techs would find evidence eventually. Every crime scene contained DNA, but it would take time, and time was what they did not have.

"I think you might be onto something. I'd like you to show me what you found, and I'd also like to call Trent. See if he has any ideas."

"I can do that," Gavin said, pulling out his phone and stepping outside.

"We'll start moving the *bopplin* over to the house," Noah said. Tobias reached for Simon. Callie was standing up to hand the infant over when her cell phone rang. She pulled it out of her handbag, and all color left her face.

Shane knew immediately it was the killer calling.

"Deep breaths, Callie. We went over how to handle this. Let it go the full four rings." He pulled out his own phone and texted Perla.

Tobias stepped outside with the baby, and Jonas went next door to quiet the children. Everyone else froze in place, their eyes locked on Callie.

She answered it the second before it went to voice mail.

Chapter 16

CALLIE SAT BACK DOWN, swallowed once, and closed her eyes as she uttered a silent prayer.

Then she opened her cell phone. "Hello."

"Took you a long time to answer." The voice was all business tonight.

Callie's left hand went to her throat, and she forced herself to look at Shane's eyes, to draw strength from his strength.

"I was in bed already. I'm not feeling well."

"I might need to see a doctor's note on that."

"It's a headache is all—a bad headache. Sometimes I get … stress headaches."

"Uh-huh. You're not playing games are you? Because my mood is tending toward lousy."

"No games."

"Turn a light on."

"What?"

"You heard me."

"What light do you want me to turn on?" Callie frantically waved a hand at Shane. He texted the instructions to Perla.

"Any light. I want to see that you're really there."

Shane nodded that it was done.

"Fine," she muttered. "Now are you finished giving orders?"

"Walk to the window so I can see you."

"Walk to the window?" She tried to put sass into her voice, when in fact she needed to stall, hoping Shane was a fast texter. They'd considered putting the call on speakerphone but were afraid the killer might pick up on a background noise. It was too risky. So instead she needed to give Shane clues as to any demands he made.

"Stop repeating everything I say and do it."

She waited. Shane nodded that he'd relayed the directions to Perla. No one in the room moved, but they all stared at one another. In the distance, one of Reuben's horses neighed.

Apparently Creeper was satisfied with Perla's shadow, because he moved on to interrogating Callie. "Where's my money?" he asked.

"It's still there. I had someone confirm it for me today, but they didn't know what they were checking. Of course I didn't ask them to bring it to me."

"Why not?" he growled.

"I was surrounded by people all day, plus that's a fair amount of money to lug around. How conspicuous do you want me to be? I don't think you want me to bring it back here. Do you?"

She tried to slow her heart rate as she waited for him to answer.

"So how are you going to get it?"

"I'm going to wait until Sunday morning. Sundays are dead around here, especially when there isn't church. This Sunday everyone's off, so—"

"I know the schedule." The voice was seething now. Callie heard the woman in the background for the first time since the call had begun. They began arguing about something, but Creeper held his hand over the receiver, and Callie couldn't make out his words, only his tone. "Sunday morning. You don't get a minute longer."

Then the line went dead.

Callie set the phone on the table and stared at it.

"What is it, Callie? What did he say? You look as if he might be lurking outside the building." Deborah reached over and squeezed her hand.

"When I told him Sunday would be better like Shane suggested — because there is no church this week — he cut me off and said he knew the schedule." She slowly met the gaze of each person in the room. "I . . . I can't describe his voice when he said it, but he was angry. More so than any other time I've heard him. What does that mean? Why would that upset him so much? If it's the money he's after . . ."

She shook her head, once again completely lost.

"Reuben, is the church schedule actually published anywhere?" Shane had disconnected with Perla after calling and speaking with her to make sure everything there was fine.

"No. There's never been a need to. Everyone here knows when to meet."

There was silence in the room, as the weight of his words sank in fully.

"So the killer is from here?" Esther asked.

Shane ticked off the possibilities on his fingers. "Either he's from here, his lady friend is from here, or one of them currently lives here now."

When no one said anything, Shane added, "We're getting closer. Might make you feel worse, but trust me. It's a good thing."

How could it be a good thing?

Silence filled the room while they each digested the evening's events.

As Callie helped the women gather up dishes and carry them over to the house, the children running along with their fathers in front of them, she kept wishing this could be over and done with. All of these people walking beside her in the dark were dear to her. She didn't want to think about anything happening to a single one of them.

It made her angry and sad at the same time.

Shane tugged on her arm, and she let out a small yelp.

"Sorry," Shane said. "I wanted to talk to you a minute before you go inside."

She nodded and handed her casserole dishes to Deborah, then stepped to a corner of the yard with Shane. Max trotted off to nose around in the bushes. The stars were incredibly bright, as if someone had taken a jar of glitter and thrown it up into the sky. She closed her eyes, focusing on the way the evening breeze cooled her face.

Shane's lips on hers were a complete surprise—warm, sweet, and enticing.

When Max bumped in between them, it was Shane who growled, then backed away, tracing her bottom lip with his fingertips. "Your dog and I need to have a talk."

She laughed, something she couldn't have imagined doing five minutes ago.

"Thanks," she said, turning her back to him and focusing on the stars again.

"Thanks? I'm not used to kissing a woman and having her thank me."

"Oh, but you are used to kissing women, huh? Some sort of hobby of yours?" Callie teased.

"Not what I meant." He wrapped his arms around her, rested his chin on the top of her head.

"Well, thank you anyway. You made me forget . . . everything, for a minute. I needed that." Her heart was thumping a beat like Max's tail beside her, and she felt like a teenage girl on her first date. But she wasn't. She was a grown woman, and she needed to tell him how much she appreciated the things he was doing for her. Sure it was his job, but he seemed to be taking a personal interest in the case.

Turning in his arms, she reached up and touched his face in the darkness. "That's three times you know."

"Three times?"

"Three times you've kissed me today. Twice in the car earlier, and just now—"

"I've been busy or it would have been more." Then he lowered his head and found her lips again. This time Max didn't interrupt them.

She'd wanted to talk to him, wanted to tell him how she was feeling. Suddenly though, it was enough to stand there in the circle of his arms. And honestly she couldn't have explained her emotions anyway. Why muck it up with words?

She allowed herself to relax and enjoy the moment. Finally she laced her fingers in his, and he walked her to the front door. Max gave her a reproachful look and one miserable little sigh before curling up on the porch. She stopped to scratch him behind the ears, plant a kiss on his head, then made her way inside. It did sort of feel like when she was in high school—except her dad wasn't waiting up for her.

Well, perhaps not her dad, but Deborah, Esther, and Melinda were—sitting in the living room with children running in and out, preparing for bed. A knowing smile passed between them as she shut the door behind her.

Esther tried to hide her amusement when she saw the expression on Callie's face. She focused instead on her son, who was nursing contentedly.

Deborah and Melinda made no effort to conceal their curiosity.

"Were you two talking about the case?" Deborah helped Mary with her nightgown, then shooed her into the bedroom the girls were using.

"*Ya.* I'm betting Shane was whispering in your ear about

escape routes as you both gazed up at the stars." Melinda pulled out her quilting as she settled into the rocking chair near the stove in the corner. Tobias had built a small fire in it though it was barely cool enough to need one.

The crackle and pop provided more than heat—it provided comfort.

Deborah and Melinda giggled, but stopped when Callie turned and placed her hands on her hips.

"Are you saying you were spying on us?"

"Not spying exactly." Deborah also pulled out her quilting. "I might have passed by the window once."

"We needed to be sure you were safe, Callie." Melinda didn't sound ashamed of herself at all.

Esther raised Simon to her shoulder, covered him with the blanket, and rubbed his back in gentle small circles. It was something that never failed to calm her, and suddenly she could picture Callie with a child—maybe several of them. "Don't be angry, Callie. They did the same when I first began seeing Tobias."

"And Seth. Even when we were young we looked out for one another." Deborah stared at the border of her quilt, frowning.

"It's true. I'd forgotten how you would follow Seth and me outside after singings."

"We allowed you your privacy," Melinda said. "It's not as if we hid in the buggy with you."

"There was that one time," Deborah murmured.

"Okay once. But after we were sure he could be trusted, we left you alone."

Callie flopped onto the couch. "So you're saying I should thank you for watching Shane kiss me."

"He kissed you? We couldn't see that. You were too hidden in the darkness," Melinda said.

"Twice just now." Callie leaned her head against the couch and tried to rest.

Esther's heart twisted some, remembering the first kiss she'd shared with Tobias—they'd been standing in her old garden. So many of the important moments in her life had happened in her garden. "Twice is *gut*. If he hadn't liked it he'd probably have stopped at once."

She stood when Simon produced a nice burp.

"Is that how you know?" Martha waited in the doorway to the sitting room, holding Joshua's hand.

Callie's eyes popped open, and she met Deborah's amused gaze.

"How you know what, *dochder*?" Deborah asked.

"If you're *in lieb*. If you've found the man you're to marry."

Callie started coughing as if she'd choked on the very idea. It was the funniest sight Esther had seen in days. Melinda reached over and patted her on the back.

Deborah stood and gathered up Joshua in her arms. "It's early to be talking about Callie and Shane marrying. They aren't even courting yet. Now you've gone and embarrassed her."

"Sorry, Miss Callie. I didn't mean to be rude." Martha stuck her bottom lip out, as if she were perturbed by the entire idea.

She walked farther into the room, and Esther saw—for a moment—Deborah as she looked over twenty years ago. With her long, dark brown hair brushed out and falling to her waist and her eyes serious and quizzical, Martha was the mirror image of her mother.

"I don't understand boys, and I heard you laughing and talking. You make it sound like something fun, but it seems to me more like something to be endured."

Callie drew in a deep breath and reached for Martha, slipping an arm around her waist. "I know the feeling, and sometimes I don't understand men very well either."

"I don't understand boys at all."

"Maybe they feel the same way about us, Martha," Deborah suggested, as she turned to carry Joshua into the other room.

"Could be *Mamm* is right, but it doesn't seem to bother boys nearly as much." Martha said goodnight, then followed her mother into the children's rooms.

After Esther put Simon in his cradle, she picked up her sewing.

"How can you girls focus on quilting when all of . . ." Callie's hands waved toward the darkened windows, "*this* is going on."

"Busy hands help push back the worries," Deborah said, as she returned to the room and picked up their quilting.

"Huh?"

"Something my *mamm* used to say when I was fussing over boys."

That started them all to laughing again, and Esther relaxed. Though she would rather have had Tobias inside with them, it was enough to know that he was outside, protecting their home.

"Melinda, I'm going to need to sit next to you if I'm going to restitch this border." Esther held the quilt out in front of her. She'd never found a project to be quite this challenging before.

"*Ya*, I was thinking the same thing. Callie, scoot down a little so Esther can sit closer."

"I can't move. I may actually sleep here."

Melinda nudged her, and she slid over with a groan, her eyes closed.

"What are you two talking about?" Deborah asked, studying her own quilt. "Why would you need to sit beside each other?"

Esther dropped her quilt into her lap, glanced at Melinda.

Melinda peered over her glasses at Deborah.

"We forgot to tell you, didn't we?"

"Tell me what?"

"Tell her what?" Suddenly Callie looked wide awake and was sitting up straighter.

"The quilts." Esther glanced down at hers. The trip she'd made to Melinda's seemed fuzzy now, seemed many days ago rather than merely hours. "We discovered the borders match up to form words."

"In German."

Deborah picked her quilt back up, ran her finger down the edge. "I thought it was some sort of design work. I hadn't figured it out yet so I was waiting."

"Same here. When I stopped by Melinda's ..." Esther tried to remember exactly when it was that they'd laid the quilts out on the floor.

"It was this morning." Melinda shook her head. "Seems like last week, but it was less than twelve hours ago."

"Wait a minute. These are the quilts you're restoring, right?" Callie moved and knelt on the floor in front of them. "The quilts from Elizabeth Hochstetler's estate?"

"Same quilts." Esther now laid her quilt down in her lap, glanced at Melinda and Deborah for a clue. Callie was becoming animated, her face flushed.

"And we received these quilts, what, about two weeks ago?"

"Two and a half, if I remember right. It was midweek." Melinda pushed up on her glasses.

Callie stood and began pacing back and forth. "Does anyone remember if Mrs. Hochstetler's death was announced in the *Gazette*?"

"Yes, of course it was." Deborah stood as well. "Callie, are you thinking Mrs. Hochstetler's death, the man's demand for money, and these quilts are somehow related?"

"They could be. He sees the announcement in the paper. Possibly the article mentions the estate, mentions our names and that we've been called to her house, and then our perpetrator shows up."

"But there's no money to speak of ..." Esther rejected the notion. It didn't seem possible. How could quilts cause a man to murder someone?

"There's the account," Melinda whispered. "I couldn't understand why Mrs. Hochstetler set up the bank account or what its purpose was. Only Mrs. Barnwell knows that answer."

"Callie, where are you going?" Esther's voice rose in concern.

"To the barn, to get Shane."

She'd reached the door before Esther called her back, disbelief filling every word. "Wait, Callie. Come back and take a closer look at these. You're bringing Shane over here, because you think three old quilts could catch a killer?"

"I'm not sure." She reached down, touched the stitching, traced the words Esther knew she couldn't read because they were in German.

They were all standing now. All staring at the old German script in their hands.

Could the quilts actually hold a clue to this mess?

Could they explain what the killer was after?

Esther honestly didn't know.

"Maybe they have something to do with this," Callie said, her fingers lingering on the aged fabric. "Maybe Shane will know the next step. It's better than sitting here waiting for a murderer to show up."

Chapter 17

MELINDA HAD AN UNREASONABLE URGE to run into the boys' room and check on Matthew and Aaron. Which was ridiculous. She could hear them in there with Deborah's boys. Occasionally a giggle from Joseph and Jacob slipped through the walls. The twins had always been able to see the bright side of things. She was glad they were all together tonight.

There seemed to be safety in numbers.

She heard her mother's voice in her mind, reminding her to trust in God. It seemed a hundred times she'd gently quoted the verse, "Lean not unto thine own understanding, Melinda."

No danger there tonight. She didn't understand any of this ...

The front door opened, and she jumped, though she knew it was Shane and Callie. Knew it before the door even opened. She'd heard their voices coming up the walk.

Why were her nerves so frayed? Because some lunatic was after her son?

Lean not unto thine own understanding.

"Callie said you think the killer's motive might have to do with the quilts and Mrs. Hochstetler's estate."

"It's another long shot," Deborah admitted. "These are unusual quilts, and we don't understand what they mean."

Shane stood over two of the quilts that had been laid out on the floor. "I've called Trent. He's looking up the exact wording of any articles relating to Hochstetler's passing. He'll send the file to my phone. In the meantime, can you tell me about the borders on the quilts?"

"They're in German," Esther explained. "Most quilts have a simple pattern around the entire border. I was trying to reinforce the stitching on mine, but I couldn't understand the pattern."

"Because there wasn't a pattern, not an obvious one anyway." Melinda knelt down on the floor and pointed to the area where the two quilts touched each other. It still surprised her when she looked at them. "It wasn't until we were comparing the two side-by-side that we understood part of each border combines to create a German script. The border on Esther's quilt is the bottom half—"

"And the border on Melinda's is the top half."

"What about Deborah's quilt?"

Deborah stood and placed hers on the opposite side. "We hadn't thought to look until just now."

Melinda pulled in a deep breath. It was obvious to all five of them, the borders matched.

"I may be the one person in this room who doesn't know German," Shane said.

"No. There are two of us." Callie knelt beside Melinda.

"Who wants to do the translation?"

Esther ran her hand along the border, her fingers touching each word as she read. "An industrious *fraa* is the best savings account." When she reached the corner, she looked up.

"Amish proverb?" Callie asked.

"*Ya.* I remember that one from my *grossmammi*." Deborah shrugged. "Not an unusual saying, but it is unusual to stitch it on a quilt."

"What does the other say?"

Melinda ran her fingers down the edge in the same way Esther had, as if touching it would bestow some blessing. "A handful of patience is worth more than a bushel of brains."

Shane rubbed at the muscle on his neck. "I'll be honest, ladies. I don't see any connection. So Mrs. Hochstetler stitched Amish proverbs on the borders of her quilts. How would that be related to our murderer? Why would it be related? She must have done this sewing years ago—"

"We've been able to date the oldest back to the mid-1900s." Callie smoothed the fabric. "I understand your skepticism, Shane. It does seem like a jump from these old pieces of cloth to a madman's quest for some unknown treasure."

Shane shrugged, sat in the rocking chair Melinda had vacated. "On the other hand, both of these quotes refer to money—"

Shane groaned. Sitting forward, he rubbed his temples with his eyes closed, then opened them wide and focused again on the quilts. "Vaguely."

"We did receive them earlier this month." Melinda wondered why that fact made her heart beat faster.

"Less than three weeks ago, Shane." Callie crossed her arms stubbornly. "And then Creeper appears. Coincidence?"

"I heard from my mother two weeks ago. That doesn't mean she's involved in this."

"But Callie is involved." Melinda was warming to the idea. She wasn't sure why. Maybe Callie's enthusiasm was contagious. "This man singled out Callie for a reason. What else has changed in her life during the last month, other than coming into possession of the quilts?"

"But they're quilts." Shane didn't exactly scoff at the word, but it was obvious he was out of his element.

The four women exchanged knowing looks.

"You tell him, Callie." Melinda sat back on her heels.

"Tell me what?"

"Do you have any idea what these are worth, Shane?"

"No. I've never given it much thought."

"I won't divulge the financial details of people in this room —"

"Go ahead and tell him." Esther stood and walked to the stove in the corner. Opening the small iron door, she put in another piece of wood. "We're all *freinden* here."

"The quilts I auctioned when I first arrived in town —"

"The ones made by Deborah and Esther and Melinda?"

"Yes. The ones we auctioned on eBay. They went for as much as four thousand dollars each."

Shane let out a whistle. "For a blanket?"

"*Ya*, we were surprised too." Melinda nodded at the memory. "The money was a big help, especially with Aaron's medical costs."

"*Englischers* don't view them as blankets or, in many instances, even quilts. They view them as art." Callie motioned toward Deborah. "When we went to Chicago for the textile display, the sale price went even higher."

"So you think these would be worth that much?"

"No." Esther sat back on the couch. "These would bring a far greater price. The stitching is more detailed than what even we can do."

"Plus they're antiques," Callie explained. "It increases the value. If the seams are reinforced ... The quilts have been stored in a trunk for many years, and they've suffered from the humidity. Quilts fare better when they're hung."

"How much more could these be worth?" Shane asked.

"I'd estimate they're each worth thirty thousand dollars, possibly. If we're lucky."

Melinda looked at Callie in surprise. She hadn't allowed herself to dwell on what the quilts might be worth, what it might mean as far as Aaron's future.

"So we could be looking at ninety thousand dollars." Shane covered his face with his hands as he peered out at the quilts through his fingers. "That's not it. This guy isn't looking for quilts. He's looking for money. He expected you to have it in a bank account or a box somewhere. That's pretty obvious from the way he trashed your apartment and the way he's talked to you."

Deborah stood and began pacing back and forth.

No one spoke for several minutes. Melinda found herself listening for the sound of the boys, something she did every night. She found herself listening for Aaron's breathing. Everything remained quiet throughout the house.

Finally Deborah returned to the middle of the room. Hands on hips, she stared down at the quilts. "Have any of you seen this design before?"

"I haven't," Shane muttered.

Callie slapped him on the arm, but he smiled, snatched her hand, and laced his fingers with hers.

"It reminds me of something I saw on the National Quilting webpage," Callie said. "They're called storybook quilts. Sometimes they're sent to schools that set up a display of quilts. Each quilt tells a story. The display includes books with each quilt, and the idea is to encourage students to read more and appreciate the history surrounding quilting."

"*Ya*, we've heard of storybook quilts," Esther said.

"But I've never seen one." Melinda cocked her head.

Deborah frowned.

Everyone leaned forward and stared at the blocks of each quilt—four squares across and five down.

"What if the money is hidden?" Deborah asked softly. "And what if these pictures tell us a story of sorts, a story of where the money could be found?"

"A story?" Esther asked.

"Oh, good grief." Shane sank back against the couch and allowed his eyes to close.

"Storybook quilts . . ." Callie began pacing again.

176

Melinda had never been good at puzzles—not like Deborah and Callie. The only puzzle she'd ever cared about was the one regarding her son's health.

What did she need to do to help him through each day?

Would this food bother him in some way?

Would that food make him stronger?

But as she gazed at the quilt squares laid out in front of them, she understood Deborah might be on to something. If she was, then it was up to Melinda to figure it out.

She needed to figure it out, or the killer would keep attacking her son and Callie.

She needed to figure it out, or they could all be in danger.

Of the people in this room, she'd been closer to Mrs. Hochstetler than anyone else.

She should be able to unravel this. Her son's safety depended on it. She needed to focus—ignore the fear coursing through her veins, and focus.

Deborah had been staring at the quilts, but she noticed when Melinda practically turned to stone beside her.

"Was iss letz?"

Melinda finally tore her eyes from the quilt.

When she did, the desperation in her friend's eyes nearly broke Deborah's heart. She hadn't forgotten what was at stake here— not exactly. But as usual, she'd become caught up in solving the mystery. She'd lost sight of the human element. She'd lost sight of her friend's suffering.

"Everything will be fine." She put an arm around Melinda. "We'll figure this out—together. Nothing, absolutely nothing, is going to happen to Aaron."

Tears filled Melinda's eyes, slipped down beneath the rim of her glasses. "First the murder, then the car, and I wasn't there to protect him either time. But this, if I could figure this out, then maybe it will all be okay again."

Pulling her into a hug, Deborah reached for the handkerchief Esther offered, slipped it into Melinda's hand. "*We* will figure this out. All of us together. Look at how hard Callie is concentrating. Her hair is starting to stick out from the effort."

"Hey!"

"I only bring it up to point out to Melinda that we're all focused." Deborah smiled.

Melinda nodded as she swiped at her cheeks.

Shane looked relieved when his phone rang. "I'll take this outside."

"Maybe we'll crack the code while he's out of the room," Callie said. "That'll show him we really might be on to something."

"Can't blame him for being skeptical. It probably sounds far-fetched to anyone who doesn't work with quilts." Esther stood and walked slowly around the three quilts. "Do the pictures in the blocks look familiar to anyone?"

"Nope." Melinda's voice sounded calmer.

"Uh-uh." Callie patted her hair.

"Wonderful stitching." Deborah knelt closer, her nose nearly touching the quilt, but she still couldn't find anything recognizable.

"Stand up. All of you stand back here with me." Esther's voice left no room for argument, so they followed her directions with some groans about growing old and tired bones.

"Now? Anything look familiar?"

Everyone shook their heads no.

"Think of the game the *kinner* play."

"Uno? Like where they match the cards?" When they all turned to stare at Melinda, she pushed on. "I've never seen a quilt pieced together this way, but they remind me of cards in a deck, shuffled randomly."

"That's not bad." Esther walked over to her cup of tea, which had long since grown cold. She took a sip and grimaced. "I was leaning more toward Dutch Blitz, what with the four decks you have—pump, carriage, pail, and plow."

"Okay, I see why your mind would head that direction." Deborah was still cocking her head, looking at the quilts with an odd expression. Then she leaned over, reached out, and ran a finger along the quilt squares. "There's a pump house and a carriage."

"And I see a pail and a plow!" Callie smiled as if she'd earned an *A* on her lessons.

Esther lowered her cup of tea slowly, afraid she would drop it now that the puzzle was beginning to fall into place.

"Not any plow. That's Mrs. Hochstetler's plow," Melinda commented.

"Huh?" Callie moved closer, a frown wrinkling her forehead.

"Look. See the broken piece here? See the flowers growing around it?"

"I wondered about that. Thought it was a way of adding color to the quilt." Esther was on the floor with them now. "I remember noticing the plow when I walked by her garden, when we were there a few weeks ago for the reading of the will."

"Her plow sits in her garden?" Callie looked from Deborah to Esther.

It was Melinda who answered. She sat on the far side of the three quilts, her arms wrapped tightly around her middle as if she were very cold. "The old rusty plow has been there for as long as I've known her. I asked her why once, and she said the iron helps the flowers grow taller and bloom brighter. She said when it broke years ago and couldn't be fixed, she asked Mr. Hochstetler to move it there for her."

"How many years ago, Melinda?" Deborah could practically hear the first real piece of the puzzle clicking into place.

"When she was but a young woman. She said her first *boppli* was just born. Must have been in the early 1940s."

"Before she sewed the quilts then."

"*Ya*. I imagine so."

"So these squares, they could be a picture of her land."

"Why though? Why would she want to put her farm on a quilt?" Esther reached for the strings of her prayer *kapp*, ran her fingers from the top to the bottom as if doing so would produce answers to questions they all needed.

Deborah knew they were close to those answers. She could feel them in the air around them.

The night sounds deepened, and they heard Shane's footsteps as he walked across the front porch.

He stepped into the room when Deborah found the answer that had been lurking at the corner of her mind.

"Maybe it's not a picture or a story. Maybe it's a map."

Chapter 18

S HANE SNAPPED THE PHONE SHUT as he walked into the house.
Things were moving quickly now. The knowledge of it thrummed
through his veins, and he wanted to be out in the Buick chasing
down the leads.

But he knew he needed to be here.

He needed to confirm what Trent had found.

And he needed to be certain Callie was okay before he left.
Callie and Aaron. Fear tightened around Shane's heart like a belt
cinched too tightly, but he pushed it away. He was not going to
allow anything to happen to either one of them.

Deborah was talking about something being a map.

"Maybe what's a map?" he asked.

"The quilts. We think they're a map of Mrs. Hochstetler's
place." Callie twirled her hair around her finger. "The squares
seem to represent different places on her farm—possibly."

"So maybe she liked sewing what she saw out her window? You
know, like we take a picture." Shane stood over the quilts, trying
to see the women's point of view. After all, they'd been right about
the newspaper article.

"That's not the Amish way, Shane." Esther's voice was soft,
gentle, and he was reminded of the times he'd spent trying to coax
details from her regarding Seth's death.

The people who killed Seth still hadn't been brought to trial. It rankled him that the case was one of the few he'd been forced to walk away from, at the insistence of his superiors. But he'd always known Esther wanted the case closed without a conviction.

Callie had tried to explain it to him once, during one of their late-night phone conversations. She said it had to do with forgiveness and grace. Shane knew about grace. He'd been raised submerged in a healthy dose of it. But that type of forgiveness? No. That was beyond what he could imagine. His training didn't allow him to imagine it.

Esther was still fingering the material in front of her. "We wouldn't quilt a picture of our own place anymore than we'd take a photograph. It would feel like boasting, and we strive to be humble."

"*Ya*, Esther's right," Melinda said. "Elizabeth Hochstetler wasn't one to brag either. No, I think if she quilted a scene, there was a reason for it — it wouldn't have been an idle venture."

"So what could her reason have been?" Shane struggled to understand what was happening, what the girls were trying to tell him, and what Mrs. Hochstetler could have been thinking.

"Perhaps she was trying to tell someone something. Or maybe she wanted to leave a record." Callie's hands were out now, waving in front of her as she tended to do when she was excited. "Storybook quilts are a controversial topic. Some insist that as far back as the Civil War, quilts were used to guide folks, like runaway slaves."

"A code?" Shane's voice went up a notch, in spite of his determination to remain neutral.

"Yes. But others argue that no such codes existed. I've done a little reading on it, but not nearly enough. The point is that no one knows if such a code did exist, because the people who did the quilting are long dead and can't attest to their true intentions."

"Same is true of Mrs. Hochstetler and these quilts," Deborah said.

"But the patterns are unusual, and it could be she quilted them for a reason. I never knew Elizabeth to do something on a whim." Melinda's voice was low, thoughtful.

"So you think the pictures might be ... what? Like a treasure map?" Shane couldn't keep the note of incredulity out of his voice now. He had a thug to catch, and it felt like the women were wasting his time chasing fantasies.

"Let's consider the interior borders again now that we're looking at the actual patterns in a different light." Deborah walked around the quilts as she spoke. "The border connecting the first and the second says—"

"An industrious *fraa* is the best savings account," Melinda recited the words.

"And what about the one connecting the second and the third?" Shane asked.

"A handful of patience is worth more than a bushel of brains."

Shane met the gaze of each woman before speaking. He was willing to admit they were on to something. That much was clear. But what? And did it really have anything to do with the killer?

No one spoke as Deborah's words faded into the night. Both proverbs were apparently everyday sayings, common among the Amish community. Both could be interpreted to focus on wealth or prosperity.

Shane decided they'd have to move on what they knew. Time was running out, and he didn't want to give their killer any additional advantage. "I just spoke with Trent. There was one article in the *Gazette* mentioning Callie in the past three months. Actually it mentioned Mrs. Hochstetler in the same piece."

"The reading of the will—" Callie's eyes widened.

"Yes. I have the wording right here." Shane pulled out his phone, thumbed through a few messages until he found it. "The reading of Mrs. Hochstetler's last will and testament took place yesterday, September 14. Most of her belongings were left to friends and family, but in one surprise request, a special gift was made to Miss Callie Harper, who wasn't available for comment at the time we went to print."

"Oh, my gosh. That could sound like she gave me a million dollars. I barely knew the woman."

Silence once more filled the room as the fire crackled.

"We're getting closer. We know why this person might think you have money. And you ladies seem to think the answer is right here in front of us." Shane stood and pulled Callie to her feet. "Get your jacket."

"Where are we going?"

"To Levi Hochstetler's farm. We need some answers, and he may be the one who has them."

While Callie grabbed her jacket, found her purse, and stopped by the bathroom, Shane peeked in on Aaron. The boys appeared to be asleep, but that didn't fool him for a minute. He'd heard them whispering before he opened the door.

At least they were safe though. They were safe for now.

It would have to be enough.

Aaron tried holding his breath while Shane stood in the doorway. Then he realized he should look like he was sleeping, and sleeping boys were probably in the habit of breathing. So he took deep breaths, hoping the covers would rise and fall and convince the detective he was out cold.

He'd played possum before. Wasn't like this was his first time, but it had been a while. Now that he was older, his *mamm* and *dat* helped him to his room, helped him out of his chair, and didn't check on him again.

They trusted him to stay put.

Unlike many of his *freinden's* houses, Aaron's house was a single story. Hannah's room was near the front of the house, next to his parents'. He shared a room with his *bruder* at the back of the house—past the kitchen. Some nights, when he couldn't sleep, he'd hear his parents walking back and forth, between their own room and Hannah's. They'd left him a special bell next to his bed in case he ever needed anything, but he'd never used it.

For one thing, Matt was always in the bed across from his. If he needed anything, Matt was there for him. Aaron didn't need a bell. He'd tried explaining that to his *mamm*. She'd smiled and said she felt better leaving the bell there all the same. He could no more have understood the reasons for the things his *mamm* insisted on than he could have understood why the chickens walked in a circular motion when he threw out the food or why Creeper had chosen Fall Festival to disrupt their lives.

"Are you asleep?" Matt asked.

"'Course not."

"Sure sounded like it to me." Joseph began laughing and threw something at Jacob, starting a pillow fight—albeit a somewhat quiet one.

"Any idea why Shane would be checking on us?" Aaron asked.

"Guess he wanted to be sure Creeper hadn't snuck into the room and snatched you."

Now that his eyes had adjusted to the darkness of the room, Aaron could make out that everyone was sitting up in their beds—everyone except Joshua, who was snoring in a crib in the corner. Aaron struggled to a sitting position and studied the play of shadow and light coming in through the window. Surely the killer couldn't find a way into the house.

"That's impossible," Jacob said as he whacked Joseph over the head with his pillow. "My *dat's* right outside the window. I saw him not ten minutes ago."

"Yup. No one gets past *Dat*. I tried sneaking out once." Joseph dodged a hit to his right shoulder. "He caught me before I had one leg out the window."

"Aren't you too young to be sneaking out the windows? And isn't your room upstairs at your house?" Matthew looked at Joseph with what Aaron thought was a mixture of annoyance and admiration, sort of like John Wayne usually looked at his sidekick.

Why was that movie stuck in his head?

"*Ya*, we're upstairs," Jacob said. "But there's a *gut* trellis running down the wall for *Mamm*'s flowers. Built nice and sturdy too."

"It was a few months ago. I'd already turned seven." Joseph shrugged as if that explained everything, but when he turned toward Matthew and Aaron, Jacob landed a shot directly on the top of his head. Joseph fell over as if he were knocked out.

"The pigs are why he was leaving. He's always worried about those pigs." Jacob shook his head as if he couldn't understand the ways of his twin brother, which was when Joseph leapt up and attacked from behind.

While the counterattack was occurring, Aaron turned to Matthew. "Are we all set for tomorrow morning?"

"I think so. Talked to Martha before she took the younger girls into the other room. Her *mamm* already asked if she wanted to go into town to help in her *aenti*'s booth. She'll have no problem sneaking away to meet us."

"And the phone?"

"Says it won't be a problem."

"Who has a phone?" The twins were suddenly no longer interested in the pillow fight. They plopped down on either side of Aaron, all eyes and ears.

Aaron tried to be aggravated with their listening in on the conversation, but it was impossible to be irritated with Jacob and Joseph. The two had been his friends for as long as he could remember. They were as loyal as Matt, and they'd never once let his sickness come in the way of a good time.

In fact, more than once he'd found himself in trouble because of them. *Freinden* didn't come any better.

He looked to Matt, who nodded.

"We're going after Creeper tomorrow."

"Using my *bruder* here as bait," Matt added. "And this time we're going to catch him."

"Martha's bringing a phone, so we can call Shane if we need him."

The twins looked at each other, silent for the space of a few seconds as the sound of their *dat* walking a patrol outside the window filled the night. When his footsteps had faded, a grin spread across each face.

"Awesome," Jacob said. "I seriously doubt this man knows what he's in for."

Joseph picked up his pillow, held it over his shoulder like a bat. "*Ya*. And if you need any help, I'll sic my pigs on him."

Chapter 19

CALLIE FOUND HERSELF BACK in Shane's old Buick. Once again he made no pretense of wanting her anywhere other than tucked up beside him.

"Have to keep you close," he murmured, opening the driver's side door so she could scoot in past the wheel, but not too far past. He left the door open long enough for her to find the middle lap belt by the glow of the dome light.

While she was fumbling with the seat belt, he checked in on the radio that was attached under the dash and talked to Captain Taylor. Before he slammed the door shut, she caught a glimpse of his grin. It settled the fireflies swirling in her stomach. She couldn't imagine what might be waiting for them at the end of the lane, but something told her it was no match for Shane.

When he cranked the ignition of the old car, she winced at the sound of the motor splitting the quiet of the evening.

"We're not going to sneak up on anyone in this car."

"If we need to sneak we'll walk or borrow someone's horse." He pulled out down the lane at a reasonably slow speed, waving once to someone she didn't see. "If we need to catch them though, this car will work fine."

"What gives with the old car, Shane? Surely you can afford a new one."

Shane gave her the slow smile that melted something deep inside her. "New car? Like that mini-SUV you bought?"

"You're not ragging on my car, are you? I like my car, and you're the one who suggested I lose the rental."

"Those were good times. Remember when I first hauled you into the interrogation room?"

She relaxed against the leather seat. It felt good to banter back and forth with him. The conversation was safe, taking her mind off her feelings and helping her forget their assailant for a few minutes.

"Yeah. I was having a little trouble accepting that I was here for good."

Shane didn't respond immediately. Just when she thought he wouldn't, he glanced at her. "Have you decided now? Decided if you're here for good?"

"This is my home, Shane. Deborah and Melinda and Esther— even you and Gavin and Trent—you're my friends." She hesitated then pushed on, perhaps because the night stole all pretenses. Or maybe because she knew their relationship had leapt past the friend point in the last twenty-four hours. "I don't have anyone I'm this close to back in Texas. I don't have any reason to return there."

Shane nodded. "And then there's Max."

This needed to end soon. She missed her dog. Missed having him in the house with her, sprawled across her feet, a nice, warm lump like house shoes with a heartbeat.

"Where'd you go?" Shane asked.

"Hmm?"

"You left for a few minutes."

"Thinking that I'll appreciate normal after this."

She didn't pull away when he wrapped his arm around her shoulders and tucked her in closer. He ran his hand up and down her arm, leaving a trail of goose bumps.

Would her life return to normal?

"I miss Max." She sighed dramatically. "I still think he would have fit in the backseat of this car."

"We will have to be going steady before I allow Max in the backseat of my car."

It was crazy, because she would turn thirty soon and Shane had just said the words *going steady* as if they were in high school. But when he did, her pulse had kicked up a notch and her palms had actually started to sweat.

"Going back to your question about the car, it was my dad's."

"Was?"

"He bought it before I was born. It's a 1971 Buick GSX."

Callie ran her hand over the black leather seats. More than forty years old, but it looked like it had come off the factory floor yesterday. "Why do you have it?"

"Growing up, we worked on it together every weekend— changed the oil, checked the brakes, even pulled the engine if we needed to. Buick made one hundred and twenty-four of these. 'Course Dad didn't realize that when he ordered it, but it quickly became a collector's item. Each year it became worth more, and each year he hung on to it. Drove it on weekends. Kept it in top shape."

"Some hobby." Callie was beginning to realize the vehicle she was riding in was more than a car. It was a connection to Shane's childhood, to his past.

"When I made detective, he handed me the keys."

"Wow."

"Yeah. Wow."

He slowed and turned down the lane that led to Levi Hochstetler's house.

"Must be worth a lot."

"More than a new mini-SUV." Shane ran his fingers through the back of her hair.

"Ever think about selling?"

"Not even once."

He pulled next to the barn and shut off the engine. The light from a kerosene lantern shone from the kitchen window, and another came on in the sitting room.

"Do you see your parents often?" She had never imagined him with parents. He'd always been Shane—the big, bad detective who was intent on making her life miserable.

Which wasn't completely true.

She'd always been afraid to acknowledge the other side of him, the human side. To do so would end what was left of their adversarial relationship, and where would she be then? Was she ready to commit to what he wanted? The thought frightened her and at the same time sent her pulse racing.

She was afraid to commit to Shane, like she'd been afraid to commit herself to Shipshewana. Correction, she was terrified of stepping any closer to the intimate side of Shane Black.

When he tipped her face up to his and kissed her lips softly, she realized it was too late to fight those fears.

"I see them twice a month," he whispered.

"See who?" Callie's mind was fuzzy from his kiss.

"My parents."

"You have parents?"

He kissed her again, then removed his keys from the ignition, walked around the car, and opened her door. "Come on, Callie Grace. Help me with these quilts. Let's see if we can put this treasure map question to rest. We have a killer to catch, and the sun will be up in another seven hours. We need to have you back at the shop before then."

Shane hated the expression on Levi and Sadie Hochstetler's face when they opened the door—cold, naked fear. It might last a second, might last longer, but he was rarely greeted by anything other than fear initially. When families opened the front door and saw him, the county detective, the first response was generally the same.

Shane's reaction to their fear might appear cold, definitely emotionless. Despite what most people thought, the veneer that looked to others like a block of ice was no more than that—a veneer. Invariably his mind would flash back to the night when he was eleven years old.

The night he had opened the door to find an officer standing on his own front porch.

The night his life had changed irrevocably.

Instead of allowing his personal feelings to intrude, he locked them down. The past was history. *That* past was ancient history serving ninety-nine years to life. He wouldn't allow it to intrude on this family's needs.

"Shane."

"Levi, I was wondering if we could speak with you."

"It's late."

"Yes, it is. I wouldn't have come by if it wasn't important."

Levi's eyes hesitated on Callie, took in the quilts they both were carrying, then peered past them, as if he might find answers in the darkness. Finally he nodded, taking his wife's arm and pulling her farther inside as he opened the door wider.

They stepped into a room that was typically Amish. Shane had grown up in the community, gone to school there, and played baseball there. He was well acquainted with plain ways and customs. Still the starkness of the Hochstetler home struck him as he walked inside, removing his Cubs cap because he knew they didn't abide wearing hats indoors.

He could have been stepping into any of a dozen homes within the Shipshewana district that he had visited in the recent past— they looked that much alike to him. Did they not miss the family photos and the drapes that softened a home against the night's darkness?

"Would you like some *kaffi*?" Sadie asked.

"No, thank you. We had dinner at Reuben's, but it might be good if we all sat down to talk this thing through."

Moving into the kitchen, they took their places around the table. Shane took the quilt Callie was carrying and set it on top of the two he had, placing them all in the empty chair next to him. He noticed a half-full cup of coffee in front of Levi's seat. Levi and Sadie had been up late discussing something before they'd arrived.

Was it related to Mrs. Knepp's murder?

How could it be?

Perhaps there was something they knew, something they hadn't reported?

Dismissing the questions, Shane quickly ran through the recent developments in the case. Sadie and Levi remained silent until he was finished.

"We saw the posters in town today," Levi admitted. "Can't say I see how this would involve us in any way."

"For whatever reason, the person we're looking for has targeted Callie. He seems to have the idea that she's come into a large sum of money. When we did a search on recent news articles, one came up with her name. It was a short piece regarding your mother's will."

Levi took his time responding. Finally he cleared his throat and glanced at his wife.

"It's all right, Levi." Sadie reached out and covered Levi's sun-aged hand with her own. "Callie will understand."

Sadie and Callie exchanged a look.

Shane had meant to ask Callie how well the two women were acquainted—but he'd allowed himself to become distracted on the way over. One more reason he needed to bottle up his emotions, to resist his feelings for Callie—at least until this case was solved.

"We thought it odd when *Mamm* named her in the will," Levi admitted. "No offense, Callie."

"None taken. I was surprised too."

"*Mamm* visited the shop, of course. All the women in my family do, but it seemed ..." Levi stared down into the coffee, didn't look up until he'd found the word he needed. "It seemed eccentric to actually leave something to an *Englischer* when she'd had little personal dealings with you."

"I understand," Callie said. "Your mother was a beautiful person and a valued customer, but I only knew her casually."

"Deborah, Melinda, and Esther knew her better?" Shane asked.

"*Ya*, of course. We're in the same district, meet together for church." Levi sat back in his chair, as if this were safer ground to cover.

"Elizabeth was particularly close to Melinda." Sadie picked up the thread. "She took a real interest in her younger son, Aaron. Always asked after him and how he was doing."

"What about the quilts, Levi? How did you feel about your mother leaving those to Callie and the girls?"

Levi's eyes flickered to the stack of quilts. "Didn't bother me so much. They're just quilts. Again, it seemed strange, but they were *Mamm*'s to do with as she pleased. I didn't even realize they were in that old trunk. Don't remember ever having seen them."

"They're actually antiques," Callie explained. "The oldest was quilted over fifty years ago."

Levi merely shrugged, so Callie stood and walked over to the stack of quilts. She unfolded one in order to reveal the top. "As you can see it's not a traditional pattern. We believe it might be a code of sorts. That your mother might have been trying to tell us something."

Levi shook his head. "Don't know why she'd do that, or why she'd use a different quilt pattern than the other women."

"The borders fit together like a puzzle, and they're German script, Amish proverbs actually. But the pictures are what we were hoping you could help us with. Do these pictures mean anything to you? There's a woman here boarding a bus, for instance. Is there anything in your family history about an important trip she took?"

Sadie had been staring at the quilt intently. "There was—"

"I don't know what you're looking for. Don't know what the quilts could mean or why she would sew them this way. Now if there are no other questions, tomorrow's Saturday and a workday for us."

Sadie looked at her husband as if he'd grown an extra pair of ears, but she held her peace.

Shane nodded to Callie, and she refolded the quilt before setting it on top of the other two.

They'd almost made it to the door when Shane turned. He could have done it at the table, but he was hoping to catch Levi off guard. By this point he was convinced the man was hiding something, though it may have been totally unrelated.

"There is one other thing," he said, as if it had totally slipped his mind. He handed the three quilts to Callie, though they reached to her chin and she looked as if she might topple backward under the weight of them. "The drawings in town are from Aaron's description. We had an artist work with him to come up with a rendering."

He reached into the pocket of his jacket, pulled out a five-by-seven envelope. "Unfortunately our perpetrator didn't stop with Mrs. Knepp. He also tried to run over Aaron earlier today, as he was crossing the street."

Sadie's hand covered her mouth. "Is he all right?"

"Yes. It did cause some panic at the festival, and the man did manage to escape. However, two different cameras were able to capture shots of him. We've been working on enhancing them."

Shane pulled out the picture as he spoke. He didn't look at the photo, didn't have to. He'd memorized the guy's features hours ago. Instead he watched Levi and Sadie Hochstetler.

On seeing the photo, Levi's face lost all color, turning first white, then a chalky gray. Sadie's hand went from her mouth to her throat, and a small cry escaped as if she'd been hurt.

"Do you know this man, Levi?"

"I do not, and I think it's time for you to leave."

"He's killed once, and he might kill again. He's after Callie, and Aaron Byer is our material witness—which means he's a prime target as well. If you know this man, you want to tell me who he is."

"I told you I didn't. Now *danki* for coming, but it's late."

Shane nodded, placed the photo on the table near their front door. "You can keep this copy. Maybe it'll jog your memory."

Then he took the quilts from Callie and walked with her into the night, toward the Buick.

He didn't start the car right away.

Instead he pulled out his cell phone and called his men at the office in Middlebury. "I want you to access everything you can on Levi Hochstetler. See if he has any brothers, cousins, or uncles who match the description of our perp. Also, call Stan Taylor and tell him I want someone watching Levi's place. If he leaves, I want to know where. If they're related, could be he'll try to meet up with our perp."

When he closed the phone, he cranked up the Buick, slipped his arm around Callie, and drove back down the lane. They were closer to solving this than when they'd arrived, and that was a good feeling. This was the part of the hunt he loved, the part where if he was smart enough, if he was vigilant enough, he could put the assailant away.

Too many ifs, but he'd take the odds on this one.

This case, he did not plan on losing.

Winning had always been important, but this time it was personal.

Personal because it was Shipshe, and to some extent Shipshe was still his town.

Personal because of Aaron, and Aaron was too much like the young boy he had once been.

Personal because of Callie.

She laid her head against his shoulder as they made their way through the night, back toward Reuben's. He'd said no to love more than once, purposely walked away from it. This time he'd waited for Callie to be ready, waited more than a year. He'd wait longer if he had to, but he wouldn't lose her to some maniac bent on finding a treasure.

Or so he told himself, as he sped through the night.

Chapter 20

ESTHER WOKE THE NEXT MORNING disoriented at first. When had she grown so used to Tobias sleeping beside her?

Amazing that love could become such an ordinary thing, like a fire banked in the stove, the horse's stall cleaned out, and someone's smile to greet you when you rolled over in bed. She wouldn't have thought it possible a year ago. Wouldn't have thought that her life—this life, married, with a father for Leah and a new baby to love and hold—would ever seem normal.

But it was normal. It was her new normal, and she didn't want anything to interrupt it.

She was married, loved, and happy.

Like Job, God had given her back all she had lost. And more.

Miracles did happen, and she was proof.

So when she woke on Saturday morning, when she opened her eyes and saw her *freinden* spread out around her room instead of her husband, her heart at first beat rapidly, then calmed because she knew the next day or possibly the day after that, everything would return to how it should be.

It was a marvel she should feel that way, but she did.

That was the miracle God had worked in her heart. He had given her back her faith in the goodness of life, and Tobias was a large reason for that, but not the only reason for it. The small *boppli* in the cradle in the corner was another part. And of course the *freinden* who were stretching and beginning to wake were the other reasons.

She hurried to the bathroom so she could be done before the others needed it, then put on the coffee. By the time it was percolating on the stove, Simon was awake and ready for his first feeding, and the morning sun had lightened the sky but had not yet peeked its way over the horizon.

"We survived the night," Callie murmured as she reached for a coffee mug.

"*Ya*, what time did you get in?"

"Late." She sat down with the coffee and clutched it as if someone might try to wrestle it away.

"Thought you had switched to tea," Deborah said, walking in and looking as fresh as ever. Nothing seemed to perturb Deborah, or at least it didn't show.

"Most days. Something tells me today I'll need coffee. Shane's putting me back in Perla's place, or rather taking Perla out of my place, in twenty minutes." She grimaced. "I need more coffee."

"Be careful today, Callie." Melinda walked into the room and went directly to where Callie nursed her coffee. She sat next to her, pulling her into a hug. "We'll all be praying, and I know Shane will be watching over you, so you'll be fine, but just be cautious."

"*Ya*, Shane isn't going to let anything happen to you." Deborah grinned mischievously.

Esther raised Simon to her shoulder when he began to fuss. Teasing Callie about her and Shane courting helped ease the tension in the room, but she knew it was simply a covering for their concern for her safety. "We agree to meet here again tonight, right?"

"Yes, but we can't do this every night, Esther. It's kind of you to offer —"

"Let's plan only for tonight, Callie. We agreed this will probably end with the festival, and no one can see further than the current day's needs. Tonight we'll meet here again and perhaps this will be done. You do what Shane says." Everyone turned to look at her, and Esther felt the heat rise in her cheeks. "What? It's not as if I'm telling her to marry him, but he will keep her safe."

"Who's getting married?" Shane stuck his head in the door, saw all the women, and raised his hands in mock surrender. "I'll be waiting in the car. Three minutes, Harper."

"Did your watch break?" Callie looked down at her coffee, still steaming in front of her. "You said I had until—"

"Three minutes. Don't make me come in there." His voice was gruff, but Esther could tell something had changed with Shane Black. Something she wouldn't have expected to ever see. Or was she imagining that? Then he turned to go, but the look he gave Callie before he left was almost tender.

Melinda sighed, confirming Esther's thoughts. "Smitten. He's completely smitten, Callie."

"He's going to be smitten if he tries to take my coffee away," Callie grumbled, pulling on her shoes. "Can I take this with me, Esther?"

"Sure. No problem." Esther topped it off with what was left in the pot on the stove. She didn't want Callie falling asleep on the way to the shop, and her eyes didn't look quite open yet.

Clutching the coffee mug, Callie shuffled out the door.

They heard her murmuring to Max on the porch.

Melinda glanced at the others in amusement. "I can't believe Shane convinced her to leave that dog here."

"Better here than back at the vet's. She doesn't want to put him in harm's way again, and this man has already gone after him once." Deborah walked to the sink and looked out the window. "That dog looks as if he's watching his best friend drive away."

"He is," Esther and Melinda said at the same time, then started giggling.

Esther was surprised they could find anything to laugh about, but perhaps it was the nervousness fluttering in their stomachs that needed to find a path of escape. Activity helped also, and within thirty minutes there was plenty of that. The house soon resembled a virtual beehive, which could happen when you had three families readying for the day. They had decided the night before that the men would go back to their chores at their respective homes. Deborah and Martha would go into town to help with the festival pie booth and at the quilt shop. Melinda would follow at noon when Deborah would return home to help Esther with preparing the evening meal.

Except something was off.

Something more than the fact that they were all starting from the same place and that a killer was afoot. From the kitchen window Esther saw the twins sneaking around the corner of Reuben's barn. Nothing unusual there. The twins probably had their pockets full of frogs.

But when Esther went out the back door to give Deborah a box of preserves for the booth, Martha was huddled up with Aaron and Matthew. Seeing Esther, she startled and turned red, then hurried off to help her mother with her younger brother.

Something was definitely going on with the children.

As the men pulled out down the lane, past the pond, Esther checked first on Simon, who was sleeping soundly, then hurried over to where Melinda was helping Deborah load her buggy.

"Do you have a minute before you go?"

The two turned and looked at her in surprise.

"I think the *kinner* are up to something. It has me worried."

"Up to something? What could they possibly be up to?" Deborah had one foot in her buggy, but she hopped backwards and frowned at her twins, dusting her hands against her dress.

"Not those two. I can take care of Jacob and Joseph. I'm worried about the older ones—Martha and Matthew and Aaron."

"Matthew asked Tobias if they could take the cart over and help their father for the morning." Melinda squinted into the rising sun, looking to see where they were. "Tobias said yes, and I agreed there was no harm in it."

"Martha's going into town with me," Deborah added. "She was here only a minute ago."

As they spoke, the three children exited the barn—Aaron already in the cart, his wheelchair fastened to the back. Matt was leading the pony. Martha was walking next to it, her head bent as if she were whispering to the boys. Something about that sight worried Esther, but she couldn't put her finger on why.

"See? That's what concerns me. Every time I've seen them they've been that way. It's as if they're planning something."

"They remind me of us when we were younger," Deborah murmured.

"Something tells me they are not planning on going to the farm." Melinda pushed up her glasses.

Melinda walked straight over to the children. "Aaron and Matthew, tell me straight. Did you lie to me earlier?"

Both boys looked up, their faces coloring as red as the fall flowers growing by the fence.

"No, *Mamm*," they murmured unconvincingly.

"So you do mean to take this cart to help your *dat* and nowhere else?"

"That's not what we said," Aaron spoke to his shoes.

"Not exactly," Matthew added.

"Look at me when you're speaking. What do you mean that's not what you said?"

"I asked if we could take the cart and pony to help *Dat,* and we do mean to go there. I just didn't exactly say we didn't mean to go anywhere else." Aaron looked pleased with himself for about five seconds, until he saw the expression on his mother's face.

Melinda knew all too well what he saw. It was the reflection of the cold fear that gripped her heart tighter than the pain of birth could squeeze a woman's abdomen, making her double over and cry out in alarm.

Had she almost fallen for this again?

What did the boys call it?

The swap?

She would make them wish they had something to swap if they didn't start telling her what they were up to right this minute. How had she been so busy she hadn't seen what they were doing?

"Matthew, what do you have to say for yourself?"

"We would have gone by there. We wouldn't have lied to you, *Mamm*."

"Not telling the entire truth is still lying. We've spoken on this before." She waited for them to tell the rest, to explain the part that had her heart hammering clear up to her throat.

But they didn't.

They fidgeted and continued to stare at the ground.

"Martha, how are you involved in this?" Deborah's voice was soft and sounded much more controlled than Melinda felt.

Everyone waited, but Martha didn't speak either. She held the pony's bridle and looked from one boy to the other, as if they might jump in and offer an answer.

"I don't know what's gotten into them." Melinda twisted her apron first one direction then the other, as if she were wringing water out of it. "Do they not understand the danger of this situation?"

"We understand it all too well," Matthew said, his eyes suddenly dark and serious and so resembling Noah's that Melinda felt a new fear, the fear that her boy had become a man when she'd been busy with other things. Which was ridiculous, since he was eleven years old.

Perhaps his maturity exceeded his years.

Perhaps helping his brother, in addition to the current trials they were all going through, had matured him faster than some.

Leah, Hannah, and Joshua were playing on the front porch, and their carefree sounds tumbled across the yard. Melinda, Deborah, and Esther stood there in front of the cart, waiting in the warmth of the morning sunlight. It was a bright fall day. A day they should have been preparing for the festival, looking forward to spending time with friends and family.

Melinda suddenly wondered what her parents were doing, whether or not they realized how much trouble had visited her family once again. She'd scarcely had time to speak with anyone, though the Amish grapevine did a good job of keeping each family aware of another's needs.

She studied the children as a slight breeze played with the hair at the nape of her neck. They squirmed under her gaze, but offered no other details to their story. Maybe she should have left the children with their extended families, but that might be bringing danger into their families' lives.

"Not speaking is fine. Might be a *gut* thing at this point," Melinda admitted. "Wait here with this buggy, and I'll follow you to our place before I head into town with Hannah."

"But——" Aaron threw a sideways glance at his brother.

"No buts. It's the least I can do to make sure my boys are safe. I'll run inside and collect my things."

Deborah crooked a finger at Martha. "If you don't mind letting go of that pony, go and sit with your *bruder*. He's staying with Esther today and after this stunt you may be too."

The girl looked back once at the boys but didn't attempt to say anything to them.

Melinda stopped halfway between the porch and the barn, halfway between the babies and her half-grown boys. Deborah's twins, Jacob and Joseph, could be seen in the field with Reuben, and even from a distance she could tell they were covered in dirt.

"How do they do it?" Deborah asked, walking up next to her. "They haven't been out there fifteen minutes."

"At least they're safe. What do you think those three were

up to?" Melinda sighed heavily, then caught herself because she sounded so much like her mother.

"Don't know, but they weren't headed only to your place. That was all I could tell by the way they were acting, and it doesn't take much of a puzzle solver to figure it out." Deborah reached out and tucked her arm through the crook of Melinda's elbow as they began walking toward the porch again. "The important thing is that we caught them before they could go anywhere they shouldn't. Maybe that makes us *gut* parents after all."

"Do you know what is worrisome?" Esther asked. "How much those three remind me of the three of us."

That statement stopped them all in their tracks.

"But we didn't—" Melinda couldn't seem to find the rest of her sentence.

"I agree with Melinda." Deborah stared back toward the boys. They hadn't moved at all. In fact, they looked almost comical, as if they were frozen there, waiting with the cart and the pony. "We never lied to our parents about our doings."

"Don't be too harsh, either of you." Esther's face took on a soft look, and Melinda thought again how much her friend had changed over the last year, since she and Tobias had wed. "They didn't lie exactly. They're *gut* children, and no doubt they thought they had *gut* reasons for what they were intending to do."

"I can't even imagine what they had planned—the three of them together. If it wasn't at your farm, Melinda, and it wasn't here, I'm guessing it was in town." Deborah looked at Martha, who was now on the porch, holding baby Joshua.

"And did we stop them, or did we merely change their plans until they can come up with another idea?" Melinda knew her boys. They were good boys, faithful to a fault, and incredibly stubborn. That was the look she'd seen on their faces—not shame, but stubbornness.

Which worried her more than the thought of their lying to her. The question was, stubborn enough to do what?

Chapter 21

DEBORAH STOPPED by her mother-in-law's farm on the way into town. Ruth had baked dozens of small, single-serve-sized cakes during the past two days. The kitchen smelled of cinnamon, lemon, apple, even blueberry. Deborah wanted to sink into a chair, accept her offer of coffee, and forget the troubles waiting in Shipshewana.

But she had offered to drive the desserts to the festival. They would be sold in the family booth and the money would be put into Ruth's jar, which she kept for the grandchildren's gifts. Ruth and Abe had been blessed with eight children, all married — except for Stephen, who was only twenty years old — and Ruth's number of grandchildren had quickly grown until she found herself with a total of forty-two.

On the Sundays when they had no church meeting, the family met at Ruth and Abe's for lunch. After the meal, Deborah would often find Ruth in the barn or down at the picnic table Jonas' father had set up years ago. She would be surrounded by her grandchildren, young and old, telling them a story from the Bible. The way she told the Scripture, Deborah barely recognized it — there was always so much adventure and romance.

The Bible was full of such things though, and Ruth had helped Deborah see that over the years.

When she'd walked into the house and smelled the baking, Deborah thought of the stories, of the grandchildren, and of the jar her mother-in-law kept. Ruth had explained that birthdays and Christmas tended to take its toll on the family budget.

She'd helped Deborah start her own jar the first year she married Jonas—though her money didn't go toward *grandkinner* yet. Still, Deborah loved knowing that doing small things like making cakes or knitting blankets for strangers could bless her own family as well as the strangers themselves.

Ruth had heard about the murder of Mrs. Knepp, and she knew Callie was involved. She didn't look surprised to hear the situation now included Deborah.

"How do you find yourself in these messes?" Ruth asked as she helped carry the cakes to Deborah's buggy.

"I was wondering the same thing at five this morning."

"When you and Jonas were young and going through your *rumspringa*—"

"We didn't go through *rumspringa*. I was always an obedient child and so was Jonas."

Ruth didn't bother to contradict her. Instead she continued her story as if Deborah hadn't interrupted. "I prayed and comforted myself by knowing there would come a day when your life would settle down."

She pushed the box of cakes into the buggy, then stood back and straightened her apron. "I suppose I thought that day had come already, but maybe it hasn't."

Deborah cocked her head, studying Ruth and trying to decide if she was being scolded or not. All she saw in the woman she'd come to think of as her own mother was love and a healthy dose of concern, probably the same expression Deborah had worn questioning Martha on the way over.

The questioning had been brief since it had produced nothing.

Martha had stared at her hands and answered in single syllables. The girl was embarrassed and remorseful but tight lipped.

Kissing Ruth's cheek, Deborah said, "*Danki*." Then she walked around to her side of the buggy and called out to Martha, who was in the barn visiting with Abe.

"For what?" Ruth asked.

"For always caring about us. For stepping in when my *mamm* passed away. And for not trying to talk me out of helping my *freinden*."

"Would it do any good?"

"No."

"Wouldn't be the right thing to do either, though there's always a temptation to protect one's own."

Martha walked out of the barn, holding her grandfather's hand.

"She favors you."

"I worry about her. She's still a child."

"Eleven years old. Sixth grade now?"

"*Ya*, but—"

"Two more years, and she'll begin to decide what type of work she'd like to do. Her quilting is *gut* like yours."

Deborah shook her head. "Seems yesterday she was building blocks on that first quilt you gave me."

Martha and Abe had stopped halfway between the barn and the buggy. They were leaning over the pasture fence, feeding an apple to one of Abe's horses. Ruth moved closer and put her hand on Deborah's arm.

"It's natural to want to protect them while you can. I wouldn't tell you not to, but you can also trust Martha. When I said she favors you, I meant more than in how she looks. She has a *gut* head under her prayer *kapp*."

Deborah was tempted to leave Martha at her in-laws', but then her daughter started telling Ruth and Abe all the things she planned to see while in town at the festival. Suddenly Deborah was eleven again, with all of her life still in front of her, and she couldn't disappoint Martha in this.

Surely it was safe or Shane would have told them.

Surely it was safe or she'd know in her heart it wasn't.

Deborah worried less as she directed Cinnamon toward the festival. The roads were busy, but with the smell of the cakes in the seat behind them, both she and Martha were smiling by the time they delivered them to Jonas' sister Kate.

Kate thanked them, then asked if Martha could stay awhile and help in the booth, as Deborah knew she would.

"Can't see why not." Deborah wasn't sure how much Kate had heard about the murder, but she knew her sister-in-law would keep a good eye on Martha. And like Ruth had reminded her, Martha was almost grown.

They talked for a few more minutes, and Deborah felt the tension leaving her shoulders as she watched the tourists, musicians, artists, and vendors. Fall Festival had always been one of her favorite times of year. Maybe this weekend would end on a good note after all.

Maybe they had blown the danger out of proportion.

Deborah walked through to the back of the booth, exited out the flap in the canvas, and climbed into her buggy. Martha was standing near Kate's oldest daughter, Sharon. Perhaps that's what Martha needed.

A little time to visit.

A little time without any responsibilities.

As she turned Cinnamon to go, she looked back and saw Martha and Sharon dip their heads closer together, as if they were sharing a secret. Sharon was a sweet girl, if a little wild. At sixteen, she was definitely in her *rumspringa*.

As she watched, though she couldn't be sure, Deborah thought she saw Sharon hand Martha something. Whatever it was, it looked like Martha slipped it into the pocket of her dress.

Aaron reached down for the chicken closest to his chair and received a sharp peck on his hand.

What had he expected? It wasn't a chick. Grown chickens pecked. His *daed* had warned him as much.

His *daed* had warned him about a lot of things.

Aaron looked around the chicken coop. Funny how nothing had changed. Looked the same as it had yesterday morning and the day before that. Same as it had last week in fact, before Creeper had come into their lives.

Aaron was the one who felt different—like those boys who had changed on the long cattle drive with John Wayne, maybe he was changing too. Maybe something inside of him had shifted when he'd seen the murder.

Scattering more feed on the ground, he rolled his chair away from the gate so the fowl would follow, then spread the rest of the feed.

His *mamm* had caught them. Didn't matter how. She had a sixth sense about such things. One thing Aaron knew—he and Matt wouldn't be going to town today unless they were with their *dat*, and that prospect didn't seem likely.

His *mamm*'s words to his *dat* still rang in his ears. "Seems the boys told you one thing and me another."

"We didn't say—" He'd stopped there, the sentence half out of his mouth. The look from his *daed* had silenced him quickly enough, and the expression on Matt's face told him it would be wiser to stay quiet.

His *daed* hadn't asked any questions at all. But his *mamm* sure had. She'd questioned them for a full ten minutes before they'd left Reuben's. Finally she'd allowed Matt to drive the cart, but insisted Aaron ride in the buggy with her and Hannah. He'd been afraid she was going to question him more, but she hadn't. The hurt look on her face had been even worse than her questions.

He'd almost broken down then, told her they meant to help. And they would help too, because they had to. But he remembered what Matt had whispered to him as she'd stood between the barn and the porch with Deborah and Esther. Matt had said, "Don't tell them our plan. No matter how badly you want to. If you tell them, you'll feel better, but we won't be able to help. Helping is more important than feeling better."

So in the end he'd sat beside *Mamm* in the buggy and felt worse than during his toughest coughing spells.

"Sounds as if they should spend the day with me," his *dat* had said.

"I'll take Hannah to your *mamm's*. I was planning on going to the shop this afternoon."

"*Ya*. Figured you might." Then he'd kissed Hannah and squeezed Melinda's arm—Aaron noticed he was always doing little things like that, as if his parents had this unspoken language between them. "Come with me, boys. There's always plenty of work."

And there had been. Aaron had never considered himself pampered, but he couldn't remember a day when he'd worked as hard as this morning. He'd actually been happy when his *daed* had pointed to the chicken feed. "Not sure that I fed them well enough this morning. Why don't you go and check on them."

It was probably an excuse to give him a rest, but Aaron wasn't about to call him on it. The day had grown warmer, and the chicken coop had a few areas of shade.

But when he was done feeding the chickens, he had to move out of the coop and to the barn. His next chore was to wash three pair of work boots—two were his *dat's* and one was his *bruder's*. Aaron found them sitting near the barn door next to a large bucket of water and a brush. Great. Maybe he could fall into the water and cool himself off.

If this was the price of rebellion, a single act would suit him fine. Settle this one situation with Mrs. Knepp's killer, and he'd walk the line for the rest of his years.

He picked up a boot and a brush, wondering what would happen if he soaked the boot in the water. When Matt touched his shoulder he almost threw the boot in the air instead.

"Little jumpy, aren't you?"

"Make some noise instead of sneaking up on a guy."

"Guess you were pretty focused on that mud."

"There's plenty of it to focus on. Think you could manage to walk around it next time?"

"Be glad you're working with boots and not horses. At least a boot will stand still for you." Matt leaned against the barn wall and studied him. "Having second thoughts?"

"No. Are you?"

"'Course not, but we're going to have to change our plans. They're not going to let us out of their sights today."

"I figured as much."

They both considered the implications of that for a few minutes. Almost against his will, Aaron's mind went back to John Wayne.

Justin called him The Duke.

He'd watched two movies starring The Duke. In both of them The Duke had been in a lot worse fixes. He'd certainly had to do worse things than feed chickens and clean muddy boots.

The Duke had fought terrible weather, fought bears, even fought bad outlaws.

"Whatcha thinking about?" Matt asked.

"Thinking this is nothing. We need to find a way to take care of the Creeper before he hurts someone else."

Matt smiled and plucked a tall weed, began chewing on it. "We'll get our chance, long as we keep our eyes open. That's why I told Martha to go ahead and pick up the cell phone. We need to be ready. If we do our work and keep our heads down, everyone will think we've forgotten whatever we had in mind. That's when we'll go after him."

As Matt turned and walked back into the barn, Aaron continued scrubbing the boot. He didn't want to leave the job half done if their chance to square things with the killer did pop up. Anything could happen in the next few hours.

One thing seemed certain.

Creeper's minutes were numbered.

Aaron could feel it.

Chapter 22

THE CROWD GATHERED in her quilt shop on Saturday was larger than ever. Callie peered out over the register and spotted Gavin in the reading corner. He once again wore his elderly guise, but this time he was dressed as a golfer waiting on his suburban wife. She wondered how she could have fallen for it before.

He was so obviously not old—she was pretty sure she could see the outline of his shoulder muscles through the polo shirt, now that she knew what to look for.

Still, from a distance, she supposed the clothes and makeup might work. Especially if the killer wasn't expecting an undercover cop to be in the store.

Swapping places with Perla had been remarkably easy. Perla had carried the trash to the alley. She was just setting the garbage cans out when the trash truck pulled up. Callie jumped off the truck Shane had put her on, and Perla jumped on in her place. The garbagemen emptied her cans and waved as usual.

It all happened so quickly Callie found herself wondering if she'd dreamed the entire thing. Except Max wasn't here by her side. Proof the nightmare was a reality. She smiled at the couple she was checking out, then glanced past them to her office. She'd gathered together a bag full of treats for Max and couldn't wait to take it to him tonight.

Except someone was in her office, bending over the bag.

"Hey. What are you doing?" Callie rushed around the counter to confront the woman.

A few inches taller than Callie was, with platinum-blonde hair tucked under a wide-brimmed, purple hat, the woman who glanced up couldn't have been older than thirty. She looked at Callie in surprise, her purple-tipped, manicured fingers going to her lips to stop a giggle from escaping—a giggle that sent a shiver zipping down Callie's spine.

She'd heard it once before, when the culprit had first called.

"Why are you in my bag? Why are you in my office?"

The woman pushed past Callie, barreling her way to the door and out into the late morning sunshine.

Callie ran after her, determined to catch one half of the Creeper-Giggles team. But the woman was already vanishing into the crowd that lined the streets, vanishing among the folks who had come to enjoy the festival.

Someone was pulling on Callie's arm, holding her back. She fought to yank free, but Gavin's voice in her ear stopped her. "Stay here. Call Shane."

He disappeared into the crowd, chasing the woman in the purple hat.

Lydia handed Callie her phone before she could ask for it. "Can you still see her?"

"No. I'm too short."

"Stand over there. On the bench."

"Would you go back inside and help the customers?"

"*Ya*, but be careful."

Running down the sidewalk to the bench, Callie excused herself as she stepped up beside an old man who was feeding pigeons. Her fingers had already found the buttons to hit in order to speed-dial Shane.

"Are you okay?" Shane asked.

"I'm fine. She was here. The woman who's helping Creeper."

"At the shop?"

"Yes, but she pushed past me and ran outside. She's headed north on Main. Gavin is chasing her. I can still see her—"

The old man on the bench scooted over and nearly knocked her off the bench.

"Excuse me, sir. I'm trying to see something here."

"Pigeons still need feeding."

"Stay focused, Callie. I'm leaving the police station now. Describe what you're seeing."

"I'm trying. She's in front of the food tent—Sir, if you hit me with any more of those bread crumbs I'm going to have to ask you to leave."

Grumbling, the old man returned to feeding the birds.

"Shane, she's past the music tent. I can barely see her purple hat—I'm serious, sir. The bread goes on the ground, not on the bench. Shane, can you arrest this man?"

"Can you see Gavin?" Shane was not easily distracted.

"He's followed her around the back of the barbeque pork tent."

"All right. I'm three blocks from you."

"Wait. She's come out the other side and now she's taking off across Main. I . . . I can't see her anymore, but—" Callie's breath caught in her chest. The birds continued pecking around her feet on the bench. She heard the old man cooing to them, but all those things faded, like a movie turned down to background noise.

"What's wrong?"

She jumped down from the bench, scattering the birds and causing the old man to stand and limp away.

"I never saw Gavin come out from behind the tent. I'm going over there."

"No, Callie. Stay where you are. Do not leave the shop. In fact, I want you to go back inside. Do you hear me?"

"Yes."

"Promise."

The words felt like pieces of glass as they left her throat. "I promise."

"I'll check on him. I'll be there in two minutes. You go back inside."

The line went dead, but she continued holding the phone, continued staring in the direction of the tent. All she could see now were hundreds of people. Gavin didn't appear anywhere in the crowd, and neither did the purple-hatted lady.

Finally she turned and walked back into the quilt shop.

Shane found Gavin lying on the ground unconscious with a four-inch gash across his forehead. Shane had already called in a description of the lady with the purple hat and available personnel were scouting the festival searching for her. Now he called for a medic on his cell phone, requesting that the emergency personnel park on the adjacent block and enter from the back of the building so as not to draw any attention. Then he called Captain Taylor. "Can you send Leroy to me?"

"Location?"

"Behind the barbeque pork tent on Main Street."

"We can have him to you in ten minutes. Who's the medic for?"

"Gavin."

"Status?"

"Four-inch laceration across the front of his scalp. He's unconscious, but his pulse and color are good. He was in pursuit of a woman Callie believes is our perpetrator's accomplice."

"I'll send someone to take Callie's statement."

"Better not. He might be watching."

"All right. How do you want to handle this?"

"I'll get the statement from Callie, but I want Leroy to gather fingerprints from the weapon."

"Which was?"

"A wood block."

"Say again."

"Wood block, Captain. You know. It's a type of musical instrument." When Taylor grunted, Shane shifted the cell to his left hand and held the pressure bandage he'd made from ripping off the hem of his shirt, applying steady pressure to Gavin's head, with his right hand. "Send Leroy in his personal vehicle. He's our best crime tech. We definitely have some footprints and if we're lucky, he'll score fingerprints as well."

"Already on his way."

Replacing the cell phone in his pocket, Shane studied the scene until the medic arrived. He hoped Gavin could be transferred without too much attention. The last thing he needed was gawkers and a crowd.

Once again he had the creeping sensation of a noose tightening. He hoped it was their perp's neck that was in the loop.

Thirty minutes later Gavin was conscious and being worked on by the medic.

"She can stitch it here. I'm fine."

Shane looked to Sylvia, who shook her head and showed him her clipboard. Fortyish with short, gray hair, she was what Shane's mom would call "sturdy." There was no nonsense about Sylvia. Shane had worked with her for at least five years — since she'd moved to Shipshe from Indianapolis. He'd seen her smile once — when Perla had slipped in the mud on the side of the road and sprained her ankle. Perla had been trying to help an Amish family who was broken down, but she knew nothing about changing the wheel on a buggy. She'd been one mad, muddy mess, and it had made Sylvia smile.

But most of the time, like right now, Sylvia was all business.

Turning her clipboard toward Shane she pointed to where she'd circled "possible concussion."

"Sorry, Andrew." Shane pushed the clipboard away. It was all he needed to see. "You have to get stitched up properly and have your head examined. I've been telling you that for years."

Sylvia's top lip twitched, but she denied the smile while she repacked her supplies.

"I can't believe I walked into her trap. I was a little behind when I followed her into the music tent and back out again. I was trying to catch up, came around the corner here, and that's the last thing I remember."

"Could have happened to any of us."

"Shouldn't have happened to me. Wouldn't have happened to me when I was enlisted. You slip up like that overseas, you come back wrapped in a flag."

"No one's wrapping you in stars and stripes today. Call the Captain when they're finished with you, and he'll send someone to pick you up."

He'd made it back to the Buick when the call came in over his radio.

"Black, we need you over here in the town's supply barn." Taylor sounded more grim than he had since they'd found Mrs. Knepp's body.

"I was headed to the quilt shop to get Callie's statement."

"You're going to want to see this."

Shane was there in five minutes, and Leroy followed him. They didn't have an overabundance of crime techs in Shipshe, but if things kept up like they had this past year, the council might look at hiring more. Not a cheery thought for a Saturday in September. The town's barn was quiet this time of day. Most folks were downtown at the festival. The back area held animals that had been in the Saturday-morning parade. The front was a storage area reserved for vendors.

Shane had no trouble finding the crime scene.

This time there was an ambulance, though no lights were blinking. Leroy began setting up immediately.

Somehow Trent had managed to beat Shane there once again.

"Shouldn't you be photographing the gospel quartet performing right now?"

"Sorry, Shane. This story's going to take precedence."

"Can we subpoena his police scanner?" Shane said to no one in particular.

"Wouldn't do much good. I'm guessing he has a backup." Taylor handed Shane the preliminary witness report, nodding toward two teenage Amish boys who were sitting on bales of hay near the door. "Those two found her when they came in to clean up the area. Their uncle had told them to do it first thing this morning, but they'd put it off."

Shane handed the report back and moved closer to the deceased. "Estimated time of death?"

"I've been here less than three minutes. You think I can give you that?" Leroy didn't even bother looking up as he continued taking photographs of the woman draped over the side of the barrel. "It looks to me like someone drowned her in two feet of water by draping her over the side of the barrel and holding her head under until the life drained out of her body. Then she was left here."

"How long ago?"

"Can't know that yet."

"I think you can guess, which is all I'm asking."

"Her skin's still warm. No rigidity and only slight discoloration. It hasn't been long. Maybe thirty minutes." Leroy sat back on his heels. "Who kills a woman in an apple barrel? Look at this. He stopped and took a bite out of a gala. At least that's what it looks like. We have one sick *hombre* on our hands."

"Yeah. Bobbing for apples is dangerous business, depending

on who you're playing with." Shane walked over to the purple hat lying a few feet away.

Their thug had left an apple with a bite out of it and the woman's hat. Why? He wasn't even trying to cover his tracks.

Or had he been interrupted by the boys?

And why had he killed his accomplice?

The closer they came to the end of Creeper's path of destruction—and it would end when the festival closed; somehow Shane knew that—the more the questions piled up around him.

It wasn't the questions that bothered him though, it was the clock ticking down in his mind.

Chapter 23

MELINDA HAD BEEN HESITANT about going into town, but Noah had assured her—with a look and a touch—that everything would be fine.

She knew the boys would not leave the farm.

There was no doubt she could trust her sons to their father's care. Now that they were onto the boys' plans, Noah wouldn't let them out of his sight.

So why the feeling of uneasiness? The turning in her stomach was hard to define—like waking in the middle of the night and knowing she'd left something important undone. But what?

As she directed her mare Ginger through the line of traffic, she wondered how she'd ever find a parking spot.

Hannah bounced on the seat beside her. Melinda had planned to take Hannah to Noah's parents, but when she'd arrived at their house, it had been empty. Somehow she'd failed to remember they were both working at the festival this weekend. Too much was on her mind. She was forgetting things, and that wasn't good.

"Look, *Mamm*. Pretty. Look," Hannah said.

The booths were beautiful with their wares set out in colorful displays against the white canvas tents. Melinda spied everything from hand-carved birdhouses to homemade desserts to T-shirts.

Then there were the smells drifting from the various food booths. Melinda's stomach began to rumble in spite of her nerves.

She had not been able to do much eating since Mrs. Knepp's murder. The meal at Esther's last night had looked wonderful, but after she'd filled her plate she'd found her appetite had fled like the last of the afternoon's warmth.

Her mind kept going back to the body, the police officers, and her son's pale form huddled in his chair.

Driving past Callie's shop she noticed the parking lot was jam-packed. "Guess we're headed to the public parking area, *boppli*. Maybe we'll see your *grossdaddi* there. Seems he was working the ten-to-two shift."

"*Daadi.*" Hannah's grin widened. She dearly loved both of her grandfathers.

Melinda was glad she'd brought the stroller. She didn't relish carrying her baby girl back through the crowd. While Hannah was walking well, she usually gave out and started crying after a block or two at the most.

When they reached the public parking area, Noah's father directed them to a spot at the far side of the lot. It was shady, and he knew Ginger would rest peacefully there while Melinda took care of business. After talking to her father-in-law for a bit, Melinda plopped Hannah into her stroller and decided to cut across the back of the auction building rather than walk through the parking lot.

They were coming around the corner of the building—Hannah already nodding off in the warmth of her stroller, clutching her foursquare quilt, which she'd had since she was an infant—when Melinda heard a familiar voice coming from within the auction building. At least it sounded familiar, but she couldn't make out exactly what the man was saying.

She pulled up short, unsure what to do.

The voice was loud. The words blunt like nails being

hammered. The man sounded angry and hurt, and his words were spoken with a sense of urgency.

"You might have hidden the truth from everyone else's eyes—with your *Englisch* clothes, your tattoos and city ways, but you can't fool me. I know who you are."

"You know nothing."

"Is that right? Did we not grow up together? Has it been that long since we shared the same supper table?"

Melinda thought to push on. She knew it was wrong to listen, but the man's voice began to crack and break and she found her feet refused to walk away. Doing so felt as if she were abandoning someone in need, someone who was bleeding and crying for help.

"What do you think I'm asking of you?" the first man continued, the older one, the one Melinda was certain she knew. "Only that you come home."

"You think this is my home? I want nothing to do with your plain life."

"Then why would you come back?"

"You know why."

"I don't."

"That's a lie!" This voice, the younger one, Melinda didn't recognize, but it seemed she should. Something tickled the back of her mind, something she couldn't quite reach. The one thing she knew was this man intended his words to harm the other, like Matthew's rocks when he used his slingshot. Even if it was to kill a snake, he slung those rocks for one purpose—to injure.

Something crashed within the room of the auction house, and Melinda pulled back instinctively.

"It's not a lie. You know me better than that. I'll tell you another truth. You're going to wish one day you were doing these things you say you hate—working a field or sitting by the lake or worshipping with the family—"

"That shows how little you know me."

"I know you're caught up in this mess."

"What would you know of that?" This was said sharply. The man was surprised, and he waited for an answer rather than slinging more words.

Quietly now, calmly, in the Amish way, the older man spoke again. Melinda found herself praying his words would sway the one who was angry. "You haven't forgotten that families stay together. That we will stick with you, help you to find a way out."

"You will help me with nothing."

"*Ya.* If you'll let us, we will. All that's needed is the one thing. All that's needed, *bruder*, is for you to come back home."

"That place isn't my home. Hasn't been for years. You disgust me, Levi. You and your ways. It's why I left, and why I'll never come back." The voice she didn't recognize grew louder as the footsteps moved closer.

Melinda had barely enough time to pull Hannah's stroller back around the corner of the building before she heard the building's door open. As she pressed her body against the wall, pulled the stroller as close to her as possible, the door slammed shut.

Steps hurried in the opposite direction.

She waited to hear if Levi would follow, but he didn't.

Finally she peeked around the corner, but all she saw was the back of a dark *Englisch* vehicle parked at the corner of the cross street and a man hurrying to open the car's door.

Was the man driving it Levi's brother?

Was this the man threatening her son? The same man who had killed Mrs. Knepp?

It seemed the killer they were hunting for might be Amish after all.

She hurried in the direction of the quilt shop. She needed to call Shane. He needed to know the identity of the man in the auction house.

Esther once again helped clear the dishes from Reuben's table on Saturday evening. It seemed they were repeating themselves. Everything was looping back over the previous evening.

But nothing was the same.

Gavin's seat was empty.

Callie seemed more angry than frightened.

And Melinda acted as if she couldn't let her boys more than three feet from her side.

"I believe I'll take the boys out to play a game of tag with the other children," Noah said.

"But it's nearly dark." Melinda glanced out the window.

"Best time if I remember right." Noah's eyes sparkled with mischief.

The boys' attention swiveled from their father to their mother and back again.

From what Esther had gathered, Noah had worked them quite hard all day after they'd been caught not telling the full truth to their parents. The other children had already scattered, but Matt and Aaron still sat at the table with little interest in their dinner. It seemed they'd barely had the energy to lift their spoons from the stew to their mouths. Now they were sitting up straight and alert.

"Can we, *Mamm*?" Matt asked.

"Please?" Aaron slowly flipped the brake on his chair back and forth.

"If your *dat* thinks it's safe ... All right, I suppose so."

The boys never heard the last three words. They were away from the table in no time. It had always amazed Esther how well Aaron maneuvered the wheelchair. Through the wall of the barn, she heard Matt call out to the other children who had already moved to the other side of the barn. Giggles and laughter followed.

"Probably you'll be needing my help," Jonas said. Stopping

behind Deborah, he added, "It will do them *gut* to run off some energy before bed."

Esther slipped the first dish into the water. "It must have been a terrible shock for you, Melinda."

"*Ya*. What if Thomas had turned around and seen you?" Deborah stepped up beside them at the sink. "I don't think he would have hurt you, but—"

"Doesn't bear thinking about." Esther scrubbed the dish harder than necessary.

"I didn't actually recognize Thomas," Melinda admitted. "It was Levi's voice I knew. When I reached the quilt shop and called Shane, he figured out the second man was Thomas."

Shane called Callie to the table. "I want you to look at this," he said, unfolding a map of Shipshewana and the surrounding area on the table. "When Thomas calls tonight, we need to be ready. Follow the script, Callie. Remember you're talking to a man who has killed twice and may be willing to kill again."

Melinda jerked at the word *killed*, nicking herself with a knife she was placing beside the sink.

"Reuben has some Band-Aids in the cabinet near you, Deborah. Could you get her one?"

"Of course."

"Let me help you." Esther pulled Melinda's finger under the faucet, to the rinse side of the sink, and turned on the cold water.

"It's nothing. I should have been paying better attention."

"I know what it was. It still surprises me to hear Thomas' name as well. To think it's one of our own. To think he could have done these things..." Esther watched Melinda's blood trickle down the drain and tried to envision how this could end well.

"Reuben has a stack of old rags next to the Band-Aids. I believe they are freshly laundered." Deborah took Melinda's hand in her own as Esther turned off the water. When she applied pressure to the small cut, fresh blood poured out, staining the cotton.

"You gals have everything under control over there, or do I need to call a medic?" Shane asked.

"Are you all right, Melinda?" Callie glanced up, worry coloring her features.

"I'm fine. It's nothing."

Max padded over to check out the excitement. It amused Esther that Callie never brought her dog into any of their houses, but Reuben insisted the Lab be allowed into his home. He said it was a barn after all. Seemed fair that Max be welcomed in where cows and horses had lain for so long.

Esther thought Reuben's reasons ran deeper. She thought on some level Reuben was thanking Callie for the fact that he was free and able to continue his life where he was most comfortable, where he was meant to be. Reuben was a gracious man, even having become a father-figure of sorts to the boy who had not reported the death of the girl on Reuben's property. Now Samuel Eby was working in the RV factory north of town and had become a frequent visitor at Reuben's home.

"Max is checking on you, Melinda." Esther reached down and gave the Lab a scratch behind his ears. She'd never been particularly fond of dogs, but Max was different. His eyes seemed so expressive, as if he understood more than they could ever guess. "She's fine, Max. I promise."

Sniffing Melinda's dress once, Max turned and padded back to Callie. Turning in a tight circle once, twice, then three times, he lay down under the table, very close to her feet.

"How did Levi and Sadie take the news, Shane?" Esther wrapped the Band-Aid around Melinda's finger, then shooed her away to the table.

Shane glanced up from the map. "Quietly."

She thought he wouldn't say any more, but then he added, "He offered to help in any way he could. I think he wants this to be over, wants his brother safely caught. I did convince him to move his family to another relative's for the next forty-eight hours."

"Do you think that's necessary?" Deborah returned to the dishes and began washing.

"Better safe. We're going to direct Thomas to an alternate location — to here." He pointed to an *X* he had marked on the map, directly over an abandoned farmstead that had sat empty for more than five years. "If worst comes to worst though, Thomas may try to contact Levi tonight. I'd rather his family not be there."

"I still don't understand how you identified him so quickly," Melinda said, staring down at her bandaged finger.

"It's been a busy afternoon," Shane admitted. "You called from Callie's shop just as I was leaving the barn —"

"Where the girl was murdered." Callie's tone was grim.

Esther stopped even pretending to wash the dishes. Turning and resting against the sink, she watched her friends, which included Shane. And when had he joined that circle? Strangely enough, she could admit to herself that somehow he had — sometime in the last forty-eight hours Shane had become part of their circle of friends.

"You couldn't have saved her, Callie. Even if you had tackled her and managed to stop her today, he would have killed her later. No doubt he'd always planned on doing it. The question was when."

"But why?" Esther asked. She could in no way imagine any reason for one person to take the life of another. This woman, this Jolene Dowden, was apparently Thomas' friend. So why would he kill her?

"Maybe he didn't want to share the money. Maybe she knows too much, and he doesn't trust her. Maybe Thomas is mentally unbalanced and she angered him in some way." Shane ran his hand around the back of his neck, massaging the muscles as he did. "We might never know, but he was careless this time, which indicates he was in a hurry. The bite marks in the apple match his dental records."

"Bite-mark analysis?" Callie's voice rose in disbelief.

"It's questionable evidence in some cases, but Thomas had a capped tooth on the front right side. With Shipshe being a small town and given the emergency nature of the investigation, we were able to check with his dentist this afternoon. The bite marks match some dental work he had done as a teen—fairly conclusive evidence I believe a judge would accept."

Silence settled like a blanket over the group as they all considered the implications of Shane's words.

"Many Amish still don't see a dentist, but Mrs. Hochstetler insisted her children go." Melinda glanced around the room. "She was very modern about some things."

"The records were a perfect match," Shane reiterated.

"And you knew to check because of the conversation I told you about?" Melinda looked miserable.

Esther thought of making her a cup of tea, but something told her this was an ache tea wouldn't fix.

"Actually I was already checking into Levi's family. I had a man following him, but pulled him off for a moment when we were chasing Jolene. That was a mistake, as I lost Levi just before he went to meet with Thomas."

"You couldn't have known," Callie offered, but Shane stopped her.

"Last night when we showed Levi the pictures, I realized he knew our perp."

"If you all could have seen Levi's face." Callie ran her finger in a circle on the map. "He turned whiter than the cloth you used on Melinda's finger."

"When you repeated the conversation to me, when you remembered Thomas calling him *brother*, it helped speed up who we were looking for within our search parameters."

"It's been years since any of us have seen him." Deborah stepped around Esther and began washing the dishes. "I thought maybe Aaron's sketch looked familiar, but I couldn't place him. He's changed so much."

Shane continued rubbing the muscle along the right side of his neck. "What's odder is that he was so careful to cover his tracks one moment — wearing gloves and a mask — then almost arrogant and cavalier the next — leaving an apple with a bite taken out of it. I'm having a hard time getting a handle on Thomas."

Melinda and Deborah exchanged looks and Esther knew in that moment what they were remembering, because suddenly she remembered it too.

Melinda spoke up first. "Shane, just before Thomas left the community, his parents tried to convince him to stay in Rest Haven, over in Goshen."

Shane stared at the women. "That didn't show on his record."

"Because he refused to go." Esther spoke up, knowing the telling would be difficult for Melinda, who was closest to Elizabeth. It had been a hard time for the Hochstetler family. "By that time, Thomas was older — "

"At least eighteen," Deborah said.

"His mood swings were dramatic. They had seen several doctors." Deborah spoke quietly, those years coming back in full color now.

"Elizabeth often asked us to pray for him." Melinda stared down at her bandaged finger. "He'd be fine when he took the medicines the doctors gave him, but often he'd forget or refuse to do so. Then the moods would grow worse. Sometimes he'd become violent. Finally Adam, Thomas' *dat*, told him he either had to go to Rest Haven or leave. He chose to leave."

Shane pulled out his notepad and added a few notes. "He must have met Jolene after he moved to the city."

"Did she have a criminal record?" Callie asked.

"Misdemeanors, but her fingerprints showed up in the database. It'll help build our case once we're able to connect the two through apartment leases, phone records, that sort of thing."

"So you have a *gut* case." Esther looked straight at Shane. It wasn't a question. She respected his work. Respected what he'd been able to do and the way he'd done it.

"Yes, we do. All that's left is to catch him, and we'll do that tomorrow, if not sooner."

The words had barely left his mouth when Callie's cell phone began to ring.

She reached to answer it, but Shane's hand covered hers.

"Tomorrow morning, ten o'clock, this spot." He tapped the map.

Curling her left hand into a fist, she answered the phone with her right.

Esther wasn't sure if anyone else noticed the difference in Callie's attitude between now and twenty-four hours ago. Esther did. Maybe because she'd been through the grieving process herself, because she'd had someone die nearly in front of her eyes. So she recognized what was happening to Callie. What she saw as she watched Callie was something she'd felt personally.

Callie wasn't afraid anymore.

Now she was angry.

Chapter 24

As CALLIE PUSHED Talk on her cell phone, she had trouble separating the different emotions she was feeling. When this had all started, when she'd come back to her shop and found Mrs. Knepp dead in her parking lot, she'd felt shame. When she'd seen Max slump to the ground, she'd experienced real fear. And throughout this entire ordeal when she'd considered the possibility that anything might happen to Aaron, she'd faced absolute terror.

Perhaps then it was the exhaustion kicking in that would explain the anger coursing through her veins now.

She'd had it with this guy.

Who exactly was he to think he could walk into their town and turn their lives upside down?

"'Bout time, Harper. I was beginning to wonder if you were actually there."

"Of course, I'm here." She glanced at Shane, who was prepared to text Perla. She was again ensconced in Callie's apartment.

"I'm tired of waiting."

"Is that why you killed Jolene?" The words shot out of Callie's mouth before she had a chance to consider how Thomas might react.

"That's none of your business." Thomas' tone chilled considerably.

233

Shane began writing her a message. He pushed the paper toward her.

Don't antagonize him.

She turned the sheet over and pushed it back.

"Seems like it is my business, since I could be next."

The string of expletives that followed caused Callie to hold the phone away from her ear. Thomas finally calmed down enough to say, "Tell me where my money is, or your dog and your friends won't see their next festival."

"Is that the best you can do? Threaten my dog and my friends?"

Shane began scribbling madly and playing charades at the same time, but Callie couldn't have stopped if he'd slapped duct tape over her mouth. Her blood was pounding through her veins. All she could picture was the lady, first in her shop, then running through the festival tents, then dead, draped over the apple barrel.

Shane had brought her a picture to identify Jolene's body rather than have her leave the shop and go to the barn. It was a sight she wouldn't forget anytime soon, and it was one more reason she had stopped fearing Thomas and started planning a way to get even.

"I won't shoot your dog this time. I'll cut him open while you watch. I'll—"

"Ten a.m. tomorrow." She gave him the crossroads for the abandoned farm.

"What's to stop me from going there without you?"

"Have at it. The place is two hundred acres."

As she was about to hit End, he threw her one final curveball.

"Ten won't work for me, Harper. I'll be there at six tomorrow evening, and don't even think about bringing anyone with you. I don't know what's gotten into your Texan boots, but you better clean them out before we meet, or I'll take care of you the same way I took care of Jolene."

The line went dead before she could think of a retort or hang up on the sociopath herself. Or was he a psychopath? She hadn't decided. Determined to hurl the phone across the room, which would have at least eased the rage pounding in her temples, she pulled her arm back, but Shane was suddenly behind her—one one arm around her waist. His other hand he closed around her fingers, which were still wrapped around the phone.

"Breathe, Callie. Don't let him win." His words in her ear were the sound of a fall breeze outside her bedroom window, calling her back, but she could barely make them out. "Breathe. That's it. Relax."

She turned around, buried herself in his arms, and—in spite of her bravado with Thomas—she realized that was where she'd like to stay.

Twenty minutes later all of the adults were once again around the table, and Captain Taylor had joined them. Callie had calmed some. Having Taylor in the room helped. She'd come to think of him as a grandfather. She couldn't help but relax when he smiled at her.

"I want to thank you all for your help and your patience during this investigation. We could have proceeded another way, could have gone with more assistance from outside authorities, brought in SWAT teams and taken a very heavy hand, but Shane wanted to do it this way. He trusted using your help, and I think he was right. Shane, why don't you outline the next twenty-four hours."

"Basically your portion is done. I'd advise the women and children to stay here again tonight, as a precaution. Thomas has agreed to meet us at the abandoned farm at six p.m. tomorrow."

"Thought it was supposed to be in the morning," Reuben said. He glanced at Callie, but she shrugged and said nothing.

"Yes, that was what I was hoping, but now it's in the evening." Shane met Reuben's gaze, then glanced down at the map that was still spread out on the table.

"Why would that be?" Reuben asked quietly. "Why would he choose later if he's so interested in the money? Seems like he'd want to grab it and be on his way."

Callie glanced up in time to see the muscle in Shane's jaw tick. Reuben's question was a good one though. She had wondered the same thing.

"Two reasons I can think of. One is control—he doesn't like to be told what to do or when to do it. The other is that he wants to leave under the cover of darkness. Probably it's both." When no one argued Shane continued, "Since there's no church meeting tomorrow, you're free to go about your regular visiting."

"Where will Callie be?" Melinda asked.

"I've asked her not to go back to the shop until we actually have Thomas in custody."

"Stay with us, Callie. Stay as long as you need." Esther reached across the table and squeezed her hand.

"Thank you." The words seemed inadequate, but she didn't know what else to say.

"Perla is at the shop now and will stay there overnight. She'll leave early in the morning, before daylight, so she can't be spotted. At approximately five-thirty in the morning, she'll drive Callie's car to the abandoned farm."

"And you'll be there?" Jonas asked.

"I'll have men on the perimeter, and by midday I'll be stationed in the middle." Shane once again pointed to the map. "There's an old windmill here. We've already checked it out. The platform is good. He won't see me unless he looks straight up, but I'll have a good view of anyone coming or going. We have two guards stationed around the clock now, in case he tries to go in early."

"What about Andrew Gavin?" Noah asked.

Captain Taylor shook his head. "I put him on forty-eight-hour leave. The concussion was more severe than we thought."

"Gavin probably fought you on that decision." Reuben crossed his arms.

Callie hadn't had the chance to call Andrew. She would later. She felt terrible about the fact that he'd been hurt. Her anger against Thomas flared again, and she took a deep breath to calm it.

"You're right," Taylor admitted. "Gavin was upset, but in the end it was my decision. He's suffered a concussion and needed twelve stitches in his head. We have plenty of personnel, especially when you include the county officers who have been helping."

Callie studied each person in the room as Shane finished up the meeting. They'd been her friends before this nightmare had started on Thursday evening, a little over forty-eight hours ago. Now they were family.

Max rolled over, settling his head on the tops of her feet where they were placed under the table.

She owed them all so much: her life, her dog's life, the success of her business.

Now Shane was saying they were done. He was giving them a free pass, except something didn't feel right.

This had all begun with Mrs. Hochstetler, Levi and Thomas' mother, and she had involved them for a reason. Glancing up, she caught Deborah staring at her.

Was Deborah thinking the same thing she was?

Deborah nodded toward the door. As everyone stood and small conversations started, they slipped out into the night.

Maybe their part in this wasn't over after all.

Deborah pulled her around the corner of the building. "I know you're plotting something. What is it?"

"Mrs. Hochstetler involved us for a reason."

"The mystery of the quilts."

"Exactly."

"It's still not solved." Deborah pulled the strings of her *kapp* through her fingers. "Kept me awake last night, even after we studied them over an hour. I think she did put something away for her family and ..."

"Hurry and say it. We're nearly out of time, and Shane is clinging to me like flypaper."

"I think maybe she put some money back for Aaron. She seemed especially close to Melinda. Maybe she felt a kinship to Aaron."

"Because of his handicap?"

"That—yes, but also because of the son she lost. She recognized the fear Melinda lives with daily."

Callie was quiet for a moment, chewing on her thumbnail as she considered Deborah's words. "That angle actually makes sense. I hadn't thought of it."

A blackbird began singing loudly in the trees lining Esther's yard. Deborah was reminded that in spite of the complications in their lives, most of the world continued on its normal course.

"What are we going to do about it?" Deborah asked.

"I say we go over there."

"What?" Deborah had known from the moment Callie lost her temper on the phone that she was about to step off the path Shane had so carefully constructed for her. She didn't know Callie had something this crazy in mind. "Go where?"

"To Levi's. He lives in the original farmhouse, the farmhouse where Mrs. Hochstetler lived when she sewed the quilts. The answers are there. I'm sure of it."

"Callie. That's dangerous."

"How can it be dangerous? Thomas is going to be at the abandoned farm—surrounded by Shane and every police officer they've rounded up for this operation."

"*Ya.* I suppose that's true."

"We don't have to stay long. We'll go tomorrow afternoon, while everyone else is visiting. I've had so many casseroles the last two days I'm having trouble buttoning my pants."

Deborah looked down at her dress, smoothed it over her stomach to check her own waistline. It was nearly dark, but Callie must have seen the gesture because she started laughing. Then Deborah started laughing. Then they were both leaning against the side of the barn trying to catch their breath and quiet themselves.

"You're going to get us caught," Callie gasped.

"And you are acting like a child." Deborah wiped at the tears stinging the corner of her eyes, but she did feel better. Tears— even tears from desperate laughter—felt better than worrying. "So we go over in the afternoon?"

"For a few minutes, with the quilts." Callie glanced back toward the barn door. "Long enough to look around."

Everyone was walking out into the yard now. Deborah could see Shane from the light spilling out of the doorway, looking for Callie. "I don't suppose that would be considered trespassing. Would it?"

"I hope not. Shane's probably looking for a reason to pull out the cuffs so he can keep a closer eye on me."

"Didn't look like you minded the attention last night when you two were cuddling in the yard." Deborah hooked her arm through Callie's and began walking her back toward the group.

"I know I'm a hypocrite. You don't have to point it out to me."

"What are *freinden* for if not to provide a mirror?"

"Please tell me that's not a proverb."

"Nope. I made it up." They began giggling again, a sound that was equal parts exhaustion, fear, and silliness. Deborah noticed both Jonas and Shane gave them an odd look.

Didn't much matter. They had a plan, and it felt better than doing nothing. It also felt like the right thing.

The mystery of the quilts had been bothering her.

Chapter 25

THE NEXT AFTERNOON, everyone had cleared out of Reuben and Tobias' farm.

Aaron couldn't believe the swap had worked. He hadn't told a soul, but he had bumped into Miss Callie the night before . . .

He'd heard Max outside, and he'd snuck out to make sure the dog was okay. He was sitting on the back porch, in his chair, with Max at his side when she walked out.

"Come out here much?" she asked.

He liked that she didn't ask how he'd got out there. People thought he couldn't get around without help, but he could if it was something important—like Max. And he was getting stronger every day. Getting into the chair on his own hadn't been that hard tonight.

"He sounded like he needed a *freind*," Aaron explained.

"I guess he misses our place a little. To tell you the truth, I do too."

They sat there like that awhile, in the dark, one on each side of Max, and then Aaron remembered what had woken him up—before he'd heard Max. It was a dream about the movie. He'd actually been one of the young cowboys.

"You ever watch John Wayne, Miss Callie?"

"Sure. My dad loved The Duke."

"Can I ask you something?" When Callie nodded, he hesitated a moment, not wanting to sound stupid, not wanting to reveal too much, but curious. And who else would he ask? Finally he plunged forward. "Why did they call him that?"

Callie laughed, reached out, and rubbed the soft spot between Max's ears. "John Wayne said it was because he was named after a dog."

Aaron thought about that a minute, his hand deep in Max's fur. "No kidding?"

"No kidding."

"Huh." Since she hadn't called him on asking about the actor, he decided to try another question. "You ever watch *The Cowboys*?"

This time she took a minute to answer. "Oh, yeah. That was one of his best."

Aaron wasn't sure he wanted to watch any more movies at Justin's. Maybe he'd suggest they play Uno or Dutch Blitz next time. This movie had stuck in his head too much for his liking. He was glad that of the two movies he'd seen, the one he'd been chasing around in his mind had been one of John Wayne's greatest.

"To tell you the truth, I still watch some of those old movies every now and then. I like them more than the new ones. There's something about John Wayne that always reminds me of a better time."

"*Ya?*"

"Yeah."

"What did you like about him?" Aaron asked.

She again took her time answering. "Like when that kid died. I hated that part. I still do. But when John Wayne said ... What was it? Death can come for you ..."

"Anyplace, anytime." Aaron couldn't have stopped the words if he'd tried.

"Yeah. Anyplace, anytime. But if you'd done all you aim to do and if you'd done your ... What was it he said? If you'd done your ..."

"If you'd done your best."

"Right. Then you'd be ready for it. Or something like that." She didn't ask how he knew the part she'd forgotten, and she didn't ask if he needed help going back inside. She just said goodnight to Max and touched him on the shoulder.

And that was when Aaron knew he was ready for whatever happened the next day. Not because of what John Wayne said in some movie, but because of people like Callie and Shane and his family. Somehow he believed everything was going to be all right.

"We're going to have extra chores for a month," he muttered.

"If we aren't killed," his *bruder* reminded him.

"It's *wunderbaar* to see you two are so cheerful about our future. Now help me load Aaron's chair." Martha was trying to put it on the back of the cart but wasn't having much luck by herself.

Matthew hurried to help her.

Aaron squirmed in the seat to watch them. The farm was deserted. Everyone had gone visiting, which was normal for Sunday afternoon.

His *mamm* thought they'd left with his *dat*.

His *dat* thought they'd left with his *mamm*.

Why had it worked today when they'd been caught the day before? Maybe because everyone thought the danger had passed with Creeper going to the deserted farm, going where Shane had laid his trap. Maybe because everyone was exhausted. Maybe because he'd prayed all night it would.

One thing was certain.

Neither of their parents expected them to try such a stupid

thing again, not after yesterday's punishment. His arms were still sore from working so hard.

But helping to stop the killer was more important than worrying about how harsh their punishment would be. What had started with them needed to end with them.

Matthew and Martha climbed up on the cart seat, and Matthew directed the pony away from the barn. They were about to pull out onto the lane when they heard a bark.

"Max?"

Trotting the cart over to the front porch they found the gold-colored dog tied to a tree. Water and food sat in the shade.

"Looks like someone else was forgotten," Martha murmured. "Miss Callie never would have left him here."

"Unless she was going somewhere she couldn't take him." Matthew stared down at the dog.

"What should we do?" Martha asked.

"I say we take him with us. Max is a *gut* guard dog." Aaron had stayed close to Max the last couple of days, when he wasn't doing extra chores.

"All right. We have enough room, barely. It's going to be crowded though." Matthew hopped down and helped Max into the cart.

They started down the lane, but stopped again when they saw Martha's *mamm* in her buggy pulled over a few feet shy of the main road. Matt directed the pony into some tall grasses and watched. Callie was sitting in the cart with Deborah. They were holding up a quilt as if they were studying it in the afternoon light.

"I thought they were gone already." Aaron turned to Martha as if it were her fault.

"They should be. They left a *gut* fifteen minutes ago. I thought they were following everyone else."

"Huh. Doesn't look like it." Matthew leaned forward for a better look. As they all watched, Deborah turned left onto the two-lane road. "Looks like they're going the opposite direction. Everyone else went to my *grossdaddi's*—to the right."

Matt said, "Giddyap," to the pony pulling their cart, hurrying to catch up to where they could see Deborah's buggy. They were almost to the main road when a Jeep pulled out with a screech. They could see where it had been parked across the road beneath some trees. The driver didn't look their way. He was completely focused on Deborah's buggy, gripping his wheel and scowling.

As he turned, he was close enough that they could make out his features.

"Why is he here? He's supposed to be at the abandoned farm!" Matt pulled down on his wool cap.

Aaron's stomach started to churn, and he thought he might lose what little he'd eaten. He heard his *bruder*'s question, felt Martha tense beside him. It seemed to him even Max's breathing changed.

But all Aaron could think about was the face he'd seen and that it was the same face that had stared at him on Thursday evening, the same face that had knelt over Mrs. Knepp. The same face that had tried to run over him with a car.

"What do we do?" Martha asked. "Do we still go to the abandoned farm?"

"Why? He's not going to be there. It's the same direction as my *grossdaddi's*. Creeper is following your *mamm* and Miss Callie." Aaron felt sick like the time he'd eaten six apples. "Why is he doing that? We heard Miss Callie tell him to go to the abandoned farm. We were sitting outside the window. Shane is there waiting for him. Who is going to protect Callie and your *mamm*?"

"We have to make a decision here, guys. I can barely see them."

"Our plan is to help catch the killer—I mean, Thomas." Martha clutched the front of the cart so hard Aaron noticed her knuckles turning white. "I say we'd better follow his car."

So Matthew turned left onto the two-lane.

At that moment, Aaron knew there was no turning back.

Melinda stared at Noah in disbelief. "What do you mean they aren't with you?"

"I thought they were with you."

"Don't tell me they did it again."

Noah checked her buggy one more time, as if the boys might appear. "Maybe they rode with someone else."

"It's the swap!" Melinda's cheeks turned a bright red. "Whatever they had planned yesterday, they're doing today!"

"Honey, stay calm. The festival is over. Whatever they had planned yesterday, they couldn't do today. Let's check with the rest of the family and ask if anyone has seen them."

Melinda tried to force the panic down into her stomach, but it refused to stay there. It kept finding its way back into her voice, her face, even her eyes.

Finally she convinced Noah to go with her to the phone shack.

"I'll look after Hannah," Esther said, moving baby Simon to her left arm so she could reach down and take Hannah's hand. "Deborah and Callie aren't here yet either. Maybe the boys are riding with them."

Melinda nodded as if that made sense, but it didn't make any sense at all. The afternoon meal was already starting. Why wouldn't Deborah and Callie be here already?

Once they were at the phone shack, she dialed the police station's number and asked to be patched through to Shane. The phone was slick in her hands and she clutched it tightly so she wouldn't drop it.

"Melinda, what's wrong?"

"I can't find the boys. Deborah and Callie are missing as well."

"What do you mean 'missing'?"

"I mean I can't find them. What do you suppose I mean 'missing'?"

"All right. I want you to stay calm."

"I'm sorry, but I'm frightened. What if something happened to them?"

"Where are you?"

"Down the road from my parents' place." She gave him the address. "We left to use the phone at the shack near the county road. What should we do? What if they're hurt?"

"Probably they're running late. I want you to go back to your parents', and I'm going to send an officer out. She'll have a cell phone, and we'll be able to stay in contact. I imagine by the time the officer arrives, the boys and Deborah and Callie will be there."

Melinda mumbled her thanks and hung up the phone.

As they made their way back in the buggy, she tried to find some comfort in what Shane had said, but she couldn't help thinking something terrible had happened.

"*Gotte* will be with them, Melinda. He's provided Shane to help us, and Shane won't let anything happen."

Melinda knew Noah was right. She felt it all the way into the marrow of her bones, so she did what was left for her to do — what was often left for a mother to do. She bowed her head and she prayed for the safety of her children.

Chapter 26

SHANE CLOSED HIS CELL PHONE, exhaustion drawing his face tight, and surveyed his assembled personnel. "That was Melinda. Her boys are missing. Deborah and Callie haven't shown either, but we need to stay focused on Thomas. We intercepted his cell phone conversation, and we know he's headed toward the abandoned farm like he should be."

"How many men do you want with you?" Taylor asked.

Shane studied the clock. Three in the afternoon. It would take Thomas over an hour to reach the designated spot from South Bend, which was where he'd been when they'd intercepted his last call. And that was if he'd left immediately after the call. Per his agreement with Callie, he wouldn't be in Shipshe for another three hours. "We're certain no one is at the farm?"

"Checked it myself an hour ago. No one's there, and we've had a man from county stationed at the front road since I left." Taylor pointed to a spot on the map where the lane leading to the old farm intersected the two-lane road. The map was actually a blown-up version from Google earth that showed each building of the property. "No one's gone in or out."

"All right. I walked the property yesterday. There's an old gate and a dirt road here." Shane pointed to the back part of the property. "It's bumpy, but manageable. Looks overgrown from the main road, and I'd like to keep it that way. If you could put a man back there on foot—"

"Done."

"I want to pull Thomas all the way in. Now that we're aware of his mental instability, there's an even greater danger of innocent bystanders getting hurt on the road. For some reason his mind has focused on the money."

Taylor studied him a moment before speaking. "He heard that his mother had died, saw the announcement in the paper … that certainly could have set him off."

"But set him off enough to kill?" Shane scrunched down another inch in the chair.

"Remember Mrs. Knepp was an accident. After that, his accomplice was probably killed in a moment of rage."

"We do know he thinks there's money hidden and that he won't stop until he has his hands on it. And we know he thinks Callie has it." Shane reached up and massaged the back of his neck. "As long as we're certain the place is empty, there's no danger in letting him drive up the lane. I want to position myself where I'll have good line of sight over the entire spread."

"Still determined to set up on the windmill?" Taylor tapped a spot between the house and the barn. "I know you checked it out, but I'm not sure it's the safest place. If he looks up, you're an easy shot."

"I'm willing to take that risk."

Taylor shook his head. "Seems too exposed."

"He won't be expecting me. There's no reason for him to look up there, and if for some reason he does, then I'll take the first shot."

"Why not find cover in the house or the barn?" Perla asked.

"I don't like their positions. If I choose one, I can't see what's happening in the other. Thomas has proven himself to be

248

cunning. I'm not going to underestimate him at the last minute. Once he's driven in, I'll call Captain Taylor, who will coordinate all personnel. It will be like pulling a trap tight."

"Where will your vehicle be?"

"I'll park it behind the old barn."

"You want men stationed inside with you?"

"No. Keep everyone else on the perimeter. I'll call you in when he's where I want him."

As the meeting broke up, Shane checked his pistol, then reached for his rifle, pocketing extra ammo as well.

"Planning on a gunfight?" Taylor stood studying him.

"Not planning on one, but I'm not going to back away from one either. Do you have a problem with that?"

Taylor didn't answer.

Shane could feel the older man's eyes on him, his expectations falling on his shoulders. Hadn't it always been that way though? Fulfilling others' hopes and needs was part of his job. Well, today his job required that he secure this town, which included keeping Deborah, Callie, and the boys from being hurt.

Thomas had already managed to get too close on several occasions. He wouldn't allow it to happen again.

The killing stopped today.

"It's not your fault he murdered the woman."

"Which one, Captain? The first or the second?" Shane looked Taylor in the eye, didn't glance away or blink when he saw the sorrow there.

"Either one. We can't control the things these people do. You know that. No matter how we wish things were different, we can't always stop them in time."

"Today I will. Yesterday I didn't, but today I will." Then he grabbed his ball cap—he'd need it if he was going to perch on a windmill—and walked out of the office to his car.

He told himself he wasn't doing this because of his past, that it had nothing to do with that scared little eleven-year-old boy he used to be. Regardless, the details of the night continued to wash over him as he drove toward the farm. He could no more have stopped them than he could have found a way to keep the afternoon sun from shining through the old Buick's windows.

It had been the middle of the summer, and the Cubs were still in the National League East. His dad had grown up in Chicago, and he'd been a Cubs man—still was a Cubs man.

As a boy, Shane watched Saturday games with his father every chance he had. Could still smell the microwave popcorn his mom would make, feel the way the old couch would sag under his dad's weight when he'd sit beside him. They'd been watching the game for over two hours when the knock came at the door.

Without saying a word, they'd run through rock, paper, scissors. Paper had covered rock—funny how he could remember that as if it were yesterday. It had fallen to him to answer—to miss out on the Cubs seventh inning at-bat. He hadn't argued. Instead he'd run to the door, expecting it to be a salesman or maybe one of the neighbor girls looking for their dog. They had two poodles and one or the other was always running off.

But as soon as he'd seen the shadow through the pane of glass lining the middle of the door, he'd known it wasn't one of the girls. When he'd pulled it open, when he'd seen the Shipshewana police uniform, Shane had known he wouldn't be seeing the end of the Cubs game. He still remembered being able to hear the announcers' voices playing in the background.

His dad had hollered something about the umpire being blind.

The officer asked him if his dad was home, and he'd nodded, but he didn't invite the man inside. Somehow he'd known, even at eleven years old, that once the man came into the house, his life—all of their lives—would change forever.

And it had.

His parents hadn't thought to send him out of the room, or perhaps it was their opinion that he was old enough to know the truth and know it from the source rather than hearing rumors. He'd never questioned them about that decision or any other that followed that fateful day.

He remembered being able to hear the Cubs game on the television still playing in the family room as they sat in the living room — a room he could only remember walking through before. His mother sat with her back ramrod straight and tears pouring down her face.

His father's hand had shaken when he'd reached out to hold hers.

And Shane, at eleven years old, had wondered how God could let tragedy strike his home. He'd wanted to go outside with his bat and smash something. He'd wanted to curl up and cry.

The officer — Officer Henry, the name popped into Shane's mind now as the abandoned farmhouse came into sight — had explained that Shane's sister, Rhonda, had walked in on a robbery. She'd stopped to buy some gas for her car and didn't realize the clerk was already dead. When she'd stepped inside the convenience store, the robber had shot her point blank. He'd fled the scene, but the owners had one of those new fancy security recorders. It was all on tape. They even had the guy's car plates. Roadblocks were up. With any luck they'd have the killer before dawn.

Someone would need to come down and identify Rhonda.

Shane rolled down his window, talked to the officer working security where the lane met the road.

"It's been real quiet." The guy was from Fort Wayne. He looked uncomfortable sitting back in the brush, his car hidden from view. "My partner's on the dirt road, the one behind the farm. He walked back there, like you said. No signs of any other car having been there either. This place is deserted."

"Good. When our killer shows up, you stay out of sight until I give the signal. Let him pass. We want Thomas as far into the property as possible before the confrontation."

The officer shot an uncomfortable glance over toward the high reeds. "Isn't this the time of year for snakes?"

"Too cool out. You'll be fine and back in town before you know it."

Shane slipped the Buick in gear and moved down the lane. He wanted to be aggravated with the officer whose mind wasn't totally on his assignment, but in truth his mind wasn't either. He was still back in his father's house, back in another time.

Perhaps that had been his first case.

The local authorities had arrested Spencer James within twenty-four hours, and they didn't need roadblocks to do it. He was holed up at a bar on the interstate, intent on drinking his way through every cent of the money he'd stolen from Skinny's Corner Stop. The man had been too drunk to offer much resistance—the weapon he'd used and cash-register bag he'd taken from Skinny's was still in his truck. The same truck that was on the video camera.

Open and shut case.

What wasn't open and shut was the hole left in the Black family.

The small lunch Callie had eaten tumbled around in her stomach like fireflies captured inside a jar. She hurried to catch up with Deborah as they made their way around the corner of the barn. Levi had left bales of hay strewn about, some still on the back of the wagon, others halfway to the door. The sun was headed toward the horizon, scattering rays through the fields.

Fields that were vacant of any movement.

Empty fields, empty yard and home, empty barn.

More than empty, everything in disarray. As Shane had promised, it looked as if everyone was gone. Levi and Sadie were at their children's home for the day. Hopefully by the time they returned later this evening, the matter of Thomas would be settled.

The unusual chaos was a reminder that they weren't merely taking a stroll on a farm or visiting on any typical Sunday afternoon.

"You still think we need to find the money?" Deborah asked. "Could be that he went for the trap. Maybe Shane has arrested him already."

"Maybe," Callie said. "But we're not here for Thomas. We're here to solve the mystery of the quilts." But worry continued to gnaw at her mind. Her instincts told her if they didn't find what Thomas wanted, and find it quickly, someone they loved was going to be hurt today. Which made no sense. Shane was taking care of Thomas. They were solving a different mystery. Weren't they?

"We've looked around the house and the animal pens," Deborah said. "How long do you think we should stay? We don't even know where to look next."

"The money, if there is money, could be anywhere on this property. I'm fairly sure this portion of the quilt refers to the barn," Callie whispered as she refolded the quilt. It was growing heavy in her arms. She would have liked to set it down, but there was no time.

"The last two places had clues in the stitching. We need to look more closely. Let's take it out into the sunlight where we can see better." Deborah pulled her away from under the eaves of the barn, out into the late-afternoon fall light.

Callie closed her eyes for a moment, feeling the warmth on her face. Had this all begun less than seventy-two hours ago? How much had she slept since then? Could she drop the quilt to the ground and curl up on top of it?

"He's coming!" Deborah squealed, pulling Callie out of her fantasy.

"Who?"

"Thomas!"

"What? Here?" Callie's pulse thundered in her veins as she swiveled her head back and forth.

"Yes. Be quiet, Callie."

They'd wandered too far from the barn's door, so they ran behind the wagon. It still held a few bales of hay, enough to hopefully hide their presence. She was growing dizzy from holding her breath. Surely Thomas could hear her heart beating.

He strode toward them, his rifle slung over his shoulder, a determined look on his face. He strode toward them as if he knew exactly where they'd gone, and perhaps he did. A pair of binoculars hung from his neck.

Callie recognized them in an instant, recognized the pink leather straps holding them around his neck. They had belonged to Mrs. Knepp.

She felt a righteous anger rising in her, an anger that burned away her exhaustion, and before she knew it she'd stood up, her head peeking above the bales of hale. Deborah jerked her back down.

"Those are Mrs. Knepp's binoculars. How dare he—"

"Sshh. He'll hear us!"

"But he already knows where we are. He's been watching. He's been following us!"

Before the matter of whether to stay hidden was settled, Levi walked out of the barn.

"Levi's not supposed to be here!" Callie fought to lower her voice.

"He must have stayed with the animals. Callie, it's not as if we're trespassing, not exactly. But we're going to have to explain to Levi what we're doing. We need to talk to him about the quilts and the story they—"

Before she could finish the sentence Levi walked between their location and Thomas, ignoring the look on his brother's face, ignoring the rifle Thomas pulled to the front.

When Thomas stopped and thumbed off the safety, Levi planted his feet and crossed his arms.

"Is that how it's going to be? You're going to shoot me with our *onkel's* rifle?"

"I will if you stand in my way, Levi. Don't test me." Thomas held the rifle at the ready, but stayed where he was—Callie guessed he was about five feet from Levi, and close enough to where they were hidden that she could make out the fact that he hadn't shaved in at least two days.

She kept her eye pressed to the gap between two bales of hay, unable to look away, vaguely aware Deborah was clutching her arm so tightly she'd probably have a bruise there tomorrow.

"These things you've done, you know they're wrong, Thomas."

"Don't call me that." Callie could see Thomas' finger move from the side of the stock to the trigger. "I go by T.J. now."

"Giving something a different name doesn't change it. I was there the night our *mamm* named you. I was also there the night she died and called out for you—"

"And were you there when they sent me away? Where were you then, big *bruder*?"

"They did no such thing, and you know it. They gave you a choice, and you chose poorly." Levi uncrossed his arms, his hands fell to his sides, and his head dropped. He looked so defeated that, for a second, Callie found herself wondering if he had suffered some sort of heart attack.

"I won't say it again." Thomas practically spat the words. "Get out of my way. I mean to have what is mine."

"And what is that, Thomas? A life of destruction? We all make decisions we regret. Must you make another? Come back, Thomas. Come back home, and we'll help you through this."

"I have murdered two people."

"And I suspect you will pay for that. The *Englisch* laws are harsh, but the killing stops here whether you turn from it or not."

Thomas repositioned the rifle. "Where's your family, Levi?"

"With *freinden*. I stayed alone. Stayed hoping I could talk some sense into you. Before you wouldn't listen, but you're out of options now. There's no one here but us, Thomas. No one for you to posture to. You might fool others into believing you're someone else—no longer the boy who once helped me with the hay, helped me with a hammer and a nail, but underneath you're the same."

Thomas laughed now. It was a harsh, broken sound. "Do I look like that same boy?"

"Your clothes don't make you different. That hunting rifle sure does not make you a different person. Come on back, Thomas. Come home. We'll find a way to make this right. We'll stand together."

"There is no *we!*" Thomas' voice exploded. "And I am not the child you remember—"

Callie thought he had been softening, that maybe there was a possibility Levi was getting through to him. She saw now that Thomas was unreachable. "Deborah, we have to get out of here."

"What?"

"While they're arguing. It's our chance to escape."

There was a possibility he wouldn't see them—if they kept the wagon between them, if they kept their heads down and moved quickly and quietly, if God cloaked them in his grace.

"Ready?"

Deborah nodded and laced her fingers with Callie's. They moved as stealthily as possible, placing each foot carefully on the ground so as not to make any noise at all. They'd crept to the corner of the barn before they heard the sound of gunfire.

Chapter 27

As THEY RAN, Callie tugged on Deborah's hand, pulling her to a stop on the path between Levi's giant barn and a stand of shade trees. "Let me catch my breath," she whispered.

"*Ya,* all right. But we can't rest here for long."

They stared at each other, eyes mirroring the same fears, the same questions. Deborah was the first to put it into words. "Who fired that shot?"

"Came from near the house. I think." Callie sank back against a tree and closed her eyes. Though she'd left her cell phone in the car, she didn't need it to guess the time. It had to be late afternoon. Darkness was still hours away, but she knew they needed to hurry, to do something. What were they doing here? What were they thinking? They should have stayed home like Shane had asked.

"Maybe it was an officer."

"Why would an officer shoot at us? Besides, they're all at the abandoned farm." Callie opened her eyes and forced herself to stand up straighter. At least she knew Max and all her friends were safe. But she and Deborah were here, and they didn't have very many options now. Two that she could think of. Hide or continue with their plan.

"Doubt whoever it was could even see us, unless they were

257

perched in a tree," Callie reasoned. "Probably they were shooting at Thomas."

"Do you think they hit him?"

"They didn't." Thomas stepped onto the path, his rifle held ready. "Drop the quilt and turn around. Both of you turn around and raise your hands up high."

Callie stared down at the quilt she'd forgotten she was holding, Mrs. Hochstetler's quilt, the storybook quilt. They'd left the other two in the buggy. This one was the final story panel. They had decided the night before that this one held the answer to the location of the treasure, if there was a treasure. And she was supposed to drop it in the dirt?

"Hearing problems, Harper?" Thomas centered the barrel of the rifle on her chest.

She looked him in the eyes for the first time and saw a complete disconnect from the reality around them. This wasn't a game for Thomas. It wasn't a treasure hunt either. It was his last hope.

Something long buried in the ground?

That was what he was banking on?

She didn't even realize she'd done as he directed and raised her hands until he smiled. "Now turn around."

His voice was low, even, but there was no mistaking that it was a command. Boots sounded against dirt, then he was standing in front of her.

He dropped a backpack on the ground next to her feet. "Unzip the main compartment and pull out the duct tape. Bind Deborah's hands behind her."

Callie noticed a look pass between them, but Deborah didn't speak.

Finally, Thomas said, "I'm sorry you involved yourself in this, Deborah."

"Mistakes are like knives, Thomas—"

"Would you be quoting the plain proverbs to me?" He laughed, but there was no humor in it. "My mistakes will serve me today. If they cut, it will be because you two did not do as you were told."

Callie looked to Deborah. She seemed awfully calm.

"Tape her hands together behind her. If she says anything else, put a piece across her mouth."

Hands shaking, Callie did as Thomas directed. He knelt in front of the quilt, picked it up with one hand, and studied it. "Why did you bring this? I was watching you. Why were you carrying it around and looking at it?"

When they didn't answer, he aimed the rifle at Deborah.

"It's a map!" The words exploded out of Callie. "We think it's a map your mother made. We were trying to follow it, to find the money."

"And where was it leading you?"

When she didn't answer immediately, he chambered a round.

"To the pond!" Callie shouted the first thing that came to mind. "We were going to the pond."

Thomas crammed the quilt into his backpack, a grin splayed across his face. "Never know when I might need an extra blanket. I'll just keep this now that we're making progress. My *bruder's* pond, huh? I guess you were lying to me earlier about already having the money. Now you're finally going to give me what I came for."

He directed Callie with his rifle, positioned her until she was standing directly behind Deborah, then he taped them together—back to back.

"Wait right here, ladies. I'll be right back. Then we'll go to the pond together."

Shane was growing restless sitting on the platform of the windmill. No sign of Thomas.

Empty lane.

Empty house.

He'd expected the man to show a bit early.

He pulled out his cell phone to call Captain Taylor, but before he could punch in the number the display lit up. It was a number he didn't recognize, and he almost let it roll over to voice mail.

Then he thought of his sister again, remembered the way Rhonda had looked that afternoon as she'd left for the mall with her friends—seventeen, long dark hair, and all her life in front of her.

"Black," he growled into the phone.

"Shane?" The voice was a whisper, so small he clutched the phone against his ear. "This is Martha. Martha Yoder."

"Martha? What's wrong?"

"We're at Levi's place. Thomas is here."

Shane slung his rifle over his shoulder and began climbing down the windmill immediately, carefully, with his one free hand. "I'm on my way, Martha. Does he know you're there?"

"No. He went back into the barn, and we're hidden—me and Matt and Aaron."

Shane's hands were sweaty, and he nearly slipped four feet from the ground. He needed to call the captain, and he needed to keep Martha on the phone. Running toward his Buick, he was glad he had parked behind the barn. It was close to the back gate. He always kept the escape route covered, even if it was a rutted dirt lane.

In this case, it provided a straight shot to Levi's place, and he would thank God for that before he fell into his bed tonight.

"Tell me what you're seeing, Martha."

"Matt wants to talk to you." There was crackling on the line as the phone was passed from Martha's hands to Matt's.

"He showed up in a Jeep with a backpack and a duffle he pulled out from the passenger seat." Matt's voice was still angry, bitter, and still reminded Shane of himself.

"Did he go in the house?"

"No. At first he followed them around—"

"Followed who?" Shane started the Buick. Instead of slowing down for the old gate, he smashed through it and hooked a right. The officer who was supposed to be guarding the dirt road was nowhere to be seen. Where had he gone? "Followed who, Matt?"

"Callie and Deborah. We would have untied them, but we were afraid we'd be caught. We didn't think we had time. It seemed smarter to just stay in front of them, and we heard Thomas say he was headed to the pond next."

Shane prayed he'd misheard the kid. There was no way a case could go this wrong in such a short period of time.

"Did you say Callie and Deborah?"

"*Ya.* Hang on. Martha needs help with Aaron's chair. I'm handing the phone to him."

More crackling and it sounded like someone dropped the phone. Then it was picked up again.

"Why are Callie and Deborah there?" Shane asked as he fishtailed out onto the two-lane road. "And what makes you think Thomas followed them?"

Aaron's voice was smaller, quieter. "We heard Thomas tell Levi he put a bug in Callie's bag."

So that's what Jolene was doing in Callie's office. She had dropped a GPS tracking device in the bag filled with toys for Max, which Callie had carried to the farm. And the phone call from South Bend? Thomas could have paid any kid twenty bucks to place that last call. How had Shane underestimated this guy?

"What's a bug, Shane?"

"Don't worry about it, kid."

"Are you on your way?"

Shane heard everything packed behind that question. The fear, the desire to trust, and the uncertainty of what to do next.

"I'll be there in . . ." he looked at his wristwatch, "seven minutes. Can you three stay hidden for that long?"

Shane was barreling down the two-lane now, his siren blaring and his speedometer reading eighty. Hopefully one of the local law enforcement officers would pick up on the fact that it was him and radio Taylor for backup. He was not disconnecting from this call. He'd have to drop the cell phone to pick up his own radio, and he wasn't going to do that either. At the moment, he was the only life line these kids had.

Why were the girls on Levi's property?

"There's something we have to do. He's taking them to the pond. Do you know where that is?"

"I can find it, Aaron. But I want you three to stay hidden until I get there."

"Someone else is here. We couldn't see who it was. Thomas and Levi were arguing, then Callie and Deborah ran from the wagon to the barn, and then there was a gunshot."

If Shane ever had Callie in his arms again he'd never let her go.

Did she have any idea how dangerous Thomas was?

Did she have any idea how much she meant to him?

The steering wheel of the Buick felt slippery in his hand, but he gripped it more firmly. The distance between them was growing shorter with every minute. He would make it there in time. He had to make it there in time.

This was beginning to resemble Shane's worst nightmare. He was supposed to confront Thomas alone, with his men circled around the farm. How had so many people managed to involve themselves?

"Looked like the shot went wild," Aaron was saying. "Deborah and Callie started running around the corner of the barn as soon as they heard it, so I don't think they were hit. Levi rolled under the wagon and didn't get up. I don't know if he's okay or not. We were going to go back to check on him ..."

Aaron pulled in a deep breath, and that was when Shane remembered how sick the kid was, how hard this must be on him.

"But then we saw Thomas go after Deborah and Callie."

"What?!"

"*Ya*, and he was hollering at them about the treasure."

Shane realized this situation was going to be very complicated. Thomas was not worried about being caught. Apparently he also wasn't worried about being killed. He had one objective—the money—and he was willing to die in order to recover it.

There was a beep on his phone followed by crackling on his radio. Shane figured it was Captain Taylor. Still he wouldn't hang up on the kid.

"Why are you going to the pond, Aaron?"

"We have to get into position before Thomas gets there."

"I want you to wait for me."

"Can't." The reception on the call faded out, then back in again. "... we saw them."

"Saw who?"

"Callie and Deborah. We were watching, and Thomas must have decided the money was back at the pond. Guess that's why he's taking them there. When we left ..." Aaron pulled in another breath, and then Matt was back on the phone.

"When we left he was tying up their hands." Matt sounded calm enough, but a little out of breath. Why was he winded? "That gave us enough time to get ahead of them. We'll meet you at the pond. Hurry or—"

The line went dead before Shane heard the rest of Matt's sentence, but Shane didn't need to hear it.

Hurry or Thomas was going to kill Callie and Deborah.

He called Captain Taylor as he pulled onto Levi's property.

It had been Taylor who'd tried to beep in while Shane had been talking to the kids.

He gave the captain the sixty-second version, left it to Taylor to reposition their forces at Levi's farm, to put his team where he wanted them, including Perla, who had earned the right to be there. Shane didn't know what had happened to the girls, but he was convinced whatever was about to occur would be over by the time help arrived.

The girls and the children were in danger.

Unless Levi had found a way to intervene.

Shane suspected he knew the identity of the mystery shooter, but the odds of anything going their way in this operation were past calculating.

Shane wasn't a hypocrite, but he wasn't a fool either. As he made his way toward Thomas, as he hurried to help the people he cared about, he began to pray.

Thomas stepped out on the trail, pulled his knife, and cut the tape that bound Callie and Deborah together. He was careful to leave the tape around their wrists intact. Picking up his bag, he nodded toward the path. "Let's go," he muttered.

Callie almost stumbled as she hurried just ahead of Deborah. She wasn't nearly as frightened as she was angry. This man had bossed her around for entirely too long. He was large, but he wasn't a giant of a man like Reuben.

What made him intimidating was the rifle and the craziness in his eyes. The craziness she had dealt with before. Hadn't Stakehorn, the original editor of the *Gazette*, been more than a tiny bit off? And Gordon Stone, the man who had killed him, hadn't been entirely sane—though he'd insisted he was merely doing his job.

Then there was Ira Bontrager. He was a sweet old man, but he'd had moments that weren't lucid.

Callie had plenty of experience dealing with folks who were one slat short of a fully functional rocker.

No, Thomas' craziness wasn't her main problem—the rifle was.

Good thing she'd taken a self-defense course.

She needed to wait for something to divert Thomas' attention, then she could rush him, knock the rifle out of his hands, and keep it out of his reach.

Which would be hard to do with her wrists taped tightly together behind her back.

Hard, but not impossible.

She couldn't help herself. She stole another glance at Deborah.

"Don't look at her. She's my insurance that you'll do what I want. Now both of you—keep walking."

As they stumbled along the path leading back toward the pond, Callie felt as if her senses were on high alert. She was aware of every bird settling in the brush, the way the sun's light filtered through the western trees, and especially the hammering of her pulse in her eardrums.

No way she was going to die at Levi Hochstetler's pond.

Her mind drifted to thoughts of Shane. *Was he in love with her?*

The question popped into her mind with the force of a firecracker blazing into the sky on a pitch-black July night.

She'd pushed the entire notion of love away because she thought she wasn't ready.

Ready?

She suddenly realized you only had to be alive to be ready.

A beating heart qualified, and she had one—for now.

What had she been waiting for? Why hadn't she told him how she felt? Why hadn't she admitted she was scared? That she didn't want to dive into life and be hurt again, be left alone again?

Why hadn't she rested in his arms while she had the chance?

God had given her so many opportunities in her life, and she had pushed them all away. She had slapped at his hand like a spoiled child, never satisfied. If she called out to him now, would he hear?

She slowed on the path, just ahead of Deborah, Thomas behind them both. Slowed and glanced back in the direction of the barn and then toward Deborah.

"Keep. Walking." He punctuated each word with a small shove. "I don't have a lot of time."

Deborah's eyes met hers, and in that moment Callie knew her friend was praying.

In that moment, she also knew it was the one thing that could possibly save them, because Thomas Hochstetler was certifiably insane. He'd stop at nothing to recover his mother's lost treasure.

They'd been over the quilts late last night and again this morning. And they'd confirmed the treasure was not at the pond before everything had fallen apart. A water source certainly did have something to do with the treasure — that was what they were looking for.

But one thing was certain.

The treasure wasn't at the pond.

Chapter 28

It seemed to Aaron that he could still hear the sound of the rifle shot echoing across the hills.

"Wonder who did the shooting." Martha's eyes were wide with alarm, but Aaron knew she couldn't be nearly as frightened as he was—her heart couldn't be hammering in her chest like his was or she'd sit down in the dirt.

"We need to focus on what we came here to do." Matthew struggled over the final hill with the wheelchair.

Martha led Max, who acted as if he were on a romp down Shipshewana's Main Street.

"No one's having second thoughts, are they?" Matthew sounded grim, and Aaron knew what he was thinking. He was thinking about Mrs. Knepp and that other lady—the younger one who had been found in the apple barrel.

"'Course not," Aaron said, then he wondered if he said it a little too quickly.

"I'm not either." Martha jogged beside them to keep up. "It's only that my *dat* is going to kill me if one of us gets—"

"Killed?" Aaron's and Matt's voices were perfectly matched in pitch and sarcasm.

"All right. It sounds stupid, but you know what I mean."

"*Ya*, we know. That's why we're going to be careful. He'll be coming this way. We know it because we overheard what he said to Miss Callie. We also know he'll bring your *mamm* and Callie with him. At least it sounded like he would as he tied their hands. No one else will be in the way. This is our chance to catch him. Our chance to fix what started three nights ago." Matt positioned the chair in an alcove surrounded by trees and small bushes.

"It'll be worth the trouble we're going to be in," Aaron agreed. He pulled in a deep, steadying breath. "It'll be worth it to end this."

Aaron was surprised to find he meant it. He'd never been so ready to have something over with. Until this moment, he'd always thought the worst thing in the world was chicken breast disease. (That was how he thought of it—and maybe why he didn't mind doing the chores out in the chicken coop, after all it wasn't the chickens' fault.) He'd been certain it was the worst thing he'd have to live with.

Now he knew it wasn't.

Disease was something you learned to deal with, like rain on the way to school or an overly hard homework assignment. It was something that maybe was *Gotte's wille*. He wasn't sure. He wasn't old enough to figure that out yet. He'd been this way as long as he could remember—struggling for breath, his body tiring out before his mind did, dependent on others.

But even Matthew was struggling for breath right now.

His *daed* tired out before he was done with the day's work, and sometimes he had to stop to rest under the big tree at the far side of the fields.

And Miss Callie was depending on Shane to keep her safe from Thomas Hochstetler.

Maybe he wasn't so different from everyone else after all.

Could be *Gotte* would even see fit to heal him at some point.

Or maybe he wouldn't.

If there was one thing he'd learned since watching Mrs. Knepp fall face first into the parking lot of Daisy's Quilt Shop, it was that he did appreciate each and every day that he awoke alive and well. *Gotte* had given him that, and it was a gift for sure. The fact that he had this disease didn't keep him from counting a day as a good one.

"Everyone remember what they're supposed to do?" Matt asked.

"I'm staying in the bushes with Max until you signal for me to release him." Aaron put one hand on Max's head. The dog settled beside his chair.

"I'm going to be positioned on the north side. If anything goes wrong, I'll head back the way we came until I pick up a signal on the cell phone." Martha pulled it out of her dress pocket and checked it one final time. "Nothing here."

"We expected that. Head on back until it works, if we need it. Hopefully we won't. I'll set up on the south side and have my slingshot ready." Matthew glanced around. "You're sure Max will stay quiet, Aaron? We can't have him giving us away."

"I'm sure. He follows hand signals real well."

"All right. If things go as planned, this will all be over by the time Shane arrives. Tonight we'll be back at home playing Dutch Blitz."

"When have things gone as planned? Not since this started," Martha muttered as she hurried off to hide in the bushes on the north side.

Max settled beside Aaron's wheel, and Matt ran around the pond, to the south. Then they all waited. From where Aaron hid, he could barely make out Matt's shirtsleeve and the white of Martha's *kapp*. He didn't think Thomas would be able to see them unless he looked right at them, and Aaron had a feeling Thomas would have eyes for one thing: what lay directly in front of him.

How could he believe treasure would be hidden near a pond?

It didn't make sense to him that a quilt would even tell a story—books, yes, but not a quilt. Where would old Mrs. Hochstetler even have hidden money out here?

He began looking around, trying to puzzle it out. Unless maybe Callie had made the entire thing up. Maybe she had wanted to move Thomas away from the house, away from Levi so he could go for help.

The pond was surrounded by a few large boulders. Mrs. Hochstetler could have buried something under one of them, but she would have needed help. She couldn't have moved one by herself. She wouldn't have submerged a treasure in the water. Would she? Could something remain in water all these years and not be ruined?

He was so busy turning the questions over in his mind that at first he didn't hear anyone approaching, didn't hear the voices in the distance. But he did notice when Max sat up and pressed against the side of his chair.

Aaron didn't say anything to the dog. Instead, he put his hand on the top of Max's head to quiet him.

Max seemed to understand. He looked up at Aaron, his eyes round and worried.

Gavin met Shane's car as he pulled on to the property.

"Did you fire the shot?" Shane asked. "And why aren't you at home?"

"I've been watching over Levi since yesterday. And yes, I fired the shot." They hurried toward the barn as Gavin explained. "I had to do something. The situation was escalating."

"Current status?"

"I don't know. I heard the call over the scanner for all personnel and called in. Taylor told me to maintain my position until you arrived."

"Hold here and scan the area." Shane hurried toward Levi, who he could see was still crouched under the wagon. Apparently he'd been hiding there since Gavin had fired his weapon to scare Thomas off. "Are you all right?"

"*Ya.* I wasn't sure who was firing."

"Gavin did that. The situation seemed to be spiraling out of control, and he wanted Thomas to back down." Shane knelt by the older man as he checked his weapon. "He explained to me that he's been staked here since Taylor put him on forty-eight-hour medical leave. Good thing he was. His shot scared your brother away from you."

"For all I knew, that crazy *bruder* of mine had another accomplice—one he hadn't killed yet." The words might have been said with some bite, but there was defeat in the older man's eyes. He stood, took a step, and cringed.

"What's wrong with your ankle?"

"Twisted it is all. Don't worry about me. I'll be fine."

"We'll help you back to the house, then I'll go after Thomas."

"He headed to the barn." Levi placed an arm around Shane's shoulder and began limping toward the front porch. "I tried talking to him. For a minute . . . for one minute, I thought I was getting through. But then that stubborn look came over his face, and I knew I'd lost him again."

Shane needed to be on that trail headed toward the pond. He motioned to Gavin for help. None of Taylor's men had caught up with them yet. Gavin jogged toward them.

"Did you see the girls again after they took off around the corner of the barn, Mr. Hochstetler?"

"Girls? What girls?" He stopped in the open area in front of the house, about twenty feet from the steps.

"Callie and Deborah," Gavin answered, moving to support Levi on one side. "They were behind the wagon. As you were talking to your brother, they ran around the west side of the barn. You didn't see them?"

"No. Your shot rang out, and I hit the ground. Didn't see anything except dirt."

Shane started shifting Levi's weight from his shoulders to Gavin's, and they'd just turned him toward the house when, suddenly, the barn exploded. Debris flew into the air and came raining down as far as the steps of the house. Hay, pieces of boards, and nails showered around them. Gavin and Shane forced Levi to the ground in one motion, covering him with their arms.

When it seemed the pieces had stopped falling, Gavin began checking Levi for injuries. Shane pulled out his cell.

"The main barn structure is on fire. We're going to need assistance from Shipshe, Chief."

"We're almost there now. I'll alert the fire department. Are there any casualties?"

"No." Shane disconnected, ice running through his veins. One look at Gavin confirmed that he could handle everything happening with Levi.

"I've got this. His injuries are minor." Gavin had already begun ripping his shirt and pressing it to the gash on Levi's forehead.

"Levi, did you have horses in the barn?"

"No. They were all in the pasture today." The man looked dazed, grim.

Gavin met Shane's gaze. "He's in shock. Go on, Shane. Go and find Callie and Deborah."

Shane skirted the barn at a trot, rifle in hand.

Whatever explosives Thomas had used had done their job well. A gaping hole now adorned the center of the western wall, and flames shot out of the roof. Fortunately they'd had rain recently. The wet grasses surrounding the barn would keep the fire from spreading.

As Shane ran down the path behind the barn, he realized how lucky they were.

Was it luck? Or had God intervened? His eleven-year-old heart fought with the faith of a man, fought and lost.

No one was trapped in the barn. Shane was sure of that. The trail was covered with fresh footprints that led away from the structure, led toward the pond.

And why had Thomas blown up the barn to begin with?

It attracted attention, drew more people to the area, and added to his list of crimes.

Through the trees, Shane spotted Levi's horses in the pasture. Then he glanced down and saw what he had hoped he wouldn't see. He knelt on the path and checked, checked to be sure he wasn't wrong.

But he knew he wasn't.

The thin steady lines, approximately two feet apart, ran steady and true. They ran straight toward the pond, and there wasn't much doubt in his mind as he hurried to catch up as to what they were.

Marks, left by Aaron's wheelchair.

He shouldn't have been surprised. The kids had told him where they were going—they'd been determined to confront Thomas—but Shane's heart still sank. He ran faster, skidding to a stop when the pond came into view.

As with every investigation, he was intensely aware that one mistake on his part could lead to someone's death.

His mind took it all in, everything in front of him, and his heart wanted to rush ahead, to take the lead. He pushed the urge back, took a knee, and forced his heart rate down.

Silently he slung the rifle around to a shooting position and peered through the scope. There was the smallest of clicks as he released the safety, but the cry of a hawk covered it.

Deborah stood in front of him on the trail, her hands bound behind her. As he watched, Martha crept forward and pulled Deborah off the trail and into the brush.

Thomas never saw it. He was too busy prodding Callie forward, onto the dock that jutted out a good ten feet into the pond.

Sunlight glittered off of Aaron's wheelchair where he was positioned to Shane's left, most of him hidden by tall grasses, trees, and Max's fur.

Where was Matthew?

Shane didn't doubt for a minute the boy was here. Considering the position of the other two, he guessed he'd be on the western shore of the pond, probably stationed behind the boulders. He scanned the pond's shores through the rifle's scope and found Matthew's wool cap—not to the west but to the south, directly opposite Thomas.

Thomas was still shouting at Callie, prodding her down the dock. He hadn't noticed Deborah was gone yet, but he would.

Shane gripped the rifle and stepped out onto the trail.

Chapter 29

DEBORAH HAD BEEN PRAYING the entire time she walked down the trail behind Callie.

Then Levi's barn had exploded, literally burst into the sky—boards, roof, and hay scattered into the air as if a tornado had come along and thrown it willy-nilly.

Callie had stumbled, Deborah bumping into her.

They stood there, pressed together, staring at the smoke rising above the tree line. The smell of fire filled the air.

What was Thomas thinking? The place would be crawling with Amish folk in twenty minutes, families intent on putting out the blaze. Now he'd never escape.

He'd pushed them on, and the pond had already come into view when Thomas stepped between them. He'd rammed the rifle into Callie's back and told her to walk out onto the far end of the small wooden dock.

When Thomas had looked at the quilt, Deborah had known they'd have to tell him something or he'd kill them where they stood outside the barn. Callie had diverted him to the pond, bought them a little time, but both Deborah and Callie knew there was no treasure in this pond. Now everything was coming to pieces.

So Deborah continued praying.

She reminded herself that God was in control, that he would provide a solution.

And she kept her eyes open, watching for a chance to escape.

When she felt small hands tugging on her arms, she thought she must be dreaming. But Martha's eyes were so wide with fright, she knew it wasn't her imagination. With her finger pressed to her lips, her daughter urged Deborah into the bushes.

Martha had pulled the thick tape off Deborah's hands and was rubbing the circulation back into her wrists.

Deborah had a dozen questions, and there was no doubt she was going to punish her daughter for being here, but all of that would have to wait. As they watched, Shane stepped out onto the trail.

At the same moment, Thomas began hollering at Callie and waving one arm in the air while he threatened her with the rifle.

"What do you mean you don't know where the treasure is? You brought me out here, Harper."

"And you were supposed to meet me at the abandoned farm."

"Where you had no intention of going. It's a good thing Jolene put the tracker in your bag or I would be there—caught no doubt by the good detective—and you'd be here. Here finding the treasure that belongs to me."

"But we didn't—"

"Shut up! It didn't work out like you planned. Now for the last time tell me where the money is!"

"I don't know."

"You do, and you'll stop lying, or—"

"She's not lying, Thomas."

Thomas jerked around, toward Shane. When he did, he grabbed Callie by the throat, dropped his rifle, and pulled a knife out of his belt. It was such a fluid motion, Deborah wondered if it was something he practiced at home, like children practiced baseball swings.

"How would you know?"

"Because I told her to set up the decoy. Because there isn't any treasure, and I think you know it, which is why this needs to end now."

"If that's true, it's going to end with her on the bottom of this pond."

"Doesn't have to be that way." Shane took a step toward Thomas, and Thomas tightened his grip on Callie's neck.

From where Deborah hid, she could see all the color leaving Callie's face.

"Give me my money, and I'll leave. Then you can have the girl." Thomas must have seen something on Shane's face, because suddenly he was smiling. "Is that what you want detective? The girl? Well, she's all yours. But not until I have what is mine."

"You can't leave the way you came, Thomas. The place is crawling with police and plain folk. You just blew up your brother's barn."

"Wasn't an accident. It was a diversion. I'll escape with what is mine while the other officers are dealing with the mess I left."

"That doesn't bother you?"

Deborah wondered why Shane was provoking him. Wasn't his job to calm the man down?

"Why should it? Even now they'll be planning to build him another. By this time next week a grander one will stand in its place. I'll waste no sympathy on Levi."

"Who is your sympathy for then? Mrs. Knepp? Jolene? Do you reserve it for the women you kill?"

"Shut your mouth, Detective, or there will be one more name to add to that list. All I want is my money, then I'll be on my way." He swiftly cut the tape binding Callie's hands, then replaced the blade at the base of her throat.

"I'm freeing your hands so you can show me where the money is. No wrong moves or the blade will go into your pretty white skin." Never taking his eyes off Callie, he added, "Detective, you need to drop the rifle and put your hands in the air. Now where's the money, Harper?"

When she still didn't speak, Thomas allowed the blade of the knife to pierce Callie's skin. A small trickle of blood made its way down her neck, and though she didn't utter a single cry of pain, Shane did as Thomas instructed.

"This is your last chance, Harper. We're going to sidestep our way to the end of this dock, so I can keep an eye on the detective while you retrieve the money." Thomas practically whispered the words into Callie's ear, but Deborah could hear them clearly. It seemed the entire world should be able to hear them, for suddenly everything was quiet. Even the birds had ceased their racket. "I want the money, and I want it right now, or I'm going to bury this blade in your throat."

What happened next occurred so quickly Deborah didn't understand it even though she was watching closely. Martha's hands were clasped in hers, Thomas' blade was pushed into Callie's neck, and Shane was standing with his hands up in a surrender position, his rifle on the ground at his feet.

Then there was the sound of a bird flying through the trees, followed by a thud and a scream.

Aaron knew the second Matt let the rock fly. He'd been staring at Thomas, refusing to be distracted by anything else that was going on around him, refusing to think about the smoke in the air from the burning barn.

This was the man who had started the nightmare.

The man who had stepped up behind Mrs. Knepp and sent her sprawling to her death in Callie's parking lot.

The man who had stared into his eyes on Thursday evening, then disappeared into the darkness.

This was the man who had killed the woman, Jolene—killed her by holding her head under water in a barrel meant to be a game.

Aaron knew Martha had pulled her *mamm* out of harm's way. He knew it was Shane who was negotiating with Thomas, though he hadn't turned to look at the man whom he had started referring to as The Law in his head.

No, he kept his eyes locked and focused on Thomas, and he kept one hand on the top of Max's head. The dog had begun trembling at the sight of Callie, but he hadn't moved, hadn't so much as whimpered. Did he realize a single sound could give away their presence? Could send the knife more deeply into his owner's neck?

Aaron kept his eyes locked on Thomas as all these terrible thoughts flew through his mind. He understood now Thomas had only one goal in mind.

Money.

It's what he had been about from beginning to end.

The pursuit of money.

And nothing would stand in his way.

Well, he wasn't the only one who could remain focused on a single goal.

Nothing would stand between Aaron and doing his job.

So he concentrated on Thomas and waited for Matt to send the rock slinging through the air.

When it hit with expert precision, blood splattered all over Miss Callie. Aaron didn't have time to think about whether the blood was Thomas' or Callie's. He did as they had planned. He released Max and uttered the words, "Go, Max. Chase."

Max needed no urging.

He flew through the air as fast as the rock had sailed from Matthew's slingshot.

He flew through the air, aiming directly for Thomas.

Thomas had dropped the knife when his hand had been hit by the rock. He was screaming and cursing and trying to stop the flow of blood.

Callie was running toward Shane, who was shouting: "Get down!"

But there was nowhere to "get down" to, so she jumped into the pond with a splash.

Aaron watched, fascinated and horrified, as Max took a final leap toward Thomas. Too late, the man looked up and saw the sixty-five-pound yellow Labrador sailing through the air toward him, teeth bared, a snarl coming from his throat so fierce it raised the hair on the back of Aaron's neck.

He rolled his chair forward in order to have a better look, and that was when he saw Shane stoop, pick up his rifle, and aim it toward Thomas.

"No!" Aaron hollered, afraid Shane would miss and hit Max.

But Shane had no intention of firing the rifle. He checked it once to ensure a bullet was in the chamber, then walked down the wooden dock, his boots echoing across the planks.

Thomas was lying on his back, clutching his hand to his chest, blood soaking his shirt, and Max stood on top of him — teeth bared in his face, barking and growling more furiously than Aaron had ever heard him.

"Get him off me. Can't you see I'm bleeding? Get this mutt off me."

Shane said nothing to Thomas. He did reach down and pull Callie out of the water.

Chapter 30

Saturday morning Melinda stood in the October afternoon sunshine, looking up at the frame of the new barn. It was literally crawling with men, all of whom had been there since sunrise.

"This is my third barn raising, and I'm still not used to the sight." Callie placed her casserole on the table, pushing it in between the other dishes.

"I can't count how many I've seen." Melinda turned and smiled at Callie. "I suppose it will always surprise me how quickly they can work to build what is needed."

"How are the boys?" Callie asked.

"*Gut.* Noah and the bishop are meeting with them once a week. Though we are glad they were there to help catch Thomas, we want them to understand the seriousness of their actions. We are a peaceful people, and what they did was not in accordance with our teachings."

Melinda reached out and touched the small row of stitches above Callie's right eyebrow. Her fingers brushed lightly over the bump. When Callie winced, she pulled her hand away. "Sorry. It still hurts?"

"Not much. Mainly my pride was bruised. To survive Thomas'

threats, rifle-waving, and his knife, only to hit my head on the side of the dock ..." She shook her head. "I've always been a klutz."

"Careful, Callie. That's my girlfriend you're talking about." Shane slipped an arm around Callie's waist, and Melinda watched her blush a deeper red than the bandana she'd tied around Max's neck.

It seemed to Melinda they made a lovely couple. She also thought Callie could use someone to look after her. Shane Black might be the perfect man for the job, and it was plain from the look in his eyes that he was more than willing to dedicate himself to the responsibility.

"Sorry I couldn't be here sooner. I wanted to ride along when Thomas was transferred."

"He's in Fort Wayne now?" Callie pushed her hair behind her ears.

"Yeah. Adalyn was making sure he was situated well."

Deborah, Esther, Trent, and Gavin joined them as Shane caught everyone up. "Since Thomas accepted the plea bargain, his case will be heard more quickly, but it's still going to be six months to a year before we know exactly what the terms of his incarceration are."

"Why so long?" Melinda asked.

"Two separate cases—one for Mrs. Knepp, the other for Jolene Dowden."

"Why did he kill Jolene, Shane? Do you know anything more about their relationship?" A frown creased Deborah's forehead.

"They'd been sharing an apartment for some time. Neighbors we've interviewed say they fought often, but as to why he chose to kill her that day during the festival ... we may never know. He hasn't said so far. He is now under a physician's care in the prison system, which includes a complete psychiatric evaluation. Perhaps we'll know eventually."

"And Jolene's parents?" Callie reached down for Max.

"We were able to contact them. Jolene ran away years ago. Her parents weren't even aware she was in Indiana."

They were all silent as they considered the two women who had lost their lives. Finally Trent raised his camera and clicked a photo of the barn raising. When everyone gave him a critical look, he said, "What? Oh, the camera."

Melinda stared down at the table, but Callie socked him in the shoulder.

"Ouch! Why did you do that?"

"Amish. No pictures. You know the drill."

"Oh. That. I'm doing a follow-up story on Thomas, and the destruction of Levi's barn is another charge Thomas will have to answer for."

"Nope. Levi isn't pressing charges." Shane pulled down on his Cubs cap.

"I'm not surprised," Deborah said. "He always held out hope for his *bruder*—hope that he would return to the plain ways, that he would come home."

She returned Joshua's hug as he ran up and threw himself around her legs. Then he was off again, running after the older children. "Is Levi still in Fort Wayne?"

"He is. After all Thomas did—the murders, blowing up his barn, trying to take all the money ... Well, Levi said we all have regrets. He wouldn't leave until Adalyn did." Shane shrugged. "He should be here any minute. Visiting hours end early on Saturdays."

The image of Levi ministering to his brother sank in around them as the sound of hammers nailing boards filled the air.

Finally Trent asked the question that had occurred to Melinda more than once. "What about the money?"

Everyone turned to stare at him.

"I know, it's a crazy thing to ask, but what about the money Thomas was after? Or was that something he made up? Was there a treasure?"

Esther, Melinda, and Deborah shared a look—a look that Callie pounced on.

"What is it? Did you figure out the last piece of the puzzle?"

"Why would you say that?" Melinda murmured, moving to the tables and straightening the long line of dishes.

"Oh, I've seen that unspoken language thing between you before. Shane, interrogate them. Make them tell us."

Shane laughed and pulled her closer. "Can't we eat dinner first? I'm starved."

They did eat dinner first. Levi arrived and sat with his wife, Sadie, at the middle of the table. After the meal, men gathered up their tools and promised Levi they would return on Monday to finish the barn. Women picked up their dishes and pulled Sadie into a hug. The words *danki* and *gern gschehne* were passed back and forth dozens of times, like a blanket of blessings wrapped around a family of friends.

By then evening had fallen.

And all who remained were Sadie, Levi, and a few of their grandchildren, who were upstairs preparing for bed. Melinda had heard the children ask their parents for permission to spend the night with their grandparents. It was a conversation repeated in many Amish homes on Saturday evenings.

Downstairs, Melinda, Esther, and Deborah sat on one side of the table—their own children taken home by their husbands. Gavin and Shane sat on the other with Callie between them. Max waited outside on the porch, curled contentedly near the door.

Sadie and Levi sat beside each other at the end of the table, looking tired and confused.

Melinda wondered if they should have waited, but the three women had agreed this was best. They had agreed the quilts' story would be revealed this evening.

"We know you're all tired," Melinda began. "But the three of us—"

She looked to her right, to Deborah, who smiled encouragement, then to her left, to Esther, who reached for her hand and squeezed it tight.

"We felt it was best if we shared what we know tonight. We have all prayed about it, and we agreed that another evening shouldn't pass with this secret in our possession, since rightfully it is yours. If you would like other members of your family to be present—"

"No. They've been through enough." Levi looked tired, ready to be done with whatever they had to say. "I spoke to them again today, and they all agreed it would be best if I handled this matter for the family."

Melinda caressed the quilt she was holding, the quilt that had been lovingly stitched so many years ago and had eventually led to such tragedy.

Sensing the direction of her thoughts, Deborah spoke up. "We asked Shane, Gavin, and Callie to be here because they have sacrificed much in the past few weeks to keep us all safe. Of course, if you'd rather this be a private matter, I'm sure they would understand."

Levi shook his head. "We owe everyone in this room, Deborah." He clutched his hands around the coffee mug. "I've spoken with Shane about this, but the way I see it, he could easily have killed Thomas a week ago by the pond."

Putting his hand into his pants pocket, he jingled his change, then continued. "The night you two came here and showed me Thomas' picture, asked me if I knew him, I told you I did not. You might think I lied to you, but I didn't. The man in that picture— he wasn't my *bruder*. He's nothing like the boy I grew up with. I saw the resemblance, but I couldn't believe—didn't want to believe it was him."

Clearing his throat, he pushed on. "Because you didn't kill him when he was threatening Callie, because of that, I will have time to try to win my *bruder*'s heart. Time to pray for him and time to minister. We owe you a tremendous debt, Shane. Andrew and Callie as well. Whatever you have to say, I welcome hearing it."

"Gavin was injured by Thomas, as was Callie." Sadie was not one given to emotion, but she accepted the handkerchief her husband handed her. "It is as it should be, with everyone here welcome."

Melinda looked at Esther. They had agreed Esther should begin with the telling of what they'd stayed this evening to share. "When I first noticed the unusual stitching of your *mamm*'s quilt, I took it to Melinda. Together we were able to figure out that the borders were German script and Amish proverbs."

"*Ya*, it's very unusual." Sadie shook her head. "Levi's *mamm* was known to be eccentric."

"We believe it was more than that." Melinda picked up the story. "The design of these quilts is also unusual. Elizabeth sewed many quilts in her life—beautiful quilts for her children and grandchildren. Quilts for charity auctions and for weddings. They were all done in the traditional Amish patterns."

"But these aren't," Sadie said.

"Correct. These three, which were left to us in the will, were done differently," Melinda said.

"They resemble storybook quilts," Callie said softly. It was the first time she had spoken. "I've had time to research them more thoroughly since the afternoon at the pond, since Thomas' arrest. Traditionally they were used to convey a secret, something the quilter wanted passed on to others but didn't want known openly ..."

Silence settled around the room as Sadie and Levi considered the idea. Melinda could see them struggle with the concept their mother would hide something from them. "Perhaps she had a good reason for not wanting to write it on a piece of paper. Maybe it could have fallen into the wrong hands."

"Like Thomas'." Levi's frown was growing more pronounced, his forehead wrinkling as he tried to follow their reasoning.

"Like Thomas, but not Thomas." Melinda adjusted the strings of her prayer *kapp*. "Remember these quilts were probably stitched before Thomas was born. Perhaps there was someone else she didn't trust in the family, or it could have been that she was paranoid about robbers or banks—"

"You're talking about a hidden treasure." Gavin sat forward, placed his palms against the table.

"Yes." Deborah looked across at the young man who had become a friend to so many within their community. "The quilts tell the story of a treasure that is hidden, kept for safekeeping here on the homestead."

"You can't be serious." Levi stood, walked to the coffeepot, and refilled his mug.

"Actually we're very serious." Esther spoke quietly, firmly. "No doubt Thomas knew about it. I don't know how. Perhaps he heard your mother mention it at some point. Maybe he overheard a conversation, but these quilts definitely tell about a treasure that is hidden, and they describe an exact location."

"I don't believe it." Levi set his mug on the counter a bit harder than necessary, its contents sloshing over the side. "*Mamm* left plenty in the bank to run the farm. And she wasn't greedy with what she left in the will. What more could there have been? Why would she do such a thing? How would she do such a thing all those years ago?"

Shane stretched his arm across the back of Callie's chair. "While we were staying at Reuben's the girls shared with me what they thought they knew, and I can't say whether it's valid or not. Obviously they've made more progress since then. What do you know about your grandparents? Or your great-grandparents?"

Levi ran his fingers through his beard. "Not much. My folks came from Pennsylvania to start over. Their parents didn't come west, but planned on joining them once they were settled. Never had the chance. They died from influenza."

Gavin scratched at the day's growth of beard on his jaw. "You say there's a map on those quilts?"

"Yes." Deborah glanced down at the quilt she held. "There's a key of sorts. Once you learn the key, it's quite easy to read."

Gavin shrugged. "So read it to us."

Chapter 31

ESTHER'S MIND WENT BACK to the day she'd driven to Melinda's, the day she'd first placed her quilt beside Melinda's and discovered the edges matched. It was like the parable in the Bible, where the woman had swept her house many times to find the lost coin.

But no one had been searching for these pieces.

No one had realized anything was lost.

Still, now the pieces were found.

As they all knelt around the three quilts that were laid out on the floor carefully lined up together, she wondered what else would be revealed this evening.

Melinda pointed to the first square, to the delicate stitching, and began to tell the story. Her hands moved over the panels of the quilts as she spoke.

"Elizabeth and Adam married in 1938." She pointed to the small dates stitched into the corner of the block, below the double wedding-ring square. "After their first year of marriage, they moved west with a small group of Amish from the Pennsylvania community."

Melinda's hands hesitated over a square depicting an Amish woman in a prayer *kapp*—no face was stitched, much like the

289

Amish dolls she sewed for Hannah. The woman on the quilt pattern was boarding a bus.

"*Ya*, that's right," Sadie whispered. "I remember her telling me once about the trip. It took two days, and then their things hadn't arrived yet as they were supposed to. However, there was an Amish community here already. The community took them in and allowed them to stay in their houses until their belongings arrived."

"No real secrets yet," Levi muttered.

Melinda continued. "The land was *gut* here. *Gotte* blessed them with fertile fields, *gut* harvests, and their first *boppli* boy."

"Me?" Levi asked.

"No." Melinda's voice fell to a whisper. "The year was 1940."

Her fingers once again traced delicate stitches that were the same color as the cloth they adorned. Finally she tapped another date stitched into the fabric. "This child lived less than one year."

Esther could practically read her *freinden*'s thoughts. Was that why Elizabeth had always had a soft spot in her heart for Aaron? Did she understand the pain of worrying over a sick child?

"Would explain the box of infant clothing I found once," Sadie said.

Melinda moved to the top of the quilt again. "Five rows in all—the first describes their marriage and trip. The second, the trials that accompanied their move. The third, the help they received from their new community. The fourth the blessings of the land. And the fifth the birth and death of their first child."

When Melinda finished speaking, Esther took up the story, moving on to the second quilt. "Trials found Elizabeth and Adam, even in Shipshewana. News arrived that Adam's parents ..." she hesitated, looked at Levi instead of at the quilt squares. "Your grandparents died suddenly."

"Of the influenza," Levi whispered.

"The year was 1941. Though there was death, there were also gifts. Your parents' many blessings were ..." Esther looked to

Deborah, who shrugged. They'd made it to the middle of the second quilt, the panel Deborah and Callie had been looking at the day Thomas had ambushed them. The quilted square obviously depicted water—blue material with blue stitching, so Callie had been able to convince him the money was hidden at the pond. "Your parents' many blessings were—"

"Showered," suggested Deborah.

"*Ya*. The blessings were showered on them, but then a relative arrived." She pointed to the next panel where a dark figure was stitched against a cloudy sky. "This person was bent on destroying all they had."

Levi stood now, running his thumbs under his suspenders. "I suspect that would be referring to my *onkel*—my *dat*'s only *bruder*. He would appear every year or so when I was young."

Accepting his handkerchief back from his wife, Levi wiped at the perspiration beading on his forehead, which appeared despite the growing coolness of the evening. No one had thought to add wood to the fire in the stove in the corner of the room. Esther thought of asking Shane to attend to it, but they were nearing the end now, and the end would take them back outside.

"I thought it odd that he never stayed." Levi was talking to them, but it was obvious his mind was back in that other time. "He never came into the house, never stayed long enough to share a meal."

He walked to the counter, took a sip of his coffee, now cold. "When I was a teenager, my *dat* hired a driver. He was gone for nearly a week. It's the one time I remember him leaving the farm for more than a day. He returned with my *onkel* in a wooden coffin. We had a proper Amish burial, here in our district, but I never learned anything about him."

"The bottom panel of this quilt indicates there was a time of peace and prosperity." Esther looked to Deborah, who turned to the third and final quilt.

"This quilt describes blessings from the hand of God." She

drew their attention to each of the squares. "Family, faith, crops, rain, *freinden*, health. All the things for which we are grateful are sewn into the panels on this quilt. Each panel has an appliqued picture and two other things—"

"A date and a tiny symbol." Sadie's nose was practically touching the quilt.

"What's this stitched here?" Levi asked, pointing to stitching above the bottom right border of the quilt.

"The numbers one, nine, five, two." Esther ran her fingers over the delicate stitching. "It's difficult to see and not noticeable unless you're looking for it. You have a *gut* eye, Levi."

"Why is it there?"

"We think that's a code, perhaps, since it's stitched into the bottom right-hand corner."

"Could it be the year that the quilt was made?" Sadie asked.

"No. The quilts were made after the birth of Levi. We know that because he is shown in the blessings of family. The final square of the last quilt."

"1955." Levi stood over the quilts, staring at them as if they were a snake that might strike at any moment. "My sisters were born 1945 through 1950. I was born in 1955 when my mother was thirty-five years old. Thomas was born a year later, and he was her last. We were her only two boys."

"You said this last quilt has something else in each panel." Sadie was practically kneeling in the middle of the quilt trying to look more closely. "I don't see anything."

"A small blue stitch. Elizabeth's symbol for water. It's in each panel."

"Are you sure you're not making this up?" Levi paced the room in agitation. "Seems a big stretch to me. For one thing, these quilts go against our tradition. *Mamm* knew that, which is probably why she kept them in a trunk. It's prideful to make such things. I suppose it's wrong to destroy them now, but I honestly don't know what to do with them, and I'm not sure I buy into the hidden-message idea."

Deborah looked to Callie for help.

Callie stepped in. "For some reason, Elizabeth felt a need to tell this story and to tell it this way, Levi. Perhaps she thought she was protecting you. As you know, I've worked with Bishop Elam in several situations regarding Deborah's, Esther's and Melinda's quilts. He's a wise and fair man. He'll be able to counsel you on what to do about your mother's quilts—if you think they should be returned to you. We have all agreed that we will honor your wishes in that matter. It's in our legal rights to give the quilts back to you, but at the very least, this is something you would want to pass down to your children and grandchildren."

"It's curious that your mother involved Callie in the will." Esther still wondered about that. The quilts she understood, but Mrs. Hochstetler's reasoning eluded her.

Shane had been sitting on the couch, leaning forward to watch as each woman took turns explaining the story of the quilts. Esther wasn't at all surprised when he reached into his pocket and pulled out a sheet of paper. Nor was she surprised when the sheet of paper turned out to be a copy of the will.

"Callie provided me with a copy of your mother's will, Levi. She received a copy of the portion that pertained to her. The wording is interesting. 'Daisy Powell's niece, Miss Callie Harper, is to receive the three quilts in the chest next to my bed. Once restored, they may be sold at Callie's discretion.'"

"Perhaps Elizabeth didn't want interference from the bishop," Esther said, though in her heart that didn't feel right either. She had known Elizabeth Hochstetler for years, and the woman had closely followed the ways of the church.

"Or maybe she knew that Callie would have the means to research storybook quilts." Melinda's eyes widened as she stared first at the quilt in front of her, then at Levi. "Elizabeth did things methodically, whether it was quilting or canning. Do you remember the year she grew three different types of bell peppers and she insisted on canning all the green ones first, then the red ones, then the yellows?"

Sadie laughed. "Oh, I remember. She was quite adamant about how things were to be done."

Shane looked back down at the paper. "She wanted each of you ladies involved. The will specifically says, 'Money from the sale of the quilts will be split five ways—one portion each to Esther Fisher, Deborah Yoder, and Melinda Byer, who will each help with the restoration, and one part to Callie, who will oversee the sales.' Perhaps because she knew you each had a passion for quilting. Maybe she knew you'd find the messages she sewed into each panel."

"I quilt adequately to warm my family, but I've never had the gift that you all do." Sadie held up her hand to stop the protests from Deborah, Melinda, and Esther. "I probably would have left the quilts in the trunk."

"I don't understand this last part," Gavin said, reading over Shane's shoulder. "'The final portion of money will be deposited in the previously established account at First Bank Shipshewana to be used as arranged with my banker, Mrs. Barnwell.'"

"I was curious about that," Shane admitted. "I talked to Mrs. Barnwell, but she guards her clients' business dealings well. She wouldn't tell me anything without a judge's court order, and I wasn't able to get one since Thomas is already in jail and no longer a threat to anyone."

"She'll tell us once we find the money," Esther said.

Everyone stopped what they were doing, turned and stared at her. "Well, isn't that obvious? Elizabeth wanted someone to find the money. At first she wasn't willing to tell you because of your *onkel*, Levi."

"And later she was waiting for Thomas to have a change of heart." Deborah glanced at Callie, who was nodding in agreement.

"But the will," Esther's voice gained confidence as the final piece of the puzzle fell into place. "The will was her safety measure, in case Thomas didn't turn around before she died."

No one said anything for the space of one, then two minutes.

It was Gavin who stretched, then looked at the clock. The tiny hands were approaching nine, and Esther knew everyone was growing tired. It had been a long day. So when he stated the obvious, she felt herself jump.

"Sounds like we should go treasure hunting then."

Chapter 32

LEVI IMMEDIATELY BEGAN shaking his head, and Melinda knew he wasn't going to go for it. Disappointment flooded through her and she wasn't sure why, other than she wanted this to be over. Tonight. She wanted this terrible thing that had begun the first evening of the Fall Festival done and forgotten.

Of course it wouldn't be.

Shane had already explained that Aaron could be called in front of the judge if there were questions about Thomas' plea bargain. As far as the first murder, Mrs. Knepp's murder, her son remained the prosecution's primary material witness.

"I still don't believe there could be a treasure," Levi was saying. "The story you tell, it sounds believable enough, but someone else could look at the quilt and tell a completely different story. It's like a child's yarn. To go traipsing around in the dark, after all these years, chasing after such things ..."

He continued to stare at the quilts from across the room. Sadie stood and went to him. "I think it might be better if we put this to rest tonight, Levi."

"Why? We have no need of a treasure. *Gotte* has provided well for us and our children."

"Levi, this gift wasn't left to us."

Melinda wasn't able to hear much of the rest. Sadie began whispering to Levi, then they both stepped out onto the porch. As they walked away, she heard Aaron's name, heard the words medical expenses. She glanced down, tears stinging her eyes. When she looked up again, Deborah reached across the quilt and patted her hand.

"It wasn't for us that I wanted to know," Melinda whispered.

"Nor I. It seems Elizabeth wanted us to unravel this puzzle, but we can't force them to travel along the trail she has laid out."

They stood and began folding the quilts while Callie carried coffee cups to the sink. Shane and Gavin discussed vacation plans now that the case was closed. Melinda realized again how much their community owed these two.

As they were gathering their things to leave, Levi and Sadie stepped back inside. "We'll look," he said.

Melinda reached again for Deborah's hand.

"One place," he added. "And only tonight. I won't be spending the rest of my days chasing after some make-believe treasure."

"You said the last quilt had a code above the bottom right corner, correct?" Sadie looked toward Deborah.

"*Ya*, the date 1952 and the symbol for water."

"Are you sure the numbers refer to a date?" Levi asked.

"No, but what else could it be?" Melinda pushed up her glasses. "A date seems most obvious."

"What could be important about 1952?" Gavin asked.

"We were at war with Korea," Shane said.

Callie tucked her hair behind her ear. "Elizabeth II became queen." When everyone stared at her she pretended offense. "What? I watch a lot of late-night History Channel."

"I have a feeling it would have been something more personal," Esther suggested.

"And something related to water." Melinda walked over and ran her hand across the quilt Deborah had folded. The center square was clearly visible—water, blessings, family, and 1952. Deborah and Callie had seemed to have discounted the pond for a very good reason, but what else could it mean?

"Could it be the pond after all?" Shane asked.

Deborah slipped a smile Callie's way. "I remembered the pond being dug when we were teens. We had a church singing out there the weekend it first rained and filled it up."

"Needed that pond for the livestock." Levi walked to the shelf running along the wall in the living room above the cast-iron stove. He picked up one flashlight for himself and tossed another to Shane. "But the pump house, now that was built in the early 1950s."

Shane caught the flashlight, tested the strength of the batteries, and nodded. "These are good."

"You're sure it was built in the '50s?" Callie asked.

"*Ya*. Had the pump serviced this last year. Carter and his son were out here. Old man mentioned he'd helped his father install the original pump in the early '50s."

"Water," Melinda said, placing her quilt on the couch.

"And blessings." Esther set her quilt on top of Melinda's.

"There's one way to find out." When Deborah's quilt was placed on top, the three quilts made for a perfect trio.

Melinda couldn't help that her pulse raced as they all walked calmly out the door, down the steps and across the yard. Max stretched—front paws out in front of him, rear high in the air—then fell into line with them. She knew it was wrong to have worldly thoughts, to care about wealth—and wealth that wasn't even hers. Regardless of what the will said, whatever was in the pump house rightfully belonged to Levi and Sadie.

Still, it was exciting to think Elizabeth Hochstetler had placed something there for safekeeping over fifty years ago, and they were about to uncover it. She couldn't help feeling God had used them in some way, used their love and talent for quilting to solve this mystery.

The question that remained was what exactly had Elizabeth hidden?

Callie held back as everyone crowded into the little pump house, fitting in around the pipes and mechanisms she couldn't begin to name.

"Come on in, Callie. You've earned a front-row seat." Gavin's voice was low, solid, and comforting. She understood, suddenly and with something of a jolt, how much she'd grown to care for him. He was the brother she'd always wanted, and she couldn't imagine not having him in her life.

Tugging on his hand, she pulled him out of the door of the shack and into the night. Max didn't make a sound, but he brushed up against her as he trotted past, settling a few feet in front of her. She could see the outline of him as her eyes adjusted to the darkness.

"Thank you, for all you've done." When Gavin didn't answer, Callie pushed on. She couldn't see his expression, but perhaps that was best. "I don't mean only during this mess, but since I've come to Shipshe. Since I was involved in Stakehorn's murder. You've always been there for me. Always been a solid friend. That's rare in this world. I realize now that God put you in my life for a reason, and I .... I want to tell you that you mean a lot to me."

He reached out then, pulled her into a side hug. "Somebody has to watch out for you. Every once in a while Shane is busy."

She laughed, wiped at tears that inexplicably wanted to fall. She didn't think she used to be this weepy. What was happening to her? Living in the country was supposed to make you hardy, but it seemed to be turning her soft and gooey.

"For what it's worth, I hope you two are happy." Gavin gave her shoulders a final squeeze, then released her.

"Aren't I a little old to be someone's girlfriend?"

"Don't rush it. You two need more time alone, time when you're not in the middle of an investigation. You'll feel better then."

When Callie shook her head, Gavin crossed his arms, stared off across the fields that were blanketed in darkness.

"You two will figure it out. Say yes when Shane asks you to go —" Gavin was interrupted by a loud commotion from inside the pump house.

"Sounds like we're missing all the action," he said. "I have a feeling you should see this."

So Callie let him lead her back inside, even though part of her was more interested in what he was about to say than in any treasure that might have been hidden for two generations.

They walked into a room flooded with light, leaving Max to take up post once more by the door.

A kerosene lamp was burning brightly and had been positioned over the pump casing.

Shane had his flashlight, as well as Levi's, trained over a three-by-three-foot square of ground next to the main machinery. They'd brushed away the dirt and found a door in the floor, which they had already managed to pry open.

"Sadie noticed the ground sounded different when she walked here," Deborah explained. "Turns out it's a root cellar."

"Not exactly full of roots," Levi called out, climbing up a short ladder with his arms full of canning jars.

He handed them to his wife carefully, as if they were fragile eggs that had survived a storm but might now shatter at the slightest touch. Sadie turned and began passing the dusty jars around the room. Levi ran his arm across his brow, then disappeared back down the ladder, returning with another armful. By the time he'd passed those out, everyone was holding a jar.

"Looks like you all were right." He wiped at the sweat and dirt on his face. "*Mamm* went to quite some trouble to hide these, for whatever reason. So even if all we have are some very old canned vegetables ..."

He paused, stared down at the quart jar in his hands a moment. When he raised his eyes, a grin played across his lips. "*Danki*. You pushed me to look for them. Her hands put them up, all those years ago, before I was even born. I don't know why my *mamm* would have hid them, but she did. And now she wanted us to find them. They were precious to her, and that makes them precious to me, even if they're only squash and carrots."

"My jar doesn't look like vegetables, Levi." Gavin had rubbed the dirt off his container and was holding it up to the light. Callie leaned closer to better see what was inside. The glass of the jar had darkened with age, but she could tell the contents were shiny and circular.

"We might as well all open them at the same time," Levi muttered.

The jars weren't fastened with wax, but the tops had been rusted on tight. Slight popping sounds filled the night as each person broke the seals age had created, which protected the contents of their jars against fifty years of weather, nearly twenty thousand mornings and nights, critters that crawled through the earthen cellar, and men and women who walked above.

Callie refused to glance up even when she heard murmured cries of surprise. She was determined to remove the top to her jar and see its contents before she looked at anyone else's.

"Stocks? Who puts stocks in a jar?"

"Mine has bills. Hundred-dollar bills."

"Where would she have gotten this much money?"

"Maybe from her in-laws — my grandparents."

The lid on Callie's jar wouldn't budge no matter how she cranked on it.

"Mind if I help you, Callie Grace?"

The words were more gentle than a caress and sent a delicious shiver down her spine. When she nodded, Shane encircled her with his arms and gave the lid of the jar one tug. It made a small popping sound as the seal broke.

"You almost had it," he lied, smiling down at her.

And suddenly she didn't care what was in the jar. She turned in his arms, gazed up into his eyes, and knew whatever was in the jar wasn't nearly as precious as what she was seeing.

Which was silly.

He'd opened a jar for her, not braved a dark night and protected her from a monster.

But the truth was that Shane had saved Callie from more than one monster. He'd saved her from at least three, and she knew — looking deep into the darkest, kindest eyes she'd ever seen — that he would defend her from more, as many more as she managed to encounter.

"Are you going to look in that jar, or stand there and hold it?" Gavin asked. "Mine had gold pieces. Imagine that. She must have had the bank get them from Fort Wayne."

Callie thrust her jar into Gavin's hands. "You can check mine for me."

Shane grinned as he passed his jar to Deborah. "Guess I'll hand over mine as well."

"You two aren't even going to look?" Deborah laughed as she juggled her jar to accept Shane's.

In the background, Callie could hear Sadie's and Levi's voices. They sounded happy. She wasn't sure what this meant to them or how it would affect the sale of the quilts. All she knew was that she needed to be alone with Shane for a few minutes.

So she slipped her hand in his and tugged him toward the door of the pump house.

"Where are they going?" Melinda asked.

"They're not curious," Deborah explained.

"We're curious all right," Shane growled.

Then he followed Callie out into the night, out under the cover of a million stars.

Epilogue

CALLIE COCKED HER HEAD and studied her fiancé as he walked out on to the back porch to join her.

"Get plenty to eat?" Shane asked.

"Of your mother's cooking? I might have to lie down in the Buick when we drive home."

He sat on the swing next to her and set it to rocking. They gazed out over the valley as the sun painted the sky golden on a perfect Thanksgiving afternoon.

"Warm enough?" Shane asked, pulling a throw blanket around her shoulders.

"I am, but you can still kiss me if you want."

So he did, and it made her toes tingle as always. Callie thought Max gave her a reproachful look, but he was as full as she was and couldn't do more than moan softly.

"Gavin told me to say yes," she admitted, when Shane stopped kissing her and returned to staring at the sunset.

"Gavin told you to marry me?"

She slapped his arm, but he grabbed her hand and wouldn't let go. "He said, 'Say yes when Shane asks you to go ...' but he never finished the sentence, and I didn't know where you were going to ask me to go."

303

"This was when we found the money?"

"And two weeks later you offered me this ring." Callie looked down at the sparkling diamond. Not too big. Not too small. Just right. Shane Black knew how to do things just right.

"I'm glad you said yes." He nuzzled her neck and she let out a yelp.

"Everything all right out there?" Shane's father asked from the kitchen.

"Yes," Callie and Shane answered in unison.

Callie thought about Shane's remark. "To marrying you or to meeting your parents?"

"Both."

"I am too." She snuggled into his arms while the stars began to make an appearance. All she could think of as her eyes grew heavy was that Deborah was right. God did have a plan. "I am too."

Acknowledgments

THIS BOOK IS DEDICATED to my grandparents John and Rose Allen. My grandfather was raised on a Choctaw reservation in Oklahoma. He met my grandmother just across the Texas border. They married and raised their family in the town of Paris. Grandmother Rose had one brother, Walter Vernon, and three sisters: Daisy, Lily, and Gertrude. When I was in grade school, we lived a few blocks away from my grandparents. Those were precious years. They let me sleep over often, cook my own eggs in the morning, and spoil their old dog. They even had a rusty barrel they burned trash in out back, and I was allowed to help. We watched *HeeHaw* and the nightly news together. I loved them dearly.

I would like to thank my team at Zondervan, including Becky Philpott, Tonya Osterhouse, Alicia Mey, and Sue Brower. This book also wouldn't be possible without the help of my agent, Mary Sue Seymour.

Cindy Barkley helped with equestrian matters. Suzanne Woods Fisher and *The Budget* freely provided Amish proverbs. Many folks from Shipshewana were willing to answer questions, including Lynn Bontrager and Kris Stutzman. You have made me feel like a welcome citizen of Shipshe!

My pre-readers have been with me through this entire series. Thank you to Donna, Kristy, and Dorsey. We need to visit Shipshe together. Family—I love you. Enough said, right? William, Kylie, Yale, and Jordyn, you make me very proud. Bobby, you know I adore you.

And finally ... *always giving thanks to God the Father for everything, in the name of our Lord Jesus Christ* (Ephesians 5:20).

Discussion Questions

1. In chapter 5, Callie attempts to explain to Deborah the heart of her relationship with Mrs. Knepp. She compares it to not being accepted into a group in high school, then admits that "in my mind there was always going to be a day—sometime in the future—when we could call a truce." Can you relate to Callie's awkwardness at not being accepted by someone or a group of people? How did you react? Has there been a time when you held on to a grudge and wished you hadn't?

2. In chapter 10, Melinda realizes, maybe for the first time, that the killer could be after her son Aaron. She has a moment of panic, and then remembers the words found in Jeremiah 29:11. Only part of the scripture is included in the chapter. The entire verse is one of my favorites.

   > "For I know the thoughts that I think toward you," declares the LORD, "thoughts of peace and not of evil, to give you a future and a hope."

   Has there been a time in your life when this scripture has brought you comfort?

3. Joshua's meltdown in chapter 11 was so much fun for me to write, because I've been there with my own child! So often when I see young mothers with young children, I'm reminded of a professor's wise words: "You're seeing three minutes of a three-hour movie." Isn't that the truth? We don't really know what's going on in someone else's life. Can you relate to Deborah's problems with Joshua, and if so, would you have handled it the same way or differently?

4. After Shane and Callie kiss, she realizes she must make a leap of faith—she can no longer straddle the fence of their relationship (chapter 13): "There was no middle ground. It was either trust and take the leap, or back up and somehow endure this thing alone."

   Callie's relationship with Shane very much parallels her spiritual journey at this point. In other words, sometimes God uses people to help us make those leaps of faith. Have you experienced a similar moment?

5. At the beginning of chapter 17, Melinda recalls her mother's advice, the biblical advice to "lean not unto your own understanding." She knows this is good advice, but knowing it and being able to do it are two very different things. What are some practical things we can do to depend on God's understanding during times of crisis?

6. In chapter 20, you read from Esther's point of view that "God had worked in her heart. He had given her back her faith in the goodness of life." This is no small thing! Esther had previously lost more than her husband, Seth, to a terrible accident. She had lost her faith in the goodness of God. Do you think it's possible to ever completely heal from such a tragedy?

7. We have a nice image of Deborah ministering to Melinda in chapter 23. "When she applied pressure to the small cut,

fresh blood poured out, staining the cotton." Sometimes it's the small daily things that remind us of Christ's sacrifice. What has occurred in your daily life recently to remind you of the gift of grace?

8. The Swap! Oh my. In chapter 25, we see that Aaron and Matt have once again pulled The Swap! Why are they doing this to their parents? Are they bad children? Do they understand it's wrong? And in this case, does the end justify the means? (P.S. did you ever do anything similar when you were a child, or since?)

9. We learn about Shane's background in chapter 26, about the tragic death of his sister, how the person who killed her was captured and imprisoned, and how that affected his family. This scene helps us to understand how Shane has become the man, and the officer, that he is. In reality, can God use something terrible in our lives for good?

10. In chapter 30, Levi reveals his attitude toward his brother. He knows he will never be able to win Thomas' freedom, but he still has hope for his salvation when he says to Shane, "Because you didn't kill him ... I will have time to try and win my *bruder*'s heart. Time to pray for him and time to minister." How is this an expression of God's grace?

About the Author

PHOTO BY JASON IRWIN

VANNETTA CHAPMAN writes inspirational fiction full of grace. She is the author of sixteen novels, including the Pebble Creek Amish series, The Shipshewana Amish Mystery series, and *Anna's Healing*, a 2016 Christy Award finalist. Vannetta is a Carol award winner and has also received more than two dozen awards from Romance Writers of America chapter groups. She was a teacher for fifteen years and currently resides in the Texas hill country. Visit Vannetta online: VannettaChapman.com, Twitter: @VannettaChapman, Facebook: VannettaChapmanBooks.